Actors' Handbook 2007-8

Edited by Andrew Chapman

This edition first published 2007 by

Casting Call Pro
138 Upper Street
London N1 1QP

www.castingcallpro.com

A CIP catalogue record for this book is available from the British Library

ISBN 978-0-9556273-0-9

Set in Rockwell
Designed and edited by Andrew Chapman (www.awrc.info)

Printed in Britain by
Antony Rowe, Chippenham

/continues...

Introduction

Acting can be one of the most rewarding and frustrating of professions. This guide is intended to make your professional life just that little bit easier. With useful introductions to some of the key areas for establishing oneself as a professional actor, and comprehensive listings for agents, service providers, theatre companies and venues, and all the UK's major acting organisations and drama schools, ***Actors' Handbook*** is designed to help you pick a path through the ever changing landscape of the professional actor.

Whether you are considering entering the profession, have just taken your first steps, or are already established as an actor, ***Actors' Handbook*** is both a useful guide to the industry and an invaluable resource to help further your career development, covering topics such as: choosing a drama school; finding work and marketing yourself; auditioning; further training, and industry related jobs for those times when you're between roles.

Actors' Handbook is brought to you by the people behind Casting Call Pro, one of the leading resources for professional UK actors. The information in this book is updated annually, more recent information can always be found at ***www.castingcallpro.com***.

If you have any questions about this book or feel an organisation or company ought to be included in future editions please send details to info@castingcallpro.com.

Acknowledgements

We are extremely grateful to the following people for their contributions. Each of the contributors bring a fresh and informative insight into what can, at times, seem a daunting and impenetrable industry. Many thanks are due to:

- Nicole Hay, projects manager at the National Council for Drama Training (NCDT) – ***www.ncdt.co.uk***
- James Berersford, co-director of The Actor's Studio – ***www.actorsstudio.co.uk***
- Claire Grogan, highly respected headshot photographer – ***www.clairegrogan.co.uk***
- Chantal Ellul, director of the Actor's One–Stop Shop, one of the UK's leading showreel providers for both edited clips and shot from scratch – ***www.actorsonestopshop.com***
- Kerry Mitchell, director of Cut Glass Productions, specialists in Voice Overs and voicereel production – ***www.cutglassproductions.com***
- James Bonallack, director of Foreign Voices, the UK's foremost agency for native foreign language voice over artists and in-house voice over production – ***www.foreignvoices.co.uk***
- James Aylett, performer and co-author of the entertaining and informative Fringe – ***www.fridaybooks.co.uk/ http://tartarus.org/james***
- Hils Barker, acclaimed stand up comic and comedy writer for Radio 4 – ***www.hilsbarker.com***.

Section 1
Drama schools & training

Choosing a drama school

Do I need to go to drama school?

Training at a reputable drama school is the best route into professional acting. Not only does it afford you an actual grounding in acting and an opportunity to practise your craft, it also gives you credibility in the eyes of casting professionals. (There are a fortunate few who have found success without studying at drama school. They have perhaps been spotted by an agent in an amateur production, but this is a lottery and not to be relied upon if you are serious about making a long-term career in acting.) Attending drama school demonstrates ongoing commitment to your calling and, as long as the school is reputable and you demonstrate a willingness to learn, you'll be better placed at the end of the course to succeed as an actor.

Choosing a course

When selecting a drama course, it is important to realise that not all drama institutions are equal. With several drama courses nationwide to choose from, it is vital to do some serious research before applying. When narrowing your options, start by looking at the institution itself: is it a university or college dedicated to drama, media or stage craft? or a private collection of teachers operating out of rented premises? Investigate how long the institution has been established and how long it has been offering a drama course. It is also important to look at who is teaching the course: do the teachers have the experience required to teach you what you need to succeed? Take time to review what facilities the institution offers: do they have their own theatre and dedicated stage staff? Finally, check the institution's pedigree by talking to past students about their experience, and check out their alumni – where are they now?

Along with your choice of institution, your course selection is also pivotal. Many courses will offer a broad cross-section of acting disciplines, while others are more specific, eg dedicated to screen

THE BENEFITS OF TRAINING

In boxed sections throughout this chapter Nicole Hay, projects manager at the National Council for Drama Training (NCDT), explains the advantages and process of finding a suitable course:

Acting is an increasingly competitive career. Equity – the actors' union – calculates that a high percentage of its members are unemployed at any given time, with actors working professionally an average of 11.3 weeks of the year. Except for those at the top of the profession, actors earn comparatively low salaries and most have to undertake temporary periods of alternative employment between engagements. To succeed, an actor needs to be intelligent, sensitive, observant and imaginative. Equally important are physical and mental resilience and self-discipline.

For those who do aspire to an acting career it is not all bad news. Despite the gloomy statistics, the personal rewards involved can be immense – how many people can claim they are making a living doing something they really want to do?

There are no formal entry requirements for becoming an actor; it is possible for untrained people to enter the profession. However, in such a competitive industry it makes sense to have as many advantages as possible including vocational training on a course accredited by the NCDT. A report carried out by the Institute of Manpower Studies on behalf of the Arts Council of England found that 86% of actors working in the profession had received formal professional training, and that the vast majority were satisfied with their preparation for working, the careers advice and guidance they had received and the overall quality of their training.

The benefits of vocational training are numerous. NCDT accredited courses provide not only the discipline, practical skills and intellectual understanding necessary for building a lasting career, but also opportunities to be seen by agents, casting directors, theatres and television companies, so vital in securing that all-important first job.

acting or stage acting. A school's website should give you a good idea of the courses they offer – look thoroughly at the course outline and if you have any questions give the school a call; they'll be happy to help with your enquiries. When choosing a course, there are a number of factors to consider. Your research should include finding out about a course's reputation by talking to people and gleaning what you can from industry publications and the internet (don't just go by the school's website which might have an inherent bias). Remember, the reputation of any particular course will fluctuate over time depending on its output of actors and its current teaching staff.

Entry is based mainly on auditions, for which you will usually be expected to select two speeches (one modern, one classical) and for which you may well be charged an audition fee (usually around £30 to £40). You will be expected to cover your own travel and accommodation costs to attend auditions.

With so many competing factors to weigh up, choosing the right drama school can be a daunting process. The National Council for Drama Training (NCDT) accredits those courses which it feels offer the highest levels of vocational training (see opposite). While competition for places on NDCT-accredited courses is fierce, their

HOW & WHEN TO GO TO DRAMA SCHOOL

Drama school courses vary from three-year degree or diploma courses to one-year postgraduate courses for people who have already attended university or have comparable prior experience. Entry is by audition – talent being the principal requirement for securing a place. For three-year courses, applicants must be 18 years and above. Many drama schools prefer to take students who are older as they are looking for people with the maturity to cope with the demands of actor training. For one-year courses, the minimum age is 21. Some students have a lot of prior experience of performing, others very little, but you must demonstrate a genuine commitment.

DIFFERENT TYPES OF COURSE

While all drama school courses aim to prepare students to enter the profession, the philosophy of actor training varies from school to school. Some place great emphasis on classical theatre training, others focus more broadly. Certain courses are specifically targeted at those who wish to make a career in musical theatre. Anyone considering applying to drama school should research their options carefully and consider the sort of career to which they are aspiring. The NCDT website (***www.ncdt.co.uk***) has links to the websites of drama schools with accredited courses and the Conference of Drama Schools website (***www.drama.ac.uk***) has a downloadable guide to professional training in drama and technical theatre.

It is important to make a distinction between vocational training courses and the vast number of performing arts courses on offer at UK universities. The Higher Education Funding Council for England funds more than 2,100 degree courses with 'drama' or 'theatre' in the title. University courses are generally more academic and may not aim to train people as actors. A one-year course accredited by NCDT may be a suitable choice for those who have already completed a drama or theatre studies degree.

WHAT IS NCDT ACCREDITATION?

NCDT accreditation aims to give students confidence that they courses they choose are recognised by the drama profession as being relevant to the purpose of their employment; and that the profession has confidence that the people they employ who have completed these courses have the skills and attributes required for the continuing health of the industry.

Students studying on an accredited course have student membership of Equity. On successful completion of the course they have automatic qualification for Equity membership provided that they are entitled to work in the UK.

graduates do tend to be better prepared for the real world of acting; in this tough, competitive environment, every advantage you can acquire is an asset.

What if I've had no other training or acting experience?

There are no formal criteria you must meet in order apply to a drama school. Fundamentally, what the schools are looking for is genuine talent and commitment. Though you are not required to have acted at school or in local amateur theatre, it certainly won't do you any harm in the eyes of casting directors, and amateur theatre can be a good way of learning more about the craft and gaining valuable experience.

Schools are generally very receptive to older applicants as they can bring life experience to bear in the acting process. As Sartre said, "Acting is a question of absorbing other people's personalities and adding some of your own experience." No bad thing, then, to have a bit of life experience under your belt.

One thing is for sure: if you don't apply, you won't be considered by the drama school, so if you have that burning passion it's time to start knocking on doors.

What about training for under 18s?

For those too young to be eligible for three-year drama school courses, the traditional route is stage school, where a range of acting, singing and dance skills is likely to be taught. Most of these are private and therefore there will be considerable fees to meet, although there may be some scholarship options. There are a few publicly funded stage schools and a number of part-time options.

Another option for younger children to discover whether acting is really for them is to attend a drama workshop. The National Association of Youth Theatres (***www.nayt.org.uk***) and the National Youth Theatre (***www.nyt.org.uk***) will help you track down suitable workshops and youth theatre groups.

What about older actors?

As with any degree-level course, most people taking it are likely to be in their late teens or twenties – but that doesn't mean there aren't opening for mature students (ie anyone into their thirties!). Check with the drama school, though – some do have age limits. Even if they don't, steel yourself for being thrown into the society of people considerably younger than yourself. If you can't find a suitable full-time course, a part-time one may be worth considering, though these are less likely to lead to career openings afterwards.

Having said that, many young actors leave the profession in the first few years for one reason or another, so there may be a little less competition for work. Actors of all ages are needed for stage and screen alike, so there's always hope – but proper training will stand you in much better stead than simply being a keen member of the local Gilbert and Sullivan society.

What about training for actors with disabilities?

There's a growing demand for actors from a broader and more inclusive spectrum of society, so disability need not be an inherent barrier to an acting career (though opportunities may still be fewer). Check with the main drama schools what their policy is – and of course what the facilities there are like for disabled people, such as hearing loops for deaf people in auditoria or rehearsal spaces, ramps for wheelchairs and so on.

The National Disability Arts Forum (***www.ndaf.org***) may be able to help with general advice, both on finding training and work as well as overcoming any potential discrimination.

There are numerous theatre companies which either welcome or specialise in employing actors with disabilities. Some of these – such as Graeae (***www.graeae.org***) and Mind the Gap (***www.mind-the-gap.org.uk***) – run some training courses themselves and are building links with drama schools to improve access to training for disabled people.

Joining a course

Applying for a course entails contacting the school, via its website, by telephone or in writing, in order to get your hands on an application form and prospectus. A standard application form will ask for your basic details, your acting experience to date and your reasons for wanting to attend the course. Check the deadline for applications as these vary from course to course and school to school. Don't leave it until the last minute – get the application in as early as you can. There's nothing to stop you from applying for more than one course, though if you've received a place on one it's polite to let the other(s) know. There should be no fees for applying, but you should bear in mind that if you're called for an audition a school will usually charge an audition fee, as explained on p10. (For general advice on auditions see p111.)

The course itself

Once you've secured your place on a course you can give yourself a pat on the back, and then get ready for the hard work: fame costs. Okay, so you might not be looking for fame, but you get the point. If you're going to get the most out of the course (for which you'll be paying either directly or indirectly), you can't rest on your laurels. This isn't the quick route to celebrity and the paparazzi.

You will be expected to attend classes, prepare, rehearse, study, and to exercise self-discipline, commitment and organisation. You'll be working with respected teachers and alongside other talented actors who will go on to work in the industry and whose path you will cross time and time again in the coming years. So take the time to look, listen and learn.

Acting courses emphasise the practical exploration of theatre, with classes revolving around physical exercises, roleplays and scenarios leading to full productions, though every course will be backed up with lectures about the history and theory of acting.

Foundation courses

Some schools and a growing number of organisations offer foundation or 'taster' courses. These can be short-term, part-time or intensive courses designed to give you an introduction to acting. It can help to have completed a foundation course before applying for drama school but they shouldn't be viewed as a substitute for a full-time drama course. You should be wary of courses promising too much for a short investment of your time and a large investment of your money. As with all other courses, check out the credibility of the institution, teachers and facilities before parting with any money.

Courses: Useful links & organisations

National Council for Drama Training (NCDT)
{t} 020 7387 3650
Visit the NCDT's website – ***www.ncdt.co.uk*** – for a full list of accredited drama courses and to download a copy of their *Applicants' Guide to Auditioning and Interviewing at Dance and Drama School* or the *Guide to Vocational Training in Dance and Drama.*

Conference of Drama Schools (CDS)
www.drama.ac.uk

Courses, Careers – why choose drama school?
www.he.courses-careers.com/drama.htm

Part-time courses
www.ncdt.co.uk/parttime.asp

Learn Direct – Actors
www.learndirect-advice.co.uk

Drama school funding

Drama school training doesn't come cheap. Standard course fees will usually start at around £3,000 per year. In addition to tuition fees you'll also have to fund course materials, accommodation, travel and living expenses. If the course is in London, as most are, you should factor in additional costs for day-to-day living expenses. Rent, in particular, is more expensive in London than other regions.

Remember, on graduation you won't be guaranteed a lucrative West End contact, and even if you get an agent from your end of year showcase you could find yourself facing considerable ongoing costs. Headshots can cost up to £300, putting together a showreel may cost an additional £300, putting on a showcase can cost another £300 and finding out about jobs through The Stage, PCR, Casting Call Pro and other services can cost you an additional £500 per year, not to mention the cost of Spotlight and Equity. That's not to say you will need to bear all these costs, but it's worth building some flexibility into your finances to ensure you can survive those tough first months after graduation.

Student Loans

Student Loans are indexed to the rate of inflation and do not have to be paid back until you have graduated and your income is over £15,000 pa. They are available to eligible full-time higher education students; two types of loan cover fees and maintenance respectively.

For courses which began after September 2006, the fees loan will cover the full amount up to £3,070 for the 2007/8 academic year. As for maintenance loans, for the year 2007/8 the maximum loan is £3,495 for students living at home with parents, £4,510 for living away from home outside London, and £6,315 for those living away from home and based in London. Eligible students are automatically entitled to 75% of the maximum, with the remainder dependent on an assessment of the

WHAT DOES IT COST TO GO TO DRAMA SCHOOL?

Drama school training is intensive and expensive. There are three main ways drama school courses are funded.

The majority of accredited three-year courses in acting, musical theatre, stage management and technical theatre are degree programmes in higher education (HE) and government state-funded. Most drama schools now offer the three-year degree courses funded by means of a parent HE institution which usually awards the qualification.

Some accredited courses are in independent drama schools which are part of the Dance and Drama Awards (DaDA) scheme, a scholarship programme funded by the Department for Education and Skills. These courses offer professional diplomas awarded by Trinity College London. The awards were introduced in 1999 to increase access to dance, drama and stage management training from all sectors of the community and provide help with fees and maintenance for talented students wishing to attend approved vocational courses at independent dance and drama schools.

It is important to be aware that the awards provide scholarships to only a percentage of students on a course and the remaining students have to fund their own places similar to full-cost courses. Each drama school is responsible for allocating its DaDA scholarships, which are given to those students who show the most talent and potential at audition. The students' financial circumstances may also be taken into consideration when an award is given, but only as a secondary factor.

A relatively small number of accredited courses are full cost or independent courses, and do not attract any government funding. The students are responsible for full fees (which average £9,000) and living costs while studying.

student's and their household's income. The amounts are reduced in the final year of study to take into account the shorter year. For up-to-date details check the government's student finance information pages at ***www.direct.gov.uk/en/EducationAndLearning/UniversityAndHigherEducation/StudentFinance/***.

Maintenance grants
If you're from a low income household you may also be eligible for a maintenance grant from the government. These are worth up to £2,765 for the 2007/8 academic year and do not have to be paid back. Again, see ***www.direct.gov.uk*** for more information about these and other possible sources of funding.

Bursaries and scholarships
Many schools have their own bursary and scholarship schemes which will vary from full course fees and some help towards living expenses to smaller awards which will go some but not all the way to covering your costs. There will only be a limited number of bursaries/scholarships given out each year, and competition will be tough, so you certainly can't rely on, or expect to receive, this kind of financial support. Check out the funding policy and opportunities for each establishment thoroughly before applying.

Charities and other sources
It is also possible to raise funds from charities, trusts and foundations – a list of these is available in a factsheet at the NCDT website (***www.ncdt.co.uk/facts.asp***).

If you are going down this route, make sure you target suitable sources of funding carefully and avoid simply sending out a standard letter to as many organisations as you can get addresses for. Your application will stand much more of a chance if you've tailored it to an appropriate body, and in an individual manner. Another route might be to think of local businesses who have shown evidence of supporting the arts – check out local newspapers and theatres to see which sponsors' logos appear, and make contact with them.

ENTERING THE PROFESSION

For graduates entering the profession the opportunities for work are many and varied. Traditionally actors gained early experience by working in regional repertory theatres, though today they are just as likely to secure their first job in television. An actor's career may also involve work in film, corporate training videos, radio, commercials, voice-overs, cruise ship entertainment, small-scale theatre touring, theatre-in-education, and West End productions. An actor's life may include employment at some point in nearly all of these areas.

Funding: Useful links & organisations

Student Loans Company
{t} 0800 40 50 10
www.slc.co.uk

Hot Courses Funding Search
www.scholarship-search.org.uk

NCDT Course Costs
www.ncdt.co.uk/cost.asp

NCDT Fundraising Factsheet
www.ncdt.co.uk/facts.asp

Students Awards Agency for Scotland
www.saas.gov.uk

Student Finance Wales
www.studentfinancewales.co.uk

Further training

There will come a point in your professional career, perhaps when you're between roles, when you might think about refresher classes or further training. It can certainly be worthwhile, both professionally and in terms of your own self-belief, to flex those acting muscles and keep your skills sharp. It's all too easy to sit back and wait for the work to come your way. While practicing techniques such as breathing and vocal exercises is useful, further training can also help you network, bring you face-to-face with other actors and professionals and keep you in the loop for auditions and castings.

There are many courses out there for specific training. You could choose to work on your skills such as singing, accents, stage combat, movement, or different acting techniques. When picking a course, find out as much information as possible about the course and school to ensure their reputability. Endorsements from other actors and word-of-mouth feedback can help in deciding which course to choose before parting with your money. Don't be shy about learning new skills – the more strings to your bow, the more versatile you are, and the more opportunities you'll be suitable for.

In some cases you may be able to learn new skills one-to-one with private tuition or coaching. Look in *The Stage* for people advertising such services (where you will also find listings for one-off workshops).

Other ideas if funding is a problem

If you're concerned about the costs of further training you could choose to team up with other actors to read through plays or replay old drama school exercises. In addition, take time to read as many plays and scripts as possible, and catch innovative shows performed by professionals and your peers. Watching others perform will keep your ideas fresh which may be useful at your next audition. The crucial thing is to view acting as a career that requires ongoing support and development.

KEEP ON GROWING

James Beresford of The Actors Studio reflects on the importance of training, networking and self-development.

With the recent upsurge in interest in becoming a performer as a career, the number of graduates leaving drama schools and universities and seeking work in the industry grows each year. Added to the ready pool of actors already searching for work, this seems to make the chance of success an ever more distant possibility, leaving many despondent and unsure of what to do and which way to turn.

To combat this many people shun formal training or skill development, favouring rather to 'go it alone', attending a sea of open auditions or working for a pittance in shows that barely muster an audience. Those who have agent's representation lose sight of what they personally can do to promote or develop their careers, believing their agent to be a miracle worker who will, unaided, transport their career to new heights!

Somewhere in the middle of this downward spiral the discovery is made that those who are successful and fulfilled in their careers are the ones who have a firm grip on the reins and are in charge of what is going on around them. Attending regular courses and workshops, networking, expanding their portfolio of plays, speeches and songs and absorbing as much information as possible all assist the jobbing actor to navigate their way through the minefield of negativity that surrounds being unemployed, and open up a whole range of different possibilities both professionally and socially.

It is important to research the courses and workshops that are available as fully as possible. Do not be afraid to ask for as much information as you need, and where possible try to attend courses run by people who are actively working within the industry. These people will not only give you valuable, up-to-date information, but they may have the potential to open doors to possible future employment.

As with many other aspects of the industry, information is passed through the grapevine! Ask what others have been doing: often the most positive feedback comes from first hand experience. There is something out there for everybody. Also bear in mind costing. Finances are always a sore point, and you may need to carefully juggle your situation in order to make things work.

The most important thing is keeping a sense of perspective on where you are. Collective learning and sharing of experiences assists everyone in any walk of life to view their situation with renewed clarity. Development whether personal or career based can only be positive, and with that, new possibilities will not be far away.

Previously an actor and then an agent, James Beresford is now manager of The Actors Studio at Pinewood Studios. Offering courses run by distinguished practitioners and expert teachers, including many directors and casting directors who are at the forefront of the film and television industries, an honest and frank appraisal of the individual's potential is always at the forefront of their philosophy. Information on The Actors Studio can be found at ***www.actorsstudio.co.uk***.

Further training: Useful links & organisations

The Actor's Centre

With a membership of 2,500 actors, The Actor's Centre is well known in the industry and has a very good reputation as one of the few institutions to cater to the ongoing needs of professional actors. In the words of The Actor's Centre, their mission is "to provide actors with professional development of the highest quality and the opportunity to enhance every aspect of their craft". Workshops and classes explore the total range of acting from classical theatre to mainstream TV. The ethos of The Actor's Centre is very much to help actors by plugging them into what's happening and what's about to happen in theatre, television, radio and film. Classes range from £17-£34 per day, with class sizes limited to a dozen.

www.actorscentre.co.uk
{t} 020 7240 3940
admin@actorscentre.co.uk

The Actor's Temple
Teaching the Meisner technique, The Actor's Temple holds regular classes, many of which are walk-in classes, though for the more popular ones you should pre-book. It's free to become a member – you then pay per class attended. Along with The Actor's Centre, The Actor's Temple enjoys a very good reputation and is, according to its founders, "committed to training professional actors to achieve more direct, intense and truthful performances".

www.actorstemple.com
{t} 020 7383 3535
info@actorstemple.com

The City Lit
The City Lit offers a wide range of classes including preparing for auditions, the Alexander technique, the Meisner technique, accents, sightreading, speaking Shakespeare, Acting in Chekhov, Acting in Shakespeare, acting for radio, clowning & performance, stage-fighting and many others.

www.citylit.ac.uk
{t} 020 7430 0544
{f} 020 7405 3347
advice@citylit.ac.uk

Theatre Royal Haymarket, Masterclasses
Each year the Theatre Royal Haymarket puts on a series of masterclasses from some of the UK's most renowned actors. Past masters have included Gillian Anderson, Anita Dobson, Simon Callow, Jeremy Irons, Kwame Kwei-Armah, Alan Rickman, Timothy West...

"Masterclass exists to give young people the chance to work with, talk to and learn from theatre's most outstanding actors, directors, designers and writers." (Theatre Royal Haymarket, Masterclasses)

Classes are free for 17-30 year olds and mature students, or if you're a Masterclass Friend (to become a Friend there's an annual donation of £45).

www.trh.co.uk
{t} 020 7930 8890
boxoffice@trh.co.uk

A-Z of drama schools & colleges

Arts Educational School London
14 Bath Road
Chiswick
London W4 1LY
{t} 020 8987 6655
drama@artsed.co.uk
www.artsed.co.uk

Courses:
B.A.(Hons) Acting, 3 years
M.A. Acting, 1 year
Details:
The School of Acting offers contemporary, industry-relevant vocational training for actors. It equips the student to a high level for a career as a professional actor in a range of performance contexts including live performance, film, television and radio. The School of Acting works to create an environment for training, which is based on trust, mutual respect and passion. The school believes that it is from within this environment that students will be secure enough to take huge creative risks. In addition, the school believes that the individual performer learns best from within the group, and that the theatre ensemble grows from the constructive input of every individual.

ALRA (Academy of Live and Recorded Arts)
Studio 1, The Royal Patriotic Building
Fitzhugh Grove
London SW18 3SX
{t} 020 8870 6475
info@alra.co.uk
www.alra.co.uk

Courses:
B.A.(Hons) Acting, 3 years
National Diploma in Professional Acting, 1 year
Details:
The courses are designed to give you the adaptability, flexibility and openness needed to sustain a career in the stage and screen industry, you will explore fully and progressively your creative, vocal and physical potential. We will instil in you the self-discipline the industry expects of you. You will be shown current working methods and practices to enable you to work effectively and professionally. You will be in continual contact with professional practitioners from all areas of the industry and you will receive lectures and workshops on the practical business of being an actor.

Birmingham School of Acting (BSSD)
G2 - Millennium Point
Curzon Street
Birmingham B4 7XG
{t} 0121 331 7220
info@bsa.uce.ac.uk
www.bssd.ac.uk

Courses:
B.A.(Hons) Acting, 3 years
Graduate Diploma in Acting (over 21s)
Details:
Birmingham School of Acting is a small specialist institution with 134 full time students on its two undergraduate acting courses and a staff of more than 60

working professionals. Birmingham School of Acting is a faculty of UCE Birmingham (University of Central England) and is accredited by the National Council for Drama Training (NCDT).

Bristol Old Vic Theatre School

2 Downside Road
Bristol BS8 2XF
{t} 0117 9733535
enquiries@oldvic.ac.uk
www.oldvic.ac.uk

Courses:
B.A.(Hons) Acting, 3 years
2yr Diploma in Professional Acting
1yr Cert HE Professional Acting
1yr Professional Acting Course for Overseas Students
Details:
Opened by Laurence Olivier in 1946, the school is an industry-led vocational training establishment preparing students for careers in acting, stage management, costume, design, scenic art, directing, theatre arts management, production management, lighting, electrics, sound, studio management, propmaking, VT editing and scenic construction. Work encompasses the breadth of theatre, television, radio, film, recording, events and trade presentations and the ever-increasing areas of employment open to a trained workforce in arts and entertainment.

Central School of Speech and Drama

Embassy Theatre
Eton Avenue
London NW3 3HY
{t} 020 7722 8183
enquiries@cssd.ac.uk
www.cssd.ac.uk

Courses:
B.A.(Hons) Acting, 3 years
Details:
Founded in 1906 by Elsie Fogerty to offer an entirely new form of training in speech and drama for young actors and other students. The choice of name – the Central School – highlighted the school's commitment to a broad range of training systems for vocal and dramatic performance. It espoused principles that were firmly held yet responsive to change. That sense of continuing critical openness to new developments is a lasting hallmark of the school.

Drama Centre London

Central Saint Martins College
Southampton Row
London WC1B 4AP
{t} 020 7514 7022
info@csm.arts.ac.uk
www.csm.arts.ac.uk/drama/

Courses:
B.A.(Hons) Acting, 3 years
Details:
Founded in 1963 by a visionary group of tutors and students, Drama Centre London offers an inspirational, passionate environment for those who are resolutely serious about acting and their careers. An Advisory Council which includes Sir Anthony Hopkins and leading directors Declan Donnellan, Adrian Noble and Max Stafford-Clark guides the school's distinctive approach. Since 1999 Drama Centre has been part of Central Saint Martins College of Art and Design, a constituent college of the University of the Arts London and an internationally renowned institution which offers the most diverse and

comprehensive range of undergraduate and postgraduate courses in art, design and performance in the country. Central Saint Martins is situated at the very heart of London, close to the theatres and opera houses of Covent Garden, the British Museum and the BBC. As University of the Arts London students, Drama Centre students have access to a range of services, including: advice on accommodation and careers; special support for international students; specialist libraries; internet and intranet facilities; a language centre; professional counselling; and support for students with disabilities.

Drama Studio London
Grange Court
1 Grange Road, Ealing
London W5 5QN
{t} 020 8579 3897
admin@dramastudiolondon.co.uk
www.dramastudiolondon.co.uk

Courses:
1 Year Diploma (over 21s)
Details:
Drama Studio London was born, in 1966, out of the need for a new, more realistic approach to actor training that took account of the professional requirements and demands of the theatre for which the students were being prepared. Over the years the goal has always remained the same: to graduate well-trained actors, technically and personally equipped to face the constantly changing demands of the professional theatre of today.

East 15 Acting School
Hatfields, Rectory Lane
Loughton
Essex IG10 3RY
{t} 020 8508 5983
east15@essex.ac.uk
www.east15.ac.uk

Courses:
B.A.(Hons) Acting, 3 years
B.A.(Hons) Physical Theatre, 3 years
1 Year Diploma (over 21s)
Details:
East 15 grew from the work of Joan Littlewood's famed Theatre Workshop. Much of the Littlewood approach was based upon the theories of Stanislavski, and the company inherited the socially committed spirit of the Unity Theatre movement, which brought many new voices into British Theatre for the first time. Theatre Workshop broke new ground, re-interpreting the classics for a modern age, commissioning new plays from socially committed writers, and creating an ensemble capable of inventing new work, such as the now legendary *Oh What a Lovely War*. Littlewood created a wonderful ensemble, who combined inspired, improvisational brilliance with method, technique, research, text analysis, and the expression of real emotions. Over the years, new training methods were evolved to strip actors of affectations, attitudes, ego trips. The quest was always to search for truth: of oneself, the character, the text.

Guildford School of Acting
Millmead Terrace
Guildford
Surrey GU2 4YT
{t} 01483 560701
enquiries@conservatoire.org
www.conservatoire.org

Courses:
National Diploma in Professional Acting, 3 years
B.A.(Hons) in Musical Theatre, 3 years
M.A. in Acting, 1 year (0ver 21s)
Details:
From the moment you start at the Conservatoire to the moment you graduate will the most challenging time in your life. Training for the profession is as tough as training to compete in the Olympics. We have to prepare you for the competition you will meet once you have graduated. The course is designed to get the best out of you and to encourage you to be versatile in your skills. We concentrate on training the whole person. Our job is to improve your strengths and tackle your weaknesses with you and our overall aim is to help you become versatile as an actor who, can sing and dance and who can work on musicals or straight plays or even in television and radio; all your classes connect to that aim. Acting is the core to all that we do and the idea behind your training is that the techniques you learn mean that you can act through singing and dancing as well as through scripts for the stage, television, film or radio.

Guildhall School of Music and Drama
Silk Street
Barbican
London EC2Y 8DT
{t} 020 7628 2571
drama@gsmd.ac.uk
www.gsmd.ac.uk

Courses:
B.A.(Hons) Acting, 3 years
MA in Training Actors (Voice) or (Movement), 2 years part-time
Details:
GSA's reputation for training multi-skilled performers gained international recognition with the inception of the Musical Theatre course in 1967. The School's ability to train the very best all round performers has gone from strength to strength under the expert leadership of Peter Barlow (Conservatoire Director) and Gerry Tebbutt (Head of Performance) who joined the School in 1994 bringing with them a new philosophy and approach to training. Their influence and that of its expert specialist staff has ensured GSA's reputation of being the leader in multi-skilled performance training.

Italia Conti Academy of Theatre Arts Ltd
Avondale
72 Landor Road
London SW9 9PH
{t} 020 7733 3210
acting@lsbu.ac.uk
www.italiaconti-acting.co.uk

Courses:
B.A.(Hons) Acting, 3 years
Details:
Founded in 1911 by the actress Italia Conti, the Itali Conti Academy of Theatre Arts trains actors for the professional stage and screen. The Academy is committed to providing an environment in which its students can be trained and educated to develop and broaden their skills to their

individual highest possible standards. Italia Conti students receive the unique benefits of training based on nearly 100 years of knowledge and experience geared to the needs of the present day.

London Academy of Music and Dramatic Art
155 Talgarth Road
London W14 9DA
{t} 020 8834 0500
enquiries@lamda.org.uk
www.lamda.org.uk

Courses:
B.A.(Hons) Acting, 3 years
Two Year Acting Course BA (Hons)
Details:
LAMDA is an independent drama school, dedicated to the vocational training of actors, stage managers and technicians in the skills and levels of creativity necessary to meet the highest demands and best opportunities in theatre, film and TV. The group work ethic is central to LAMDA's teaching. The training does not deconstruct the student in order to rebuild a LAMDA product but encourages and develops innate skills. The courses are practical not academic. Class times are Monday - Friday 9am - 5.30pm with some evening and weekend classes. All classes are compulsory.

Manchester Metropolitan University School of Theatre
Mabel Tylecote Building
Cavendish Street
Manchester M15 6BX
{t} 0161 247 1305
enquiries@mmu.ac.uk
www.artdes.mmu.ac.uk

Courses:
B.A.(Hons) Acting, 3 years
Details:
The course offers students the opportunity to develop and match new and existing skills to a professional acting career. Workshops, seminars, and public performances are designed to synthesize component skills that include voice, movement, acting, textual analysis, and research. The course aims to nurture instinctive ability in an environment that allows for the development of new skills whilst simultaneously enabling individuals to recognise particular strengths and abilities. The final year of the course is entirely performance based with students working with both staff and guest directors from across Europe in the preparation of a series of public performances. Former students include Sir Anthony Sher, Julie Walters, David Threlfall, Richard Griffiths, Bernard Hill, Steve Coogan, John Thomson, Noreen Kershaw, Amanda Burton and Adam Kotz.

Mountview Academy of Theatre Arts
1 Kingfisher Place
Clarendon Road
London N22 6XF
{t} 020 8881 2201
enquiries@mountview.ac.uk
www.mountview.org.uk

Courses:
B.A.(Hons) Acting, 3 years
Acting (1 Year Postgraduate Diploma)
Classical Acting (1Year MA)
Details:
Founded in 1945, Mountview is now recognised as one of the country's leading Academies of Theatre Arts, offering an extensive and stimulating training for those

interested in pursuing a performance, directing or technical theatre career. Mountview's courses are structured to give students a thorough grounding in all aspects of their chosen field. Our students are trained to a high level to develop a range of skills which will enable them to bring thought, energy and commitment to their professional work, giving them the tools to succeed in a competitive industry.

Oxford School of Drama

Sansomes Farm Studios
Woodstock OX20 1ER
{t} 01993 812883
info@oxforddrama.ac.uk
oxford.drama.ac.uk

Courses:
Three Year Diploma in Acting
One Year Acting Course
Details:
We offer practical, hands-on training to talented students who are committed to forging careers as actors. In order that we are able to provide the best possible training we have decided not to run degree courses. This means that we don't have pressures put upon us to increase our number of students as is so often the case in drama schools which enter into partnership with a university. It also means that our courses can remain truly vocational, with no element of essay-writing. However, we do understand that our students want recognition of their achievements in the form of a national qualification, so both our three-year and one-year courses offer vocational qualifications accredited by Trinity College London which are equivalent to degrees (level 6 and level 5 on the National Qualifications Framework respectively).

Queen Margaret University College

Clerwood Terrace
Corstorphine
Edinburgh EH12 8TS
{t} 0131 317 3247
dramaadmin@qmu.ac.uk
www.qmuc.ac.uk
Courses:
BA/BA (Hons) Acting and Performance, 3 to 4 years
Details:
The School offers a dynamic programme of training geared towards professional work in the arts and entertainment industries and a lively and inquisitive practical study of contemporary theatre and links with the industry are strong. In both undergraduate and postgraduate education, the aim is to develop graduates who are critical and reflective independent practitioners and are immediately employable within the theatre and performance sectors. Furthermore, as a school we believe that it is vital that our work reflects contemporary working practice and therefore, where appropriate, students collaborate across programmes on a variety of projects.

Rose Bruford College

Lamorbey Park
Burnt Oak Lane
Sidcup DA15 9DF
{t} 020 8308 2600
enquiries@bruford.ac.uk
www.bruford.ac.uk

Courses:
B.A.(Hons) Acting, 3 years
Details:
The programme is designed to produce an artist who is flexible and articulate, able to

work in a variety of genres and repertoires with the ability to apply skills as demanded by a text and its performance conditions.

Royal Academy of Dramatic Art
62-64 Gower Street
London WC1E 6ED
{t} 020 7636 7076
enquiries@rada.ac.uk
www.rada.org

Courses:
B.A.(Hons) Acting, 3 years
Details:
The three year course is a training for students who wish to earn a living working not only in the more traditional outlets but in the many alternative areas of theatre, film, television and radio. It is an arduous course with a minimum working day of 10 am to 6.30 pm with individual classes in the evening. The objective is to encourage development of individual skills at the highest level and to utilise those skills in contributing unreservedly to the development of the group by actively participating in the content and conditions of its working life. The course divides itself roughly into two parts; intensive work on individual skills and the application of those skills to work on group projects and productions for public performance.

Royal Scottish Academy of Music and Drama
100 Renfrew Street
Glasgow G2 3DB
{t} 0141 332 4101
dramaadmissions@rsamd.ac.uk
www.rsamd.ac.uk

Courses:
3 year undergraduate acting course
Details:
The School of Drama is a dynamic, leading edge place of training and development for emergent artists. It is one of the UK's premiere schools and has a rapidly evolving international profile. It aims to nurture and promote the development of artists of excellence, enabling them to pursue fruitful and meaningful careers in a national and international context, thereby making a contribution to the cultural landscapes.

The Royal Welsh College of Music and Drama
Cathays Park
Cardiff CF10 3ER
{t} 029 2039 1327
drama.admissions@rwcmd.ac.uk
www.rwcmd.ac.uk

Courses:
B.A.(Hons) Acting, 3 years
Postgraduate Diploma in Acting for Stage, Screen and Radio, 1 year
Details:
Established in 1949 at Cardiff Castle, the college is the National Conservatoire of Wales. We provide specialist practical and performance-based training that enables students to enter and influence the music, theatre and related professions. We offer an exceptional environment in which to pursue a professional acting course. Our established teaching team is made up of highly-experienced professional practitioners, who will help you develop the physical and emotional resources that will enable you to respond to the wide-ranging demands of the contemporary acting professions. We have designed this course to equip you with the full range of knowledge and skills you will need to succeed in theatre, film, TV and radio.

Section 2
Agents

The agent's role

Good agents are industry veterans who will put you forward for suitable upcoming auditions (often not publicly advertised) and protect your interests from unscrupulous producers. A good agent will work alongside you to help you develop a financially stable and fulfilling career. While it is not obligatory to get an agent, it is advisable. If casting directors (see the next chapter for more about them) are the doorways to the acting world then casting agents are the keys.

What does an agent do?
Their primary role is to put you forward for castings and help get you work. They will use their contacts and keep their ears to the ground to raise your profile and maximise the number of auditions and interviews you are considered for. Privy to opportunities that are generally kept out of the public realm, they have close relationships with the all-important casting directors.

The other important role of an agent is to negotiate fees on your behalf. Your agent should know the market rate for a particular production and the business of reaching an agreed fee should be their area of expertise. They will also be responsible for the contract itself. Not only will they be working on your behalf to get you the best deal (and their own, because of course they are dependent on the commission they make from you for their own living), they will be saving you from having to go through the often tricky nitty-gritty of fees and contracts, freeing you to concentrate on the main job in hand – the actual acting.

There should be no joining fee for signing-up with an agency, so be wary of those who try to get you to part with any money up front. The actors' union Equity advises against signing up with anyone who asks for money at this stage. (For more information about Equity see p176.)

Most agents work on a sole representation basis – ie you're represented only by that one agent. Any work you get (whether through the agent or your own networking and contacts) will be subject to commission, which varies from agency to agency. The rate of commission is generally between 10% and 20% – but remember that larger agencies, and indeed the more successful smaller ones, will also charge VAT on top of that.

No matter how much you resent seeing a slice of your earnings being given over to the Inland Revenue and a further slice to your agent, especially if it's acting work you've got through your own efforts rather than via the agent, don't try to hoodwink them by withholding details of acting work to avoid commission. This is a rocky road that's likely to lead to the break-up of the partnership.

Some agencies will give you a contract to sign. Make sure you read it through properly and, if you're happy, sign two copies, keeping one for yourself. An important part of the contract to look out for is the notice period for leaving an agency – there may be a period where you have left but are still obliged to pay commission, so check the details carefully.

Personal managers

Some agents are members of the Personal Managers' Association (PMA), offering a wider range of services to their clients – but remember that personal managers are not necessarily the same as agents. Personal managers will work with an actor one-to-one to field contact with the press, arrange tours and so on, as in the music industry, but may not have the same relationship with possible sources of work as an agent does.

Getting an agent

Ask fellow actors (and teachers if you have attended a drama course) for recommendations and tips; check websites; view agency websites (see if they are open to new clients or if their lists are closed) and utilise all the resources at your disposal (see Section 7 of this book; you can also search for agents at the Casting Call Pro website – ***uk.castingcallpro.com*** – and that of The Agents' Association, ***www.agents-uk.com***). Agencies vary from the very large such as ICM with hundreds of (often prestigious) clients, to much smaller ones with a staff of only one or two and a client list of perhaps a few dozen.

Think about whether the size of the agency matters to you: larger ones are likely to have a greater reach, but may not be able to spare time for prolonged personal contact with clients. Conversely, a smaller agency can make you feel more cared for – but have fewer contacts. Either way, always be friendly in your dealings and get to know the staff.

Once you've drawn up your target shortlist, write to the agencies with a covering letter, your CV and a professional black and white photograph. Write your name and contact details on the back of the photograph, too. Don't email the agency unless they specifically invite it, and avoid phoning unless to check whether they are currently taking on new clients.

It's helpful, though more time-consuming, to tailor your approach to individual agents (see the advice writing a covering letter in Section 3). Address your letter to a specific person – contact names are listed in the directory of agents after this chapter. Be straight-to-the-point (without being rude) in your letter. Ensure you check the postage required before sending your package as a CV, headshot and cover letter will require more than just a standard 1st class stamp. No agency will thank you for obliging them to pay a shortfall in the postage!

In your covering letter explain why you feel this agency is right for you and highlight any showcase or productions you'll be performing in in the near future, should the agent wish to see you on stage. Be aware that due to the sheer volume of interest they receive, and because their main responsibility is to their existing clients, agents can't see every production, so be patient and don't be put off by a standard 'our lists are full' reply.

There is a limit on the number of actors an agent can represent. For this reason they are careful about whom they represent and will be looking for actors whom they believe show potential and will be successful. Depending on their existing client list, they may feel they have reached capacity in certain areas (eg age, look etc.), though most agents would be willing to take on an extra client if they feel they have exceptional talent. In your letter, mention that you can supply a showreel on request.

An agent may respond by saying that you look interesting but are not suitable at that particular time (for a variety of reasons), but to keep in touch. This is sound advice: you can send an updated CV and headshot every now and then to keep you on their radar (but make sure you don't badger them to the point of irritation!).

Keep sending out letters and working your contacts. It can be dispiriting but if you're deterred by this initial rejection you have a long road ahead of you when it comes to casting auditions. Representation and roles may not come immediately, but that's not to say it won't happen. Your watchwords should be self-belief and perseverance.

Some agencies may expect you to come for an interview before they take you on – as always, dress smartly and be confident without being pushy, and turn up on time!

The actor/agent relationship

The relationship between an agent and an actor is vital to the ongoing success of the partnership. Dialogue is the key to a good working relationship with your agent. A good agent will let you know what they're putting you forward for and may also be able to offer you advice and give you post-audition feedback from the casting director. Equally, you should let an agent know how a casting went. The more feedback you give them, the better you can plan ahead and prepare for future castings.

There will be, unless you're very lucky, periods of unemployment during which you may be tearing your hair out. It's natural to wonder if your agent is doing all they can for you and to question your representation. Remember, though, that this is the nature of the industry you've chosen. Agents can sing your praises and get you a foot in the door but after that it's up to you. The truth is that many, many actors may be put forward and considered for a role, but the part will be given to only one. That you don't get a part is not the fault of your agent.

If you feel you're simply not being put forward for things and are effectively lying dormant on your agent's books then it's a good idea to raise this with them. In many cases your concerns will be addressed and allayed. (It's not in an agent's interest to ignore you – an out of work actor brings no revenue!) In some cases there may be a parting of the ways, mutual or otherwise, and you choose to seek new representation. Try to part on good terms and leave the door open. The acting profession is swift-moving and you'll run into the same people time and time again, so it makes good sense to try to keep people on your good side and maintain amicable relations.

The relationship between an agent and their actors is a two-way street. The agent's reputation depends not just on their negotiating skills and rapport with casting directors, but also their clients. You are representing them and so should be professional and avoid behaviour and situations that may reflect badly on the agent.

The PMA (***www.thepma.com***) has a code of conduct which member agencies adhere to, making the responsibilities of each party clear. The most important part of your relationship with any agent is to stay in touch (without making a nuisance of yourself) – communication will usually clear things up. If you're a member of Equity, you can download the organisation's helpful 'You and Your Agent' booklet from the members' section of the website ***www.equity.org.uk***.

Self-marketing

Your agent is a vital part of your ongoing efforts to get work. This doesn't mean you should cease marketing yourself: keep sending out letters, networking and checking websites and publications for castings. It's to your advantage to market yourself as best you can and to keep plugging away. The agent isn't your sole route to work, so don't be tempted to sign up and assume you can relax and let them do all the work. Agents are likely to respond well to proactive clients, as long as you don't try to interfere with their way of doing things.

A-Z of agents

10 Twenty Two Casting
PO Box 1022
Liverpool L69 5WZ
{t} 0870 850 1022
{f} 0151 207 4230
nick@10twentytwo.com
www.10twentytwo.com
Contact: Nick Durham
Founded: 2002
No. of clients: 2000

21st Century Actors Management
E10, Panther House
38 Mount Pleasant
London WC1X 0AN
{t} 020 7278 3438
mail@21stcenturyactors.co.uk
www.21stcenturyactors.co.uk
Contact: Penny Sands
Founded: 1991
No. of clients: 20
Notes: Apply as and when; enclose hard copies of CV/headshot.

41 Management
3rd Floor
74 Rose Street Lane North
Edinburgh EH2 3DX
{t} 0131 225 3585
{f} 0131 225 4535
mhunwick@41man.co.uk
www.41man.co.uk
Contact: Maryam Hunwick

9ine Partners Ltd
Move
{t} 0845 055 1979
{f} 020 8749 7441
karenb@9inepartners.com
www.9inepartners.com
Contact: Karen Beaufort-Lloyd
Founded: 2005
No. of clients: 50

A & B Personal Management
Suite 330
Linen Hall
162-168 Regent Street W1B 5TD
{t} 020 7434 4262
billellis@aandb.co.uk
Contact: Bill Ellis
Founded: 1982
Notes: As and when, email contact initially.

A & J Management
242a The Ridgeway
Botany Bay
Enfield EN2 8AP
{t} 2083420542
{f} 020 8342 0842
info@ajmanagement.co.uk
www.ajmanagement.co.uk
Contact: Jackie Michael
Founded: 1985
No. of clients: 600
Notes: Moving into extras and walkons.

A.D.A Enterprises
78 St Margarets Road, Twickenham
Middlesex TW1 2LP
{t} 020 8892 1716
{f} 020 8892 1716
snert@hotmail.com
Contact: Tricia Evans
Founded: 1983
Notes: As and when across the board.

A.R.C. Entertainments
10 Church Lane
Redmarshall
Stockton on Tees TS21 1EP
{t} 01740 631292
arcents@aol.com
www.arcents.co.uk
Contact: Carol M Mottershead
Founded: 1998

Academy Castings
Blue Square
272 Bath Street
Glasgow G2 4JR
{t} (00)+(0)141 354 8873
{f} (00)+(0)141 354 8876
robert@academycastings.co.uk
www.academycastings.co.uk
Contact: Robert Szemis
Founded: 2003
No. of clients: 50
Notes: Film, Television, commercials.

Access Artiste Management
PO Box 39925
London EC1V 0WN
{t} 020 8505 1094
info@access-associates.co.uk
www.access-associates.co.uk
Contact: Sarah Bryan
Founded: 1999
No. of clients: 80

Act Out Agency
22 Greek Street
Stockport
Cheshire SK3 8AB
{t} 0161 429 7413
ab22@aol.com
Contact: Kieran McPeake
Founded: 1995
No. of clients: 40

Actitude
Studio 233
186 St. Albans Road
Herts WD24 4AS
{t} 020 8728 3484
{f} 020 8728 3484
actitude.info@virgin.net
www.actitudemanagement.co.uk
Contact: Rai Rossetto
Founded: 2004
No. of clients: 20

ActNatural
PO Box 25
St Agnes TR5 0ZN
{t} 01872 552 552
info@actnatural.co.uk
www.actnatural.co.uk
Contact: Lesley Kazan
Founded: 2002
No. of clients: hundreds

Actors' Creative Team
Albany House
82-84 South End
Croydon CR0 1DQ
{t} 2082398892
office@actorscreativeteam.co.uk
www.actorscreativeteam.co.uk
Contact: Dawn Rhodes-Shaw
Founded: 2001
No. of clients: 18

Actors International
Conway Hall
25 Red Lion Square
London WC1R 4RL
{t} 020 7242 9300
{f} 020 7831 8319
mail@actorsinternational.co.uk
Contact: Kay Potter
Founded: 2000
No. of clients: 80

Actors World Casting
13 Briarbank Road
London W13 0HH
{t} 020 8998 2579
katherine@actors-world-production.com
Contact: Katherine Pageon
Founded: 2005
No. of clients: 60

After Dark Management Agency
9 Greek Street
London W1D 4DQ
{t} 01708 55 22 65
afterdarkma@aol.com
www.afterdarkma.co.uk
Contact: Omar Shaker
Founded: 2005
No. of clients: 100
Notes: dancers, models, actors.

All Talent UK
Central Chambers
93 Hope Street
Glasgow G2 6LD
{t} 0141 221 8887
{f} 0141 221 8883
enquiries@alltalentuk.co.uk
www.alltalentuk.co.uk
Contact: Kay Gannon
Founded: 2005
No. of clients: few hundred
Notes: model agency also.

ALW Associates
1 Grafton Chambers
Grafton Place
London NW1 1LN
{t} 020 7388 7018
{f} 020 7813 1398
alweurope@onetel.com
Contact: Carol Paul
Founded: 1995
No. of clients: 50

am:pm the actors' agency
S2 Central Park
33 Alfred Street
Belfast BT2 8BD
{t} 028 90235568
{f} 028 90235568
mark@ampmactors.com
www.ampmactors.com
Contact: Mark McCrory
Founded: 2004
No. of clients: 70
Notes: open books April then every 3rd month.

Amanda Andrews Agency
30 Caverswall Road
Blythe Bridge
Staffordshire ST11 9BG
{t} 01782 393889
amanda.andrews.agency@tesco.net
Contact: Amanda Andrews
Founded: 2000
No. of clients: 30

American Agency
14 Bonny Street
London NW1 9PG
NW1 9PG
{t} 020 7485 8883
{f} 020 7482 4666
americanagency@btconnect.com
www.americanagency.tv
Contact: Ed Cobb
Founded: 2000
No. of clients: 60

Amethyst Management
4 Pauls Lane
Southport
Merseyside PR9 9 QE
{t} 01704 549979
sharonamethystsharon@yahoo.co.uk
Contact: Tom Gray

Founded: 2007
No. of clients: 40

ANA Actors
55 Lambeth Walk
London SE11 6DX
{t} 020 7735 0999
{f} 020 7735 8177
info@ana-actors.co.uk
www.ana-actors.co.uk
Contact: Sandie Bakker
Founded: 1995
No. of clients: 35

Andrea Wilder Agency
23 Cambrian Drive
Colwyn Bay
Conwy LL28 4SL
{t} 07919 202401
{f} 070922 49314
casting@awagency.co.uk
www.awagency.co.uk
Contact: Andrea Wilder
Founded: 1998
No. of clients: 20

Andrew Manson Personal Management
288 Munster Road
London SW6 6BQ
{t} 020 7386 9158
{f} 020 7381 8874
post@AndrewManson.com
www.andrewmanson.com
Contact: Andrew Manson
Founded: 1984
No. of clients: 80

APM Associates
PO Box 834
Hemel Hempstead
HP3 9ZP
{t} 01442 252 907
{f} 01442 241 099
apm@apmassociates.net
www.apmassociates.net
Contact: Linda French
Founded: 1989
No. of clients: 70

Arena Personal Management
Panther House
38 Mount Pleasant
London WC1X 0AP
{t} 020 7278 1661
{f} 020 7278 1661
arenapmltd@aol.com
www.arenapmltd.co.uk
Contact: Susan Scott
Founded: 1985
No. of clients: 18

Astral Actors Management
7 Greenway Close
London NW9 5AZ
{t} 020 8728 2782
info@astralactors.com
www.astralactors.com
Contact: Liz Felton
Founded: 2004
No. of clients: 40
Notes: no cold CVs without invite to see something or showreel.

Atmosphere Entertainments
17-19 Bedford Street
Covent Garden
London WC2 9HP
{t} 020 7868 5588
ailsya@atmosphere.uk.com
www.atmosphere.uk.com
Contact: Maxine Lankitus
Founded: 2000
No. of clients: 120
Notes: corporate, commercial ents speciality acts etc.

Audrey Benjamin Agency
278A Elgin Avenue
London W9 1JR
{t} 020 7289 7180
aud@elginavenue.fsbusiness.co.uk
Contact: Audrey Benjamin
Founded: 1985
No. of clients: 40

Barrie Stacey Promotions
Apt.8 Shaldon Mansions
132 Charing Cross Road
London WC2H 0LA
{t} 020 7836 4128
{f} 020 7836 2949
hopkinstacey@aol.com
www.barriestacey.com
Contact: Barrie Stacey
Founded: 1966

Bloomfields Management
34 South Molton Street
London W1K 5BP
{t} 020 7493 4448
{f} 020 7493 4449
www.bloomfieldsmanagement.com
Contact: Emma Bloomfield
Founded: 2004
No. of clients: 40
Notes: Hard copies only with SAE.

Bodens
99 East Barnet Road
New Barnet
Herts EN4 8RF
{t} 020 8447 0909
{f} 020 8449 5212
info@bodensagency.com
www.bodensagency.com
Contact: Adam Boden
Founded: 1979
No. of clients: 70

Brian Taylor Associates
50 Pembroke Road
Kensington
London W8 6NX
{t} 020 7602 6141
{f} 020 7602 6301
briantaylor@nqassoc.freeserve.co.uk
Contact: Brian Taylor
Founded: 1970
No. of clients: 80

Brood Management
3 Queen's Garth
London SE23 3UF
{t} 020 8699 1071
{f} 020 8699 1107
broodmanagement@aol.com
Contact: Brian Parsonage Kelly
Founded: 2003
No. of clients: 40

Byron's Management
76 St James Lane
London N10 3DF
{t} 020 8444 4445
{f} 020 8444 4040
byronscasting@aol.com
www.byronsmanagement.co.uk
Contact: Cat Simmons
Founded: 1995
No. of clients: 140

C K Casting
22 Oakland Place
Buckhurst Hill
Essex IG9 5JZ
{t} 020 8554 2316
carmelthomas@ckcasting.co.uk
www.ckcasting.co.uk
Contact: Kerry Goodyear
Founded: 2004
No. of clients: 125

Canongate Actor and Model Management
9 Waters Close
Leith
Edinburgh EH6 6RB
{t} 0131 555 4455
{f} 0131 555 2021
al@canongate.com
www.canongate.com
Contact: Alistair George
Founded: 2004
No. of clients: 100

Christopher Antony Associates
The Old Dairy
164 Thames Road
London W4 3QS
{t} 020 8994 9952
{f} 020 8742 8066
info@christopherantony.co.uk
wwww.christopheranthony.com
Contact: Chris Sheils, Kerry Walker
Founded: 2005
No. of clients: 20

Chrystel Arts
6 Eunice Grove
Chesham
Bucks HP5 1RL
{t} 01494 773336
{f} 01494 773336
chrystelarts@beeb.net
Contact: Chrissi Minter
Founded: 2000
No. of clients: 30

Cinel Gabran Management
P.O. Box 5163
Cardiff
Wales CF5 9BJ
{t} 0845 0 666605
{f} 0845 0 666601
info@cinelgabran.co.uk
www.cinelgabran.co.uk
Contact: David Chance
Founded: 1988
No. of clients: 70
Notes: Closed to English language at the moment, more Welsh language wanted.

Circuit Personal Management Ltd
Suite 71, SEC
Bedford Street
Stoke on Trent ST1 4PZ
{t} 01782 285388
{f} 01782 206821
mail@circuitpm.co.uk
www.circuitpm.co.uk
Contact: David Bowen
Founded: 1988
No. of clients: 24
Notes: Email or post or give us a ring!

Claypole Management
PO Box 123
Darlington DL3 7WA
{t} 0845 650 1777
{f} 08701 334784
claypole_1@hotmail.com
www.claypolemanagement.co.uk
Contact: Sam Claypole
Founded: 1999
No. of clients: 50+

Clic Agency
LL54 7NF
{t} 01286 831001
clic@btinternet.com
www.clicagency.co.uk
Contact: helen pritchard
Founded: 2006
No. of clients: 50
Notes: Actors taken from all over.

Clive Corner Associates
3 Bainbridge Close
Ham TW12 5JJ
{t} 020 8332 1910
CornerAssociates@aol.com
www.cornerassociates.cwc.net
Contact: Clive Corner
Founded: 1987
No. of clients: 70

Cloud Nine Agency
96 Tiber Gardens
Treaty Street
London N1 0XE
{t} 020 7278 0029
{f} 020 7278 0029
cloudnineagency@blueyonder.com
www.cloudnineagency.co.uk
Contact: Linda Morgans
Founded: 1995
No. of clients: 60

CMP Management
8/30 Galena Road
Hammersmith
London W6 0LT
{t} 020 874 10707
{f} 020 874 11786
info@ravenscourt.net
Contact: Christopher Price
Founded: 1999
No. of clients: 100
Notes: 16+

Collis Management
182 Trevelyan Road
London SW17 9LW
{t} 020 8767 0196
{f} 020 8682 0973
marilyn@collismanagement.co.uk
Contact: Marilyn Collis
Founded: 1992
No. of clients: 60

Complete Artistes
Northern & Shell Tower
4 Selsdon Way
London E14 9GL
{t} 020 7308 5351
{f} 020 7308 6001
lisa.dawson@nasnet.co.uk
Contact: Lisa Dawson
Founded: 2006
No. of clients: 5

Cops on the box
BM BOX 7301
London WC1N 3XX
{t} 020 8650 9828
{f} 07710 065851
info@tvcops.co.uk
www.cotb.co.uk
Contact: Steve Duffy
Founded: 1993
No. of clients: 200
Notes: Very specialised - see website.

CPA Management
The Studios
219b North Street
Romford
Essex RM1 4QA
{t} 01708 766444
{f} 01708 766077
david@cpamanagement.co.uk
www.cpamanagement.co.uk
Contact: David Bishop
Founded: 1995
No. of clients: 30

Crescent Management
10 Barley Mow Passage
London W4 4PH
{t} 020 8987 0191
{f} 020 8987 0207
mail@crescentmanagement.co.uk
www.crescentmanagement.co.uk

Contact: Steve Hedges
Founded: 1993
No. of clients: 22
Notes: Hard copies preferable.

CS Management
7 Cannon Road
London N147HE
{t} 020 8886 4264
{f} 020 8886 7555
carole@csmanagementuk.com
www.csmanagementuk.com
Contact: Carole O'Shea
Founded: 2001
No. of clients: 150
Notes: CV + photographs.

Dalzell and Beresford
26 Astwood Mews
London SW7 4DE
U.K. SW7 4DE
{t} 020 7341 9411
{f} 020 7341 9412
mail@dbltd.co.uk
Contact: Simon Beresford
No. of clients: 30

Debbie Edler Management
37 Russet Way
Peasedown St. John
Bath BA2 8ST
{t} 01761 436631
{f} 01761 436631
dem2005@eircom.net
dem.1colony.com
Contact: Dave Edler
Founded: 1995
No. of clients: 150

Denmark Street Management
Packington Bridge Workspace
Unit 11, 1b, Packington Sq
London N1 7UA
{t} 020 7354 8555
{f} 020 7354 8558
mail@denmarkstreet.net
www.denmarkstreet.net
Contact: Sarah O'Leary
Founded: 1985
No. of clients: 20
Notes: general, but particularly females, and men under 25.

DGPM
The Studio
107a Middleton Road
London E8 4LN
{t} 020 7241 6752
{f} 020 7241 6752
infodgpm@aol.com
Contact: David Graham
Founded: 2006
No. of clients: 16

Dick Horsey Management Limited
Cottingham House
Chorleywood Road
Rickmansworth WD3 4EP
{t} 01923 710 614
{f} 01923 710 614
roger@dhmlimited.co.uk
www.dhmlimited.co.uk
Contact: Roger de courcey
Founded: 1993
No. of clients: 30

DP Management
1 Euston Road
London NW1 2SA
{t} 020 7843 4331
danny@dpmanagement.org
Contact: Danny Pellerini
Founded: 2005
No. of clients: 60
Notes: post only. TV, film, theatre, musical.

dQ Management
Suite 21, Kingsway House
134-140 Church Road
Hove
East Sussex BN3 2DL
{t} 01273 721221
{f} 01273 779065
info@dqmanagement.com
www.dqmanagement.com
Contact: Peter Davis
Founded: 2003
No. of clients: 50

Edge Haine Artists
86 Margaret St.
London W1W 8TE
{t} 020 7580 7488
{f} 020 7580 7499
alastair@handembroidery.com
Contact: Edge Haine
Founded: 2005
No. of clients: 10

EKA Management
The Warehouse Studios
Glaziers Lane
Culcheth WA3 4AQ
{t} 0871 222 7470
{f} 01925 761097
kate@eka-agency.com
www.eka-agency.com
Contact: Kate Sinclair
Founded: 1995
No. of clients: 50

Elinor Hilton Associates
BAC
Lavender Hill
London SW11 5TN
{t} 020 7738 9574
{f} 020 7924 4636
info@elinorhilton.com
www.elinorhilton.com
Contact: Elinor Hilton
Founded: 2003
No. of clients: 50
Notes: happy for applications by email and to look at showreels.

Elliott Agency
94 Roundhill Crescent
Brighton
East Sussex BN2 3FR
{t} 01273 683882
info@elliottagency.co.uk
www.elliottagency.co.uk
Contact: Amanda Holmes
Founded: 1980
No. of clients: 500

Emma Sharnock Associates (E.S.A)
York House, 29 York Road
Tunbridge Wells
Kent TN1 1JX
{t} 01892 539007
{f} 01892 539007
esa-agency@btconnect.com
www.esa-agency.co.uk
Contact: Emma Sharnock
Founded: 2005
No. of clients: 50

Emptage Hallett
14 Rathboine Place
London W1T 1HT
{t} 020 7436 0425
{f} 020 7580 2748
mail@emptagehallett.co.uk
www.emptagehallett.co.uk
Contact: Michael Hallett
Founded: 1996
No. of clients: 90
Notes: post only.

Et-nik-a Prime Management & Castings Limited
30 Great Portland Street
London W1W 8QU
{t} 020 7299 3555
{f} 020 7299 3558
info@et-nik-a.com
www.et-nik-a.com
Contact: Aldo Arcillia
Founded: 2000
No. of clients: 60

Eva Long Agents
107 Station Road, Earls Barton
Northants NN6 0NX
{t} 07736 700849
EvaLongAgents@yahoo.co.uk
Contact: Eva Long
Founded: 2004
No. of clients: 30
Notes: Prefer email applications.

Explosion Entertainments
111 Woodland Way, Ongar
Essex CM5 9ET
{t} 07789 377405
peter@explosionentertainments.org
www.explosionentertainments.org
Contact: Peter Airey
Founded: 1999
No. of clients: 600

First Act Personal Management
2 Saint Michaels
New Arley, Coventry
Warwickshire CV7 8PY
{t} 01676 540285
firstactpm@aol.com
www.spotlightagent.info/firstact
Contact: John Burton
Founded: 2003
No. of clients: 27
Notes: post only.

Frances Ross Management
Higher Leyonne
Golant
Fowey PL23 1LA
{t} 01726 833004
{f} 01726 833004
francesross@btconnect.com
Contact: Frances Ross
Founded: 2001
No. of clients: 20

Fresh Agents Ltd
Suite 5. SAKS House 19 Ship Street
Brighton BN1 1AD
{t} 01273 711777
lauren@freshagents.com
www.freshagents.com
Contact: lauren Lambe
Founded: 2000
No. of clients: Many

Gag Reflex Management
102 Oldham Street
Manchester M4 1LJ
{t} 0161 228 6368
{f} 0161 228 1652
lee@gagreflex.co.uk
www.gagreflex.co.uk
Contact: Lee Martin
Founded: 2004
No. of clients: 15

Global Artists
23 Haymarket
London SW1Y 4DG
{t} 020 7839 4888
{f} 020 7839 4555
info@globalartists.co.uk
www.globalartists.co.uk
Founded: 1996
Notes: application via letter or through the website.

Goldielle Promotions
68 Lynton Drive
Hillside
Southport PR8 4QQ
{t} 01704 566604
goldielle@yahoo.co.uk
www.goldiellepromotions.com
Contact: Elinor Pedlar
Founded: 2004
No. of clients: 40

Grays Management
Panther House
38 Mount Pleasant
London WC1X 0AP
{t} 020 7278 1054
{f} 020 7278 1091
e-mail@graysmanagement.idps.co.uk
www.graysman.com
Contact: Mary Elliot-Nelson
Founded: 1989
No. of clients: 75
Notes: postal applications only.

Hall James Personal Management
20 Abbey Close
Pinner
Middlesex HA5 2AW
{t} 020 8429 8111
{f} 020 8868 5825
info@halljames.co.uk
www.halljames.co.uk
Contact: Sam Hall
Founded: 2006
No. of clients: 25

Hamilton Hodell
Fifth Floor, 66 - 68 Margaret Street,
London W1W 8SR
{t} 020 7636 1221
{f} 020 7636 1226
christian@hamiltonhodell.co.uk
www.hamiltonhodell.co.uk
Contact: Christian Hodell

Harvey Voices
54-55 Mragaret Street
London W1W 8SH
{t} 020 79524361
info@harveyvoices.co.uk
www.harveyvoices.co.uk
Contact: Emma Harvey
Founded: 2006
No. of clients: 90
Notes: voiceovers. Previously Speak Ltd - all details changed!

Hilary Gagan Associates
187 Drury Lane
London WC2B 5QD
{t} 020 7404 8794
{f} 020 7430 1869
hilary@hgassoc.freeserve.co.uk
Contact: Hilary Gagan
Notes: no emails - post applications.

Hobson's International
62. Chiswick High Road
London W4 1SY
{t} 020 8995 3628
actors@hobsons-international.com
www.hobsons-international.com
Contact: Several
Founded: 1986
No. of clients: 600

Image Management
94 Roundhill Crescent
Brighton BN2 3FR
{t} 01273 680689
mail@imagemanagement.co.uk
www.imagemanagement.co.uk
Contact: Adam Campbell
Founded: 2003
No. of clients: 60

Industry Casting
332 Royal Exchange
Manchester M2 7BR
{t} 0161 839 1551
{f} 0161 839 1661
mark@industrypeople.co.uk
www.industrycasting.co.uk
Contact: Mark Potts
Founded: 2002
No. of clients: 300

Inspiration Management
Room 227 The Aberdeen Centre
22-24 Highbury
London N5 2EA
{t} 020 7704 0440
mail@inspirationmanagement.org.uk
www.inspirationmanagement.org.uk
Founded: 1986
No. of clients: 20
Notes: hard copy by post photo, CV, letter plus state why a co-op.

International Artistes
4th Floor, Holborn Hall
193-197 High Holborn
London WC1V 7BD
{t} 020 7025 0600
{f} 020 7404 9865
info@internationalartistes.co.uk
www.internationalartistes.co.uk
Contact: Laurie Mansfield
Founded: 1945
No. of clients: 300

International Creative Management Inc
4-6 Soho Square
London W1D 3PZ
{t} 020 7432 0800
television@icmtalent.com
www.icmtalent.com
Contact: Human Resources
No. of clients: 1975

International Theatre and Music Ltd
Garden Studios
11-15 Betterton Street
Covent Garden, London WC2H 9BP
{t} 020 7470 8786
{f} 020 7379 0801
info@internationaltheatreandmusic.com
www.internationaltheatreandmusic.com
Contact: Claire Lloyd
Founded: 1981
No. of clients: 65
Notes: musical theatre books currently open.

Ion Entertainment
8 Bridge House
Bridge Street
Sunderland SR1 1TE
{t} 07811 122633
info@ionentertainment.co.uk
www.ionentertainment.co.uk
Contact: gareth Hunter
Founded: 2005
No. of clients: 15

Jaclyn Agency
52 Bessemer Road
Norwich NR4 6DQ
{t} 01603 622027
{f} 01603 612532
info@jaclyn2000.co.uk
www.jaclyncastingagency.co.uk
Contact: Henrietta Cassidy
Founded: 1956
No. of clients: 500

Janet Howe Casting
56 Iron Market
Newcastle Under Lyme
Staffs ST5 1PE
{t} 01782 661777
{f} 01782 661666
info@janethowe.com
Contact: Janet Howe
Founded: 1997
No. of clients: 50

Janet Plater Management Ltd
D Floor Milburn House
Dean Street
Newcastle Upon Tyne NE1 1LF
{t} 0191 221 2490
{f} 0191 233 1709
info@janetplatermanagement.co.uk
www.janetplatermanagement.co.uk
Contact: Janet Plater
Founded: 1997
No. of clients: 65

Janice Tildsley Associates
47 Orford Road
London E17 9NJ
{t} 020 8521 1888
{f} 020 8521 1174
info@janicetildsleyassociates.co.uk
www.janicetildsleyassociates.co.uk
Contact: Janice Tildsley
Founded: 2003
No. of clients: 70
Notes: Send photo, CV.

JB Associates
4th Floor, Manchester House
84-86 Princess Street
Manchester M1 6NG
{t} 0161 237 1808
{f} 0161 237 1809
info@j-b-a.net
www.j-b-a-net
Contact: John Basham
Founded: 1997
No. of clients: 70

Jeremy Hicks Associates
114-115 Tottenham Court Road
London W1T 5AH
{t} 020 7383 2000
{f} 020 7383 2777
info@jeremyhicks.com
www.jeremyhicks.com
Contact: Jeremy Hicks
Founded: 1990
No. of clients: 25

Jigsaw Arts Management (JAM)
64-66 High Street
Barnet
Hertfordshire EN5 5SJ
{t} 020 8447 4534
{f} 020 8447 4531
admin@jigsaw-arts.co.uk
www.jigsaw-arts.co.uk/agency
Contact: Debbie Morris
Founded: 2005
No. of clients: 35

John Doe Associates
London W10 4AR
{t} 020 8960 2848
info@johndoeassociates.com
www.johndoeassociates.com
Contact: Shae Potter
Founded: 2004
No. of clients: 150
Notes: CVs will be considered.

Johnston & Mathers Associates
PO Box 3167
Barnet EN5 2WA
{t} 020 8449 4968
{f} 020 8449 2386
johnstonmathers@aol.com

www.johnstonandmathers.com
Contact: Dawn Mathers
Founded: 2001
No. of clients: 50

K Talent
Suite 109 The Bridge
12-16 Clerkenwell Road
London EC1M 5PQ
{t} 020 7324 6350
mwildey@kentsgroup.com
www.kentsgroup.com
Contact: Melissa Wildey
Founded: 2003
No. of clients: 50
Notes: CVs, headshot and showreel.

KD Entertainments
80 Axiom Avenue
Westwood
Peterborough PE3 7EJ
{t} 01733 269 397
keithdaniels221279@hotmail.com
www.kdentertainments.co.uk
Contact: Keith Daniels
Founded: 2006
No. of clients: 15

Keddie Scott Associates Ltd
107-111 Fleet Street
London EC4A 2AB
{t} 020 7936 9058
{f} 020 7936 9100
fiona@ks-ass.co.uk
www.ks-ass.co.uk/
Contact: Fiona Keddie, Anna Loose
Founded: 2003
No. of clients: 100

Keddie Scott Associates-Wales
3 Orchard Place, Canton
Cardiff CF11 9DY
{t} 029 2021 9396
{t} 07917 272298
wales@ks-ass.co.uk
www.ks-ass.co.uk
Contact: Sarah Harding Colin Scott
Founded: 2006
No. of clients: 10
Notes: Preferably apply by post with SAE refer to website.

Kelly Management
7 Lownes Courtyard
Boone Street
London SE135TB
{t} 020 8297 2822
kellymanagement@btinternet.com
Contact: Robert Kelly
Founded: 2006
No. of clients: 25

KEW Personal Management
PO Box 48458
London SE15 5WW
{t} 020 7277 1440
info@kewpersonalmanagement.com
www.kewpersonalmanagement.com
Contact: Kate Winn
Founded: 2005
No. of clients: 35

Ladida Management
1st Floor Swiss Centre
10 Wardour Street
London W1D 6QF
{t} 020 7287 0600
{f} 020 7287 0300
m@ladidagroup.com
www.ladidagroup.com
Contact: Rebecca Gillett
Founded: 2005
No. of clients: 50

Laine Management
Laine House
131 Victoria Road
Salford M6 8LF
{t} 0161 7897775
elaine@lainemanagement.co.uk
www.lainemanagement.co.uk
Contact: Samantha Greeley
Founded: 1982
No. of clients: 800
Notes: Postal applications

Lee Morgan Management
The Strand, Golden Cross House
8 Duncannon Street
London WC2N 4JF
{t} 020 7484 5331
{f} 020 7484 5100
leemorganmgnt@aol.com
leemorganmanagement.co.uk
Contact: Lee Morgan
Founded: 2005
No. of clients: 40

Leeds Limelight Agency
18 King Edward C rescent
Horsforth
Leeds LS18 4BE
{t} 07904 090722
robert@leedslimelight.com
www.leedslimelight.com
Contact: Robert Kelso
Founded: 1998
No. of clients: 9
Notes: Email / website approach.

Leigh Management
14 St Davids Drive
Edgware
Middlesex HA8 6JH
{t} 020 8951 4449
{f} 020 8951 4449
leighmanagement@aol.com
Contact: Michelle Leigh
Founded: 1982
No. of clients: 80
Notes: must be in Spotlight, please only apply if you are currently appearing in something.

Liberty Management
4 Oxclose Drive
Dronfield
Derbyshire S18 8XP
{t} 0114 2899151
{f} 0114 2899151
office@libertymanagement.co.uk
www.libertymanagement.co.uk
Contact: Elaine Hollings
Founded: 2005
No. of clients: 70

Links Management
34-68 Colombo Street
London SE1 8DP
{t} 020 7928 0806
{f} 020 7928 0806
agent@links-management.co.uk
www.links-management.co.uk
Contact: John Holloway
Founded: 1984
No. of clients: 22

Lisa D Management
PO Box 4050
Bracknell
Berkshire RG42 9BZ
{t} 01344 643 568
{f} 01344 643 568
agents@lisad.co.uk
lisad.co.uk
Contact: Lisa Dennis
Founded: 2000
No. of clients: 50

Liz Hobbs Management Ltd
65 London Road
Newark
Notts NG24 1RZ
{t} 08700 702 702
{f} 0870 333 7009
enquiries@lizhobbsgroup.com
www.lizhobbsgroup.com
Contact: Liz Hobbs
Founded: 1990
No. of clients: 50

Looks London Ltd
12a Manor Court
Aylmer Road
East Finchley
London N2 0PJ
{t} 020 8341 4477
{f} 020 8442 9190
lookslondonltd@btconnect.com
www.lookslondon.com
Contact: Amanda Ashed
Founded: 2003
No. of clients: 180

Mad Dog Casting Ltd
Third Floor
15 Leighton Place
London NW5 2QL
{t} 020 7482 4703
info@maddogcasting.com
www.maddogcasting.com
Contact: Mad Dog
Founded: 1999
No. of clients: 2500

Main Artists
34 South Molton Street
London W1K 5BP
{t} 020 7495 4955
{f} 08701 280003
andrew@mainartists.com
www.mainartists.com
Contact: Andrew Allen
Founded: 2006
No. of clients: 48
Notes: No phone calls. Applications by post

Markham & Marsden Ltd
405 Strand
London WC2R 0NE
{t} 020 7836 4111
info@markham-marsden.com
www.markham-marsden.com
Contact: David Marsden
Founded: 1990
No. of clients: 60
Notes: Hard copies preferred.

MBA
Concorde House
18 Margaret Street
Brighton BN21TS
{t} 01273 685970
mba.concorde@virgin.net
www.mbagency.co.uk
Contact: Andrea Todd
Founded: 1960's
Notes: No emails. Send hard copies.

McLaren Management Ltd
McLaren House, Lochay Drive
Comrie, Crieff
Perthshire PH6 2PE
{t} 01764 671 137
{f} 01764 670 719
enquires@mclarenmanagement.co.uk
www.mclarenmanagement.co.uk
Contact: John McLaren
Founded: 2000
No. of clients: 30

MFL Agency Ltd
Windsor House
21 Richmond Place
Ilkley LS29 8TJ
{t} 01943 430 740
mfl.agency@blueyonder.co.uk
Contact: Jolanda Burns
Founded: 2003
No. of clients: 60

MGA Management
11/4 Abbdey Street
Edinburgh
EH7 5XN
{t} 0131 466 9392
murray@themgacompany.com
www.mga-management.com
Contact: Murray Grant
Founded: 2006
No. of clients: 10

Mitchell Maas McLennan
The Offices of Millennium Dance 2000
Hampstead Town Hall Centre
213 Haverstock Hill , London NW3 4QP
{t} 01767 650020
{f} 01767 650020
agency@mmm2000.co.uk
Contact: Zoe Traves
Founded: 2005
No. of clients: 40
Notes: apply in writing.

MV Management
Ralph Richardson Memorial Studios
Kingfisher Place, Clarendon Road
Wood Green, London N22 6XF
{t} 020 8889 8231
theagency@mountview.ac.uk
www.mvmanagement.co.uk/
Contact: Yvonne I'Anson
Founded: 2001
No. of clients: 19

Nancy Hudson Associates Ltd
50 South Molton Street
London W1K 5SB
{t} 020 7499 5548
agents@nancyhudsonassociates.com
www.nancyhudsonassociates.com
Contact: Nancy Hudson
Founded: 1999
No. of clients: 70

NE Representation
38 Coniscliffe Road
Darlington
County Durham DL3 7RG
{t} 01325 488385
{f} 01325 488390
theresa@nerepresentation.co.uk
www.nerepresentation.co.uk
Contact: Theresa Stinson
Founded: 2006
No. of clients: 350

New Faces Ltd
2nd Floor, Linen Hall
162-168 Regent Street
London W1B 5TB
{t} 020 7439 6900
{f} 020 7287 5481
val@newfacestalent.co.uk
www.newfacestalent.co.uk
Contact: Val Horton
Founded: 2000
No. of clients: 200

NJR Management
PO Box 147
Malvern
Worcs WR13 6HE
{t} 01684 541887
{f} 01684 541886
nikki@njrmanagement.com
www.njrmanagement.com
Contact: Nikki Reeves

Founded: 2004
No. of clients: 30

North West Actors
36 Lord Street
Radcliffe
Manchester M26 3BA
{t} 0161 724 6625
{f} 0161 724 6625
northwestactors@btinternet.com
www.northwestactors.co.uk
Contact: Richard White
Founded: 2007
No. of clients: 10

NorthOne Management
HG08 Aberdeen Studios
Highbury Grove
London N5 2EA
{t} 020 7359 9666
{f} 020 7359 9449
actors@northone.co.uk
www.northone.co.uk
Contact: robin middleton
Founded: 1986
No. of clients: 24
Notes: prefer postal applications.

Nyland Management
20 School Lane
Heaton Chapel
Stockport SK4 5DG
{t} 0161 442 2224
nylandmgmt@freenet.co.uk
Contact: Patrick & Tony Nyland
Founded: 1986
No. of clients: 60

Oi Oi Agency
Pinewood Film Studios
The Coach House, Pinewood Rd
Bucks
{t} 01753 655514
info@oioi.org.uk
Contact: Julie

oneaction
40 Elfrida Crescent
Bellingham
London SE6 3EW
{t} 07753 690 222
smitheagle@btinternet.com
Contact: Dean Smith
Founded: 2006

OnScreenAgency.com
No.199
2 Lansdowne Row, Mayfair
London W1J 6HL
{t} 020 7193 7547
{f} 020 7493 4935
info@onscreenagency.com
www.onscreenagency.com
Contact: Dean Salvara
Founded: 2004
No. of clients: 15

Ordinary People
16 Camden Road
London NW1 9DP
{t} 020 7267 7007
{f} 020 7267 5677
info@ordinarypeople.co.uk
www.ordinarypeople.co.uk
Contact: Sarah Robbie
Founded: 1988
No. of clients: 1000

Otto Personal Management Ltd
Office 2, Sheffield Independent Film
5 Brown Street
Sheffield S1 2BS
{t} 0114 275 2592
admin@ottopm.co.uk
www.ottopm.co.uk
Contact: John Langford
Founded: 1985
No. of clients: 35

Pat Lovett Associates
43 Chandos Place
Covent Garden
London WC2N 4HS
{t} 020 7379 8111 / 0131 478 7878
{f} 020 7379 9111 / 0131 478 7070
info@pla-uk.com
www.pla-uk.com
Contact: Dolina Logan
Founded: 1981
No. of clients: 150

Paul Telford Management
3 Greek Street
Soho
London W1D 4DA
{t} 020 7434 1100
{f} 020 7434 1200
info@telford-mgt.com
Contact: Paul Telford
Founded: 1993
No. of clients: 50

Pelham Associates
The Media Centre
9-12 Middle Street
Brighton BN1 1AL
{t} 01273 323010
{f} 01273 202492
petercleall@pelhamassociates.co.uk
www.pelhamassociates.co.uk
Contact: Peter Cleall
Founded: 1993
No. of clients: 65
Notes: Letter CV etc.

PFD
Drury House
34-43 Russell Street
WC2B 5HA
{t} 020 7344 1010
postmaster@pfd.co.uk
www.pfd.co.uk
Contact: Human Resources
Founded: 1999

PHA
Top Floor
136 Englefield Rd
London N1 3LQ
{t} 020 7424 5832
paddypatou@hotmail.co.uk
Contact: Patrick Hambleton
Founded: 2006
No. of clients: 45

Purely Talent
26 Westmore Road
Tatsfield
Kent TN162AX
{t} 01959 573080
purelypartyevent@aol.com
Contact: Louise McRandal
Founded: 2006
No. of clients: 10

Ray Knight Casting
21a Lambolle Place
London NW3 4PG
{t} 020 7449 2478
{f} 020 7722 2322
casting@rayknight.co.uk
www.rayknight.co.uk/
Contact: Ray Knight
Founded: 1988

Reality Check Management Ltd
97 Charlotte Street
London W1T 4QA
{t} 020 7907 1415
{f} 020 7907 1423
info@realitycheck-m.com
www.realitycheckmanagement.com
Contact: Angelina Riccio
Founded: 2005
No. of clients: 400

Red Canyon Management
{t} +44 07939 365578
showkins@redcanyon.co.uk
www.redcanyon.co.uk
Contact: Sarah Howkins
Founded: 2005
No. of clients: 20

Rhino Management
Studio House
Delamare Road
Cheshunt, Herts EN8 9SH
{t} 01992 642225
{f} 01992 642277
kevin@rhino-management.co.uk
www.rhinomanagement.co.uk
Contact: Kevin Sands
Founded: 2003
No. of clients: 78
Notes: email or post.

Richard Kort Associates
Theatre House
2-4 Clasketgate
Lincoln LN2 1JS
{t} 01522 526888
{f} 01522 511116
richardkort@dial.pipex.com
www.richardkortassociates.com
Contact: Richard Kort
Founded: 2005
No. of clients: 50

Rossmore Personal Management
70-76 Bell Street
London NW1 6SP
{t} 020 7258 1953
agents@rossmoremanagement.com
www.rossmoremanagement.com
Contact: Alison Lee

Royce Management
29 Trenholme Road
London SE20 8PP
{t} 020 8778 6861
{f} 020 8778 6861
office@roycemanagement.co.uk
www.roycemanagement.co.uk
Contact: Amanda Fisher
Founded: 1980
No. of clients: 40

RSM Artistes Management
15 The Fairway
Leigh on Sea SS9 4QN
{t} 01702 522647
info@rsm.uk.net
www.rsm.uk.net
Contact: Cherry Parker
Founded: 1996
No. of clients: 26
Notes: Hard copies only.

RWM Management
1919 Havelock Street
London N1 0DA
{t} 020 7278 8271
kate.whaley@virgin.net
Contact: Kate Whaley
Founded: 2000
No. of clients: 60
Notes: Letters only.

Sandra Harris Associates
171 Cranley Gardens
London N10 3AG
{t} 020 8444 6506
{f} 020 8444 2848
Sandra@highlyacclaimed.co.uk
Contact: Sandra Harris
Founded: 2005
No. of clients: 8
Notes: Email preferable.

Sandra Reynolds Agency
62 Bell Street
London NW1 6SP
{t} 020 7387 5858
{f} 020 7387 5848
info@sandrareynolds.co.uk
www.sandrareynolds.co.uk
Contact: Tessa Reynolds
Founded: 1975
No. of clients: 400

Sandra Singer Associates
21 Cotswold Road
Westcliff-on-Sea
Essex SS0 8AA
{t} 01702 331616
sandrasingeruk@aol.com
www.sandrasinger.com
Contact: Sandra Singer
Founded: 1983
No. of clients: 120

Scott Marshall Partners Ltd
2nd Floor
15 Little Portland Street
London W1W 8BW
{t} 020 7637 4623
{f} 020 7636 9728
smpm@scottmarshall.co.uk
Contact: Manon Palmer

Sharon Foster Management
15A Hollybank Road
Birmingham B13 0RF
{t} 0121 443 4865
mail@sharonfoster.co.uk
www.sharonfoster.co.uk
Contact: Sharon Foster
Founded: 2006
No. of clients: 20

Shelly Eden Associates
The Old Factory, Lyttelton Rd,
London E10 5NQ
{t} 020 8558 3536
Shellyeden@aol.com
Contact: Tom Byrne
Founded: 2000
No. of clients: 15

Shepperd-Fox
5 Martyr Road
Guildford GU1 4LF
{t} 07957 624601
info@shepperd-fox.co.uk
www.shepperd-fox.co.uk
Contact: Jane Shepperd
Founded: 2005
No. of clients: 40

Shining Management Ltd
12 D'Arblay Street
London W1F 8DU
{t} 020 7734 1981
{f} 020 7734 2528
info@shiningvoices.com
www.shiningvoices.com
Contact: Jennifer Taylor
Founded: 2002
No. of clients: 60
Notes: Voice overs.

Simpatico Roleplay Agency
8 Manor Park, Histon
Cambridge CB4 9JT
{t} 01223 575259
steve.attmore@ntlworld.com
www.simpaticoagency.com
Contact: Steve Attmore
Founded: 2001
No. of clients: 30

Soul Management
10 Coptic Street
London WC1A 1NH
{t} 020 7580 1120
info@soulmanagement.co.uk
www.soulmanagement.co.uk
Contact: Thomas Adams
Founded: 2004
No. of clients: 30

Stage and Screen Personal Management
20B Kidbrooke Grove
Blackheath SE3 0LF
{t} 07958 648 740
stageandscreen1@yahoo.co.uk
www.stageandscreen.mfbiz.com
Contact: Orit Sutton
Founded: 2004
No. of clients: 12
Notes: Hard copies, CVs.

Stage Centre Ltd
41 North Rd
London N7 9DP
{t} 020 7607 0872
stagecentre@aol.com
Contact: John Dunlop
Founded: 1982
No. of clients: 22
Notes: Prefer people to be in shows when they get in touch.

Stephanie Evans Associates
Rivington House
82 Great Eastern Street
London EC2A 3JF
{t} 0870 609 2629
{f} 0870 609 2629 *
steph@stephanie-evans.com
www.stephanie-evans.com
Contact: Stephanie Evans
Founded: 2003
No. of clients: 50

Susi Earnshaw Management
68 High Street
High Barnet
London EN5 5SJ
{t} 020 8441 5010
{f} 020 8364 9618
castings@susiearnshaw.co.uk
www.susiearnshaw.co.uk
Contact: Susi Earnshaw
No. of clients: 300

Take Flight Management
22 Streatham Close
Leigham Court Road, Streatham
London SW16 2NQ
{t} 020 8835 8147
{f} 020 8835 8147
info@takeflightmanagement.com
www.takeflightmanagement.com
Contact: Morwenna Preston
Founded: 2003
No. of clients: 40

Thames Valley Theatrical Agency
Dorchester House, Wimblestraw Road
Berinsfield
Oxon OX10 7LZ
{t} 01865 340333
{f} 01865 340333
donna@thamesvalleytheatricalagency.co.uk
www.thamesvalleytheatricalagency.co.uk
Contact: Donna Thomson
No. of clients: 100

The Acclaim Actors Agency
Ground Floor
23 May Road.
Twickenham Green TW2 6RJ
{t} 020 755 88 311
info@acclaimactors.co.uk
www.acclaimactors.co.uk
Contact: James Potter
Founded: 2006
No. of clients: 19

The Actors Group
21-31 Oldham Street
Manchester M1 1JG
{t} 0161 834 4466
enquiries@theactorsgroup.co.uk
www.theactorsgroup.co.uk
Contact: Co-Op
Founded: 1980
No. of clients: 21

The BWH Agency Ltd
Barley Mow Centre
10 Barley Mow Passage
Chiswick, London W4 4PH
{t} 020 8996 1661
{f} 020 8996 1662
info@thebwhagency.co.uk
www.thebwhagency.co.uk
Contact: Joe Hutton
Founded: Oct-04
Notes: Hard copies include SAE for return.

The Castings Factory
1 Victoria Street
Liverpool L2 5QA
{t} 0151 227 3866
info@castingsfactory.co.uk
www.castingsfactory.co.uk
Contact: tara maguire
Founded: 2006
No. of clients: 250

The Central Line
11 East Circus Street
Nottingham NG1 5AF
{t} 0115 9412937
centralline@btconnect.com
www.the-central-line.co.uk
Contact: Kim Gillespie
Founded: 1983
No. of clients: 14

The Commercial Agency
12 Evelyn Mansions
Carlisle Place
London SW1P 1NH
{t} 020 7233 8100
anne@thecommercialagency.co.uk
www.thecommercialagency.co.uk
Contact: Anne Shore
Founded: 2002
No. of clients: 150

The Identity Agency Group
112a Chobham Road
Stratford E15 1LZ
{t} 020 8555 5171
casting@identitydramaschool.com
www.identitydramaschool.com
Contact: Philip Dempsey
Founded: 2003
No. of clients: 50

The Narrow Road Company
21 / 22 Poland Street
London W1F 8QH
{t} 020 7434 0406
{f} 020 7439 1237
agents@narrowroad.co.uk
Contact: Victoria Long
Founded: 1986
Notes: Hard copies only.

Tim Kent Associates Ltd
Pinewood Film Studios
The Coach House, Pinewood Rd
Bucks SL0 0NH
{t} 01753 655517
{f} 01753 655622
castings@tkassociates.co.uk
Contact: Tim kent Julie Fox
Founded: 2002
No. of clients: 20

Tim Scott Personal Management
284 Grays Inn Road
London WC1X 8EB
{t} 020 7833 5733
{f} 020 7278 9175
timscott@btinternet.com
Contact: Tim Scott
Notes: Hard copies include SAE for return.

Underbelly Productions
83 Charlotte Street
London W1T 4PR
{t} 020 7580 0154
{f} 020 7580 0155
brett@underbelly.co.uk
www.underbelly.co.uk
Contact: Brett Vincent
Founded: 2005
No. of clients: 11
Notes: Email.

Valerie Brook Agency
10 Sandringham Road
Cheadle Hulme
Cheshire SK8 5NH
{t} 0161 4861 631
{f} 0161 488 4206
colinbrook@freenetname.co.uk
Contact: Colin Brook
Founded: 1996
No. of clients: 120
Notes: Hard copies only.

Vincent Shaw Associates
186 Shaftesbury Avenue
London WC2H 8JB
{t} 020 7240 2927
{f} 020 7240 2930
info@vincentshaw.com
www.vincentshaw.com
Contact: Andy Charles
Notes: Hard copies include SAE for return.

Waring & McKenna
11-12 Dover Street
London W1S 4LJ
{t} 020 7629 6444
dj@waringandmckenna.com
www.waringandmckenna.com
Contact: Waring McKenna
Notes: Hard copies only.

Wendy Lee Management
2nd Floor
36 Langham Street
London W1W 7AP
{t} 020 7580 4800
wendy-lee@btconnect.com
Contact: Wendy Lee
Founded: 1999
No. of clients: 40

West Central Management
Panther House
38 Mount Pleasant
London WC1X OAP
{t} 020 7833 8134
{f} 020 7833 8134
mail@westcentralmanagement.co.uk
www.westcentralmanagement.co.uk
Contact: Leigh Kelly
Founded: 1980
No. of clients: 25

Williamson & Holmes
9 Hop Gardens
St Martin's Lane
London WC2N 4EH
{t} 020 7240 0407
{f} 020 7240 0408
jackie@williamsonandholmes.co.uk
www.williamsonandholmes.co.uk
Contact: Jackie Williamson
Founded: 2006
No. of clients: 30

Willow Management
151 Main Street
Yaxley
Peterborough PE7 3LD
{t} 01733 240392
{f} 01733 240392
pb@willowmanagement.co.uk
www.willowmanagement.co.uk/
Contact: Peter Burroughs
No. of clients: 70
Notes: Very specialised – actors 3ft-5ft or very tall.

Co-operative agencies

A co-operative agency is one run by actors themselves: a group of actors (usually 20 or so) working together to represent each other. Work such as answering the phone, administering the office and working contacts will be undertaken on a rota basis. Many co-operative agencies will charge commission at the lower end of the scale (closer to 10% than 20%), which can be attractive to an actor. While they can and do work, co-operative agencies may not always carry the same clout with casting directors as the more traditional agencies.

If the potential disadvantage of joining a co-operative agency is being less influential than mainstream agencies, there are advantages too: one is that members have more day-to-day involvement with their career management. Everyone in the co-op is invested in success and motivated by similar goals. Another advantage is that co-ops sometimes pursue a broader range of work, such as corporate and educational opportunities.

Think carefully about why you might want to join a co-op – that's sure to be one of the questions its existing members ask you in an interview. Don't be offended if you're asked to go through a probationary period – it's only reasonable that a group of people with a particular dynamic will want to make sure, for both parties' sake, that things will work out. Good communication between members of a co-op is vital to its success.

A-Z of co-operative agencies

1984 Personal Management

Based in: London
{t} 020 7251 8046
info@1984pm.com
www.1984pm.com
1984 is a co-operative personal management agency representing approximately 20 actors across film, theatre, television and commercials.

Actors Alliance

Based in: London
{t} 020 7407 6028
actors@actorsalliance.fsnet.co.uk
www.actorsalliance.co.uk
Actors alliance is a co-operative agency providing representation to its members in the entertainment industry. Our aim is to provide helpful and accurate recommendations to casting professionals in the fields of film, television, theatre and corporate work.

Actors' Creative Team

Based in: London
{t} 020 8239 8892
office@actorscreativeteam.co.uk
www.actorscreativeteam.co.uk
Actors' Creative Team is a co-operative agency established in 2001 and is jointly owned and run by professional actors. Each member acts as an agent, representing colleagues and finding them work in every area of the profession.

Actors Direct

Based in: Manchester, Leeds, London, South-West
{t} 0161 237 1904
actorsdirect@aol.com
www.actorsdirect.org.uk
Founded in 1994, Actors Direct has 25 members, with roughly equal numbers of men and women, mainly based around the north-west of England. Members are expected to have excellent office skills and a strong sense of team spirit. The group does not represent under 16s or walk on artists. Actors Direct is actively seeking submissions from mixed race, oriental, black and Asian actors.

Actors Network Agency (ANA)

Based in: London
{t} 020 7735 0999
info@ana-actors.co.uk
www.ana-actors.co.uk
ANA was established in 1985 and represents 20-30 actors in film, theatre, television and commercials.

Actorum

Based in: London
{t} 020 7636 6978
info@actorum.com
www.actorum.com
Actorum was established in 1974 by Danny Schiller and Vivienne Burgess. We were the first actors' co-operative in the United Kingdom. Over 30 years on, Actorum remains the premiere co-operative agency, constantly aiming to provide a first class, personal, knowledgeable and dynamic service to the industry.

Alpha Personal Management
Based in: Londcon
{t} 020 7241 0077
alpha@alphaactors.com
www.alphaactors.com
Alpha Personal Management was established in 1983, and is a co-operative personal management agency representing approximately 20 actors across film, theatre, television and commercials.

arena personal management
Based in: London
{t} 020 7278 1661
arenapmltd@aol.com
www.arenapmltd.co.uk
arena is a professional, hard working, actors' co-operative agency established in the 1980s. We represent professionally trained or experienced performers. We do not represent extras, models, dancers or children.

AXM
Based in: London
{t} 020 7261 0400
info@axmgt.com
www.axmgt.com
We are a non-profit organisation that exists to represent its members' interests in film, television, theatre, presentation, roleplay, voiceover and all other areas of performance arts. We are always interested in hearing from actors from all backgrounds who wish to join us.

Cardiff Casting
Based in: Cardiff
{t} 02920 233321
admin@cardiffcasting.co.uk
www.cardiffcasting.co.uk
Cardiff Casting, established in 1981, represents approximately 20 actors across film, theatre, television and commercials.

CCM
Based in: London
{t} 020 7278 0507
casting@ccmactors.com
www.ccmactors.com
Established in 1993, CCM represents approximately 20 actors across film, theatre, television and commercials. When not working, we take turns in the office – this is normally one day a week fulfilling the following tasks; liaising with casting directors; submitting clients for current castings; and actively searching for opportunities within the industry.

Circuit Personal Management
Based in: Midlands/North West
{t} 01782 285388
mail@circuitpm.co.uk
www.circuitpm.co.uk
Circuit is an Actors' Co-operative established in 1988. Our client list is primarily Midlands and North-West based, working throughout the UK in theatre, television, radio, voice-over, film and corporates (both video and role-play).

City Actors Management
Based in: London
{t} 020 7793 9888
info@city-actors.freeserve.co.uk
www.city-actors.freeserve.co.uk
London's premier co-operative agency was established in 1982 and continues to thrive.

Crescent Management
Based in: London
{t} 020 8987 0191
mail@crescentmanagement.co.uk
www.crescentmanagement.co.uk
Crescent Management is a theatrical agency dedicated to supplying professional, trained, talented actors for the stage and screen. Established since 1991 and representing approximately 25 actors.

Denmark Street Management
Based in: London
{t} 020 7354 8555
mail@denmarkstreet.net
www.denmarkstreet.net
Established in 1985, Denmark Street Management has developed over the years to become one of the UK's leading co-operative agencies - specialising in providing highly skilled professional actors for theatre, film, television, commercials and radio.

Direct Line Personal Management
{t} 020 8694 1788
daphne.franks@directpm.co.uk
www.directpm.co.uk
Founded in Leeds in 1985, Direct Personal Management represents a range of actors of varying ages and types. All are experienced Equity members. Our clients work in theatre, film, television, radio, voice-over, video and corporate projects. We do not represent extras or walk-ons. Many of our actors are from the North of England and we also represent actors from London and other areas including Wales. Our actors work throughout the United Kingdom and also internationally.

Frontline Management
Based in: London
{t} 020 7261 9466
agents@frontlinemanagment.org
www.frontlinemanagement.org
Frontline was formed in 1986 as an actor's co-operative, making 2007 our 21st anniversary.

IML
Based in: London
{t} 020 7587 1080
info@iml.org.uk
www.iml.org.uk
ML is a co-operative actors' agency, registered as a Friendly Society. It was founded in 1980, making it one of the oldest co-ops, as well as being one of the UK's most successful

Inspiration Management
Based in: London
{t} 020 7704 0440
mail@inspirationmanagement.org.uk
www.inspirationmanagement.org.uk
We are an actors' co-operative agency, established in 1986, and have become one of the most respected and longest-running co-operatives in the country. Based in Islington (within easy reach of London's West End) we have over twenty members, representing a wide range of skills and experience.

Links Management
Based in: London
{t} 020 7928 0806
agent@links-management.co.uk
www.links-management.co.uk
Established in 1984 and currently representing 17 actors, with work areas including film, television, theatre and commercials.

North of Watford
{t} 01422 845361
info@northofwatford.com
www.northofwatford.com
North Of Watford Actors' Agency is a co-operative agency representing actors living and working all over the United Kingdom.

NorthOne Management
Based in: London
{t} 020 7359 9666
actors@northone.co.uk
www.northone.co.uk
NorthOne Management was founded as an actors agency in 1986. Since then its founding members have moved on, but bequeathed a wealth of accumulated experience, which the current members enjoy. It is only by the collective co-operation of the members that NorthOne flourishes, whether as an actor or an agent. This prerequisite of co-operation and involvement, we believe, also makes the actor a more professionally aware member of the industry.

Otto Personal Management
Based in: Sheffield
{t} 0114 2752592
admin@ottopm.co.uk
www.ottopm.co.uk
Otto Personal Management is an actors' co-operative management which was set up in Sheffield in 1985 and is now based in the heart of Sheffield's Cultural Quarter. Our actors have a wide and varying history in all aspects of the media industry. Theatre, Film, Television, Radio, Voice over, Multimedia and Corporate Videos etc.

Park Management
Based in: London
{t} 020 7923 1498
actors@park-management.co.uk
www.park-management.co.uk
Park Management is a small boutique style agency representing actors in film, television and theatre. We look after the careers of a small number of actors who we develop strong long term relationships with. We attend showcases where we look for specific casting types to fill gaps in our list. For this reason we ask actors not to contact us unless you are appearing in a production at a venue central to London.

Performance Actors Agency
Based in: London
{t} 020 7251 5716
performance@p-a-a.co.uk
www.p-a-a.co.uk
Founded in 1984, Performance Actors Agency has built an outstanding reputation of providing actors to the industry. Run by actors, for actors, Performance Actors Agency represents talented, committed, and hard working performers who have chosen to be part of a team. Our members' work includes film and television, the Royal Shakespeare Company, repertory theatre and the West End, corporate work, radio and voiceovers.

RbA Management
Based in: Liverpool
{t} 0151 708 7273
info@rbamanagement.co.uk
www.rbamanagement.co.uk
RbA Management (formerly Rattlebag Actors Agency) was launched in 1995 and has grown to become one of the leading agencies in the north of England, with credits in TV, film, commercials, theatre and radio. RbA Management is interested in hearing from professional actors with a base in the northwest of England. The agency does not deal in extra or walk-on work.

Rogues and Vagabonds
Based in: London
{t} 020 7254 8130
rogues@vagabondsmanagement.com
vagabondsmanagement.com
We are one of the oldest co-operative agencies in London and pride ourselves in our first class reputation of providing clients of the highest calibre.

Stiven Christie Management
Based in: Edinburgh
{t} 0131 228 4645
info@stivenchristie.co.uk
www.stivenchristie.co.uk
Formed in 1983, the business was originally called The Actors Agency. It was established by a group of young Scottish based actors who wished to learn more about the overall industry within which they were working and to aid them in this process the new agency was set up as a co-operative partnership. We promote our talent across the entire spectrum of performance media. Our clients can be found in film, television, radio, theatre, commercials, voice-over, presentation and role-play projects. The Agency is run as a commercial enterprise by the partners Douglas Stiven and Simon Christie who work from the offices located in Dunfermline and associates in Edinburgh and London

The Actors File
Based in: London
{t} 020 7278 0087
mail@theactorsfile.co.uk
www.theactorsfile.co.uk
The Actors File Co-operative Personal Management was created 21 years ago. As one of the first waves of co-operatives in Britain it was at the forefront of the changing face of representation. We do our utmost to stay there, remaining competitive and accessible. Started by five actors (three of whom are still with us) we now represent around 25 actors covering a wide range of types and skills.

The Actor's Group
Based in: Manchester
{t} 0161 8344466
enquiries@TheActorsGroup.co.uk
www.theactorsgroup.co.uk
The Actors' Group was formed in 1980 and was the first co-operative actors' agency outside of London. TAG (as the agency quickly became known) continues to work in all media nationally and internationally. Since its inception the agency has provided actors for work on the stages of the RSC, the RNT, The Old Vic, The Young Vic, The Royal Court and practically every regional Rep, as well as small/middle scale theatre, children's theatre and TIE, film and television. Our experienced

membership ranges from young actors, to those middle-aged as well as established older actors. The age range spans 18 to 72.

The Central Line

Based in: Nottingham
{t} 0115 941 2937
centralline@btconnect.com
www.the-central-line.co.uk

The Central Line is a co-operative personal management agency formed in 1983 and based in Nottingham. We supply actors nationwide – most of them have London bases and are flexible and responsive

West Central Management

Based in: London
{t} 020 7833 8134
mail@westcentralmanagement.co.uk
www.westcentralmanagement.co.uk

Established in 1984. Co-operative management representing 15-20 actors. Areas of work include theatre, musicals, television, film, commercials and corporate. Members are expected to work 4 days in the office per month. Will consider attending performances at venues within Greater London with 2 weeks' notice. Accepts submissions (with CVs and photographs) from actors previously unknown to the company sent by post or e mail. Will also accept invitations to view individual actors' websites.

Section 3
Applying for work

Casting directors

Casting directors are employed by directors and producers to sieve through the pool of acting talent and suggest the most appropriate actors for the part. Their job is to know the acting talent inside out and to facilitate meetings between potential candidates and the director. Armed with a character breakdown, they usually work with casting agents to shortlist suitable candidates who they think will match the role's requirements and the director's expectations.

By and large, casting directors will be brought in for specific projects (eg a film or theatre production) rather than employed on ongoing contracts. There are more than 250 casting directors in the UK, some working as individuals freelancing to production companies and others as part of larger collectives or companies. Many casting directors pride themselves on an encyclopaedic knowledge of actors and are renowned for keeping detailed notes on whoever crosses their path.

In the majority of cases the casting director does not choose or have final say over who gets a role. This is up to the director and the producer. It is in the casting director's interests to be on the side of the actor, as their reputation will be consolidated by a successful casting. The vision and choices displayed by a casting director will reflect well on them and enhance their standing in the industry, just as a poor pool of talent for casting sessions can damage their credibility.

In addition to sourcing actors, a casting director is also responsible for liaising with agents, directors and actors to schedule castings. They will often sit in on the castings and may give the actor tips beforehand on what the director will be looking for. It's important to listen to these – never forget that it's usually in the casting director's interest to get you the job just as much as it is yours, and they are likely to know more about what the director and producer will respond to.

Approaching casting directors

You can approach casting directors directly with a CV, photo and covering letter, but in many instances they will prefer to work through agents. Often they will request that your agent sends a showreel before deciding whether or not to bring you in for a casting.

They will, however, constantly be on the look out for promising new actors, and some may attend a production you are in or may occasionally be willing to meet with you if your CV is of a suitably promising calibre.

Rather than bombarding every casting director across the nation with your details unannounced, find out first whether they accept unsolicited contact from actors at all – some do, some don't. A brief, polite phone call or email should establish this, and remember to stick to what they say: some may want submissions by post only, others may accept them by email.

Details of many casting directors can be found at the Casting Directors' Guild website – ***www.thecdg.co.uk*** – though bear in mind the site is not directly aimed at actors. You could also keep an eye out in show and TV credits for casting directors' names.

CVs

To maximise your chances of being called in for an audition, it is vital you spend the time constructing a professional CV. While a headshot can give an employer some idea of your facial characteristics, the CV should show your versatility, experience, dependability and professionalism. Professionalism really is key here: no matter how suitable you may be for a role, a poorly spelt, structured or printed CV can quickly remove you from consideration.

The CV should start with your contact details and those of your agent if you have one. Where possible include your email address and mobile phone number, as casting directors often need to get in contact with potential cast at very short notice and a quick response time can be critical in securing an audition slot.

Next come your key physical characteristics, such as age, playing age, build, height, weight, hair color, eye color, ethnicity and native accent – though don't go overboard on the detail as your photograph will reveal some of it anyway. A simple statement such as 'tall with slim build' can sometimes convey more than a list of statistics. If you do decide to include your weight and height remember to include them in both metric (metres and kilos) and imperial (feet and pounds) format.

Whether you put your date of birth is debatable; some people think it can limit your options by precluding you for some roles in the mind of a casting director, whereas others think it should be included as a simple yardstick.

Finally you may wish to include your Spotlight number, your Equity status (whether or not you are a member) and whether or not you hold a valid UK driving licence in this section.

Playing age

Regardless of whether you include your actual age, you will need to include your playing age. Don't try to overstretch at this point and be honest: a playing age of 16 to 35 is simply unrealistic – do you really think you look both 16 and 35? A good rule of thumb is to limit the age range to a maximum of 10 years. Another test is to get independent advice. Send your photo to teachers, friends and colleagues and ask them to tell you honestly how old you look.

Credits and training

After these key contact details and physical characteristics you should include your credits and training. Again, some people prefer to put training first, others credits – it's up to you. As long as each section is clearly laid out and the CV isn't too long it shouldn't matter unduly, though we'd recommend that you lead with your credits – whatever your field, any employer or agent will look for your experience above all else. *The ideal CV length is one page*, so if you do need to cut back on credits, omit the oldest and least prestigious.

Credits should include the role you played (put this first), the production, the director, the venue, theatre company and the date (just the year will do). The norm is to list the most recent credits first as these are the most telling and the most relevant and there's no point keeping your big guns at the foot of the CV. If you have a number of credits across different genres you might want to list them under different sections (eg film, theatre, television, radio, corporate, commercials).

Above all, get the details right: historians may have identified more than 50 variations of the name Shaxper, but in the business 'Shakespeare' is what they expect! Avoid amateur productions if possible, or at least put these below professional experience.

Remember, first impressions are hard to reverse, so keep your CV clear, focused and honest. Don't exaggerate your role and certainly don't claim experience you've never had. Sure, a credit may slip through the net but most won't. Actors, agents, directors and casting directors are continually networking, working together professionally and meeting socially. There's every chance that lies will be found out and come back to haunt you.

Your training should include the institution, the course and the dates you attended and, if relevant, any awards or distinctions you received. It's not obligatory to include referees, though if you have a particularly prestigious referee (eg a respected actor, tutor or industry professional) it may help to include them.

Other skills

Additional skills and interests can be listed in a different section. These can be useful if you have genuine skills such as sporting abilities (horse riding is the classic), musical abilities or particular interests which may be valuable to a role. If you are confident in a range of regional or national accents, list these too, but you really need to be sure of your accuracy, or you'll soon get caught out. Don't list skills you don't have – at best you'll end up looking foolish, at worst you'll earn the reputation as a chancer or a liar. Applying for work is one part of acting where your ability to pretend should be suppressed!

Each of these sections should be clearly marked, with bold section titles so the reader can quickly establish where the key information can be found. However, don't go crazy with fancy layouts, big boxes and wacky typefaces – what people want to see is the information.

Check and check again

Before sending your CV to anyone, check the spelling and accuracy of all the information listed. Pass it to friends and family for a second opinion and further spell checking. Finally, ensure your name is clearly visible at the top of all pages. It should be clear from your layout that the document is a CV, so no need for the label "CV" anywhere – simply focus on the key information.

In general, *remember the 15-second rule*: that's probably how long your CV will be looked at in the first pass, and if you can get through to the second stage of a longer look, you're well on the way. Fifteen seconds might seem depressing – but think how quickly all of us form impressions of other people when we meet them.

Keep your CV simple and informative – this doesn't have to mean it's anonymous, and a good CV always reaches a balance between conveying the details of your experience and showing what sort of person you are.

Online CVs

A number of websites offer an online CV service. Professionally formatted, these CVs or online profiles generally allow you to enter then amend your credits, training, and at least one photo. Some of these websites include your CV in an online directory which is searchable by industry professionals and can offer a good level of exposure. Online CVs, to which you can direct people either with a link via email or a URL they can look up, can reduce the laborious task of faxing and mailing out your CV. Services of this kind specifically for actors include Spotlight and Casting Call Pro – see Section 7 for more details.

Bear in mind that this method of communication doesn't find favour with everyone. Some people won't want to receive CVs via email, preferring the more traditional paper copy. In general, any agent or casting director who specifies that they don't want submissions by email is perhaps less likely to be well disposed to going to a website for your details. If you're a young actor and used to doing everything online, remember that not everyone in the industry does things that way – acting is a field where personal contact counts a great deal.

Covering letters

Together with your headshot and your CV, the covering letter is your calling card. As such, it's important to set the right tone and create a good impression. While it's true that a good letter can really do you favours, it's also true that a bad, poorly presented letter can result in your application being dumped in the bin. Agents, directors and casting directors receive a mountain of unsolicited approaches and won't be able to devote more than a few moments to each, therefore it's essential that you don't give them any reason to dismiss your approach.

You might think that spelling and grammar are irrelevant and the real substance is in your acting ability, but before you get to show off your talents you need to be called to audition. You'll not get that far if you have been ruled out of the selection process by writing a poorly phrased, poorly presented letter riddled with mistakes. You'll be doing yourself a serious disservice if you send off a letter that's unprofessional in appearance and content.

BASIC DOs

- print rather than handwrite (unless you have exceptionally clear handwriting which would make you stand out)
- buy good quality paper (consider having a professional letterhead printed, too)
- personalise the letter with the name of the recipient
- check spelling and grammar
- check the factual content – eg names/addresses/contact nos
- read, read and read again before posting
- send it in a clean envelope and write the address neatly and legibly, with your return address on the back
- photocopy or keep an electronic copy for future reference and to keep tabs on who you've contacted.

Given that there will be dozens, hundreds or thousands of other letters you might wonder how you can distinguish yourself, and set your submission apart from the others. The tone of a letter is one of the most important elements and yet one of the hardest to get right. You don't want to sound sycophantic, arrogant, outlandish or zany. Including a keepsake or memento or some other such wacky device might raise a momentary smile in the office, but it's also likely to land you in the bin.

Instead, take an entirely professional approach. Start by finding out the name of the person to whom you're writing, and ensuring you know how to spell it correctly. Address your contact by their full name rather than by their first name or title.

Write in the first person singular (I) and adhere to the usual rules of grammar and letter writing. A standard letter will often start with your address at the top right, then the recipient's address (at the left-hand side of the paper) with the date opposite or beneath, followed by the greeting (*Dear Matt Barnes*), the body of the letter and concluded "Yours sincerely", with a space for your signature and beneath that your name (printed). As you begin writing the body of your letter, be

BASIC DON'Ts

- don't address your letter to a generic title – eg Dear Sir/Madam
- don't be overly familiar/informal
- don't write a bog-standard, top and tailed letter which is clearly a generic mailing to all and sundry
- don't use meaningless or cliched phrases synonymous with dull covering letters – eg "for your perusal", "I implore/beseech you", "you'll regret it if you don't give me the..."
- don't forget to sign the letter – an easy omission
- don't forget to include any other important materials – eg headshots/CV...
- ...but don't include anything else in the hope of getting attention
- don't forget to stamp the letter with the correct postage.

yourself but keep in mind that yours will be one of many and that the agent/director won't have the time or patience to read an essay. A letter should consist of a couple of clear, succinct paragraphs outlining why you are interested in the role/agency and why you think you're suitable and should be considered. Lay the text out neatly and clearly. Finally, consider inviting the recipient, if they're someone particularly influential, to an upcoming show you're in.

If you're sitting there thinking all this advice is obvious and you don't need it, remember that people overlook these watchwords time and time again – and they miss out on work because of it.

If your letter is accompanied by a headshot and CV, they'll have an idea of your look and your career to date, so don't simply parrot what the CV says. Writing a good letter is a fine line between being arid/uninformative and irritatingly verbose and/or self-aggrandising. When writing, try to think how it will come across to the reader, a person who doesn't know you. As with your CV, the letter is a balance between coming over as cold and clinical or being too gimmicky. Be to the point... but also be human. Once again, it's a good idea to run your draft by a friend or colleague for a second opinion before sending it.

Email letters

Email covering letters may lack the tactile and visual benefits of a good quality piece of letterheaded paper – but the rules of writing remain the same. Be brief and informative, explaining what you're applying for and why you'd be suitable, but don't make it sound like it's you that's the machine rather than the computer. It's worth putting your phone number in a signature at the bottom of the mail – some people like to put a voice to the applicant. Take extra care to read and spell-check an email letter, as you won't be able to beg the postman to stop it going out: pushing the button too quickly is all too easy.

If you're attaching a CV and photo, make sure you use standard file formats such as Word and JPG – never expect the recipient to be an IT expert. Most importantly, make sure they accept email submissions at all.

Headshots

The industry standard for photos is a black and white 10 x 8" (25 x 20cm) headshot taken by a professional photographer. The headshot will usually take in the top of your shoulders (but shouldn't include the rest of your body) in a natural pose straight to camera, clearly displaying your entire face. Most importantly the photo should look like you. If you can't replicate the look on the photo when you're called into audition at 6am on a Sunday then your headshot is not doing you any justice. You need a headshot which shows the casting director exactly what you look like. If you have a birthmark, mole or wrinkle don't try and edit it out, embrace your individuality and let your headshot provide the casting director with an honest representation of who you are.

Choosing a photographer

A good photographer may well cost in excess of £250 for a session (and don't forget to check if they're VAT registered), so this is not something to take lightly. It may sound expensive but it really does need to be done properly. Before calling a photographer check their website to see if they offer any discounts to students, recent graduates, or Equity, Spotlight or Casting Call Pro members. Note also that some casting websites offer their own photography service – Casting Call Pro, for example, offers professional headshots to members for £50.

Word-of-mouth recommendation counts for a lot – assuming there's no commission involved, actors will only refer photographers whose work they're happy with. Ask other actors where they've had their headshots done, see which names crop up again and again and look out for those who offer a professional, friendly service at competitive rates. In addition, use online and offline directories to search for examples of photographers' work, their prices and their location. These days you'll find that most photographers and studios have a website with

A PHOTOGRAPHER'S TIPS

*Professional headshot photographer Claire Grogan (**www.clairegrogan.co.uk**) offers some useful pointers.*

As an ex-actor myself I understand only too well the importance we all place on our headshots. We search for that elusive shot, the one that utterly captures our personality and uniqueness, the photo that covers every possible casting and makes us look absolutely fantastic! A lot to ask for, I know, but here are a few points to consider.

When choosing your photographer make sure you look at lots of different examples of their work and then choose one whose photos you really like with a style that you feel would suit you. Chat to them first on the phone and find out costs, location, how long the session times are and whether there's anywhere to change tops or adjust your hair/make up etc.

In terms of the film versus digital question, there's not a huge difference; both are great for Spotlight. I still prefer film but that's just a personal choice. Remember that final images from a film shoot can also be put on a CD as a digital scan – just ask your photographer if they can do this for you.

When deciding what to wear for your main shot choose a couple of fairly neutral/classic tops that you feel good in. Think carefully and honestly about your casting potential so you can wear a couple of other appropriate things to subtly suggest different looks such as professional/gritty/romantic etc. These work well for additional photos on your Spotlight portfolio. For females I recommend a fairly natural make-up to start with and then add more if you want a slightly more glam look later in the shoot. For males, just a bit of cover-up if you need it on the odd blemish or under-eye shadows.

Prepare yourself well for the shoot and try to get a good night's sleep – you won't get the best results if you turn up bleary eyed! Try as much as possible to relax and be yourself during the shoot; that way you should end up with some great shots to choose from.

examples of their work which you can browse before parting with any cash. If you are considering going to a studio ask which photographer you'll be working with and try to see examples of their work. Taking an actor's headshot is a pretty specific skill and something entirely different from modelling shots or wedding photography. Make sure your photographer knows what taking an actor's headshot involves and always ask to see examples of past work.

What is included

When negotiating a fee – and it is worth an initial approach to see if there's room for negotiation – remember to factor in the number of shots the photographer will take, the number of prints included and the cost of extra copies: you don't want to be disappointed to receive five prints when you'd been expecting ten.

The photographer will own the rights to any of the photos they take of you, even though you pay for the initial session – another good reason to check how many prints you will get, as you are likely to have to pay for extra copies. Check at the start whether the photographer's charges for these are competitive. If you want to reproduce the picture in any form (eg online, in Spotlight, at Casting Call Pro or as publicity for a show) you will need to get permission from your photographer. They should also be credited whenever you display or print the picture: this is a legal obligation.

During the session

Make sure you get a good night's sleep before the session and arrive wearing clothes which make you feel comfortable, confident and relaxed. Ensure the clothes don't distract from your face (no loud shirts or patterned blouses). You may consider taking a collection of tops to ensure they capture the right 'you'. Don't wear too much make-up and don't get your hair cut the day before – give a new cut time to settle in. It is also sensible to avoid props, backgrounds and accessories – in fact, avoid anything which draws attention away from your face. Most good photographers will be able to advise you on such things, so do listen to them, as the good ones will have been doing this for many years.

Do make sure you look clearly at the camera, particularly so that your eyes can be seen fully – though don't stare or look vacant, of course! Your eyes are like the style in which you write your covering letter – they reveal a lot of your personality at a glance. Aim for a hint of a smile rather than something too full-on, otherwise it will come across as a bit 'too much' and perhaps mean your eyes are less noticeable.

Opinions differ on whether natural or artificial light works best, but many casting directors will prefer the former. Discuss it with your photographer – some will even take your picture out of doors.

Choosing a shot

When choosing a shot select one which looks most like you and which you think best reflects your look and talents. Ask the opinion of people you trust. While family and friends can be helpful and supportive, they may not be the best judges; better to ask fellow actors, your agent or the photographer.

If you've been given a digital image, check the size of the file: don't go emailing huge files of more than 1Mb to people as it can slow up their connection or go over their storage limit. If you're not confident with these technicalities, ask the photographer.

A-Z of photographers

10 out of 10 Photography
14 Forest Hill Business Centre
Clyde Vale
London SE23 3JF
{t} 0845 123 5664
pauljneed@hotmail.com
www.pauljneed.co.uk
Contact: Paul J Need

10x8
East Dulwich
London SE22 9LF
{t} 020 8299 9707
wolf@10x8.com
www.10x8.com
Contact: Wolf Marloh

Actors photography
Prestwich Manchester M25 9GL
{t} 07776 233218
ian-vernon@freeuk.com
www.ian-vernon.freeuk.com/actors.html
Contact: Ian Vernon

Actors World Photographic
Ealing W13 0HH
{t} 020 8998 2579
photo@actors-world-production.com
www.actors-world-production.com
Contact: Daniel Pageon

Adam Parker
1 Hoxton House
34 Hoxton Street
London N1 6LR
{t} 020 7684 2005
ccp@adamparker.co.uk
www.apfolio.com
Contact: Adam Parker

Andrew Chapman Photography
198 Western Road
Sheffield S10 1LF
{t} 0114 266 3579
andrew@chapmanphotographer.eclipse.co.uk
www.bipp.com/AndrewS.Chapman
Contact: Andrew Chapman

Angus Deuchar Photographer
Wimbledon
London SW19 1EP
{t} 07973 600728
Angus@ActorsPhotos.co.uk
www.actorsphotos.co.uk
Contact: Angus Deuchar

Brendan Harrington Photography
3 Brannock Heights
Newry BT35 8DH
{t} 028 30266408
brendanharrington@btinternet.com
www.brendanharringtonphotography.com
Contact: Brendan Harrington

Brent Helsel Photographie
80b Three Colt Street
Docklands
London E14 8AP
{t} 020 7987 6521
brent@brenthelsel.com
www.brenthelsel.com
Contact: Brent Helsel

Bridget Jones
Colney Hatch Lane
London N10 1BA
{t} 07967 633432
bridgetjones88@btinternet.com
Contact: Bridget Jones

C. Moore Photography
125 Hartington Road
London SW8 2HB
{t} 020 8740 9594
studio@caseymoore.com
www.caseymoore.com
Contact: Casey Moore

CarolinePhotos
10 Elm Drive
Chobham Surrey GU24 8PP
{t} 01276 857633
info@carolinephotos.com
www.carolinephotos.com
Contact: Caroline Cooper

casting-image.com
London E5 8JH
{t} 07905 311 408
photo@casting-image.com
www.casting-image.com
Contact: John Walton

Charlotte Colman Photography
London W5
{t} 07764 604 537
charlotte@charlottecolman.co.uk
www.charlottecolman.co.uk
Contact: Charlotte Colman

Chris Baker Photographer
Barnet N1 1QP
{t} 020 8441 3851
chrisbaker@photos2000.demon.co.uk
www.chrisbakerphotographer.com
Contact: chris baker

Christopher Holmes Photography
4 Exchange Court, Fleece Inn Yard
Highgate Kendal LA9 4TA
{t} 01539 730064
chrisholmesphoto@btinternet.com
www.chrisholmesphoto.co.uk
Contact: Chris Holmes

christophernicholson.com
Flat 5, Winscombe Hall
19 Disraeli Road, Ealing
London W5 5HS
{t} 07956 466138
info@christophernicholson.com
www.christophernicholson.com
Contact: Christopher Nicholson

Claire Grogan
Archway
London N19 3LG
{t} 020 7272 1845
claire@clairegrogan.co.uk
www.clairegrogan.co.uk
Contact: Claire Grogan
{t} 07932 635381

Clive Moore Photography
London SW24DH
{t} 07788 815649
clivemooreuk@hotmail.com
www.clivemoore.com
Contact: Clive Moore

Curran Matthews Photography
41 Berrymead Gardens
London W3 8AB
{t} 020 89923242
info@curranmatthews.com
www.curranmatthews.com
Contact: Curran Matthews

David Lowdell Photography
70a Towngate
Wyke, Bradford
West Yorkshire BD12 9JB
{t} 01274 690301
david@dlpbradford.com
www.dlpbradford.com
Contact: David Lowdell

David Peters Digital Ltd
Unit 14 Fordhouse Road Trading Estate
Steel Drive
Wolverhampton WV10 9XB
{t} 01902 397739
dp@davidpeters.co.uk
www.davidpeters.co.uk
Contact: David Peters

David Price Photography
30d Longley Road
London SW17 9LL
{t} 07950 542 494
info@davidpricephotography.co.uk
www.davidpricephotography.co.uk
Contact: David Price

Department-S
P.O Box 727
Kenley
Surrey CR8 5YF
{t} 020 8668 0493
mouse@mailbox.co.uk
mysite.wanadoo-members.co.uk/ producers/exhibitionmain.html
Contact: Russell Brennan

Derek Brown Photography
Annandale Road
London SE10 0DB
{t} 020 8488 6856
castcallpro@derekbrown.co.uk
www.derekbrown.co.uk
Contact: Derek Brown

Digital Studios
45 Tower Avenue
Chelmsford CM1 2PW
{t} 0870 777 04 08
info@digitalstudios.co.uk
www.digitalstudios.co.uk
Contact: Vincent Leleu

doubletake
19 Bakers Row
London EC1R 3DG
{t} 0870 429 9625
astrid@doubletake-uk.com
www.doubletake-uk.com
Contact: Astrid Harrisson

Eamonn McGoldrick Photographer
3 Mount Hooly Cres
North Queensferry
Fife KY11 1JW
{t} 07810 482491
contact@eamonnmcgoldrick.com
www.eamonnmcgoldrick.com
Contact: Eamonn McGoldrick

Elaine Turner
Baldock
Hertfordshire SG7 6RU
{t} 077147 62718
eac@elaineturner.co.uk
www.elaineturner.co.uk
Contact: Elaine Turner

Elliott Franks Photography
15a Campbell Road
Bow
London SW19 1WW
{t} 07802 537 220
elliott@elliottfranks.com
www.elliottfranks.com
Contact: Elliott Franks

Fatimah Namdar
49 Holmesdale Road
London N6 5TH
{t} 020 8341 1332
fn@fatimahnamdar.com
www.fatimahnamdar.com/
Contact: Fatimah Namdar

Fourth Wall Photography
9 Marchwood Crescent
Ealing W5 2DZ
{t} 020 8991 1089
fourthwallphoto@aol.com
Contact: David Mosby

Fraser Photography
North West, CH2 3BP
{t} 07737 066537
fraserphotos@yahoo.co.uk
Contact: Lindsay Fraser

Gap Photography
228 Uxbridge Road
London W12 7JD
{t} 07956 521334
giovanni@gapphotography.com
www.gapphotography.com
Contact: Giovanni Pincay

Garnham Photography
{t} 07711 941208
martingarnham@aol.com
www.garnhamphotography.co.uk
Contact: Martin Garnham

Gary Treadwell
4, The Heathers
Foxhole, St Austell
Cornwall PL26 7SA
{t} 01726 824166
gtreadwell@btinternet.com
www.gtreadwell.com
Contact: Gary Treadwell

Gemma Mount Photography
Woodstock Building
9b Windermere Road
Archway N19 5SG
{t} 0208 342 9318
gemma@gemmamountphotography.com
www.gemmamountphotography.com
Contact: Gemma Mount

Gorm Shackelford
London N1 9BD
{t} 07963 948915
ges@gormshackelford.com
www.gormshackelford.com
Contact: Gorm Shackelford

Harry Rafique Photography
18 Grove End Gardens
Grove End Road
London NW8 9LL
{t} 020 7266 5398
harry@hr-photographer.co.uk
hr-photographer.co.uk
Contact: Harry Rafique

Helen Jones Photography
9 Milton Court
Parkleys Richmond TW10 5LY
{t} 07973 8415476
enquiries@helenjonesphotography.co.uk
www.helenjonesphotography.co.uk
Contact: Helen Jones

Hugh Macdonald
London N7 9LD
{t} 07773 764708
hugh@brokenpipefilms.com
www.brokenpipefilms.com/photography
Contact: Hugh Macdonald

Hyde End Studios
298 Hyde End Road
Spencers Wood Reading RG7 1DN

{t} 0118 9885088
simon@hyde-end.com
www.hyde-end.com
Contact: Simon Kemp

Indraccolo Photo
138 Upper Street
London N1 1QP
{t} 020 7354 0699
info@indraccolophoto.co.uk
indraccolophoto.co.uk
Contact: Diego Indraccolo

inner light studio
16 Reservoir studios
547 Cable Street
London E1W 3EW
{t} 020 7780 9838
info@stephanierushton.com
www.stephanierushton.com
Contact: Stephanie Rushton

J.K.Photography
17 delamere Rd
Wimbledon
London SW20 8PS
{t} 07816 825578
jkph0t0@yahoo.com
www.jk-photography.net
Contact: James Keates

Jack Blumenau Photography
72 High Street
Ashwell
Hertfordshire SG7 5NS
{t} 01462 743508
blumenrat@aol.com
Contact: Jack Blumenau

John Clark
(Studio Location)
79 Fairfield Road
London E3 E3 2QA
{t} 020 8854 4069
john@johnclarkphotography.com
www.johnclarkphotography.com
Contact: John Clark

John Nichols Studio
868 Wilmslow Road
East Didsbury (next to railway station)
Manchester M20 5NL
{t} 0161 446 2002
868online@gmail.com
Contact: john nichols

John Tudor Photography
91 Dock House, Victoria Quays
Leeds LS10 1JJ
{t} 0784 111 3574
john@johntudorphotography.co.uk
www.johntudorphotography.co.uk
Contact: John Tudor

Jon Campling Headshots
London SW16 5DJ
{t} 020 8679 8671
photo@joncampling.com
www.joncampling.com
Contact: Jon Campling

Jonathan Littlejohn
14 Panmure Place
Edinburgh EH3 9JJ
{t} 0131 229 5079
littlejohnjonathan@hotmail.com
groups.msn.com/JonathanLittlejohn
Contact: Jonathan Littlejohn

Jonathan Nunn
Kennington Park Road
London SE11 5TS
{t} 07788 427843
info@jonathannunn.com
www.jonathannunn.com
Contact: Jonathan Nunn

Julia Wates Photography
The Lodge, Riverview Gardens
Barnes
London SW13 8QY
{t} 020 8741 0046
juliawates@hotmail.com
www.julia-watesphotography.com
Contact: Julia Wates

Karl Weber Photography
3 Major Terrace
Seaton
Devon EX12 2RF
{t} 01297 21227
karl.weber@virgin.net
www.karlweber.co.uk
Contact: Karl Weber

Karla Gowlett
London Coliseum
St Martin's Lane
London WC2N 4ES
{t} 07941 871271
kgowlett@hotmail.com
www.karlagowlett.co.uk
Contact: Karla Gowlett

Kate Walsh Photography
3 Carriage Place
Stoke Newington
London N16 9JX
{t} 020 7690 3074
kate.a.walsh@gmail.com
www.kateawalsh.com
Contact: Kate Walsh

Kelly Young Photography
BR3 4LW
{t} 020 8650 3705
Kelly@bennyoung.freeserve.co.uk
Contact: Kelly Young

Kevin Bird Photography
116 Clapham Common Northside
London SW4 9SW
{t} 07900 018326
birdkevin@hotmail.com
www.kevinbirdphotography.co.uk
Contact: Kevin Bird

Kim Thorn Photography
40 Trevelyan Way
Berkhamsted
Hertfordshire HP4 1JH
{t} 07984 804492
enquiries@kimthornphotography.co.uk
www.kimthornphotography.co.uk
Contact: Kim Thorn

Kirsten McTernan
42a Brook Street
Riverside
Cardiff CF11 6LH
{t} 02920 206325
kirsten@kirstenmcternan.co.uk
www.kirstenmcternan.co.uk
Contact: Kirsten McTernan

koenigma
2 Littlemead, Broadmayne
Dorchester
Dorset DT2 8US
{t} 07919 140818
ian@koenigma.com
www.koenigma.com
Contact: Ian Koenig

Latte Photography
1 clos-yr-eos, South Cornelly
Porthcawl CF33 4RJ
{t} 01656 743007
chris.bbbb@tesco.net
www.latte444.com
Contact: Chris Bumstead

LB Photography
36 Nutley Lane
Reigate
Surrey RH2 9HS
{t} 01737 224578
postmaster@lisabowerman.demon.co.uk
Contact: Lisa Bowerman

LFX Photography
TW9 4DT
{t} 07752 358106
fxphotography@gmail.com
fayethomas.com
Contact: Faye Thomas

Linsey O'Neill Design
111 Brampton Road
Poole
Dorset BH15 3RF
{t} 01202 680312
linsey@linsey-oneill-design.co.uk
www.linsey-oneill-design.co.uk
Contact: Linsey O'Neill

LJUP
F9 Ashgrove House
Elland Road
Elland
West Yorkshire HX5 9JB
{t} 0870 428 7543
lj@ljup.com
www.ljup.com
Contact: Leonard J Urbani

Lou Mensah
London SE14 5HW
{t} 020 7771 1712
lou.mensah@btinternet.com
Contact: Lou Mensah

Louise O'Shea Photography
41 Ferme Park Road
London N4 4EB
{t} 07966 236188
louiseoshea@mm.st
www.louiseoshea.com
Contact: Louise O'Shea

LWE
London
London E8 2EG
{t} 07900 073089
info@lwelephant.co.uk
www.lwelephant.co.uk/photography
Contact: Arnis Balcus

Lynn Herrick Photography
189 Alexandra Park Road
London N22 7BJ
{t} 020 8349 3632
lynn@herrick-photo.co.uk
www.herrick-photo.co.uk
Contact: Lynn Herrick

M.A.D. Photography
Enfield Chase
Enfield North
London EN2 7HS
{t} 0208 363 4182
mad.photo@onetel.net
www.mad-photography.co.uk
Contact: Mark Davis

Marcos Bevilacqua Photography
Unit 6
2 Lansdowne Drive
London E8 3EZ
{t} 020 7683 095
info@marcos-book.com
www.marcos-book.com
Contact: Marcos Bevilacqua

Margaret Yescombe Photography
Tennyson Road
London NW6 7RU
{t} 07834 524 525
info@margaretyescombe.com
www.margaretyescombe.com
Contact: Margaret Yescombe

Mark Brome Photographer
Aston Works
Back Lane, Bampton
Oxfordshire OX18 2DQ
{t} 07885 950725
click@markbrome.com
www.markbrome.com
Contact: Mark Brome

Mark Farrington Photography
The Old Bakery
Tidmarsh
Reading RG8 8ES
{t} 0118 9844320
mark@medialink.co.uk
Contact: Mark Farrington

Matt Jamie Photography
17B Witley Road
London N19 5SQ
{t} 07976 890 643
photos@mattjamie.co.uk
www.mattjamie.co.uk/portraits
Contact: Matt Jamie

Mcneil Designs
McNeil Designs, 3 Westhill Arcade,
Hastings, East Sussex
TN34 3EA
{t} 01424 430055
info@mcneildesigns.co.uk
www.mcneildesigns.co.uk
Contact: Oliver McNeil

MH Photographic
Studio 28, Shepperton Studios
Studios Road
Shepperton
Middlesex TW17 0QD/TW19 7NU
{t} 07817 142 281
info@actors-headshots.com
www.actors-headshots.com
Contact: Mike Holdsworth

Michael Pollard
SK2 6BT
{t} 0161 456 7470
info@michaelpollard.co.uk
www.michaelpollard.co.uk
Contact: Michael Pollard

Middleton Mann Photography
26 Rasper Road
Finchley
London N20 0LZ
{t} 07930 331373/020 8445 2927
mid@middletonmann.freeserve.co.uk
Contact: Middleton Mann

My Headshots
38A Fen Rd.
Milton, Cambridge
Cambs CB4 6AD
{t} 01223 561795
martyn@myheadshots.co.uk
www.MyHeadshots.co.uk
Contact: Martyn Rayner

Natasha Greenberg
4 Auckland Road
London SE19 2DL
{t} 07932 618111
natashagreenberg@mac.com
www.ngphotography.co.uk
Contact: Natasha Greenberg

Neil Fortescue
4 Fenn Close
Frating
Essex CO7 7GB
{t} 07791 520724
neil@neilfortescue.com
www.neilfortescue.com
Contact: Neil Fortescue

Nick Gregan Photography
Studio 3
10a Ellingfort Road
London E8 3PA
{t} 020 87533 7994
nickgregan@btconnect.com
www.nickgregan.com
Contact: Nick Gregan

Nkphotographer
15 Blegborough Road
Streatham
London SW16 6DL
{t} 07782 20 20 72
nina@nkphotographer.com
www.nkphotographer.com
Contact: Nina Katinka Fredriksen

Olyden Johnson Photography
Suite 22,Continental House
497 Sunleigh Road, Alperton
Middlesex HA0 4LY
{t} 020 8932 3880
oj@olyden.com
www.olyden.com
Contact: Oly Johnson

Paul Barrass Photography
Unit 6 10a Ellingfort Road
London E8 3PA
{t} 020 8533 1492
paul@paulbarrass.co.uk
www.paulbarrass.co.uk
Contact: Paul Barrass

Peter Simpkin
London N10 2AS
{t} 020 8883 2727
petersimpkin@aol.com
www.petersimpkin.co.uk
Contact: Peter Simpkin

Phil Crow
12 Vine Street
Lincoln LN2 5HZ
{t} 07787 155852
phil@philcrow.com
www.philcrow.com
Contact: Phil Crow

Rafe Allen Photography
London SE4 1DZ
{t} 07980 840757
email@rafeallen.com
www.rafeallen.com
Contact: Rafe Allen

Remy Hunter Photography
Belsize Park, north west London - zone 2
London NW3
{t} 020 7431 8055
remy_hunter@hotmail.com
www.remyhunter.co.uk
Contact: Remy Hunter

Richard Gallagher
London
{t} 07748 430022
dickie.gallagher@gmail.com
www.dickiegallagher.co.uk
Contact: Richard Gallagher

Richard Williams Photography
Aylesbury HP20 2JR
{t} 07710 780152
Richard.Williams@10by8.com
www.10by8.com
Contact: Richard Williams

Rob Savage Photography
122b Avenue Mansions
Alexandra Park Road
Muswell Hill N10 2AH
{t} 07901 927597
contact@robsavage.co.uk
www.robsavage.co.uk
Contact: Rob Savage

Robert Gooch
Essex RM19 1QW
{t} 07976 965577
info@robertgooch.com
www.robertgooch.com
Contact: Robert Gooch

Rocco Redondo
Studio 5
25b Vyner Street
London E2 9DG
{t} 07770 694686
rocco@roccoredondo.co.uk
www.roccoredondo.com
Contact: Rocco Redondo

Rockwell Media UK
Flat 3,58 Abbotsford Street
Blackness
Dundee DD21DA
{t} 01382 434711
rockwellcm@blueyonder.co.uk
www.rockwellmedia.co.uk
Contact: Donald Suttie

Rory Buckland Photography
West Midlands & East Sussex
B9 4AA
{t} 07887 897 749
info@rorybuckland.com
www.rorybuckland.com
Contact: Rory Buckland

Rosie Still Photography
391 Sidcup Road
Eltham
London SE9 4EU
{t} 020 8857 6920
rosie391@talktalk.net
www.rosiestillphotography.com
Contact: Rosie Still

S.Grandvaux Photography
31 cuddington
Deacon Way
London SE17 1SR
{t} 07737 065105
stephanegrandvaux@yahoo.com
Contact: Stephane Grandvaux

Sam Clark Photography
Axworthy Cottage
Lewdown
Okehampton EX20 4EB
{t} 01566 783 233
sam@farlap.co.uk
www.samclarkphotography.com
Contact: Sam Clark

School of Art
34 St Oswalds place
London SE11 5JE
{t} 020 7793 9315
info@alexfranck.com
alexfranck.com
Contact: Alexander Franck

Scorching Image Photography
283 - 287 Bexley Road
Northumberland Heath, Erith
Kent DA8 3EX
{t} 0870 432 1338
information@scorchingimage.com
www.scorchingimage.com
Contact: Dave Wise

Shambhala
London NW3 4HL
{t} 07930 10 12 99
shambhala.photo@gmail.com
www.photo.net/photos/Shambhala
Contact: Shambhala M.

Sheila Burnett
20A Randolph Crescent
London W9 1DR
{t} 020 7289 3058
sheilab33@ntlworld.com
www.sheilaburnett-photography.com
Contact: Sheila Burnett

Shoot The Moon Photography
Concept House
Naval St
Manchester M4 6AX
{t} 0161 205 7417
elaine@shoot-the-moon.co.uk
www.stmphotography.co.uk
Contact: Elaine Dunstan

Shoreline Imaging
SY4 3HR
{t} 01743 341199
info@shorelineimaging.co.uk
www.shorelineimaging.co.uk
Contact: Tom Card

Shot By The Sheriff Photography
62A East Dulwich Grove
East Dulwich
London SE22 8PS
{t} 0800 03 777 03
photos@shotbythesheriff.co.uk
www.shotbythesheriff.co.uk
Contact: Keith Sheriff

Simeon Lloyd Photography
Beach View House
Freshwater
East Pembrokeshire SA71 5LE
{t} 01646 672376
studio@simeonlloyd.com
www.simeonlloyd.org.uk
Contact: Simeon Lloyd

Simon Stanmore Photography
79 Colson Road
Loughton
Essex IG10 3RQ
{t} 020 8508 2850
modelling@simonstanmore.com
www.simonstanmore.com
Contact: Simon Stanmore

SJS Photography
47 Colin Park Road
London NW9 6HT
{t} 07733 107146
info@sjsphoto.co.uk
www.sjsphoto.co.uk
Contact: Stuart Slavicky

Sophie Baker
31 Brookfield
5 Highgate West Hill
London N6 6AT
{t} 020 8340 3850
sophiebaker@totalise.co.uk
Contact: Sophie Baker

Stan Gamester Photography
24 Eleanor Street
Cullercoat, North Shields
Tyneside NE30 4PG
{t} 0191 2901380
info@stangamester.co.uk
www.stangamester.co.uk
Contact: Stan Gamester

Steve Johnston Photography
75 Haverhill Road
London SW120HE
{t} 077 7599 1834
info@castingphoto.co.uk
www.castingphoto.co.uk
Contact: Steve Johnston

Steve Morgan
Fernhill
Hebden Bridge HX7 7AB
{t} 07798 553272
steve@stevemorganphoto.co.uk
www.stevemorganphoto.co.uk
Contact: Steve Morgan

Steve Ullathorne Photography
16 Bowden Street
London SE11
{t} 07961 380 969
steve@steveullathorne.com
www.steveullathorne.com
Contact: Steve Ullathorne

Stevebrayphoto
TW3 2EU
{t} 020 8755 4156
info@stevebrayphoto.co.uk
www.stevebrayphoto.co.uk
Contact: Steve Bray

stevenleephotography
London SW18 1PR
{t} 0781 084 8470
svllee@gmail.com
www.stevenleephotography.com
Contact: Steven VL Lee

Stuart Allen Photography
London/Midlands/SW/SE
S053 3DW
{t} 07776 258829
info@stuartallenphotos.com
www.stuartallenphotos.com
Contact: Stuart Allen

Studio One
2 Trinity Street
Enfield EN2 6NS
{t} 07939 827243
info@Studio1-London.co.uk
www.Studio1-London.co.uk
Contact: Warren Vince

Studio Shots
12 Ashworth Square
Wakefield
West Yorkshire WF1 4SN
{t} 07796 681935
info@studio-shots.co.uk
www.studio-shots.co.uk
Contact: Craig Lomas

Suzannah Lea Photography
Haslemere
Surrey GU27 1QA
{t} 07702 839995
suzannah.lea@googlemail.com
www.suzannah-lea-photography.com
Contact: Suzannah Lea

T.I.S.M.ART
7 Findon Close
Wandsworth
London SW18 1NQ
{t} 0796 3628274
artifacts10@aol.com
Contact: Libby, or Ian Tucker

talentShots
2 minute walk from Piccadilly Circus
London W1F 9EL
{t} 07956 175 863 for bookings
info@talentshots.co.uk
www.talentshots.co.uk
Contact: Pepe Escuredo

The Light Studios
Cooper House
2 Michael Road
Fulham SW6 2AD
{t} 020 7610 6036
thelightstudios@yahoo.com
www.lightstudios.org
Contact: Daniel Garnett

The-Artyard
Flat 1
54 Chaucer Rd
Bedford MK40 2AP/MK45 3JX
7764497206
lougirling@hotmail.com
www.the-artyard.com
Contact: Louise Girling

TM Photography
Suite 228
Business Design Centre, 52 Upper Street
London N1 0QH
{t} 020 7288 6846
info@tmphotography.co.uk
www.tmphotography.co.uk
Contact: Tony Meehan LBIPP

tojam media
{t} 07710 055318
info@bandphotography.co.uk
www.bandphotography.co.uk
Contact: Simon Murray

Tony Preece Photography
188 High Road
Leyton
London E10 5PS
{t} 07939 139097
andonis@ntlworld.com
www.tonypreece.com
Contact: Tony Preece

Vincent Abbey Photography
6 Lynton Road
Chorlton
Manchester M21 9NQ
{t} 0161 860 6794
vabbey@yahoo.com
www.vincentabbey.co.uk
Contact: Vincent Abbey

Wildpear Studio
70 Hill Street
Richmond TW9 1TW
{t} 020 8948 2300
studio@wildpear.com
www.wildpear.com/
Contact: Neal Criscuolo

YelenaVG photography
Exeter EX4 2PU
{t} 07855 584336
yelena_vg@yahoo.co.uk
www.geocities.com/yelena_vg
Contact: Yelena Grigorenko

Showreels

With broadband connection speeds improving and DVDs cheap to reproduce, showreels have become an increasingly important way to market yourself. A showreel provides "moving image evidence" of what you are like as a performer. Without it, a casting director or agent can only assess you on the strength of your CV and photograph, which by their two-dimensional nature can only provide part of the picture.

When it comes to all types of screen casting, nothing is more helpful to those casting than being able to see you on camera. So much so, that increasingly casting professionals will only call a person in to audition if they have seen their showreel beforehand. The showreel makes up a key third of your marketing or "job application" package.

Content

Showreels are usually created from a collection of past work, showcasing your range as an actor. Ideally your showreel will consist of clips from broadcast work. However, if you don't have sufficient clips from your body of work you could consider getting a showreel made for you from pieces shot specifically for the showreel. Many of the leading showreel companies now offer 'shoot from scratch' services in which they'll work with you to shoot your choice of scenes. If you have some previous material but not all of it is usable,

TOP PREPARATION TIP

The following process is definitely worth doing: it will save you valuable time and money in your showreel edit and will also help your thought processes when it comes to finalising your clips. Having identified your clips, log where they are on the individual DVDs or tapes, eg: 'Gladiator Clip 3 – starts at: 10 mins and 2 secs, finishes at: 10 mins and 25 seconds'. If you're using VHS, reset the time counter before finding the clip.

CHOOSING YOUR BEST CLIPS

*In boxed sections in this chapter Chantal from the Actor's One-Stop Shop (**www.actorsonestopshop.com**) provides expert advice on how to approach compiling your showreel:*

You're looking for clips which will best show you off. They should show some range, you should be clearly visible within them, and as much as possible they should show you speaking. Working on the basis of, say, an end four-minute product, when looking through your past work you should keep in mind that essentially you're looking for around eight 30-second clips.

Any clip longer than 30 seconds will feel drawn out. If you're doubtful about this, try watching three or four reels in succession, and you'll quickly notice that 30-second clips feel the 'right length'. In fact, the real rule of thumb is between 10 and 30 seconds. This variable clip length ensures that your end reel will feel pacey, as the viewer is not lulled by the predictability of exactly 30-second clips throughout.

Now, because material, like life, doesn't fit neatly into pre-determined chunks, you might find that in reality you have a great clip which is, say, one minute long that you would like to use. The answer in this case is to split the scene into two 30-second segments – and then maybe show one part at the start of the reel and the other towards the end.

This brings us to another key point. When creating a showreel you should not be 'trying to tell a story', ie the running order of the clips should not be dictated by a narrative sequence. It's fine, in other words, if you have two segments of a particular film - one from the start and the other from the end of the film – to reverse the order in the actual showreel.

This is because when creating a showreel the main thrust is to show-off your various performances, not the original films.

SHOT-FROM-SCRATCH REELS

When opting for filming a reel from scratch, the number of scenes you choose to film will largely be dictated by your budget. However, given that the name of the game is to incorporate as quickly as possible some actual past work – even if only of a low-budget nature – we'd advise opting for just one or two scenes. Typically, each would be around one to two minutes long. The advantage here is that as the scenes are being shot specially for you, the focus of any scene will be on you. For this reason, it's perfectly acceptable to present even just one scene to agents and/or casters.

You want something that looks credible on camera – as though it might have been 'lifted' from a fuller-length film or TV production. You should select material on the basis of role-type – ie choose a script which will allow you to portray the kind of character you might reasonably be cast as. Modern scripts work best and generally you should avoid well-known ones or theatre pieces. The former will distract the viewer by inviting comparison with the more famous portrayal of that script, while the latter will usually require skilful adaptation for camera.

Do not be afraid to write something especially for the purpose, or perhaps to get a friend to. If you opt for a monologue, ensure, nevertheless, that there is interaction with the listening character, and that it's believable why the other character is non-speaking. An option might be to give the 'listener' one or two feed/ interjectory lines – which, incidentally, will also help your performance.

If going for two scenes, make sure they are not only a character contrast, but a visual contrast – by filming in two different-looking locations and changing your outfit – not to mention your 'co-star'. It may sound like an obvious tip, but learn you lines thoroughly. Being on camera can be nerve-wracking enough without having to scrabble for your lines.

Think also about your appearance. Overall, unless the character you are playing dictates otherwise, you should be well-groomed and look your best on camera.

showreel producers can also help you combine this with material shot from scratch. Some also offer script consultation and direction which are worth considering to ensure you choose suitable material and to get the perfect performance.

When thinking about scripts and scenes it's generally better to concentrate on scenes showing you playing characters you are likely to be cast as. So rather than trying to show your entire range in a showreel, focus on portraying these characters – play to and showcase your existing strengths. Too much versatility makes it difficult for a casting director to picture you in the role, so put your best character forward.

Always use the services of a professional company; there is an art to putting together a professional looking showreel. A showreel that looks like it was cobbled together by a friend won't do you any favours. It really is worth going to the expense of using a professional company which specialises in showreels for actors.

Before deciding on a company, try to view samples of their work to give you an idea of the quality of the finished product. As ever, if you can get personal recommendations from other actors you know, so much the better.

Make the showreel informative and entertaining as this will help maintain a casting director's attention. The first 30 seconds of your showreel are the most important. It's often sensible to start with a brief collage of the work about to be shown, ensuring the casting director gets a quick overview of your talent right from the start.

Alternatively, you might consider opening with a still of your headshot or a long close up, over which you can place your name. At all points in your showreel it should be clear that the focus is on you as it is you who is being showcased, not the other actors. With this in mind, include plenty of close-ups.

Length

Your showreel should ideally be three to four minutes long, with the maximum length of each clip not exceeding 60 seconds, ideally only 30 seconds and of varied length (see box on p101). Try not to exceed six minutes in length; casting directors don't have the time to watch a mountain of showreels from start to finish. Better a pacey three-minute reel than a five-minute one which seems to drag. Keep it clean, keep it simple and keep it relevant.

Format

If you are considering creating a new showreel, you'll want to end up with both a DVD (or CD-ROM) version of your showreel which you can post to casting directors and a 'streamed' version which you can upload to your website or to websites which offer a hosting service.

The DVD version of your showreel will look pretty standard – but take the time to ensure the box and DVD come with personalised designs

COPYRIGHT

Given that an actor's showreel is intended for the personal promotion of the actor and not intended to be sold for commercial gain or broadcast, it's not usually expected to secure copyright clearance – and in fact the diversity of the source material involved would in any case tend to make it impractical.

But you should be tactful in any dealings with potential employers, so it often doesn't go amiss to let people know you're collating work for your showreel anyway – and, especially on a low budget film, it's a good idea to let it be known from the outset that one of the key reasons you'll be working on the production is because you'd like a copy of it 'for your showreel' (it may even prompt them to be more honourable about ensuring you get a copy of the end work!).

If you have the opportunity, do check with the broadcaster's rights department – just because you were in a programme or film doesn't mean you have automatic rights to take an extract for viewing in a different format.

WHAT TO DO ONCE YOU'VE GOT YOUR REEL

Be aware that once you've put together your new showreel, you are now the proud owner of a powerful marketing tool. Don't rest on your laurels: get out there and make it work for you! Your basic task is to ensure that as many people as possible see it. Besides any agents you may approach with it, on your list of recipients should be anyone who's ever cast you, shortlisted you, or shown any interest in you as an actor. Casting directors, producers, directors, heads of production companies – you should consider anyone who may have casting influence.

In addition, any job application you make should include your new reel – whether or not the job advert requests it.

Go global with it: get it out on the net. There are various web directories which, for a basic charge, will allow you to have an online reel. You can even email it (but do ensure it's properly 'streamed' first or you might provoke angry reactions from casters whose mailboxes you've overloaded).

Keeping your reel current is a good idea. Apart from the obvious benefit of keeping your presentational material fresh, regular updating has the added advantage of giving you the perfect 'excuse' to keep in touch with casters on an ongoing basis.

which have your name and contact number clearly visible. As most showreel companies will charge you for subsequent copies of your DVD, take the price of DVD duplication services into account when selecting a service provider.

Streamed or internet showreels should be in WMV (Windows Media Video) or QuickTime format, and a typical file size for a two- to three-minute showreel should be around 6Mb.

Usually a showreel editing facility will be able to handle all the regular formats but check with them beforehand if you have a more untypical format eg VHS-NTSC (used in the United States).

Your contact details should be clearly visible at the start and end of the showreel and on all packaging. Where possible try to include your headshot on the CD cover or DVD case.

Costs

Editing previous material is likely to be charged by the hour (probably between £40 and £80 ph), which is why getting your material organised properly important is vital – see the box on p100.

If you need material shot from scratch, it will probably cost a few hundred pounds for each scene – make sure you know where you stand on this before proceeding with a showreel company, and discuss all the details with them. Ideally you won't want to film too many new scenes, in the hope that you'll soon have new material from real work that can be spliced into a updated showreel in due course.

Given that the costs for producing a showreel are high, it's vital that you choose a company with suitable experience of working with actors, and that the end results present you in the best possible way.

Voicereels

*This chapter was kindly provided by Cut Glass Productions (**www.cutglassproductions.com**).*

If you want to get into the voiceover industry (see p137), your first step will be to create a top quality voicereel to send out to agents, production companies and casting directors. This is your chance to showcase your vocal abilities, and is a powerful 'calling card'. A well put together reel makes an impression - and you won't be considered for voiceover jobs without one.

It's important to get your voicereel right. Even if you have a fantastic voice, if the reel is badly produced or directed, drags on for 10 minutes with boring material, uses the same backing music/scripts as hundreds of other showreels, or doesn't show any variation, it is likely to end up in a frustrated agent's bin!

Your voicereel should showcase your natural voice as much as possible, so it's a good idea to make the most of your natural accent and voice qualities. If a casting director wants a 'northern voice' they usually prefer it to be a genuine one. Occasionally, however, a job may call for one actor to voice several different voices – and if you do have an excellent ear for accents it might be a good idea to try these out in a single animation style piece/narration on your voicereel.

The recording session

You should feel comfortable and relaxed in your chosen recording environment. It is vital that you are given enough time to experiment with material, especially if you are recording a voicereel for the first time.

Good direction and production skills are vital. The director should gently guide you in what suits your voice, what is working for your voice, and what isn't. You might find your voice is just right for intimate, soft-sell ads and promos, but not punchy hard-sell. You may also discover your voice and delivery style is extremely well suited to documentary work. It should be a one-to-one journey – a flexible, creative process between you and the person directing the session.

Recording a voicereel isn't something that should be rushed through in a single hour, or even two. If you are in a studio that rushes you in and out of the door, you probably aren't getting enough guidance, help and direction, and it will be obvious on the finished product.

Your voicereel

Your finished voicereel should be around four minutes long. Any longer, and you will have lost the casting director's attention. It should be edited, together with music and sound effects, to show your voice to its maximum potential. Your reel should contain a mix of commercial ads, documentaries and narrations. A punchy 60-90 second 'montage' that sits at the beginning of the reel is also a good idea, to give a quick snapshot of your abilities.

If you are looking to get into radio drama at the BBC, they ask for a different kind of voicereel altogether, featuring dramatic pieces and no commercials. This should still be punchy, show your best possible vocal range, and be well produced.

Commercial opportunities

In an age of high-speed broadband, having a voicereel to hand has become an important way for an actor to market themselves. The industry has expanded so much that you don't need to be a high profile celebrity in order to get voiceover work. Digital technology has opened up endless possibilities for the voiceover artist: mobile entertainment, animations, narration, e-learning… and there are more commercials, documentaries and factual entertainment shows than ever before.

Although lucrative, the voiceover industry is a competitive industry, just like acting. If you are prepared to market yourself, have a great voice and an individual, well-produced showreel, you are several steps ahead of the competition!

A-Z of voice/showreel providers

A1 Vox
{t} 020 7434 4404
info@a1vox.com
www.a1vox.com
Type: voicereels

Actor's One-stop Shop
{t} 020 8888 7006
info@actorsonestopshop.com
www.actorsonestopshop.com
Type: showreels, voicereels

Bernard Shaw
{t} 01227 730 843
info@bernardshaw.co.uk
www.bernardshaw.co.uk
Type: voicereels

Blank Canvas Media
{t} 0845 094 0352
info@blankcanvasmedia.co.uk
www.blankcanvasmedia.co.uk
Type: showreels

Brownian Motion Pictures Ltd
{t} 020 8677 6059
production@brownianmotion.co.uk
www.brownianmotion.co.uk
Type: showreels

Crying Out Loud
{t} 020 8980 0124
simon@cryingoutloud.co.uk
www.cryingoutloud.co.uk
Type: voicereels

Cut Glass Productions
{t} 020 8374 4701
info@cutglassproductions.com
www.cutglassproductions.com
Type: voicereels

EditBeyond
{t} 07772 759036
contact@editbeyond.co.uk
info@blankcanvasmedia.co.uk
Type: showreels

Harrogate Independent Films
{t} 01423 889632
h.i.f@btinternet.com
www.harrogateindependentfilms.com
Type: showreels

Hats Off Studios
{t} 01993 898620
michael@hatsoffstudios.com
www.hatsoffstudios.com
Type: voicereels

Moving Heads Ltd
{t} 0845 838 1439
info@webcastit.tv
www.movingheads.tv
Type: showreels

November Reels
{t} 020 7870 7595
info@november-reels.com
www.november-reels.com
Type: showreels

One Voice Productions ltd
{t} 0870 9770 699
info@onevoiceproductions.co.uk
www.onevoiceproductions.co.uk
Type: showreels

Original Image
{t} 020 7494 0777
info@originalimage.co.uk
www.originalimage.co.uk
Type: showreels

Round Island
{t} 07701 093 183
mail@roundisland.net
www.roundisland.net
Type: showreels, voicereels

Showreels UK
{t} 07929 596948
postmaster@showreelsuk.co.uk
www.showreelsuk.co.uk
Type: showreels

ShowReelz
{t} 01727 752 960
brad@showreelz.com
www.showreelz.com
Type: showreels

Silver-Tongued Productions
{t} 020 8309 0659
info@silver-tongued.co.uk
www.silver-tongued.co.uk
Type: voicereels

Small Screen Showreel
{t} 020 8816 8896
showreels@smallscreenvideo.com
www.smallscreenvideo.com
Type: showreels

Stop&play
{t} 020 7226 7736
info@stopandplay.net
www.stopandplay.net
Type: showreels

Take Five Studios
{t} 020 7287 2120
info@takefivestudio.com
www.takefivestudio.com
Type: showreels

The Reel Deal Showreel Co.
{t} 020 8647 1235
www.thereel-deal.co.uk
Type: showreels

The Showreel
{t} 020 8995 3232
info@theshowreel.com
www.theshowreel.com
Type: voicereels, showreels

The Showreel Doctor
{t} 01473 715576
0788 3790 427
www.sheilasreels.info
Type: showreels

Twitch Films
{t} 020 7266 0946
post@twitchfilms.co.uk
www.twitchfilms.co.uk
Type: showreels

VTS International
{t} 020 8440 4848
paul@vtsint.co.uk
www.vtsint.co.uk
Type: voicereels

Auditions & interviews

When attending interviews or auditions it's vital to be punctual: plan how you are going to get there, and allow extra contingency time for unexpected delays en route. The casting director may well have allocated specific time slots and the last thing you want is to miss yours. If you're a little early, you will have time to compose yourself.

Arrive well-presented and ready to perform, and introduce yourself clearly. Make eye contact with the casting director and try not to be too nervous. There are ways of dressing appropriately for a part, in such a way as to chime with what you think the character might wear, but unless it's been specifically requested, which is unusual, you should turn up as yourself rather than in costume. First impressions count and are difficult to overturn.

Preparation can really help in building confidence. Learn your lines, practice the piece again and again until you know the words backwards and inhabit the character instinctively. It's difficult to overemphasise how much familiarity with your material can help build confidence and ultimately deliver a good performance.

Under-preparing can have disastrous consequences. Not only will it make you look unprofessional, but if you go into the audition knowing you've not prepared then you may very well find your mouth drying and the words disappearing while the casting director is looking on and, if not shaking their head, then wondering why you're wasting their time.

Practise in front of your friends – in a lot of cases, you may think you have learned a monologue, but as soon as you are in that audition, you have so many distractions that it's easy to forget your lines. Practice might not make perfect but it will sure go a long way! Practice pacing yourself to avoid being breathless or too ponderous.

Auditions

In the audition you'll often be expected to have prepared two contrasting pieces, of about two to three minutes each, to show your range. You may have been given some guidance beforehand indicating the style of piece to perform, or you may have a shortlist of speeches/scenes from which you can pick. If you have free range to choose, select something with which you're familiar, a scene or speech you can contextualise and a character you know and care about. In addition to these prepared pieces you may also be asked to sight-read a scene or monologue.

If you're unsure whether or not to address your monologue to the panel or to a spot on the wall, the best thing to do is to ask. Some people hate it when you address a monologue to them, others don't mind. The key is to determine which they would prefer before you start. If they ask you not to address the monologue to them, then pick a spot on the wall a little above their heads.

Take a couple of seconds to gather yourself before you start and when you finish your monologue, don't say "that's it!", don't apologize and don't make excuses, just take a second or two to pause and the panel ought to know when you have finished.

You're bound to be nervous but try and remain relaxed and confident. The people you'll be performing to are not your enemies, they're human beings and they'll appreciate that auditions are a nerve-wracking experience. Make your nerves and energy work for you, harnessing and utilising them to focus on your performance. You may have your own techniques for steadying the nerves such as mental imagery or breathing patterns.

While directors may have pre-conceived notions of what they're looking for, or the part may demand certain physical characteristics, there are numerous cases of actors going into an audition and successfully making a part their own with their own unique performance.

Be prepared to 'think around the scene' – understanding the motivations of the character will help you perform it, and will also help if you are invited to discuss the scene afterwards.

Auditions for musical theatre can be a somewhat different experience, from a hectic and anonymous 'open audition' for a big West End production down to a more personal presentation. For the former, don't be angry if your singing is cut short – it doesn't necessarily mean they don't like it.

If you are going for a smaller regional show, make sure you talk to director and choreographer equally. Prepare yourself beforehand with a suitable repertoire of different songs, and try to warm your voice up before the actual audition if you can. As for the dance element, the main point will be to see how you move and hold yourself. Don't wear heavy clothing!

Interviews

Do your background research in preparation for an interview. Find out about the director and as much as you can about the production. Consider other productions the director has undertaken and actors they have worked with. Have they a particular style? What do you think the character is like? Prepare yourself for any common questions such as 'Why do you think you're right for the role?'

Talk about the play or the script if you have read it. Show your enthusiasm and keenness and don't be shy about asking any questions you may have. The interview is a two-way process, providing an opportunity for you to find out more as well as for the director/tutor to assess you.

If there is more than one interviewer, address them all equally. Try not to let personalities get in the way – you're here to show your enthusiasm and skills, so there's not point in getting involved in any disagreements (not that you necessarily have to agree with everything they say – informed discussion can be very positive).

Never feel you have to fill every silence: a common mistake in interviews is to talk nervously at nineteen-to-the-dozen.

Rejection

Being considered for a part, auditioning and then not getting the part is a fact of life for an actor. Rejection is inevitable. This can be painful, especially if you were particularly set on a part for which you thought you were perfect. It's something you'll have to get used to. You certainly won't be alone.

It helps to think of it not as rejection, which can cement a negative perception, but rather to think of it along the lines of "I wasn't chosen this time, roll on next time". The reason you weren't chosen may not be to do with your audition; it could be that you weren't, in the end, physically what the director had in mind or that somebody else was absolutely ideal and shone out. Never let being turned down for a part dent your determination to get the next one!

Attending auditions – including those for which you don't get the part – helps to get your name and face out there and may lead to future recalls and auditions.

Section 4
Sources of work

Unpaid work

In acting the competition is fierce and paid work doesn't always come thick and fast, so new actors often take on unpaid roles to build their reputation, reviews and experience.

The scale and professionalism of unpaid theatre productions and films varies enormously, from a single person who is writer/director/crew with little or no experience of putting a piece together, to much more professional set-ups with full equipment, sound recordists, lighting camera people, a cast of actors, a director, writer. On unpaid productions you'll often find that it's not just the actors working for free – the crew may also be doing it as a labour of love and to learn more, expand their contacts and CV, just like you.

If you're looking to join in with an unpaid production, it will help to know that other people in the team are aiming for professional careers, too. Don't be tempted into thinking that 'amateur dramatics' will help you keep your hand in, for example: do it for fun by all means, but it is unlikely to help your career progression or boost your CV in a way that the industry will warm to.

Student films

Student films can be a great way of learning; simply by being in front of a camera, working with a script, a director and other actors. Everyone has to start somewhere and some of the people you work with on a student project may go on to be the leading lights of tomorrow.

If you're between jobs they can be a means of keeping your skills sharp and of networking with other actors and industry creatives. (It can be the kind of experience you don't get on a course or in your usual environment working with actors and technicians with whom you're familiar.)

As well as the actual on-set experiences, the film is likely to be viewed by a whole host of other people in the business, actors, teachers, directors, so it's another showcase for your talents.

The nature of the project could be anything from an end-of-year student film to a low/no budget film which may go on to get some kind of distribution or lead to members of the cast and crew gaining representation and the film reaching a wider audience (eg via a short film competition), gaining greater exposure for all involved.

Another option is to 'go it alone' with your own fringe theatre show at one of the festivals – see Section 5 for some specific advice on this.

The downside

The flip side of unpaid work is that you may find yourself traipsing halfway across the country, working with less than professional cast and crew and all for the grand reward of a copy of the finished film for your collection. A casting agent or director may look at your CV and see only a string of non-paid credits and not give you a second glance.

As with work as an extra (see the next chapter), you run the risk of being pigeon-holed and boxing yourself into a particular type of work, not making the transition from unpaid to paid, professional work. Having said this, most people recognise that you have to start somewhere and you can always omit work from your CV if you feel it won't be to your advantage to include it.

SOURCES OF UNPAID WORK

Various websites list casting calls. Mandy (***www.mandy.com***), for example, lists a wide range of primarily unpaid work and is well worth looking at on a daily basis. Casting Call Pro (***www.castingcallpro.com***) provides automated unpaid casting call alerts to your email inbox for free. Shooting People (***www.shootingpeople.org***) provides a daily email listing of film and TV casting calls, primarily for student or unpaid productions but with the occasional paid call. It's well worth the £30 annual subscription.

Part-time work

Part-time and temporary work can be a godsend in the acting profession. As well as helping towards the rent it gives you a greater degree of flexibility to attend those all-important interviews and auditions. The obvious drawback with part-time work is that it's not going to let you live like a king or queen.

Part-time jobs usually pay pro rata, so your income will be substantially less than if you were working full time. It's a cliché that the majority of actors take up part-time work in a bar as a waiter or hostess. Like most clichés, there's some truth in it. The shift nature of this and similar types of promotional work you help in fitting auditions around your work commitments.

As well as registering with temping and promotions agencies, a number of which are detailed below, plus corporate role-play firms (see p120), there are a number of other avenues you can pursue. Examples include market research and mystery shopping. These types of jobs often pay cash in hand and you're usually looking at between £30 to £50 per hour.

Extra work

Another classic source of part-time work is of course as an extra, 'walk on' or 'supporting' actor. Make no mistake: although there are people who earn some sort of a living doing loads of 'background' work (though they are often not professional actors), it's tiring work, time-consuming and requires keeping unusual hours. TV and film scenes with extras often start at the crack of dawn and go on for ages as a scene is retaken over and over again. You won't get the chance to hob-nob with the stars!

Having said all that, walk-on work can earn you £100 a day, which could be what gets the bills paid, and can be interesting experience particularly if you want to see what TV and film work is like.

PART-TIME WORK: USEFUL LINKS

PromoJobs Pro is a free site, listing promotional jobs and temporary work for actors, models and promotional staff ***www.promojobspro.com***

Offtowork offers opportunities in the hospitality industry in London and Birmingham.
www.offtowork.co.uk

N20 provides promotional, modelling and entertainer services.
www.n2o.co.uk

Turns specialises in part-time work for 'resting' actors.
www.turns.net

Murder mystery actors: professional actors always required throughout the UK for ongoing as-and-when murder mystery events.
www.knightstemplarevents.co.uk

Making Waves is one of the UK's leading youth and student marketing and PR agencies.
www.makingwaves.co.uk

Chaperonesuk is for chaperones and child minders looking for work and for people looking to hire chaperones and child minders.
www.chaperonesuk.co.uk

NOP Mystery Shopping: visit, make phone calls or internet enquiries to various establishments, posing as a prospective shopper or purchaser of some product or service.
www.cybershoppers.nop.co.uk

Extra work is sometimes advertised in local newspapers, but you will find more opportunities at web directories such as StarNow (***www.starnow.co.uk***) or ***www.starsinmyeyes.tv***. Total Talent (***www.total-talent.com***) is a directory where you can list your profile for free for casting directors to look at. There are also numerous specialist agencies for walk-on work. For more information and a list of such agents, see the National Association of Supporting Artistes' Agents at ***www.nasaa.org.uk***.

Roleplay & corporate training

In addition to acting for stage, screen and radio there are other professional outlets such as roleplaying and corporate training videos. Roleplaying is now commonplace in the business environment and seen by many companies as a valuable means of motivating and educating their employees, from sales reps through to CEOs and from multinational corporations to local authority departments.

There are companies dedicated to providing roleplay actors to businesses, working with the business on the brief then collaborating with the actors to develop tailored roleplay scenarios designed to help the company achieve its aims. Typically, workshops will be run by a trainer aided by actors and delivered to an audience who will usually be asked to participate. The workshops may be run with the aim of improving the morale of employees or instructing them on very specific skills which will be employed in their work, such as sales, customer support techniques or preparing for and giving presentations.

This kind of work puts you in front of an audience and requires you to get into character, improvise and interact, skills vital to the actor. And of course it can carry you through the lean times between roles. Equity doesn't cover or advise on rates for roleplay as it doesn't fall within their categorisation of professional acting work, so you'll sometimes find rates of pay are quite low.

Many businesses also find confident and outgoing actors helpful at trade shows, exhibitions and for marketing presentations to help demonstrate new products and services to the trade or the public.

A-Z of roleplay providers

Act Up
{t} 020 7924 7701
info@act-up.co.uk
www.act-up.co.uk
Act Up started in 1999. We are an independent organisation specialising in communication and acting training. We run short, part-time courses and bespoke, on-site training for people in business. All the trainers are established, professional actors.

ActorFactor
{t} 01626 336166
info@actorfactor.co.uk
www.actorfactor.co.uk
ActorFactor provides many different services; actors, facilitators, theatre skills, drama, performance, forum theatre, role play. ActorFactor uses interactive experiential simulation, such as role play, in an environment that promotes learning and development, ultimately to achieve successful change.

Barking Productions
{t} 0117 908 5384
info@barkingproductions.co.uk
www.barkingproductions.co.uk
Barking Productions is a highly acclaimed creative development and corporate entertainment company, run by professional actors and specializing in drama-based training. Barking Productions has worked with a wide range of clients from blue chip and public service organizations to medium and small companies.

Buzzword Films
{t} 01395 446895
info@buzzword-films.co.uk
www.buzzword-films.co.uk
Buzzword Films is a producer and distributor of high quality interactive training films focusing on a range of important social and health issues

CragRats
{t} 01484 686451
info@cragrats.com
www.cragrats.com
CragRats deliver learning and communication programmes, working with people of all ages and disciplines to create engaging learning experiences which appeal to a range of learning styles. Established in 1989, CragRats now has over 300 professionally trained actors involved in their learning experiences.

Creative Forum
{t} 0845 4301308
info@creativeroleplay.co.uk
www.creativeroleplay.co.uk
Creative Forum offers bespoke training programmes and conference themed performances using theatre, role-play and drama techniques. The training is high impact, memorable and issue led.

Dramatic Solutions
{t} 0121 224 7677
admin@dramaticsolutions.co.uk
www.dramaticsolutions.co.uk
Dramatic Solutions was created in 2001 when Richard da Costa and Colin Rote met working on a production of Rumplestiltskin. Understanding the power drama has to communicate and the impact it can have on the issues facing business today, they formed the company to utilise this powerful medium in corporate environments. Since then Dramatic Solutions has helped numerous businesses achieve their objectives using imaginative and memorable events and programmes focused on improving business performance.

Impact Factory
{t} 020 7226 1877
enquiries@impactfactory.com
www.impactfactory.com
Delivering courses on presentation skills, effective communication, team building, leadership development, public speaking, assertiveness skills, confidence and self esteem to name but a few.

ImpAct on Learning
{t} 01484 660077
feedback@impactonlearning.com
www.impactonlearning.com
Founded on solid principles of quality and reliability, ImpAct on learning has established an enviable reputation for exceeding client expectations. Every training workshop, dramatic presentation or event is thoroughly researched and reviewed to ensure the client brief is accurately interpreted. ImpAct on Learning now services a diverse range of clients in the public sector. It has a committed policy of product development to meet the changing needs of its ever increasing customer base.

Interact
{t} 020 7793 7744
info@interact.eu.com
www.interact.eu.com
Interact is the UK's leading exponent of the use of theatre-skills in business. Interact work in close partnership with many organisations in the UK and Europe, to deliver creative solutions to training and development need.

Just Roleplayers
{t} 020 8471 8616
help@justroleplayers.com
www.justroleplayers.com
Just Roleplayers represents an experienced team of professional actor roleplayers, with a wide cross section of experience, from law to health and from marketing to finance. Professional roleplay is a highly effective and well established method of developing communication skills which draws upon the abilities of professional actors to bring reality to roleplay training sessions.

Laughlines
{t} 0845 170 1600
info@laughlines.net
www.laughlines.net
Our actors are available for all types of corporate work. We can take on any role-play situation and write the scripts to tailor it for your subject matter. Our work is usually comedy based, as this seems to make a bigger impact. We have many satisfied clients including Shell.

NV Management

{t} 01608 674181
hello@nvmanagement.co.uk
www.nvmanagement.co.uk

Specialists in providing professional actors for the business world and also offering an enticing range of related services including bespoke training films, streaming videos for the web, interactive seminars and much more.

ProActive Roleplay

{t} 020 8761 3804
enquiries@proactiveroleplay.com
www.proactiveroleplay.com

ProActive Roleplay looks to bridge the gap between the corporate training industry and the acting profession and is able to do this given the professional backgrounds of the two founder members who trained as professional actors at the Bristol Old Vic Theatre School and since graduating have combined appearing regularly as actors in theatre and television with their work in the training industry. Prior to embarking on acting careers they both built a considerable history of working in industry, ranging from public sector to private industry management.

RolePlayUK

{t} 01780 761960
www.roleplayuk.com

RoleplayUK's actors are trained to apply specific acting techniques developed by Sanford Meisner. These techniques examine how to react to stimuli provided and encourage a naturalistic reaction rather than a performance.

Scenario

{t} 020 7431 2824
enquiries@scenarioroleplay.co.uk
scenarioroleplay.co.uk

Founded in 2005 to provide professional actors for role-play in training and business situations across London, the UK and the Republic of Ireland, Scenario now works with the NHS, GMC, universities, legal firms, schools, colleges and businesses across a wide range of applications.

Steps

{t} 020 7403 9000
mail@stepsdrama.com
www.stepsdrama.com

Founded in 1992, and originally known as Steps Roleplay, we began by providing professional role players for assessment centres and skills practice. The company has grown and developed since then and we now offer a range of drama based initiatives. The company was re-branded as Steps Drama Learning Development in 2001. We now have a senior management team of six, with support from in-house project managers as well as an administrative and accounting team. All our programmes are designed with the clients' specific learning objectives in mind and delivered by an experienced team of professional actors (all of whom are trained by Steps), facilitators, consultants and associate trainers.

The Performance Business
{t} 01932 888 885
info@theperformance.biz
www.theperformance.biz
We are always looking for actors who can portray authentic business roles. We welcome CV submissions from actors of all types. It is essential that you have worked in a business environment.

Turning Point Training
{t} 01392 446456
turningpointco@aol.com
www.turningpointtheatre.co.uk
Established in 1990 Turning Point Theatre Company and Turning Point Training make theatre-based training programmes, video and DVDs on specific health and social issues. Projects are created in collaboration with health agencies, the corporate and voluntary sectors. Our unique training programmes have addressed many important issues including retirement, ageism, bereavement and loss, mental illness, drugs and alcohol awareness, teenage pregnancy, carers, racism and child protection.

Theatre in Education

Theatre in Education (TIE) uses theatre to explore educational or social issues with children and young people. Specialist TIE companies often travel around the country, presenting workshops at schools, arts centres, community halls or smaller local theatres, and can provide an ongoing source of work for the suitably motivated actor. TIE programmes have traditionally covered issues such as racism or gender, but nowadays can equally focus on issues such as road safety, bullying or smoking, as well as more formal educational topics.

TIE work is likely to draw upon a wide range of skills, such as playing many different parts, singing, playing musical instruments or helping young people take roles themselves. Actual sessions can vary greatly in length, from short workshops to extended half- or full-day workshops. The touring nature of this work can also mean that it is exhausting – and a driving licence is probably a must.

In some cases teaching experience might be an asset, too – certain TIE companies look for it when recruiting, particularly when their work relates to specific aspects of the National Curriculum. Some companies (such as Oily Cart) also specialise in working with young people who have learning disabilities. You may be expected to attend a special workshop before you can be considered for joining some groups.

TIE can bring great rewards for the actor, and many end up sticking to this field for their whole careers, though if you're hoping for stardom this might not be the route, and rates of pay can be variable. Liking work with young people is of course a prerequisite.

A-Z of TIE companies

Actionwork
{t} 01934 815163
info@actionwork.com
www.actionwork.com
Actionwork is one of the South Wests leading theatre-in-education companies and performs to schools throughout North Somerset, Somerset, the South West, England, the UK and other parts of the world. Recent international tours included visits to Japan and Malyaysia. Through theatre-in-education we can explore many different topics, social issues, and PSHE programmes. All of our shows are backed up with workshops and can include lesson plans, evaluation reports and a variety of other resources.

Aesop's Touring Theatre Company
{t} 01483 724633
info@aesopstheatre.co.uk
www.aesopstheatre.co.uk
Aesop's Touring Theatre Company specialises in Theatre in Education, touring schools, art centres and theatres nationally throughout the year with plays and workshops specifically written and designed for Nursery, Infant and Junior age groups. The company aims to educate young audiences through the powers of entertainment and imagination whilst, at the same time, encouraging children to question and think for themselves. A high standard of professionalism is maintained by employing experienced actors with specialist skills and considerable enthusiasm.

Arc
{t} 020 8594 1095
nita@arctheatre.com
www.arctheatre.com
For more than 20 years Arc has specialised in creating and performing theatre that challenges assumptions and causes real change in the way that people relate to one another at work, at school and in the community. As a pioneering organisation we were instrumental in bringing the issue of racism in football to the forefront of public awareness. The organisations that we work with are those that seek to move forward and achieve a lasting difference, whether it be in the field of diversity, inclusion, education, health, criminal justice or community cohesion.

Barking Dog
{t} 020 8883 0034
info@barkingdog.co.uk
www.barkingdog.co.uk
Drawing on its vast experience of presenting and devising children's shows and drama, The Barking Dog Theatre company performs at around 250 schools each year. Other venues include: The Barbican Centre, Cambridge City Festival, The Maltings St Albans, Colchester Arts Centre and many other theatres, arts centres and outdoor events.

Big Fish
{t} 020 8269 1123
info@bigfishtheatre.co.uk
www.bigfishtheatre.com
Our mission is to produce high quality innovative theatre productions and drama experiences for young people in London. Through its activities, the company seeks to challenge social injustice and inspire personal and community growth and change.

Big Wheel
{t} 020 7689 8670
info@bigwheel.org.uk
www.bigwheel.org.uk
Big Wheel shows are funny, fresh and focused – which makes them an ideal way to deliver information. We have been presenting schools workshops since 1984. Our tried-and-tested show formats connect with the audience using contemporary pop-culture references and parody. Students have the opportunity to explore sensitive issues and consequences in a safe environment; young people facing challenging decisions and dilemmas are able to share views and consider the facts throughout the show, as well as having a fantastic, memorable time. Big Wheel shows are an example of TIE at its most effective.

Bigfoot
{t} 0870 0114 307
info@bigfoot-theatre.co.uk
www.bigfoot-theatre.co.uk
Bigfoot Theatre Company is a UK wide organisation that promotes theatre arts as a tool to educate and empower children and teachers alike. We exist in order to offer quality creative learning experiences that are accessible, sustainable and far reaching.

Bitesize
{t} 01978 358320
admin@bitesizetheatre.co.uk
www.bitesizetheatre.co.uk
Bitesize was set up in September 1992 by Artistic Director Linda Griffiths to specialize in theatre for young people. Our aim is to produce high quality, accessible shows for a schools audience and so our annual programme of between ten and twelve productions contains a mixture of shows from new writing to Shakespeare. It includes educational shows based on National Curriculum requirements, adaptations of Classic Stories and entertaining seasonal shows.

Black Cat Puppet Theatre
{t} 01535 637359
diana@blackcat-theatre.co.uk
www.blackcat-theatre.co.uk
The Black Cat Theatre company was set up in 1985 and operates from a small village on the edge of the Yorkshire Dales. Founder member Diana Bayliss works as a solo puppeteer/performer, often in collaboration with other artists. The company provides puppet and shadow theatre performances, workshops, residencies and training in schools, theatres and community venues throughout the UK.

Blah Blah Blah!
{t} 0113 2740030
manager@blahs.co.uk
www.blahs.co.uk
Based in Leeds for twenty years we have been taking theatre to young people across the country and internationally. Combining creative freedom with stark realism, our plays have provoked, captivated and communicated with hundreds of youth centre and school audiences. The company was created in Leeds in 1985 by three graduates from the Drama, Theatre and Television course at King Alfred's College, Winchester.

Box Clever
{t} 020 7357 0550
admin@boxclevertheatre.com
www.boxclevertheatre.com
Box Clever is a touring theatre company which performs to over 70,000 young people per year, touring to schools, colleges and theatres across the UK. Our work is broad and contemporary, across many different disciplines including dance, film and music. Led by the writer-in-residence, Michael Wicherek, the company has a particular focus on new writing and creating pathways by which young people become active participants in theatre projects, both within and outside formal education.

Bzents
{t} 01664 434565
enquiries@bzents.co.uk
www.bzents.co.uk
Bzents specialises in high quality and innovative entertainment for children, families, corporate events, summer fairs and historical events.

C&T
{t} 01905 855436
info@candt.org
www.candt.org
C&T was formed in 1988 by four Drama graduates from University College Worcester (now University of Worcester). Collar and TIE (as the company was then called) soon developed a strong reputation in Worcestershire and the West Midlands for touring plays in the grand tradition of Theatre in Education. Over the last ten years, we have been continuously developing new ideas, placing digital technologies at the heart of the drama, and giving young people a new sense of confidence that drama does connect to their experience, and that they do have a creative contribution to make to their community.

Chaplins
{t} 020 8501 2121
enquires@chaplinspantos.co.uk
www.chaplinspantos.co.uk
Touring children's pantomime company, entertaining children of all ages throughout the UK, able to perform in all venues, including schools.

Classworks
{t} 01223 249100
info@classworks.org.uk
www.classworks.org.uk
Classworks was founded in 1983 as Cambridge Youth Theatre by Claudette Bryanston and Jenny Culank to provide a creative outlet for young people aged 15-25 years. The professional touring arm of the company tours at least once per year and is hosted by some of our leading national venues and arts centres, carrying the flag for the best in young people's theatre.

CragRats
{t} 01484 686451
info@cragrats.com
www.cragrats.com
As education specialists we design and deliver programmes for schools and other educational environments. We use a range of creative techniques such as theatre roadshows, interactive workshops, media, competitions and awards, special events and much more to make your project powerful and unique. Working with young people is just one element of our service – we connect with teachers, parents and the wider community.

CREW
{t} 0845 260 4414
info@crew.uk.net
www.crew.uk.net
Our team are committed to bringing you the very best in educational drama. Promising consistent quality, excitement and learning in over 15 workshops CREW inject drama, humour, and life into all areas of the Primary National Curriculum. With workshops covering Victorians, Romans, healthy living and many more.

Freedom Theatre
{t} 01225 445577
info@freedomtheatre.co.uk
www.freedomtheatre.co.uk
Freedom Theatre Company is a professional theatre company and a registered charity based in Bath. The company is committed to excellence and integrity at all levels and is available to bring professional, live theatre to schools, prisons, churches and theatre venues across the region.

Freshwater Theatre
{t} 020 8525 7622
info@freshwatertheatre.co.uk
www.freshwatertheatre.co.uk
Freshwater Theatre Company is proud to have become one of the most respected theatre-in-education companies in the UK. Over the last ten years the company has brought educational drama to thousands of children in primary and special needs schools all over London and the south east, providing unforgettable entertainment and learning.

Golden Egg Productions
{t} 020 8262 8889
www.goldeneggproductions.com
Golden Egg Productions a touring theatre company for audiences age 3-18 years. It is made up of dedicated and experienced actors and theatre professionals with extensive backgrounds in young people's theatre and education. We have front line experience which enables us to know what children want and also what is most important to our customers: quality, reliability and value for money.

Half Moon Young People's Theatre
{t} 020 7265 8138
admin@halfmoon.org.uk
www.halfmoon.org.uk
Half Moon Young People's Theatre aims to produce and present professional theatre for and with young people that informs, challenges and shapes their artistic potential, placing these creative experiences at the core of our policies and practices. The company principally serves London and works exclusively with young people from birth to age 17, placing a particular emphasis upon engaging those often excluded in terms of culture (ethnicity) and ability (disability).

Hobgoblin
{t} 020 8542 4850
info@hobgoblintheatrecompany.co.uk
www.hobgoblintheatrecompany.co.uk
Hobgoblin Theatre Company is a young and dynamic group of actors committed to bringing entertaining, educational theatre into your school. We have all trained professionally and are members of Equity, as well as having extensive experience of Theatre In Education. We write all of our plays ourselves to ensure that they have a firm historical basis that directly supports the National Curriculum. Each of the hour long plays brings the past to life through vibrant characters and engaging stories, during which time the children are involved interactively through decision making and discussion.

ImpAct on Learning
{t} 01484 660077
feedback@impactonlearning.com
www.impactonlearning.com
ImpAct on Learning is a communications and training provider using theatrical techniques. We use drama to help education providers deliver messages, to motivate or challenge students.

Jacolly Puppet Theatre
{t} 01822 852346
theatre@jacolly-puppets.co.uk
www.jacolly-puppets.co.uk
Jacolly Puppet Theatre is a professional touring company based in Devon, England, which has toured widely on both sides of the Atlantic since 1977. Educational productions are mainly for primary schools and currently include environmental issues, biodiversity, road safety and bullying.

Kinetic Theatre
{t} 020 8286 2613
paul@kinetictheatre.co.uk
www.kinetictheatre.co.uk
Kinetic Theatre Company Ltd is a professional Theatre-in-Education company touring musical plays geared to the National Curriculum for Science to Primary schools and theatres throughout the UK. Our purpose is to supplement science teaching practices in a fun, dramatic yet educational way.

Kipper Tie
kippertie2004@aol.com
www.molesbusiness.com
Kipper Tie Theatre was formed by writer/director Bernie C. Byrnes and writer/composer Jim Fowler in Newcastle upon Tyne. Our aim is to

produce immersive, educational, exciting and above all entertaining theatre for children of all ages. Our energetic approach, which mixes acting with dance, music and mime, is attracting increasing recognition and has led to our skills being 'loaned out' to companies producing theatre for adults.

Lantern
{t} 020 8944 5794
www.lanternarts.org
Lantern Theatre Company have many shows under their belts and offer a range of performances for different ages and areas of the curriculum. Recent developments have included receiving grants to perform in hospices and hospitals. Lantern Theatre Company enjoys performing in special needs schools and playschemes.

Live Wire Productions
{t} 01224 592777
info@livewireproductions.org.uk
www.livewireproductions.org.uk
Award winning Live Wire Productions, an ensemble science Theatre in Education company, was founded in 1994 and is a unique resource for schools, the community and organisations seeking to improve an understanding of basic scientific principals as a prerequisite to change in attitudes through drama. All 36 commissioned productions produced by the company to date cover a wide range of subjects where each performance is customised to the group, audience, class etc ensuring that the optimum impact is achieved and that the key messages relevant to the needs of those in attendance are delivered.

London Bus Theatre
{t} 01208 814514
kathy@londonbustheatre.co.uk
www.londonbustheatre.co.uk
The London Bus Theatre Company is one of the leading TIE groups in the UK and can offer schools and colleges drama workshops and DVDs/videos on issues such as bullying, drugs, anti social behaviour and interview techniques. The London Bus Theatre Company converted to a CIC in July 2006 and is one of the leading Theatre in Education groups in the UK. Our funding is from LEAs, community funds and trusts as well as Police Forces and PCTs. We are in constant demand as our work is of the highest quality and has proved to be cost effective for crime and disorder and substance misuse initiatives. BP, Umbro, KeyMed and the Co-operative group have sponsored a wide range of projects since 2001.

Loud Mouth
{t} 0121 4464880
info@loudmouth.co.uk
www.loudmouth.co.uk
Loud Mouth Educational Theatre Company use theatre to explore young people's issues and views. Our interactive education and training programmes are well researched, lively and accessible, with sessions aimed at adults as well as young people. Loud Mouth tours nationally and internationally and has gained a reputation as one of the country's premier theatre in health education companies.

M6 Theatre Company

{t} 01706 355 898
info@m6theatre.co.uk
www.m6theatre.co.uk
M6 Theatre Company is dedicated to the development and presentation of innovative and relevant, high quality theatre for young people. M6 uses theatre as a positive, creative and active learning medium to assist young people's understanding and enrich their imagination.

Magic Carpet

{t} 01482 709939
jon@magiccarpettheatre.com
www.magiccarpettheatre.com
Magic Carpet Theatre has been presenting shows and workshops since 1982. We tour children's theatre productions and workshops to schools all over the UK and abroad.

Monster Productions

{t} 0191 2404011
info@monsterproductions.co.uk
www.monsterproductions.co.uk
Monster Theatre Productions Ltd is proud to be one of the UK's leading producers of children's theatre for the under sevens and providers of youth theatre programmes. To date we have given literally thousands of children their first experiences of theatre. Using a unique blend of puppetry, performance, interaction and live music we provide young children with an enchanted cornucopia of modern myths and visual magic to appreciate and share with their families.

Oily Cart

{t} 020 8672 6329
oilies@oilycart.org.uk
www.oilycart.org.uk
From its beginning in 1981, Oily Cart has challenged accepted definitions of theatre and audience. In particular we have created delightful, multi-sensory, highly interactive productions for the very young and for young people with complex disabilities.

Onatti

{t} 01926 495220
info@onatti.co.uk
www.onatti.co.uk
Performs French, Spanish and German language plays for all UK and ROI Secondary School and also UK primary schools.

Pals Production

{t} 01858 446 557
info@palsproductions.co.uk
www.palsproductions.co.uk
PALS Productions is a young and dynamic company bringing animated theatre in education to schools across the UK. PALS have a whole host of performances and workshops for key stages 1 and 2 which are all curriculum linked; from history to literature. PALS also perform a variety of open-air performances throughout the summer suitable for adults and children.

Pilot Theatre

{t} 01904 635755
info@pilot-theatre.com
www.paradoxtheatre.co.uk
Pilot Theatre - the company that created the award winning Lord of the Flies, Beautiful Thing, East is East and Rumble

Fish - is a national touring theatre company resident at York Theatre Royal.

Polka Theatre
{t} 020 8543 4888
admin@polkatheatre.com
www.polkatheatre.com
Polka Theatre is one of the few venues in the UK which is dedicated exclusively to producing and presenting high quality theatre for young audiences. Since our doors opened in 1979, this unique venue has offered children a first taste of the thrilling, challenging and inspiring world of theatre. Every year, over 100,000 children discover theatre at Polka.

Proper Job
{t} 0870 990 5052
mail@properjob.org.uk
www.properjob.org.uk
Proper Job produces high quality theatre using the biomechanical technique. Our productions tour to community venues including schools and normally include full costume, impressive sets, lighting, music and are fully blacked out to provide a memorable experience for audience and participants. We aim to maximise the full participative potential of performance in theatre through our drama workshops exploring specific issues such as citizenship, local democracy, stereotyping, sex and relationship theatre and substance misuse.

Quantum Theatre
{t} 020 8317 9000
office@quantumtheatre.co.uk
www.quantumtheatre.co.uk

Quicksilver Theatre
{t} 020 7241 2942
talktous@quicksilvertheatre.org
www.quicksilvertheatre.org
Quicksilver Theatre is a children's theatre company who commission and produce new plays and perform them to children the length and breadth of Britain and abroad, providing many with their first experience of live theatre.

Small World
{t} 01239 61595
info@smallworld.org.uk
www.smallworld.org.uk
These are the sorts of things that we do: participatory theatre, arts and culture for development, performances, arts and refugees, workshops, training, puppet and mask making, facilitating participatory consultations, PLA & PRA processes, evaluating arts and development projects, intergenerational projects, processions, carnivals, consultantcy, cabaret, giants and giant shadow puppets, healthy eating and arts projects, multimedia events, installations and more.

Tag Theatre

{t} 0141 429 5561
info@tag-theatre.co.uk
www.tag-theatre.co.uk

TAG Theatre Company is one of the major players in the children and young people's theatre sector in Scotland. TAG continues to offer an exceptionally broad range of highest quality theatre productions and participatory projects designed to engage and inspire Scotland's children and young people. Established in 1967, TAG draws upon unparalleled experience in generating memorable creative experiences for our young citizens both within and outwith the formal education sector. Each year, TAG brings outstanding professional performances to audiences in theatres and schools across the country. All our performance work is supported by fully integrated, cutting edge education programmes.

The Key Stage

{t} 01342 892951
info@thekeystage.co.uk
www.thekeystage.co.uk

The Key Stage is a Theatre in Education company visiting schools across the UK. Our key aim is to make learning fun! Through comedic, exciting and fast-paced theatrical shows, The Key Stage endeavours to both educate and entertain. Every show is accompanied with detailed teachers' notes and suggested educational activities - these can be used in conjunction with the play to enhance the learning experience as a pre or post show lesson.

The Play House

{t} 0121 464 5712
info@theplayhouse.org.uk
www.theplayhouse.org.uk

The Play House creates opportunities for children, young people and their families to engage in high quality drama and theatre to explore and make sense of the world they live in. We do this through two touring companies – Language Alive! and Catalyst Theatre – and a range of projects such as The Healthy Living Centre and international projects like For Tomorrow.

Theatre Centre

{t} 020 7729 3066
admin@theatre-centre.co.uk
www.theatre-centre.co.uk

Theatre Centre exists to commission and present new pieces of professional theatre specifically created for young people. The company was founded in 1953 by Brian Way whose observations of the unimaginative fare offered to children by London theatres led him to explore a more innovative approach.

Theatre in Education Tours

{t} 01934 815 163
tie@tietours.com
www.tietours.com

Tie Tours is an international theatre and training company. We provide shows and workshops to explore many issues including bullying racism and violence. Innovative, exciting, educational and great fun. Established in January 1995, the company has attracted many diverse talented people to its ranks. Exciting shows, amazing workshops: we have performed all over the UK to a variety of people in a variety of venues including schools, youth clubs, community centres, hospitals, open-air housing estates, parks, theatres and festivals.

Thrift
{t} 01635 41119
office@thriftmusictheatre.co.uk
www.thriftmusictheatre.co.uk
Although Thrift root their work in theatre, the emphasis in all of their projects is the learning experience. We try to develop theatre as a medium for developing entrepreneurial activity, teaching young people that experiment is good, certainty does not matter and ways of finding creative solutions to problems. We seek to find ideas for Theatre in unusual and sometimes difficult places, being inspired by things that most people would never see or notice, anywhere & everywhere. In buildings and architecture; the sounds and rhythms of the street; colours, spaces, people walking past in a hurry.

Paid work

Much work in forthcoming productions will be filtered through casting directors and agents, but there are various other avenues which you can pursue to find out about auditions and what's in the production pipeline.

Casting Call Pro

138 Upper Street
London N1 1QP
{t} 020 7288 2233
info@castingcallpro.com
www.castingcallpro.com

Casting Call Pro (CCP) was established in 2004 and offers an online CV service, casting alerts, peer networking, and a variety of industry guides and resources. It currently lists 20,000+ actors and is used by hundreds of production companies, casting directors and employers. Standard membership includes a profile listing in the directory and is free. Premium membership is £15+vat per month or £100 +VAT for a year.

CastWeb

7 St Lukes Avenue
London SW4 7LG
{t} 020 7720 9002
info@castweb.co.uk
www.castweb.co.uk

Established in 1999, CastWeb is a casting breakdown service with castings sent out by email. Eligibility for subscription membership requires one of the following: "a current entry in the industry casting directory Spotlight, or membership of the actors' union Equity, or a suitable CV submitted to Castweb for approval". A monthly subscription is £17.95 + VAT, with reductions for 3, 6 or 12 months.

Equity Job Information Service

Guild House
Upper St Martins Lane
London WC2H 9EG
{t} 020 7379 6000
www.equity.org.uk

Up to the minute breakdowns available to all Equity members. See also Equity, p176.

PCR

PO Box 100
Broadstairs CT10 1UJ
{t} 01843 860885
info@pcrnewsletter.com
www.pcrnewsletter.com

Something of an industry standard, PCR is a weekly newsletter listing what's in pre-production or casting. Prices range from £29 for 5 weeks to £260 for a full year. PCR also publish Theatre Report, covering fringe and repertory theatre (from £11.50 for three months), and Filmlog.

The Stage

47 Bermondsey Street
London SE1 3XT
{t} 020 7403 1818
admin@thestage.co.uk
www.thestage.co.uk

Published weekly, *The Stage* carries industry news, articles and castings. Some job ads are free at the website; subscription to the newspaper (from £14 quarterly, £53 a year) gives full access.

Voiceover work

*This chapter was kindly provided by James Bonallack, director of Foreign Voices (**www.foreignvoices.co.uk**).*

How can you succeed in the voiceover business? You've got a brand new voice or showreel with a trendy mix of commercials, corporates and narratives and now you're ready to sit down behind the mic and start earning the big money. Let's start with the good news: if you're Jenny Eclair, Tom Baker or Jack Dee it's easy – your agent calls you, you turn up at the studio where people make a huge fuss of you, you voice a 30-second commercial and then when the cheque arrives you think there's one zero too many on the end. If not, much as with anything else in life, you'll get out what you put in – if you're lucky. Having a great voice is the easy bit – making money with it is a whole different story. This snapshot of the UK voiceover industry will help you make some informed decisions and perhaps avoid some painful mistakes.

Getting started is the most difficult part. People will not be beating a path to your door; you're going to have to get them interested in you and, more importantly, your voice and what you can do with it.

Three golden rules

A producer is looking for three things in a voice. First, that you have a voice that's worth paying for, which means that your voice will have certain qualities. It doesn't mean smooth or rich or sexy or hard sell or sporty or that your voice is recognizable. It doesn't mean that you can narrate or sight read effortlessly for hours. It doesn't even mean that you are studio savvy and know what the engineer wants before he does! It simply means that your voice has got a certain something that he or his client feels fits their requirement which is why your reel has got you a phonecall and which is why you are nervously pacing down a Soho side street looking for a studio with a name like Beach (if they think they're trendy) or Digital Sound and Video Mastering Ltd (if they don't care who thinks they're trendy).

FEES FOR VOICE WORK

Here are some basic rules which will preserve your sanity and hopefully improve your bank balance. Voiceover sessions are calculated by the hour and then the half hour, half day or day rate. Never work for less than £50 an hour on any project that is of a commercial or corporate nature. This accounts for 95% of all voiceover sessions.

Jobs at the lowest end of the pay scale include voice telephony, charity work, talking books, language tapes and other semi-commercial products. Don't be misled, though: there are well paid projects out there in abundance in all of those areas.

Better paid work includes corporates, broadcast (idents, continuity, documentary talking heads and narrations), commercials for radio and TV and computer games. There are dozens of different types of paid work for voiceover artists but the top end is where you want to be. If you give your voice to a commercial or to a product that people are parting with their hard earned cash to buy then the chances are that you will be getting a buyout (common) or royalties (less and less common).

As a rule of thumb you should be happy working in a band from £130-£180 per hour depending on who you are working for and what kind of work you are doing. Again, check the internet and voiceover portals especially for more detail. Try Equity and Usefee TV (***www.usefee.tv***) especially for radio, TV and advertising usage deals.

Your approach to the client regarding rates is also important. A 'voice' that works efficiently and overlooks a modest overrun with good humour will be asked back. For their part, producers are usually very fair and honest but there are horror stories. (One company offered a voice artist £250 to do 24 internet ads. Luckily they found out from another voice just leaving the studio that the fee should have been in the region of £2500 once usage was taken into account.)

The second thing the producer is expecting is that you do what it says on your demo or voiceover CV. That means if you say you narrate well then you had better be able to narrate well. If it says you're as cheap as chips because you've only done a bit of hospital radio before you decided to become a voice actor then his expectations will be very much less. The point is don't say you're a genius if you're not – you'll be found out!

Finally, the third thing they want from you is that you can take direction. That simply means read what it says on the script unless it's obviously not correct; listen to what you are being asked to do and do it without a fuss and to the best of your abilities. As you gain experience you'll develop confidence about voicing your opinions but to begin with concentrate on getting the right result and showing willing.

Voiceover agents

One of the questions I hear most from new voices is "How do you find a voiceover agent?". Start by sending your demo to agents and anyone else who might be useful – but call first. There is virtually no chance that an agent will take you on if you send your demo in unsolicited. Your chances improve when you take the trouble to ask intelligent questions about their business and how you could be of use to them, supported by a clear voice CV and a short demo with your phone number on the CD and on the box spine.

But do you really need an agent just yet? It sounds odd but actually they are going to be a lot more interested in you if you've got some solid voicing experience under your belt before you start to pester them for representation.

Certainly a good agent will greatly improve your earnings and supply you with regular work but equally there are many voices languishing unused on agency books. I can think of one agency in particular which has 100 or more voices on its books. Their top people work regularly but the rest don't get a look in – the agent is too busy worrying about his star clients. Agencies do hire but they tend to hire by developing relationships with voices they know.

With the advent of online voiceover portals many agencies are booking voices without actually going to the trouble of representing them. The relationship builds and eventually they slot into the agency by default.

(By the way that's a two way street. Many savvy voices are now representing themselves and are represented by more than one agent to find as many outlets as possible for their voice. Having said that, the traditional model of putting all your work via one agent is under threat but still very much in place at the top of the food chain. If you have a top agent you won't want to upset them by touting for work outside of that relationship.)

Internet portals

If you're at all familiar with voiceover portals you'll instantly see the advantages. You're on the internet 24/7; you have your own URL (web address) without having to set up your own site; you can be searched by producers in various ways and you can take advantage of other online databases to send your link to potential clients. The better portals will offer free advice and information about aspects of the industry and directories of relevant contacts. Several portals are very established while the newer ones (***www.voicespro.com*** and ***www.voicefinder.biz*** being my two favourites) have highly advanced features and appear much more functional than their older rivals.

Studios are strange places populated by sound engineers who don't see much sunlight. But remember they are your friends. They make you sound good; they help you drop in just after where you inexplicably fluffed for the fifth time and they make you come across as being better than you probably are. Learn the jargon and get a reputation for turning up early and being professional. These are the shortcuts to recommendations and repeat business. The same goes for producers and the money people who pay your invoices – network with anyone who might be useful!

As you develop your skills and find you have a good client base you might want to think about setting up a home studio, perhaps even with an ISDN capability. This is particularly useful for voices that do a lot of radio spots or who live outside London. The advantages are that you are more competitive and can save the production company time by editing your own .WAV files. This makes using you convenient and in all probability very good value. The disadvantage is that you could find yourself very isolated as the business is very much one of networking in the pub after the session.

Here it is in a nutshell: be proactive and be professional. The industry is very competitive and luck and timing play a big part.

Section 5
Fringe & comedy

The Edinburgh fringe

This chapter – a guide to what to expect from the Edinburgh fringe – was kindly provided by James Aylett, a seasoned fringe performer and co-author of fringe *(Friday Books,* **www.fridaybooks.co.uk***):*

Performing at the Edinburgh Festival Fringe can feel like both a month-long party and a prison sentence. Although it offers a melting pot for some of the most creative people across Britain and beyond to showcase brilliantly imaginative theatre, it's potentially the most demanding and exhausting way of fulfilling your desire to act. For a start the work doesn't stop at performing – the casts of fringe productions are generally required to muck in and help with pretty much everything else, from publicising the show to carrying the company keyboard up the Royal Mile.

As if that wasn't already more than a full-time job, you naturally want to try and experience some of the wealth of artistic experimentation going on in the same city. Shows run until the early hours; the bars are open until 3am and the clubs until 5am; parties happen on a nightly basis and there's no waiting around until the next afternoon for things to begin again. Is it any wonder that several hundred people go mad every year?

It's worth pointing out that Edinburgh fringe shows rarely offer huge amounts of money even to the most qualified actors, partly because the large number of Fringe shows results in a rather thin spread of the profits; an expenses-paid profit-share production is the most you can hope for, and not a bad deal when you consider even just the expense of living in Edinburgh during the fringe. The large number of shows at the fringe (some 1800 in 2006) also means that productions really have to work to get people to see them – while some of the larger Edinburgh venues can guarantee a more consistent chance of getting audiences, the old adage about many fringe shows having an audience of three people still holds true.

So why go at all? The easy answer is that if reading the above paragraphs fills you with dread, maybe you shouldn't. You'll probably hate it. But if you think you can cope with the challenges, there's a lot to love – and it remains a great place to develop your acting experience and, if you're persistent enough, to get seen. The intense atmosphere, the chance to perform a show in the same venue for a month and the need to keep focused on the task in hand all act as an invaluable training ground for budding performers of all varieties, which is why so many known actors, writers, musicians and comedians cite the fringe as a great stepping stone in their careers.

But perhaps the biggest appeal of the fringe is simply that it has a creative atmosphere that nowhere else can match. It is three weeks of unbelievably sustained artistic activity which combines an element of competitiveness with a healthy sense of camaraderie (perhaps brought on by a joint sense of suffering) among a huge number of people who really care about what they're doing. The shows are of variable quality, but there are more risks taken and ideas tried out than in any of the big funded arts festivals (something which is usually clear when comparing the fringe to the offerings of the overshadowed Edinburgh International Festival which happens at around the same time).

Publicity

Taking a show to Edinburgh is not really about performing a show. It's about publicising a show. This becomes obvious the minute you arrive there. However early you get there, somebody will always have got there before you in readiness to shove a piece of cardboard in your face – probably taking advantage of the fact that you haven't yet learned to say no.

People flyer you everywhere, all the time. If you're acting at the fringe, the chances are you'll end up flyering as well. You can choose to make this the most miserable experience you've ever had, by treating it as a horrific duty and getting rid of your flyers with the same relish as stuffing envelopes. But this doesn't make for the best

REVIEWS

One of the more realistic reasons for going to Edinburgh is to come back backed up by a couple of nice reviews. Not only do they actually help sell tickets for the show you're in, but they look terribly nice on your website and indeed your CV. And, surprisingly given the number of the shows at the fringe, most people can expect to get their show mentioned in at least one publication (whether it's a personal mention depends on the size of the cast, the quality of your performance and whether the reviewer likes the look of you).

SkinnyFest and Three Weeks are printed especially for the fringe and are the most likely chance you have of being reviewed. The Scotsman tries to get round as many shows as possible (though if you're not eligible for their Fringe First awards you're at a distinct disadvantage) and recently broadsheets better known south of the border have been increasing their coverage, notably The Guardian and The Independent.

If you're up in Edinburgh mainly for the sheer ego-boosting joy of seeing your name in print, you should focus your flyering upon the people wandering up and down the Royal Mile conspicuously wearing press passes. Unfortunately press passes seem to be quite easy to get hold of, and you often end up with a man from Plumbing Weekly coming to see your show for free without the slightest intention of recommending it to his large readership of plumbing enthusiasts.

publicity, because people on the street probably decide not to go and see your show. Alternatively, by telling people all about what you are doing and why they should come to see it, you might engage their interest. It's also a better way of making friends.

There are also people who spend several hours devising clever and wacky ways to get people to take their flyers. Variations of the old "please could you hold this for a moment" then running away routine are rife. Or disguising flyers as pieces of cake. Or kidnapping and drugging people then tattooing publicity blurb onto their bodies. This is all good, clean fun, but at the end of the day you have only succeeded in foisting yet more onto them about which they are none the wiser except that whatever it's advertising is being put on by some cunning bastards.

As far as the bums-on-seat-per-flyer hit rate goes, nothing beats personal contact. On the other hand, the wackier ways of getting rid of flyers can get a group noticed and offer the opportunity to have a bit of fun. But go carefully – flyering done properly (or indeed improperly) is extremely hard work (harder, some would argue, than the performing in the show itself). Try to avoid flyer-induced exhaustion or insanity, as it's a pity when the energy used up on publicity results in a drop in the quality of a performance.

The other main type of print publicity is posters, which work as follows: you put up a poster. Somebody else puts a poster up over the top of it. You put up another poster over the top of that one… and so on. The people with the most posters visible are not those who put the most posters up, but those who do it most regularly. It's that simple. The actual areas you can put posters up in are rather limited these days; since the venues themselves are now ultra-competitive, you are never going to be allowed to put up posters at any venue other than your own.

The alternative outdoor fringe box office has a place where posters can be displayed, otherwise there is only really the much-fought over poster space on the Royal Mile to use. Some pubs, cafes, bars etc are also happy for posters and flyers to be left on their premises, but it's a good idea to ask. Other surfaces may look tempting – those shiny blue fringe-sponsored bins may seem to be crying out for one of your lovely posters – but people are employed to remove them, and will. Fly-posting is illegal and some pretty hefty fines are threatened for doing it; on the other hand, the fact that the promoters of respected big-name acts are particularly guilty of fly-posting suggests that nothing at all is being done about it, which is annoying because, let's face it, it's not difficult to track down the culprits.

You might find yourself doing some actual performing as a publicity tactic, either on the street itself or on specially designed outdoor stages. This is all good and well, but again requires care, again in case you end up doing your actual show with very little energy or motivation left, and also in case you end up putting people off you altogether. Casts who go about chanting excerpts from their reviews or specially designed slogans get extremely irritating after a while – a production of *A Midsummer Night's Dream* which goes around greeting people "Hail, mortal!" is crying out to be culled. In any case, it is rare for anyone to successfully distil their show into a 20-minute performance which works in the open air. For this reason, the little stages, fun though they be, mainly benefit the fringe organisers and sponsors – and of course the punters, who treat the whole thing as free entertainment.

Doing the shows

After a day of draining intellectually and physically demanding work, deprived of sleep and most likely food and drink as well, performers at the Fringe have to throw themselves into the equally draining, physical and intellectual task of performing. Unless they happen to be in a morning show, in which case they have to get up frightfully early. And it's not as if the shows themselves are ever plain sailing. The fringe is full of idiosyncrasies, in addition to which each venue will add its own idiosyncrasies just because they can. Throw in a load of thespians with extra idiosyncrasies and you're in for a pretty idiosyncratic time.

One such idiosyncrasy is the way venues manage to cram so many shows into one day by having them virtually back to back. As if it wasn't already hard enough putting on a show in the distinctive high-pressure atmosphere of the fringe, people end up setting up everything for it in under five minutes at the same time as another show is getting all of its things out of the way. For shows involving a lot of props, big sets and complex technical set-ups, it is particularly nightmarish. You have to expect to pull your weight at these times, and there's no point in grumbling that you're an actor and need to get into character – everybody will be too busy to listen anyway.

WHAT TO SEE

Even the most avid fringe-goer couldn't hope to see every one of the shows on offer. So how do you even begin to choose? The first place to look is the fringe brochure. This handy guide lists everything that is on over the course of the festival, detailing all the vital information like locations and times, and helpfully split into different (albeit occasionally misleading) categories. Go through the brochure and circle the shows that look as though they will interest you. Then ignore it, because the show descriptions are written by the people who are putting them on, so they often lie and rarely describe the show you're going to see.

Reviews give you an idea of the quality of any given show, but they're naturally the opinions of individuals, and one man's inspired piece of cutting-edge physical theatre is another man's dance music-fuelled strobe nightmare. So ignore them as well.

People doing shows are in a pretty good position to give you a rough idea of what their show contains. But they will also be desperately trying to sell you a ticket however poor they really believe their show to be, so you can pretty safely ignore them too. A better way to find out about shows is to listen to what everyone else is talking about. Shows that are either brilliant or truly dreadful provide hours' worth of conversation, so if everyone is talking about a show, it's a fairly safe bet that it's going to be for one of those reasons. Even then, you can't be sure.

The best advice I can give is to take risks. You can stick to the big venues and the well-known names if you want (and you'll pay for the privilege) but not a single one of the most memorable shows we've seen was a sure-fire hit. The fringe is all about trying things out, and if you discover a little-known, poorly-attended piece of theatre that somehow achieves perfection then it's an experience that you could never repeat in London's West End. The chances of disappointment are high; but the risk is worth it for the times when you strike gold.

Learning to keep performances fresh time after time is part of what being a professional is all about, but the extreme pressures of the fringe arguably make it even harder. Give yourself the space you need (if not in the mad rush immediately before the show, then in a suitable alternative time). Be as positive as possible during the show, and if you do have problems with somebody or something, wait until an appropriate time to share it with the world.

Tempting though it is to cope with shows by getting drunk before them, this will make everybody else very cross. Get drunk after the show. Do some voice exercises to assist you when you're competing with the orchestra of electric fans set up to cope with the fact that you are in a venue which has come to resemble a sauna (and wash your clothes occasionally). Most importantly, get some sleep.

And during any show, whether you are performing or spectating, enjoy it. It's the reason you're at the fringe, so you might as well get something out of it.

How do people live?

The fringe is essentially one big party. For many, the fringe lifestyle also mostly involves going to parties. And there are lots of parties. It's therefore important that you find out where the parties are, and if necessary work out how to crash them. If you want a quieter evening you might try crashing a performer bar instead. You might even see somebody famous.

But there are practical considerations, like having somewhere to live for the entire month. If you're cast in a fringe show it will almost certainly be somebody else's problem to find you accommodation – and if that's not part of the deal you must be aware that you'll end up forking out at least another £650 and you need to start looking in March rather than June if you don't want to be in a sleeping bag on the Meadows (a cheaper option is to blag space from other groups – if you're actually performing though, it's not such a good idea, because you're never going to perform well if you're sleeping on a kitchen table).

The sensible shows hire a flat, ideally close to the city centre and best of all within a few minutes' walk from their venue. Some groups share accommodation (particularly comedians, who tend to be there on their own anyway). Some groups share beds (particularly comedians, who need the warmth and companionship of another body at night to overcome the self-loathing that is behind their art).

As a performer you're well advised to check out the exact deal here as well – groups on a budget have a tendency to cram several people into one bedroom, which can increase the risk of tension and, in extreme cases, madness; people need time on their own, and this may be difficult in a cramped flat.

BEYOND THE FRINGE

If you spend all your time at the fringe doing shows, you'll miss out on some of the other great things on offer. Don't do that – it's an essential part of the fringe experience to wallow in everything that's on, especially as some of them are free. The circus-like entertainments which take place along the Royal Mile throughout August are professional and sometimes awe-inspiring. Sometimes you even see scientologists (though they're not always free if you get too close).

Like many major fringe festivals, the Edinburgh fringe has a smaller but occasionally interesting international festival going on at the same time (though it's mainly located on the fringes). There are also several other types of festival running at the same time, notably the book festival, film/TV festival and art festival, all of which offer a breather from the fetid thespian cloud hanging over the city. You might even go and see the Edinburgh military tattoo if the relentless bagpipers busking Scotland the Brave don't sate your appetite for tourist-friendly clichés.

It's also rumoured that somewhere in the Edinburgh fringe there is a city, which has got bits that exist outside the month of August.

Some accommodation is drab, some is palatial. Quite a lot in Edinburgh seems to be somewhere in between – either a well appointed flat nestling halfway up a damp dingy staircase that looks just like the one in *Shallow Grave*, or an enormous apartment carved out of Georgian townhouses that nonetheless is a little rundown, with peeling paint, appliances that need encouragement, and a strange box room that has no obvious purpose (although groups on a budget will ask somebody to sleep in it). And why would you prefer large-yet-seedy over unassuming-but-well appointed? Because they're great for parties, of course.

What not to go to the fringe for

The fringe is not about famous people. So it's a shame that so many think it is about famous people, or at least becoming a famous person. Yes, it has its success stories, and is still the place that agents, casting directors and talent scouts hang out in the hope of finding the next Tom Stoppard or Stephen Fry. However, with the sheer number of performances at the fringe, getting an agent to see you in a show is every bit as difficult as it is in an ordinary London fringe theatre. If you happen to be planning to go to the Edinburgh fringe in the hope of finding fame and fortune, now is the time to reconsider. It will just be an expensive route to disappointment.

If you go to the fringe in the hope of finding an agent, you must be prepared to write to anyone who looks in the slightest bit promising, and you should do it well in advance of the fringe; if you're lucky they'll at least be sending a representative up to Edinburgh for a few days so they may be able to fit you into their schedule. The same goes for casting directors, and you can expect the same politely-worded but infuriating rejection letters from them both.

You might also hope to get seen by a talent scout; the problem is, you never really know where they're going to be or who they are, and they tend to visit shows that are doing quite well or that really interest them – just like any ordinary punter. You'll know who they are if they come to your show and like it, but that doesn't help you get them to your show in the first place. Your best bet is to hang around a big venue to see if you can spot anyone with a clipboard or a special pass, then flyer them with your most charming pitch. The only downside is that you may end up spending a long time flyering the boiler man.

It does happen, though – people get spotted at the fringe. There are people whose careers are launched by that one fortunate time when a casting director couldn't get a ticket for Paul Merton so went to see them in *Bacmeth – the Dyslexic Tyrant* instead, discovered their talent and cast them in a big television drama which propelled them into the limelight and won them a Golden Globe for the second series.
It just doesn't happen to very many people.

And yet...
If I have said nothing else of importance, it is that it's okay, and indeed fun, doing shows to an audience with four people in it. It may be that your hard work is rubbished by the press and sinks into obscurity within minutes of the final performance. But you have given those four people an experience that they will take away with them for better or for worse. It's not fame – but it's a tiny bit of recognition on the broad canvas of the arts.

I was once given a flyer for a one-woman show by two breathless, excited girls. They explained that they weren't involved in the show in any way, but had been to see it and liked it so much that they had taken a stash of flyers to hand out to other people. They had been the only two people in the audience, and they felt it ought to be seen by many more.

Later that day, I saw the woman actually performing the show in costume looking pissed off and bitter, trying to give out flyers. Of course she looked pissed off and bitter – she was only getting two people in her audiences and that is why she wasn't happy.

But the two breathless girls were happy.

Stand-up comedy

*As a new act in 2001, Hils Barker (**www.hilsbarker.com**) made it to the final of* So You Think You're Funny?, *Channel 4's national stand-up competition. She went on to co-write groundbreaking sketch show* Radio9 *for Radio 4 (aired in 2004–2006), and has appeared in and written for BBC TV comedy such as* The Message, The Late Edition *and* The Comic Side of Seven Days. *She is also a stand-up on the London and national circuit and here brings advice 'from the coal face'.*

People come at stand-up from so many different areas of life it feels presumptuous to describe how to go about it. Why people do it is maybe more interesting. It's got me thinking that being a comedian is not so much a job, more of a condition and it's just a question of when you accept the fact, throw out your social life and start hanging out at clubs called things like 'BrouHaHa' and 'Primrose Hillarity'. I did my first gig at a biker's pub in Islington called the 'Purple Turtle'; it wasn't so much stand-up, more a monologue of five minutes of 'jokes' that I had written, delivered firmly to the back wall and at high speed so no-one could heckle. But I loved it, and after that I was hooked. The first gig raised more questions than it answered: "Where can I do this again?" "How can I do it better?", "Who *names* these clubs?"

Other questions might be: what are you looking to achieve through doing stand-up, and is it possible to earn a living from it? As hinted above, it's different for everyone. Comics vary so much in style that someone who is perfect for one club may go down terribly in another, and understanding that this doesn't make you crap is really important. Similarly, some comics are live stand-ups through and through; others will want to move into TV and radio, writing or sketch comedy. All of them, though, are probably motivated by having ideas and opinions that they want to 'get out there'.

It's possible to make a great living from stand-up if you're regularly playing all the bigger clubs, such as the Comedy Store, Jongleurs or the Glee, and even if you're not, there are so many clubs at the moment that you can earn a living if you're any good and you gig frequently. Having said that, it can take a good few years to get to either level, because obviously when you start out no-one will pay an inexperienced comedian, and often it costs you money to travel to gigs and do try-out spots for promoters. But as with acting, no-one gets into it because they think it's going to make them any money. You do it for the sheer fun and because you like showing off.

Open mic spots

The first step towards getting started is probably to buy your local listings guide (in London it's *Time Out*, Glasgow and Edinburgh *The List*, and so on), get familiar with the comedy section and start turning up at clubs. Go and watch comedy at all levels, from open mic nights to the Comedy Store. It will inspire you, make you laugh, give you an idea of how to shape your material, and also, you start meeting people.

Find out who runs the clubs where you can get yourself a five-minute spot, and either call them or talk to them on the night. In *Time Out*, you can tell more or less which clubs are for newer acts – they normally have a lot more than the standard three or four comics on the bill, or there'll be a thing saying 'interested acts should call'.

After you've done your first few open spots, I think it's massively encouraging to know that assuming you're in any way funny (and you must be, or you probably wouldn't be interested in doing it in the first place) anything is possible through hard work and fanatical dedication. I use those words advisedly; you can start getting a lot of stage time just by being the one who turns up, and there really will be a lot of new acts who turn up obsessively. I know I did when I started out, and it's true that you don't really make much progress as a comic otherwise. The best way to improve is by turning up at gigs as many nights per week as you can spare, either to get on the bill or just to watch.

It might sound dull but when you really want to play the gigs, nothing works better than a bizarre combination of quasi-stalking tactics and hardcore diary management. (Once you're up and running, with any luck you can get an agent who is brilliant enough to do all that for you.) You could also do one of the various comedy courses on offer (see box).

Good and bad gigs

Don't set too much store by reviews, whether they're negative or positive. There may be reviewers or promoters who think you're shit one minute then brilliant the next, or vice versa. But it's worth reminding yourself that every wonderful comedian who is now a household name or widely accepted as a genius has been through that process, and has had nights where people think they're terrible. As a student at the Edinburgh festival in 1998, I saw one of my favourite stand-ups, a hilarious person, get booed off stage at a gig. I remember mentioning it, shocked, to a stand-up acquaintance, who

COMEDY WORKSHOPS

I did a sort of comedy workshop when I started out, where new acts and people who were thinking of starting stand-up, brainstormed ideas once a week. It was fun, but not a very professional approach, and I know there are courses which cover everything from choosing your comedy persona, to joke-writing techniques, networking and so on. That can be really useful, but it can also be a bit prescriptive. A lot of people think it's better if your comedy persona emerges organically from the kind of material you write, rather than slamming a style onto a new act, which can ring pretty false. Also, don't assume that everyone who runs a course (or indeed a gig) is in it for the love of comedy. Most are, but if you're going to get advice from someone, make sure you think they're a like-minded person.

The advantages of the comedy course are that you meet people straight away who are also trying to do what you're doing, so you've got an instant network to talk through ideas with, bitch about stuff, and celebrate / commiserate with. There are so many gigs, especially the early ones, where all you want to do afterwards is analyse every last detail with another comedian.

was starting to do pretty well. His reaction was simply, "And?... Bad gigs happen to everyone."

Up until that point, it just hadn't occurred to me that people probably got better as comedians via a brutal learning curve. I mean, it kind of had, but I'd mainly seen comedy videos and not much of the real live thing. In a way, though, it was liberating to learn that even when you've sort of made it you can still have bad nights. I think it was this piece of knowledge – that comics can watch other comics having a bad gig, but still know that the person on stage is a good comedian – that made me think it might be possible to give stand-up a try.

Agents

It's probably best to wait for an agent to come to you, but you can definitely hurry that along by emailing them and asking them to come and watch you gig, or by entering as many stand-up competitions as possible. There are no rules, though. There are some comics who have been gigging for ten years who don't have or need an agent. If you want to write and perform stuff for TV it can help, but then so can writing material and sending it to script editors and producers at Radio 4 or BBC 7.

It's also worthwhile thinking about what you have as a comic that is unique (remember your personality, which onstage may be a persona, can be just as important as your material, and make audiences buy into weird ideas or even average jokes). If you have long hair and write jokes like Bill Bailey, great, but that major breakthrough may be postponed until Bill Bailey retires. Unless you're a woman, in which case, brilliant; a career as 'the female Bill Bailey' is all set to go.

Also 'as a woman' though, you've got to get used to every reviewer or random person at a party saying, "So, is it hard/different/interesting being a female stand-up?" If you can learn a sarcasm-free answer to that, and the unisex one – "Where do you get your material from?" – and make it look spontaneous every time, you've probably mastered the hardest part. Welcome to the gang...

A-Z of festivals

This is by no means a comprehensive list of the many arts festivals that take place around Britain and Ireland, but focuses instead on fringe festivals where new productions are likely to be welcomed, as well as events that feature comedy and street theatre. Remember that some of the smaller festivals can come and go over time. It's best to contact organisers a good six months before the actual festival if you're hoping to be involved.

Aberdeen International Youth Festival
Custom House
35 Regent Quay
Aberdeen AB11 5BE
{t} 01224 213800
info@aiyf.org
www.aiyf.org
Month: August
Youth orchestras, choirs, music groups, dance and theatre groups can apply to take part in the festival by sending an application form and a recording of a recent performance. Groups must be of amateur status and made up of young people not over the age of 25 years.

ArtsFest (Birmingham)
{t} 0121 464 5678
mail@artsfest.org.uk
www.artsfest.org.uk
Month: September
The UK's largest free arts festival features strong elements of street theatre and comedy, and potential participants with these skills are invited to make contact via forms available at the website.

Arundel Festival Fringe
www.arundelfestival.org.uk
Month: August-September
Established fringe festival alongside the official Arundel Festival (***www.arundelfestival.co.uk***). Contact via the form at the website.

Ashbourne Festival
PO Box 5552
Ashbourne
Derbyshire DE6 2ZR
{t} 01335 348707
info@ashbournearts.com
www.ashbournearts.com
Month: June-July
2007 saw the festival's first comedy night, so there could be opportunities in that area in the future,

Bath Fringe Festival
admin@bathfringe.co.uk
www.bathfringe.co.uk
Month: May-June
Provides a banner for fringe events alongside the main Bath festivals, and arranges some of the bookings.

Belfast Festival at Queen's
25 College Gardens
Belfast BT9 6BS
{t} 028 9027 2600
g.farrow@qub.ac.uk
www.belfastfestival.com
Month: October-November
Ireland's largest international arts festival, with many theatre and comedy acts. Fringe events have been run in the past.

Bewdley Festival
Snuff Mill Warehouse
Park Lane
Bewdley
Worcestershire DY12 2EL
{t} 01299 404808
admin@bewdleyfestival.org.uk
www.bewdleyfestival.org.uk
*Month:*October
Festival featuring drama, comedy, music and visual arts, with a range of fringe events.

Brighton Festival Fringe
12a Pavilion Gardens
Castle Square
Brighton BN1 1EE
{t} 01273 260804
info@brightonfestivalfringe.org.uk
www.brightonfestivalfringe.org.uk
Month: May
It could be a performance, a show, an exhibition, an event, a gig or an open house – more than 500 events took place in 2006. Full guide for participants at the website.

Brouhaha International Street Festival (Merseyside)
The Alima Centre
35 Sefton Street
Liverpool L8 5SL
{t} 0151 709 3334
info@brouhaha.uk.com
www.brouhaha.uk.com
Date: August
Carnival arts organisation involved in events around the country and focused on its own carnival in Liverpool.

Bury Fringe Festival
12 Green Lane
Great Barton
Bury St Edmunds IP31 2QZ
secretary@buryfringe.com
www.buryfringe.com
Date: April
See www.buryfringe.com/fringeforum for information for performers.

Bury St. Edmunds Festival
Angel Hill
Bury St. Edmunds
Suffolk IP33 1XB
{t} 01284 757630
info@buryfestival.co.uk
www.buryfestival.co.uk
Month: May
Not a fringe festival per se, but includes a comedy strand. See also Bury Fringe Festival.

Buxton Festival Fringe
124 Brown Edge Rd
Buxton SK17 7AB
{t} 01298 71368
Info@buxtonfringe.org.uk
www.buxtonfringe.org.uk
*Month:*6 July 2007 - 22 July 2007
Provides an opportunity for artists to perform or exhibit in an environment that is low cost and an atmosphere that is receptive. Performers make their own arrangements with venues and pay an entry fee.

Cambridge Fringe Festival
TWFCC
Fourwentways
Little Abington
Cambridge CB1 6AP
{t} 01223 323 522 or 01223 837 891
info@camfringe.com
www.camfringe.com
Date: July-August
An open access festival, welcoming professionals, semi-professionals and amateurs alike.

Canterbury Festival
Christchurch Gate
The Precincts
Canterbury CT1 2EE
{t} 01227 452853
info@canterburyfestival.co.uk
www.canterburyfestival.co.uk
*Month:*October
International arts festival which also has a fringe.

Chelsea Festival
The Crypt
St Luke's Church
Sydney Street
London SW3 6NH
{t} 020 7349 8101
info@chelseafestival.org
www.chelseafestival.org
Month: July
Has a small programme of comedy events.

Dublin Fringe Festival
Sackville House
Sackville Place
Dublin 1
{t} +353 1 817 1677
graham@fringefest.com
www.fringefest.com
Month: September
A curated fringe festival where artists must apply with examples of previous work – full details at the website.

Dublin Theatre Festival
44 East Essex Street
Temple Bar
Dublin 2
{t} +353 1 677 8439
Email: info@dublintheatrefestival.com
www.dublintheatrefestival.com/
Month: September-October
The oldest English-speaking theatre festival in the world, reaching its 50th anniversary in 2007. Includes 'Theatre Olympics', a fringe-like range of extra events. See also Dublin Fringe Festival.

Ealing Comedy Festival
020 8825 6064
events@ealing.gov.uk
www.ealing.gov.uk/services/leisure/ealing_summer/
Month: July
Established London comedy festival, focusing on well-known names.

Edinburgh Festival Fringe
180 High Street
Edinburgh EH1 1QS
{t} 0131 226 0026
admin@edfringe.com
www.edfringe.com
Month: August
The Edinburgh Festival Fringe is officially the largest arts festival in the world. In 2006 hundreds of groups participated putting on 1,867 different shows with a total of 28,014 performances in 261 venues. Anyone can apply to perform.

Exeter Summer Festival
Civic Centre
Paris Street
Exeter EX1 1JJ
{t} 01392 265205
general.festivals@exeter.gov.uk
exeter.gov.uk/festival
Month: June
Mainly a music and dance festival, but with a good range of comedy events too.

Grassington Festival of Music and Arts
Riverbank House
Threshfield
Skipton BD23 5BS
{t} 01756 752691
arts@grassington-festival.org.uk
www.grassington-festival.org.uk
Month: June
Mainstream arts festival which includes street theatre elements.

Hay Fringe Festival
Ice House, Brook Street
Hay-on-Wye HR3 5BQ
info@hayfringe.co.uk
www.hayfringe.co.uk
Month: May-June
Poetry, theatre and street performance coinciding with the Hay Literature Festival.

Hebden Bridge Arts Festival
New Oxford House
Albert Street
Hebden Bridge HX7 8AH
{t} 01422 842684
hbfestival@gmail.com
www.hebdenbridge.co.uk/festival
Month: June
General arts festival also featuring street theatre and comedy.

Hotbed Festival (Cambridge)
The Junction
Clifton Way
Cambridge CB1 7GX
{t} 01223 249300
office@menagerie.uk.com
www.menagerie.uk.com
Month: July
This is the Cambridge New Writing Theatre Festival with the aim "to celebrate the energy and excitement that comes from commissioning, producing and witnessing new plays".

London International Festival of Theatre (LIFT)
19-20 Great Sutton Street
London EC1V ODR
0) 20 7490 3964
info@liftfest.org.uk
www.liftfest.org.uk
Month: June (2008)
International theatre festival which has been running every other year since 1981, as well as supporting artists throughout the year.

Llangollen Fringe Festival
01978 860600
contact@llangollenfringe.co.uk
www.llangollenfringe.co.uk
Month: July
"If you want to put some music on, run a workshop, get into busking, stage an art show, organise a lecture, lead a guided walk or anything else as part of the Fringe in 2007 e-mail us and we'll do our best to make it happen."

Manchester International Festival

131 Portland Street
Manchester M1 4PY
{t} 0161 238 7300
info@manchesterinternationalfestival.com
www.manchesterinternationalfestival.com
Month: June-July
This showcase for new music also features comedy and theatre performances.

National Student Drama Festival

19-20 Rheidol Mews
London N1 8NU
{t} 0207 354 8070
info@nsdf.org.uk
www.nsdf.org.uk
Month: March
Showcase for student drama. Submissions are invited from students of any subject, aged 16 or over, or if they are directing a show within two years of graduation.

Norwich Fringe Festival

01603 621935
info@norwichfringefestival.co.uk
www.norwichfringefestival.co.uk
Month: September-October
Started in 1998. Submission form available at the website.

Oxfringe

oxfringe@gmail.com
www.oxfringe.com
Month: March
New fringe organisation which began with literary and performance poetry alongside main Oxford Literature Festival, likely to expand to promoting theatre and comedy in 2008.

Pulse Fringe Festival (Ipswich)

01473 261142
ctaylor@wolseytheatre.co.uk
www.pulsefringe.com
Month: June
Showcasing comedy and drama in the East of England.

Reading Fringe Festival

enquiries@readingfringefestival.com
www.readingfringefestival.com
Started in 2005, the Reading Fringe is open to everyone.

Salisbury International Arts Festival

87 Crane Street
Salisbury SP1 2PU
{t} 01722 332241
info@salisburyfestival.co.uk
www.salisburyfestival.co.uk
Month: May-June
International arts festival with theatre and comedy elements.

Sedburgh Festival of Books & Drama

c/o Sedburgh Book Town Ltd
72 Main Street
Sedburgh LA10 5AD
{t} 015396 20125 / 20034
booktown@sedburgh.org.uk
www.sedburgh.org.uk
Month: August-September
New festival focused around books, with theatre elements.

Stockton Riverside Fringe Festival

www.fringefestival.co.uk/
Month: August
This free music festival now has a comedy tent.

Swansea Fringe Festival
c/o The Dylan Thomas Centre
Somerset Place
Swansea SA1 1RR
{t} 01792 474051
info@swanseafringe.com
www.swanseafringe.com
Month: September-October
"Anyone can perform, from the established to the emerging." Details at the website.

Wexford Fringe Festival
Wexford Chamber of Industry & Commerce
{t} 053 9122226
www.wexfordfringe.ie
Month: June
Coincides with the Wexford Opera Festival, and embraces comedy and street theatre.

Windsor Fringe
info@windsorfringe.co.uk
www.windsorfringe.co.uk
Month: September-October
Has been encouraging new talent in music, dance, comedy, drama and art since 1969.

Section 6
Living as an actor

The business of you

Naturally as an actor your focus is always going to be on your performances – that's why you're doing all this! But it's important to remember that you are also running a business. As with any self-employed person (unless you're lucky enough to have a full-time job with a theatre company you respect), whether a freelance writer, a plumber or a taxi driver, this means that there is background admin to be done, as well as the business of promoting yourself.

When you start out, acting may only take up a smallish proportion of your time, and you might have a 'day job' of some kind to tide you over – but income you make as an actor often (but not always – see below) counts as self-employment, and of course you will need to make time for applying for more acting work. In this chapter we'll provide a quick survey of some of the main issues which you should consider.

Self-employment
When you 'go it alone', it's not just a question of finding the work and banking the money: you still need to pay tax, for one thing. From a tax point of view, you may well be both employed and self-employed – it depends partly on how you are paid. In some cases you may find your tax is paid at source (PAYE) before you get the money, and historically the Inland Revenue has been keen to see 'entertainers' as a special case to be treated as employees – it means you can claim fewer expenses.

Now that self-assessment is well-established, however, it's quite likely that work where your tax isn't deducted at source will be regarded as self-employment. The most important thing to do is talk to HM Revenue & Customs – their telephone helpline staff are renownedly helpful and not at all like the intimidating 'taxman' of old. Call them on 08459 154515 to talk through the issues and register as self-employed if appropriate.

The HMRC website also has loads of advice on this subject: see ***www.hmrc.gov.uk/employment-status/*** for a starting point. In the section under 'special cases', you'll find that it says "entertainers who are not employed under a contract of service or in an office with emoluments chargeable to tax... as employment income are treated as employed earners provided their remuneration consists wholly or mainly of salary. If it does not, they retain their self-employed status."

If the Revenue sends you a self-assessment form (for declaring income in a particular tax year, ie 6 April in one calendar year to 5 April in the next), you may need then to fill out sections both for 'employment' and for 'self-employment'. These need to be submitted by the end of the January after the tax year in question (though that's changing to the earlier time of September in the next year or two).

Payment (for any tax not taken at source) is made in two halves in January and July 'on account' for the following tax year. As well as tax, you will need to pay National Insurance. Remember: there are fines for being late with payments. The Revenue is currently encouraging people to use its online submission service rather than the traditional paper format.

All this can get very confusing. There's a simple solution: go and see an accountant! Also, if you're a member of Equity, get hold of its 'Advice and Rights Guide' for reference.

Accountants

The most important thing is to keep records of your work and income, and the relevant dates. You don't have to become obsessed with double-entry bookkeeping (though it could help) – but keep a clear record of income and outgoings related to work. This means invoices, payslips, details of cheques, and receipts for anything work-related. In terms of the latter, promotional items such as photographs and showreels ought to be tax deductable as expenses – if you're self-employed. Don't take our word for it, however: get an accountant.

Accountants are experts at things like expenses and will almost always think of things that wouldn't occur to you however much you might have read up on the subject. You can find a list of accountants specialising in finances for actors at the end of this chapter.

As a general rule, using the services of an accountant will pay for itself: having your tax return prepared will probably cost in the region of £300, but they can usually save you that and more on tax deductable expenses. Many accountants will invite you for a free initial meeting to discuss your affairs, and you can take things from there. Take any correspondence from the Revenue with you, and details of income and outgoings.

Other finances

Given the precarious lifestyle you've chosen, it's wise to bone up on other financial issues. Do you want to take out a mortgage to buy a home, for example? It's perfectly possible, and these days lenders are much less prejudiced about the self-employed than they used to be. Nevertheless, they will want to see recent accounts, perhaps for the last three years, and several months' worth of bank statements. Make sure you have all this information well organised.

Even if you're only renting a property, letting agents are getting increasingly stern about checking up on this stuff. Often they expect a 'guarantor' (someone who will cover the payments if you default), such as a parent, even for tenants well into adult life. If you have someone suitable to cover you like this, make sure you speak to them beforehand!

Another dirty word to people in creative fields is 'pensions'. You might be young and care-free now, but how will you sustain yourself in old age (assuming you don't become the next Inspector Morse)? It's worth thinking about how to save now to avoid a crisis later on. For all of these issues, you're best off talking to an expert again. Check out ***www.unbiased.co.uk*** to track down an independent financial adviser (IFA) in your area.

Marketing yourself

Section 3 of this book will give you a basic grounding in creating your main self-marketing kit: CV, photograph and show/voicereel. Registering with web-based services such as Spotlight is now a key part of your armoury, too. Some, such as Casting Call Pro, also offer premium services such as providing you with your own website – a great way to update people on your work and attract more.

There's more to it, though. Plumbers can often rely on word-of-mouth alone. Taxi drivers usually have their clients standing around waiting for them. Self-employment in the creative industries isn't usually that simple, largely because there's so much competition (and you're providing a service that people 'enjoy' rather than 'need').

This means being smart: always be on the lookout for opportunities to promote yourself. This doesn't mean being overconfident or excessively pushy – rather, get talking to people, make connections, show an interest, and give people reasons to want to talk to you again. If you're looking for work in the corporate field (see p120), consider getting business cards and a letterhead printed. Remember that people take you according to how you present yourself – try to talk to them in their 'language'.

Part of being professional is being organised, too. Make sure it's easy for people to get in touch with you – phone, email – and don't give them reasons to think less of you, such as a silly outgoing answerphone message. Keep track of your appointments and make sure you're always on time for them. Also, keep a record of people in the industry that you've met and their contact details, and maybe even a diary of performances you've seen – it all helps you to feel part of something, and you never know when a name in a file might be just the connection you need to help you get work.

Beating the blues

Everyone knows the clichés about actors working in fast-food outlets when they're 'between jobs'. Hopefully this book will have given you some solid guidance to get more rewarding work than that, but if not, never despair, and always come back fighting when you've been turned down for something.

Beyond applying for acting jobs, make sure you go and see other productions, too: seeing a really good performance or production can lift your spirits and remind you just why you're in this business! Also, it's important to take time out and enjoy yourself, however well or badly work is going.

Your general well-being is vital and will make you more resilient in the face of disappointment, not to mention more dynamic as a performer. Keep yourself fit and healthy: eat well, and get plenty of exercise. Doing classes such as pilates or yoga can help here, or join a gym, or simply go swimming, cycling or running regularly. All this will help you keep your body in tone, which will show in your work. We don't want to sound like your mother here, but these things really count. Time after time studies show it's things like this that keep people happy rather than making pots of cash – not that the latter wouldn't help now and then.

Acting is a unique job that brings happiness to thousands of audiences every year, and the more positive you are in the gaps between work, the more you'll be part of a 'feedback loop' that keeps you buoyant too, and at the peak of your performance.

A-Z of accountants

Bowker Orford

Based in: London
{t} 020 7636 6391
mail@bowkerorford.com
www.bowkerorford.com
We are founder members of the Institute of Chartered Accountants Entertainment and Media Group. We have been acting for clients in the music business for over 30 years and have extensive experience acting on behalf of performers, music publishers and all related areas. As a result we have a good knowledge of copyright, royalty accounting and tax issues. We have in excess of 500 actors as clients, including many household names, and we act for a number of theatrical production companies and theatrical agents.

Breckman & Company

Based in: London
{t} 020 7499 2292
grahamberry@breckmanandcompany.co.uk
www.breckmanandcompany.co.uk
Breckman & Company, chartered certified accountants, have specialised in the Arts and Entertainment Industry for over 40 years, for both individuals and companies. We are based in the West End of London, near the heart of Theatreland.

Centre Stage (London)

Based in: London
{t} 0845 603 5401
accounts@centrestage-accountants.com
www.centrestage-accountants.com
Centre Stage is a firm of Chartered Accountants specialising in the Entertainment Industry. Our experience over many years has led us to believe that there is a need for the kind of specialism we can offer due to the many unusual aspects of the entertainment industry. For example, many actors hold down other jobs, many temporary, often during or between acting jobs, but are treated as self-employed.

Centre Stage (Manchester)

Based in: Manchester
{t} 0161 655 2000
accounts@centrestage-accountants.com
www.centrestage-accountants.com
See above.

David Evans Chartered Accountants

Based in: North West
{t} 01200 428460
david@evansaccountants.com
www.evansaccountants.com
David Evans Chartered Accountants has acted for individuals and businesses involved in creative work, as well as charities involved in community arts, for over 10 years. We have a wealth of experience and expertise.

Goldwins

Based in: London
{t} 020 7372 6494
info@goldwins.co.uk
www.goldwins.co.uk
For many years, we have been successfully offering specialist accounting, taxation and financial services to people in the entertainment professions right across the UK.

Indigo

Based in: Sussex
{t} 01403 892683
info@indigotax.com
www.indigotax.com
At Indigo we have clients from a wide spectrum of industries. However, we pride ourselves on our knowledge of accountancy in the music or entertainment industry and many of our clients are musicians, performers, producers, writers or are otherwise involved in multimedia business.

Mark Carr & Co (Hove)

Based in: Hove
{t} 01273 778802
info@markcarr.co.uk
www.markcarr.co.uk
Our principal expertise is supplying accounting and taxation services to the entertainment industry. We act for actors, dancers, writers and agents among other professions within the industry.

Mark Carr & Co (London)

Based in: London
{t} 020 7717 8474
info@markcarr.co.uk
www.markcarr.co.uk
See above.

Martin Greene

Based in: London
{t} 020 8360 9126
info@martingreene.co.uk
www.martingreene.co.uk
As with all aspects of the entertainment industry, we work closely with lawyers on all contractual, tax planning and commercial matters. These include intellectual property exploitation and protection, recording and licensing contracts.

MGI Midgley Snelling

Based in: London & Weybridge
{t} 020 7836 9671
email@midsnell.co.uk
www.midsnell.co.uk
Since our formation, we have built a strong tradition of delivering specialist services to clients associated with the entertainment industry and have a thorough knowledge and understanding of this unique industry.

Saffery Champness

Based in: London
{t} 020 7841 4000
info@saffery.com
www.saffery.com
Our specialist media and entertainment team act as enthusiastic and trusted advisers to the creative industries sector, to both businesses and individuals operating within it. The group possesses particular experience in the fields of advertising, marketing and PR, film and broadcasting, music, publishing, sport, theatres, and talent agencies.

Sloane & Co

Based in: London
{t} 020 7221 3292
mail@sloaneandco.com
www.sloaneandco.com
Sloane & Co., founded in 1974 by David Sloane, is a firm of Accountants offering a wide range of financial services of particular concern to organisations and individuals working in the entertainment field.

Spencer Davis and Co
Based in: London
{t} 020 8863 0009
info@accountancyformusicians.co.uk
www.accountancyformusicians.co.uk
Spencer Davis and Co is an accountant based in Harrow, London. We provide a full and comprehensive range of accountancy services for performing artists including musicians, actors, jugglers and fire eaters.

Taylorcocks (Bournemouth)
Based in: Bournemouth
{t} 0870 770 8111
bournemouthenquiries@theaccountants.co.uk
www.theaccountants.co.uk
For many years we have provided specialist accounting, taxation, business and financial advice to the leisure and entertainment industry. Our knowledge and experience mean that we understand the special requirements of the sector.

Taylorcocks (Farnham)
Based in: Farnham
{t} 0870 770 8111
farnhamenquiries@theaccountants.co.uk
www.theaccountants.co.uk

Taylorcocks (Portsmouth)
Based in: Portsmouth
{t} 0870 770 8111
portsmouthenquiries@theaccountants.co.uk
www.theaccountants.co.uk

Taylorcocks (Portsmouth)
Based in: Oxford
{t} 0870 770 8111
oxfordenquiries@theaccountants.co.uk
www.theaccountants.co.uk

Taylorcocks (Reading)
Based in: Reading
{t} 0870 770 8111
readingenquiries@theaccountants.co.uk
www.theaccountants.co.uk

Section 7
Organisations & resources

Equity

Equity, formed in 1930, is the trade union for actors and the entertainment profession. Its 35,000+ members include actors, singers, dancers, choreographers, stage managers, theatre directors and designers, variety and circus artists, television and radio presenters, walk-on and supporting artists, stunt performers and directors and theatre fight directors. Equity works on behalf of actors, lobbying to secure minimum terms and conditions of employment. In addition to its ongoing campaigning for better pay and conditions, Equity offers a casting service, advice and insurance.

To qualify for membership you must have undertaken professional acting work. Subscription fees are 1% of your gross earnings (with a minimum of £125 and a maximum subscription of £2025) plus a one-off £25 joining fee. If you're on a full-time accredited drama course you're eligible for student membership (£15 per year). Outlined below are some of the main benefits of joining Equity (taken from the Equity website).

Pay & conditions
Equity negotiates minimum terms and conditions with employers across all areas of the entertainment industry. Copies of contracts and agreements are available from Equity offices for a small charge.

Help & advice
Equity can help you throughout your career, offering a range of services as well as advice. Its staff have detailed, specialist knowledge and are happy to give advice to members and their agents on contracts and terms of engagement.

Equity card
The universally recognised symbol of your status as a professional in the entertainment industry.

Legal and welfare advice
Free legal advice on disputes over professional engagements including personal injury claims. Free advice on National Insurance, taxation, benefits, pensions and welfare issues.

Publications
A quarterly magazine is sent free of charge to all members, keeping you in touch with Equity initiatives and activities. Equity also produces a wide range of information leaflets which are always available to members.

Medical support
All members can use the British Performing Arts Medicine Trust Helpline to access advice and information on performance-related medical, psychological and dental problems.

Royalties & residuals
Equity distributes royalties, residuals and other payments to members for TV and film re-runs, video sales and sound recordings.

Registers
Equity compiles a large number of specialist registers which are made available to casting directors and employers.

Job information
Equity members can access a service giving them information on job availability across the industry.

Campaigns
Equity campaigns vigorously on behalf of its members on a wide range of national, local and specialist issues and has a strong track record of success.

Your professional name
Equity reserves your choice of professional name when you join, as long as it is not already in use by another member.

Insurance

Public liability of up to £5 million, backstage cover and accident cover are available free to all members as long as they are in benefit. Call First Act Insurance on 020 8686 5050 for more information.

Rights, copyright & new media

Equity monitors national and international developments in intellectual property rights, campaigning for adequate recognition of performers' statutory rights.

Charities

Equity runs two charities, the Equity Benevolent Fund and the Evelyn Norris Trust, which exist to help members in times of trouble. Call 020 7379 6000 for more information. Equity also supports other organisations which provide help specifically for performers.

Pensions

The Equity Pension was set up in 1997 and if a member chooses to join, the BBC, ITV companies, PACT TV companies and West End theatre producers will pay into it when you have a main part with one of them. There is a similar scheme in place for opera singers and dancers in the standing companies.

Discounts

Equity members are entitled to discounts on a range of services and goods including hotels, car breakdown recovery, ticket prices and others.

Equity

Guild House
Upper St Martins Lane
London WC2H 9EG
{t} 020 7379 6000
{f} 020 7379 7001
www.equity.org

Spotlight

Founded in 1927, Spotlight is the current industry standard for UK actors in terms of recognition and reputation. Spotlight produces both an annual book and a CD which lists more than 30,000 actors and is used by thousands of TV, film, theatre and radio professionals. Membership also entitles you to an advice resources staffed by Spotlight. Once registered you'll appear in *The Spotlight Book*, published annually, and have an online profile which you can login to with a pin number to keep your details up to date.

Casting professionals can search the online database by a range of characteristics (eg credits, physical attributes and skills). Spotlight is often the first port of call for casting directors and industry professionals whether looking to cast for a particular production or a more general browse and to keep abreast of who is out there, the old hands and the new kids on the block. It is strongly recommended that you join Spotlight – not to do so can be a false economy and entry will ensure that you are in the main 'shop window' for the UK acting profession.

The Spotlight Link is a system which allows industry professionals to post casting breakdowns to registered casting agents who can then submit their clients.

Contacts is a directory of industry resources and professionals published by Spotlight. Categories include agents, casting directors, photographers and theatres. It currently costs £11.50 (+ P&P).

How do I join Spotlight?

Preliminary application forms can be printed off online or requested by post. Once submitted, these are then vetted. If your application is successful your online entry should appear within 21 days and your profile included in the next available offline directory (*The Spotlight*

Book). You don't need to have an agent but "Spotlight only accepts entries from artists who have recognised training and/or professional acting experience".

How much does it cost

Costs vary depending on when you join. Below are the current (2007) prices (inclusive of VAT).

January - March:	£182
April - June:	£172
July - August:	£152

The Spotlight
7 Leicester Place
London WC2H 7RJ
{t} 020 7437 7631
info@spotlight.com
www.spotlightcd.com

Casting Call Pro

Established in 2004 and now with 20,000+ professional actors and 10,000+ casting professionals, Casting Call Pro has quickly become one of the largest networking resources for the UK acting industry. Actors can create a comprehensive online profile which displays credits, physical characteristics and skills, photos and, where applicable, links to their Imdb entry and Spotlight page. Once listed in the directory, actors can be searched and contacted by casting directors. Using cutting edge software, Casting Call Pro employs sophisticated searching and matching technology to provide casting professionals with actors who fit their requirements.

The site also has a section for casting alerts where agents can place character breakdowns. The team at Casting Call Pro then alert actors who fit the bill via email to the new casting. Actors can then apply via the site, sending a covering letter direct to the casting director and an automated link to their online Casting Call Pro profile. A tracking system allows them to see when their application has been viewed. This also logs all views from casting professionals searching the directory, giving real time reporting to the actors.

Membership includes entry into the actors' database, searchable by industry professionals, and access to resources and directories including photographers, theatres, drama schools, peer networking tools, substantial discounts on key services (eg headshot sessions for £50+VAT), and a host of online resources for the actor.

Minimum requirements for registration

(Members must meet at least one of these criteria)

- Equity membership
- training at an accredited drama school
- three professional credits.

Subscription fees

Standard membership gives actors a listing in the directory and is free. The optional premium package allows members to access paid casting alerts, upload up to 20 photographs, showreel and voicereel clips, create a castingcallpro email address (eg mattbarnes@castingcallpro.com) and their own URL (web address). Premium subscription is currently £15+VAT per month or £100+VAT for a year.

Casting Call Pro
138 Upper Street
London N1 1QP
{t} 020 7288 2233
info@castingcallpro.com
www.castingcallpro.com

A-Z of useful organisations

Actors' Benevolent Fund
6 Adam Street
London WC2N 6AD
{t} 020 7836 6378
{f} 020 7836 8978
office@abf.org.uk
www2.actorsbenevolentfund.co.uk
The role of the Actors' Benevolent Fund is to care for actors and theatrical stage managers unable to work because of poor health, an accident or frail old age. The fund has been in place for over 120 years.

Actors' Charitable Trust
Africa House
64 Kingsway
London WC2B 6BD
{t} 020 7242 0111
robert@tactactors.org
www.tactactors.org
TACT helps the children of actors under the age of 21 with grants, advice and support.

Agents' Association
54 Keyes House
Dolphin Square
London SW1V 3NA
{t} 020 7834 0515
{f} 020 7821 0261
association@agents-uk.com
www.agents-uk.com
The largest professional trade organisation of its kind in the world. Our member agents represent and book all kinds of performers, celebrities and musicians within all areas of the light entertainment industry.

Artsline
54 Chalton Street
London NW1Ê1HS
{t} 020 7388 2227
{f} 020 7383 2653
admin@artsline.org.uk
www.artsline.org.uk
Artsline is a disabled led charity established twenty-five years ago to promote access for disabled people to arts and entertainment venues promoting the clear message that access equals inclusion.

BECTU
373-377 Clapham Road
London SW9 9BT
{t} 020 7346 0900
{f} 020 7346 0901
info@bectu.org.uk
www.bectu.org.uk
BECTU is the independent union for those working in broadcasting, film, theatre, entertainment, leisure, interactive media and allied areas. The union represents permanently employed, contract and freelance workers who are primarily based in the United Kingdom.

British Academy of Dramatic Combat
3 Castle View
Helmsley
North Yorks YO62 5AU
workshopcoordinator@badc.co.uk
www.badc.co.uk
The BADC is the longest established stage combat teaching organization in the United Kingdom. The BADC also enjoys international recognition as a provider of excellence in teaching quality, curriculum design and assessment rigour. The BADC is dedicated to the advance of the art of stage combat in all forms of performance media.

British Arts Festival Association
2nd Floor
2B Charing Cross Road
London WC2H 0DB
{t} 020 7240 4532
info@artsfestivals.co.uk
www.artsfestivals.co.uk
BAFA is a vibrant membership organisation covering the widest span of arts festivals in the UK. These include some of the large international cultural events such as the Edinburgh International Festival and Brighton Festival through to small dynamic festivals such as the Winchester Hat Fair and the Corsham Festival in Wiltshire.

British Council
10 Spring Gardens
London SW1A 2BN
{t} 020 7930 8466
{f} 020 7389 6347
general.enquiries@britishcouncil.org
www.britishcouncil.org
The organisation was set up in 1934 to promote a wider knowledge of the United Kingdom abroad, to promote the knowledge of the English language, and to develop closer cultural relations between the United Kingdom and other countries.

Casting Directors Guild
{t} 020 8741 1951
www.thecdg.co.uk
The Guild is a professional organisation of casting directors in the film,television, theatre and commercials communities in the UK who have joined together to further their common interests in establishing a recognised standard of professionalism in the industry, enhancing the stature of the profession, providing a free exchange of information and ideas, honouring the achievements of members and standardisation of working practices within the industry.

British Film Institute (BFI)
Belvedere Road
South Bank
London SE1 8XT
{t} 020 7255 1444
library@bfi.org.uk
www.bfi.org.uk
The BFI promotes understanding and appreciation of Britain's rich film and television heritage and culture.

Conference of Drama Schools (CDS)
The Executive Secretary
P O Box 34252
London NW5 1XJ
{t} 020 7722 8183
{f} 020 7722 4132
info@cds.drama.ac.uk
www.drama.ac.uk

The Conference of Drama Schools comprises Britain's 22 leading drama schools. CDS exists in order to strengthen the voice of the member schools, to set and maintain the highest standards of training within the vocational drama sector, and to make it easier for prospective students to understand the range of courses on offer and the application process. Founded in 1969, the 22 member schools offer courses in acting, musical theatre, directing and technical theatre training.

Conservatoire for Dance and Drama (CDD)

1-7 Woburn Walk
London WC1H 0JJ
{t} 020 7387 5101
{f} 020 7387 5103
info@cdd.ac.uk
www.cdd.ac.uk

The Conservatoire for Dance and Drama (CDD) is a new higher education institution, founded in 2001. It was established to protect and promote some of the best schools offering vocational training in dance, drama and circus arts. The CDD offers courses in acting, stage management, classical ballet, theatre directing, contemporary dance, lighting, costume and scenic design. Entry to the schools is very competitive but they seek students who have the talent, skill and determination to succeed regardless of their background.

Council for Dance Education and Training (CDET)

Old Brewer's Yard
17-19 Neal Street
London WC2H 9UY
{t} 020 7240 5703
{f} 020 7240 2547
info@cdet.org.uk
www.cdet.org.uk

Founded in 1979, the Council for Dance Education and Training is the national standards body of the professional dance industry. It accredits programmes of training in vocational dance schools and holds the Register of Dance Awarding Bodies – the directory of teaching societies whose syllabuses have been inspected and approved by the Council. It is the body of advocacy of the dance education and training communities and offers a free and comprehensive information service, Answers for Dancers, on all aspects of vocational dance provision to students, parents, teachers dance artists and employers.

Drama Association of Wales

The Old Library
Splott
Cardiff CF24 2ET
{t} 029 2045 2200
{f} 029 2045 2277
aled.daw@virgin.net
www.amdram.co.uk/daw

Founded in 1934 and a registered charity since 1973, the Association offers a wide and varied range of services to Community Drama. Among others, members include amateur and professional theatre practitioners, educationalists and playwrights.

Foundation for Community Dance
LCB Depot
31 Rutland Street
Leicester LE1 1RE
{t} 0116 253 3453
{f} 0116 261 6801
info@communitydance.org.uk
www.communitydance.org.uk
The Foundation for Community Dance is a UK-wide charity, established in 1986, to support the development of community dance, providing information, advice and guidance for dance artists, organisations, students and communities about community dance and the issues they face.

Fringe Theatre Network
Imex Business Centre
Ingate Place
London SW8 3NS
{t} 020 7627 4920
helenoldredlion@yahoo.co.uk
www.fringetheatre.org.uk
Fringe Theatre Network (FTN) was founded in 1986 as Pub Theatre Network when fringe venues felt the need for an organisation to support them, keep them in touch with each other and present their case on their behalf. FTN was registered as a charity in 1987 and exists to support and promote fringe theatre in London by providing services, support and a network of contacts for venues, producing companies and individuals working on the fringe and thereby to increase the viability and professionalism of fringe theatre, and by representing fringe theatre as an umbrella organisation which can act and speak on behalf of fringe theatre to statutory authorities, funding bodies, policy makers and other arts organisations.

Independent Theatre Council (ITC)
12 The Leathermarket
Weston Street
London SE1 3ER
{t} 020 7403 1727
{f} 020 7403 1745
admin@itc-arts.org
www.itc-arts.org
The ITC is the UK's leading management association for the performing arts, representing around 700 organisations across the country. The ITC works closely with Equity on agreements, contracts and rights for performers.

National Association of Youth Theatres
Darlington Arts Centre
Vane Terrace
Darlington DL3 7AX
{t} 01325 363330
{f} 01325 363313
naytuk@btconnect.com
www.nayt.org.uk
NAYT (National Association of Youth Theatres) supports the development of youth theatre activity through training, advocacy, participation programmes and information services.

National Council for Drama Training (NCDT)
1-7 Woburn Walk
Bloomsbury
London WC1H 0JJ
{t} 020 7387 3650
{f} 020 7387 3860
info@ncdt.co.uk
www.ncdt.co.uk
The National Council for Drama Training is a partnership of employers in theatre,

broadcast and media industries, employee representatives and training providers. The aim of the COUNCIL is to act as a champion for the drama industry, working to optimise support for professional drama training and education, embracing change and development.

National Operatic and Dramatic Association (NODA)
58-60 Lincoln Road
Peterborough PE1 2RZ
{t} 0870 770 248
{f} 0870 770 2490
everyone@noda.org.uk
www.noda.org.uk
The National Operatic and Dramatic Association (NODA), founded in 1899, is the main representative body for amateur theatre in the UK. It has a membership of some 2500 amateur/community theatre groups and 3000 individual enthusiasts throughout the UK, staging musicals, operas, plays, concerts and pantomimes in a wide variety of performing venues, ranging from the country's leading professional theatres to village halls.

National Youth Theatre
443-445 Holloway Road
London N7 6LW
{t} 020 7281 3863
{f} 020 7281 8246
info@nyt.org.uk
www.nyt.org.uk
The National Youth Theatre was established in 1956 to offer young people the chance to develop their creative and social skills through the medium of the theatrical arts which includes acting and technical disciplines. The National Youth Theatre is now an internationally acclaimed organisation, providing opportunities to all young people aged 13-21 in the UK, regardless of background.

Performing Rights Society
Copyright House
29-33 Berners St
London W1T 3AB
www.mcps-prs-alliance.co.uk

Personal Managers Association (PMA)
1 Summer Road
East Molesey
Surrey KT8 9LX
{t} 020 8398 9796
www.thepma.com
The PMA is the professional association of agents representing UK based actors, writers, producers, directors, designers and technicians in the film, television and theatre industries. Established in 1950 as the Personal Managers' Association, the PMA has over 130 member agencies representing more than 1,000 agents.

Northern Actors Centre
21-31 Oldham Street
Manchester M1 1JG
{t} 0161 819 2513
{f} 0161 819 2513
info@northernactorscentre.co.uk
www.northernactorscentre.co.uk
The NAC provides workshops for actors and other professionals in theatre, television, film and radio to enable them to continuously maintain and develop their craft once their initial training has been completed. Areas covered include physical, vocal, studio techniques, characterisation, approaches to specific styles, genres and authors, career management.

Skillset
Prospect House
80-110 New Oxford Street
London WC1A 1HB
{t} 020 7520 5757
info@skillset.org
www.skillset.org
Skillset is the Sector Skills Council for the audiovisual industries (broadcast, film, video, interactive media and photo imaging). They conduct consultation work with industry, publish research and strategic documents, run funding schemes and project work, and provide information about the challenges that face the industry. They also provide impartial media careers advice for aspiring new entrants and established industry professionals, online, face to face and over the phone.

Society of Teachers of Speech & Drama
73 Berry Hill Road
Mansfield
Nottinghamshire NG18 4RU
{t} 01623 627636
stsd@stsd.org.uk
www.stsd.org.uk
The STSD was established soon after the Second World War from the amalgamation of two much earlier Associations formed to protect the professional interests of qualified, specialist teachers of speech and drama, to encourage good standards of teaching and to promote the study and knowledge of speech and dramatic art in every form.

Theatrical Management Association
32 Rose Street
London WC2E 9ET
{t} 020 7557 6700
{f} 020 7557 6799
enquiries@solttma.co.uk
www.tmauk.org
TMA is the pre-eminent UK wide organisation dedicated to providing professional support for the performing arts. Members include repertory and producing theatres, arts centres and touring venues, major national companies and independent producers, opera and dance companies and associated businesses. The association undertakes advocacy on behalf of members to authorities to promote the value of investment in the performing arts. The association also facilitates facilitating concerted action to promote theatre-going to the widest possible audience.

Section 8

Theatrical venues

A

Abbey Theatre & Arts Centre
Pool Bank Street
Nuneaton
Warwickshire CV11 5DB
{t} 024 76 327359
boxoffice@abbeytheatre.co.uk
www.abbeytheatre.co.uk

Abbey Theatre, The
Westminster Lodge
Holywell Hill
St. Albans AL1 2DL
{f} 01727 812742
manager_@_abbeytheatre.org.uk
www.abbeytheatre2.org.uk
Capacity: 230
Founded: 1967

ABC Glasgow
300 Sauchiehall Street
Glasgow G2 3JA
{t} 0141 332 2232
boxoffice@abcglasgow.com
www.abcglasgow.com
Capacity: 1250

Aberdeen Arts Centre
33 King Street
Aberdeen AB24 5AA
{f} 01224 626390
enquiries@aberdeenartscentre.org.uk
www.digifresh.co.uk
Capacity: 350

Aberdeen Music Hall
Union Street
Aberdeen AB10 1QS
{t} 01224 641122
tickets@aberdeenperformingarts.com
www.musichallaberdeen.com
Founded: 1822

Aberystwyth Arts Centre
Penglais
Aberystwyth SY23 3DE
{t} 01970 622882
aeh@aber.ac.uk
www.aberystwythartscentre.co.uk
Capacity: 312
Founded: 1973

Abraham Moss Centre
Crescent Road
Manchester M8 5UF
{f} 0161 908 8315
g.davis@manchester.gov.uk

Academy Theatre
Take2 Centre
Birdwell, Barnsley
South Yorkshire S70 5TU
{t} 01226 744442
enquiries@theacademytheatre.co.uk
www.theacademytheatre.co.uk

Academy Theatre
7 Market Place
Shepton Mallet BA4 5DQ
info@academytheatre.co.uk
www.academytheatre.co.uk
Capacity: 270
Founded: 1970

Acorn Theatre
Parade Street
Penzance TR18 4BU
{t} 01736 363545
admin@acorn-theatre.co.uk
www.acornartscentre.co.uk
Capacity: 150
Founded: 1987

Acoistic Music Centre
St Bride's Centre
10 Orwell Terrace
Edinburgh EH11 2DY
{f} 0131 557 1050
admin@edfringe.com
www.acousticmusiccentre.com

Actors Centre, The
1A Tower Street
London WC2H 9NP
{t} 020 7240 3940
info@acshowcase.co.uk
www.actorscentre.co.uk

ADC Theatre
Park Street
Cambridge CB5 8AS
{t} 01223 359547
boxoffice@adctheatre.com
www.adctheatre.com

Adelphi
The Strand
London WC2E 7NA
{t} 020 7344 0055
info@adelphitheatre.co.uk
www.adelphitheatre.co.uk
Capacity: 1500
Founded: 1930

Adelphi
1-3 Hunslet Road
Leeds LS10 1JS
{t} 01845 574183
Leedscityfringe@aol.com
www.theadelphi.co.uk
Capacity: 120
Founded: 1900

Alban Arena
Civic Centre
St Albans
Hertfordshire AL1 3LD
{f} 01727 865 755
alban.arena@leisureconnection.co.uk
www.leisureconnection.co.uk/centre/4/86/alban_arena.html

Albany
Douglas Way
Deptford
London SE8 4AG
{t} 020 8692 4446
admin@thealbany.org.uk
www.thealbany.org.uk
Capacity: 200
Founded: 1930

Albert Halls
Victoria Square
Bolton BL1 1RU
{t} 01204 334400
albert.halls@bolton.gov.uk
www.alberthalls-bolton.co.uk
Capacity: 676
Founded: 1985

Aldwych Theatre
Aldwych
London WC2B 4DF
{t} 020 7379 3367
www.aldwychtheatre.com
Founded: 1905

Alhambra Theatre and Studio
Morley Street
Bradford BD7 1AJ
{t} 01274 432000
alhambra-theatre@bradford.gov.uk
www.bradford-theatres.co.uk
Capacity: 1400
Founded: 1914

All Saints' Church
122 Oakleigh Road
London N20 9EZ
{t} 020 8445 8388
allsaints.net@boltblue.com
www.allsaints.uk.com/index.php?m=10&p=10

Alma Tavern Theatre
18-20 Alma Vale Road
Clifton
Bristol BS8 2HY
{t} 0117 973 5171
info@theatre-west.co.uk
www.theatre-west.co.uk/index.php?page=alma
Capacity: 50

Almeida
Almeida Street
London N1 1TA
{t} 020 7359 4404
info@almeida.co.uk
www.almeida.co.uk
Capacity: 325
Founded: 1837

Alnwick Playhouse
Bondgate Without
Alnwick NE66 1PQ
{t} 01665 510785
info@alnwickplayhouse.co.uk
www.alnwickplayhouse.co.uk
Capacity: 700
Founded: 1925

ALRA Theatre
R.V.P. Building
Trinity Road
Wandsworth SW18 3SX
{t} 020 8870 6475
{f} 020 8875 0789
enquiries@alra.co.uk
www.alra.co.uk
Capacity: 100
Founded: 1979

Alsager Arts Centre
MMU Cheshire, Hassall Road
Alsager
Stoke-on-Trent ST7 2HL
a.a.c@mmu.ac.uk
www.alsagerartscentre.org.uk/home

Altrincham Garrick Playhouse
Barrington Road
Altrincham WA14 1HZ
{t} 0161 928 1677
info@garricktheatre.fsnet.co.uk
www.garricktheatre.co.uk

Amadeus Centre, The
50 Shirland Road
Little Venice
London W9 2JA
{f} 020 72661225
info@amadeuscentre.co.uk
www.amadeuscentre.co.uk
Capacity: 55
Founded: 1989

Andrew Sketchley Theatre
189 Whitechapel Road
London E1 1DN
{t} 020 7377 8735
ask@the-academy.info
www.the-academy.info
Founded: 1985

Angel Theatre
Walnut Tree Avenue
Woodbridge
Suffolk IP12 2GG
{t} 01394 420272
tracy@angeltheatre.plus.com
Capacity: 351

Anvil
Churchill Way
Basingstoke RG21 7QR
{t} 01256 844244
box.office@theanvil.org.uk
www.theanvil.org.uk
Capacity: 1389
Founded: 1994

Apollo
Queen Caroline Street
London W6 9QH
{t} 0870 6063400
venuebookings@clearchannel.co.uk
www.london-apollo.co.uk
Capacity: 3632
Founded: 1932

Apollo
17 Wilton Road
London SW1V 1LG
{t} 0870 400 0650
venuebookings@clearchannel.co.uk
www.apollovictoria.co.uk
Capacity: 2208
Founded: 1930

Apollo Theatre
Apollo Theatre
Shaftesbury Avenue
London W1V 7DH
www.apollo-theatre.co.uk
Founded: 1932

Arc Theatre
College Road
Trowbridge BA14 0ES
{t} 01225 756376
{f} 01225 777148
theatre@arctheatre.org.uk
www.arctheatre.org.uk
Capacity: 220
Founded: 1998

Arcadian, The
Hurst St
Birmingham B5 4TD
{t} 0121 622 5348
duncan@glee.co.uk
www.glee.co.uk

Arches
253 Argyle Street
Glasgow G2 8DL
{t} 0141 221 4001
info@thearches.co.uk
www.thearches.co.uk
Capacity: 104
Founded: 1991

Archway Theatre
The Drive
Horley
Surrey RH6 7NQ
{t} 01293 784398
arch@archwaytheatre.co.uk
www.archwaytheatre.co.uk

Arcola Theatre
27 Arcola Street
London E8 2DJ
{t} 020 7503 1646
info@arcolatheatre.com
www.arcolatheatre.com
Founded: 2000

Arena Theatre
Wulfruna Street
Wolverhampton
West Midlands WV1 1SE
{t} 01902 322380
{f} 01902 322599
arena@wlv.ac.uk
www.arenatheatre.info
Capacity: 150
Founded: 1999

Armagh Theatre and Arts Centre
Market Street
Armagh City
Co. Armagh BT61 7AT
{t} 028 3752 1820
admin@themarketplacearmagh.com
www.marketplacearmagh.com

Arnolfini
16 Narrow Quay
Bristol BS1 4QA
{t} 0117 917 2300
boxoffice@arnolfini.org.uk
www.arnolfini.org.uk

Artrix
School Drive
Bromsgrove B60 1AX
{t} 01527 577330
artrixadmin@ne-worcs.ac.uk
www.artrix.co.uk

Arts Centre
Biddick Lane
District 7
Tyne & Wear NE38 8AB
{f} 0191 219 3466
Matthew.blyth@sunderland.gov.uk
www.artscentrewashington.com
Capacity: 110

Arts Depot
5 Nether Street
Tally Ho Corner
North Finchley N12 0GA
{t} 020 8369 5454
info@artsdepot.co.uk
www.artsdepot.co.uk
Capacity: 400
Founded: 2004

Arts Theatre
6-7 Great Newport Street
London WC2H 7JB
{t} 020 7836 2132
jorigg@artstheatre.com
www.artstheatrelondon.com
Capacity: 360
Founded: 1927

ArtsEd
14 Bath Road
Chiswick
London W4 1LY
{t} 020 8987 6666
{f} 020 8987 6699
shortcourses@artsed.co.uk
www.artsed.co.uk/facilities
Capacity: 150
Founded: 1990

Ashcroft Arts Centre
Osborn Road
Fareham
Hampshire PO16 7DX
{t} 01329 223100
ashcroft@hants.gov.uk
www.ashcroft.org.uk/programme/young.html
Capacity: 150

Assembly @ Assembly Hall
Mound Place Edinburgh
Edinburgh EH1 2LX
{t} 0131 623 3030
info@assemblyrooms.com
www.assemblyrooms.com

Assembly @ George Street
Assembly Rooms, 54 George Street
Edinburgh EH2 2LR
{t} 0131 623 3030
info@assemblyrooms.com
www.assemblyrooms.com

Assembly @ St George's West
58 Shandwick Place
Edinburgh EH2 4RT
{t} 0131 623 3030
info@assemblyrooms.com
www.assemblyrooms.com

Assembly @ The Queen's Hall
Clerk Street
Edinburgh EH8 9JG
{t} 0131 623 3030
info@thequeenshall.net
www.thequeenshall.net

Assembly Hall
Crescent Road
Tunbridge Wells TN1 2LU
{t} 01892 530613
boxoffice.aht@tunbridgewells.gov.uk
www.assemblyhalltheatre.co.uk

Assembly Hall
Union Place
Worthing
{t} 01903 206206
West Sussex BN11 1LG
theatres@worthing.gov.uk

Assembly Rooms and Guildhall Theatre
Assembly Rooms
Market Place
Derby DE1 3AH
{f} 01332 255446
boxoffice@derby.gov.uk
www.assemblyrooms-derby.co.uk

Astor Theatre Arts Centre
Stanhope Road
Deal CT14 6AB
admin@astortheatre.co.uk
www.astortheatre.co.uk

Atherstone Memorial Hall
Atherstone Leisure Complex
Long Street, Atherstone
North Warwickshire CV9 1AX
atherstoneleisurecomplex@northwarks.gov.uk
www.northwarks.gov.uk/site/scripts/documents_info.php?documentID=152&pageNumber=6
Capacity: 316

Attfield Theatre
The Guildhall
Bailey Head
Oswestry SY11 1PZ
{t} 01691 690222
info@attfieldtheatre.co.uk
www.attfieldtheatre.co.uk

Augustine's
41 George IV Bridge
Edinburgh EH1 1EL
{t} 08452 26 27 21
edvenue@paradise-green.co.uk
www.paradise-green.co.uk

Avalon Theatre
Cornwall College
Pool
Redruth TR15 3RD
{t} 01209 616381
www.avalontheatrecompany.co.uk

Avenue House Grounds
Avenue House
17 East End Road
Finchley N3 3QE
{t} 020 8455 4640
info@avenuehouse.org.uk
www.avenuehouse.org.uk
Capacity: 200
Founded: 2002

Avondale Theatre
72 Landor Road
London SW9 9PH
{t} 020 77333210
admin@italiaconti.com
www.italiaconti.com/facilities.html
Capacity: 152
Founded: 1911

Aylesbury Civic Centre
Market Square
Aylesbury HP20 1UF
{t} 01296 486 009
aabbott@aylesburyvaledc.gov.uk
www.aylesburycivic.org
Capacity: 650

B

Babbacombe
Babbacombe Downs
Torquay TQ1 3LU
{t} 01803 328 385
info@babbacombe-theatre.com
www.babbacombe-theatre.com
Capacity: 1494
Founded: 1939

Baby Belly
The Caves
Niddry St South, off Cowgate
Edinburgh EH1 1QR
{t} 020 7580 0150
info@smirnoffunderbelly.co.uk
www.smirnoffunderbelly.co.uk

Bacon Theatre
Dean Close School
Shelburne Road
Cheltenham GL51 6HE
{t} 01242 258002
admin@bacontheatre.demon.co.uk
www.bacontheatre.co.uk
Capacity: 566
Founded: 1991

Bangor Studio Theatre
38a Central Avenue
Bangor BT20 3AW
{t} 028 9145 4706
mail@bangordramaclub.co.uk
Founded: 76

Barbican
Silk Street
London EC2Y 8DS
{t} 020 7638 4141
tickets@barbican.org.uk
www.barbican.org.uk

Barlow Theatre
Oldbury Rep
Spring Walk
Langley B69 4SP
{t} 0845 358 2200
info@olburyrep.org
www.oldburyrep.org

Barn Theatre
Burnt Oak Lane
Sidcup DA15 9DF
{t} 020 8308 2616
boxoffice@bruford.ac.uk
www.bruford.ac.uk/what_venue.html
Capacity: 97

Barn Theatre
Handside Lane
Welwyn Garden City
Herts AL8 6ST
{t} 01438 840553
www.barntheatre.co.uk

Barn Theatre, The
70 High St
West Molesey

Surrey KT8 2LY
{t} 020 8941 1090
fcbrown@hotmail.com
www.thebarntheatre.co.uk
Capacity: 85
Founded: 1977

Barons Court
28a Comeragh Road
London W14 9RH
{t} 020 8932 4747
{f} 0171 603 8935
baronstheatre@hotmail.com
Capacity: 60
Founded: 1991

Barrett Marsden Gallery
17-18 Great Sutton Street
London EC1V 0DN
{t} 020 7336 6396
info@bmgallery.co.uk
www.bmgallery.co.uk

Barrington Centre
Ferndown Community Association
Penny's Walk, Ferndown
Dorset BH22 9TH
{f} 01202 870165
admin@fbarringtoncentre.co.uk
www.barringtoncentre.co.uk/home/index.asp

Basildon Park
Lower Basildon
Reading
Berkshire RG8 9NR
{t} 0870 428 8933
basildonpark@nationaltrust.org.uk
www.nationaltrust.org.uk/main/w-vh/w-visits/w-findaplace/w-basildonpark
Capacity: 700
Founded: 1978

Bateman's
Burwash
Etchingham
East Sussex TN19 7DS
{t} 0870 240 4068
{f} 01435 882811
batemans@nationaltrust.org.uk
www.nationaltrust.org.uk/main/w-vh/w-visits/w-findaplace/w-batemans.htm
Capacity: 500
Founded: 1940

Battersea Arts Centre
Lavender Hill
London SW11 5TN
{t} 020 7223 6557
{f} 020 7978 5207
boxoffice@bac.org.uk
www.bac.org.uk
Capacity: 300
Founded: 1893

Beau Sejour Leisure Centre
Amherst
St Peter Port
Guernsey GY1 2DL
{f} 01481 747298
cultureleisure@gov.gg
www.freedomzone.gg

Beck Theatre
Grange Road
Hayes
Middlesex UB3 2UE
{t} 0870 380 0017

Bedales Olivier Theatre
Bedales School
Steep, Petersfield
Hants GU32 2DG
{t} 01730 711510
j.barker@bedales.org.uk
www.bedales.org.uk/schoolSite/bedArts/BedArts_theatre.html
Founded: 1996

Bedford
77 Bedford Hill
Balham
London SW12 9HD
{t} 020 8682 8940
{f} 020 8682 8959
info@thebedford.co.uk
www.thebedford.co.uk

Bedford Corn Exchange
St Paul's Square
Bedford MK40 1SL
{f} 01234 269519
centralboxoffice@bedford.gov.uk
www.bedfordcornexchange.co.uk

Bedford School Theatre
De Pary's Avenue
Bedford MK40 2TU
{t} 01234 269519
theatreboxoffice@bedfordschool.org.uk
www.bedfordschool.org.uk/theatre
Capacity: 170278

Bedlam
11b Bristo Place
Edinburgh EH1 1EZ
{t} 0131 225 9893
hire@bedlamtheatre.co.uk
www.bedlamtheatre.co.uk
Capacity: 92
Founded: 1980

Bedworth Civic Hall
High Street
Bedworth CV12 8NF
{t} 01203 376707
peter.ireson@nuneaton-bedworthbc.gov.uk
www.civichallinbedworth.co.uk
Capacity: 400
Founded: 1975

Belgrade Theatre
Belgrade Square
Coventry CV1 1GS
{t} 024 7625 6431
admin@belgrade.co.uk
www.belgrade.co.uk
Capacity: 800
Founded: 1958

Belton House
Belton House
Grantham
Lincolnshire NG32 2LS
{t} 01909 511061
{f} 01476 579071
belton@nationaltrust.org.uk
www.nationaltrust.org.uk/main/w-vh/w-visits/w-findaplace/w-beltonhouse.htm
Capacity: 700
Founded: 1984

Benn Hall
Newbold Road
Rugby CV21 2LN
{f} 01788 533719
janeberry@dcleisure.co.uk
www.thebennhall.co.uk
Capacity: 700

Berwyn Centre
Ogwy Street
Nantymoel
Bridgend CF32 7SD

{f} 01656 841393
arts@bridgend.gov.uk
Capacity: 296

BFI IMAX Cinema
1 Charlie Chaplin Walk
South Bank, Waterloo
London SE1 8XR
www.bfi.org.uk/whatson/imax
Capacity: 477

BFI National Library
BFI
21 Stephen Street
London W1T 1LN
www.bfi.org.uk/filmtvinfo/library/visiting

BFI Southbank
Belvedere Road
South Bank, Waterloo
London SE1 8XT
www.bfi.org.uk/whatson/southbank

Bharatiya Vidya Bhavan
4a Castletown Road
London W14 9HE
{f} 020 7381 8758
events@bhavan.net
www.bhavan.net
Capacity: 295
Founded: 1972

Biggar Puppet Thatre
Broughton Road
Biggar
Lanarkshire Ml12 6HA
{f} 01899 220750
admin@purvespuppets.com
www.purvespuppets.com/biggar_puppet_theatre.html

Bingley Little Theatre
Main Street
Bingley BD16 2LZ
{t} 01274 431576
Administration@bradford-theatres.co.uk
www.bingleylt.co.uk
Capacity: 360

Birchvale Theatre
Southwick Road
Dalbeatti DG5 4AR
{t} 01556 610654
birchvale@dalbeattie.com
www.dalbeattie.com/birchvale

Birmingham Alexandra
Station Street
Birmingham B5 4DS
{t} 0121 643 1231
esther.blaine@clearchannel.co.uk
www.ticketmaster.co.uk/venue/189386

Birmingham Botanical Gardens
West Bourne Road
Birmingham B15 3TR
{t} 0121 4541860
admin@birminghambotanicalgardens.org.uk
www.birminghambotanicalgardens.org.uk
Capacity: 500
Founded: 1987

Birmingham Repertory
Centenary Square
Broad Street
Birmingham B1 2EP
{t} 0121 236 4455
info@birmingham-rep.co.uk
www.birmingham-rep.co.uk
Founded: 1971

Bishopsgate Institute and Foundation, The
230 Bishopsgate
London EC2M 4QH
{f} 020 7392 9250
events@bishopsgate.org.uk
www.bishopsgate.org.uk/events.asp?

Blackfriars Arts Centre
Spain Lane
Boston
Lincolnshire PE21 6HP
{t} 01205 363108
{f} 01205 358855
admin@blackfriars.uk.com
www.blackfriars.uk.com
Capacity: 230
Founded: 1966

Blackheath Halls
23 Lee Road
London SE3 9RQ
{t} 020 8463 0100
piershenderson@blackheathhalls.com
www.blackheathhalls.com

Blackie, The
Great Georges Community
Cultural Project
Great George Street
Liverpool L1 5EW
{f} 0151 709 4822
staff@theblackie.org.uk
www.theblackie.org.uk/blackieinfo.htm

Blackpool Grand
33 Church Street
Blackpool FY1 1HT
box@blackpoolgrand.co.uk
www.blackpoolgrand.co.uk
Capacity: 1894
Founded: 1100

Blackwood Miners' Institute
High Street
Blackwood
Gwent NP12 1BB
{f} 01495 226457

Blake Theatre
Almshouse Street
Monmouth NP25 3XP
{t} 01600 719401
{f} 01600 772701
boxoffice@theblaketheatre.org
www.theblaketheatre.org
Capacity: 500
Founded: 2001

Blenheim Palace
Woodstock
Oxfordshire OX20 1PX
{f} 01993 810570
Operations@blenheimpalace.com
www.blenheimpalace.com

Bloxwich Library Theatre
Elmore Row
Bloxwich
Walsall WS3 2HR
info@walsall.gov.uk
www.walsall.gov.uk/index/leisure_and_culture/walsalllive/walsall_live_venues.htm

Blue Elephant, The
59A Bethwin Road
Camberwell SE5 0XT
{t} 020 77010100
info@blueelephanttheatre.co.uk
www.blueelephanttheatre.co.uk
Capacity: 66
Founded: 1999

Bollington Arts Centre
Wellington Road
Bollington
Macclesfield SK10 5JR
www.bollingtonartscentre.org.uk

Bolton Little Theatre
Hanover Street
Bolton BL1 4TG
{t} 01202 513361
info@blt.org.uk
www.blt.org.uk
Capacity: 160

Bonaly Outdoor Centre
71 Bonaly Road
Edinburgh EH13 0PB
{t} 0131 441 1878
info@bonaly.org.uk
www.bonaly.org.uk/edin/main.htm

Bongo Club, The
37 Holyrood Road
Edinburgh EH8 8BA
{f} 0131 558 7604
info@thebongoclub.co.uk
www.thebongoclub.co.uk

Bonington Theatre
Arnold
Nottingham NG5 7EE
{f} 0115 9560731
www.bonington-theatre.co.uk

Borough Theatre
Town Hall
Cross Street
Abergavenny NP7 5HD
{t} 01873 850 805
boroughtheatre@monmouthshire.gov.uk
www.abergavenny.net/theatre
Capacity: 338
Founded: 1870

Bournemouth International Centre
Exeter Road
Bournemouth BH2 5BH
{t} 0870 111 3000
boxoffice.bic@bournemouth.gov.uk
www.bic.co.uk
Capacity: 4500
Founded: 1984

Bournemouth Little Theatre
11 Jameson Road
Winton
Bournemouth BH9 2QD
fghsh@tiscali.co.uk
www.bournemouthlittletheatre.co.uk

Bowhill House
Selkirk
Scotland TD7 5ET
{t} 01750 22204
bht@buccleuch.com
www.bowhilltheatre.co.uk

Boxmoor Playhouse
72 St John's Road
Hemel Hempstead HP1 1NP
{t} 0845 3301634
boxmoorplayhousewebmaster@ntlworld.com
www.boxmoorplayhouse.co.uk
Capacity: 150
Founded: 1990

Brentwood Theatre
15 Shenfield Road
Brentwood CM15 8AG
{t} 01277 230833
{f} 01277 230833
admin@brentwood-theatre.org
www.brentwood-theatre.org
Capacity: 100
Founded: 1993

Brewery Arts Centre
Highgate
Kendal LA9 4HE
{t} 01539 725133
admin@breweryarts.co.uk
www.breweryarts.co.uk
Capacity: 260
Founded: 1993

Brewhouse Theatre
Coal Orchard
Taunton TA1 1JL
{t} 01823 274608
{f} 01823 323116
boxoffice@thebrewhouse.net
www.thebrewhouse.net
Capacity: 352
Founded: 1977

Brick Lane Music Hall
443 North Woolwich Road
London E16 2DA
{t} 020 7511 6655
{f} 020 7476 6333
info@bricklanemusichall.co.uk
www.bricklanemusichall.co.uk
Capacity: 200
Founded: 1992

Bridewell Theatre
Bride Lane
Fleet Street
London EC4Y 8EQ
{t} 020 73533331
info@stbridefoundation.org
www.bridewelltheatre.org
Capacity: 150
Founded: 1994

Bridgewater Hall
Lower Mosley Street
Manchester M2 3WS
{t} 0161 907 9000
{f} 0161 950 0001
admin@bridgewater-hall.co.uk
www.bridgewater-hall.co.uk
Capacity: 2330
Founded: 1996

Bridgwater Arts Centre
11-13 Castle Street
Bridgwater
Somerset TA6 3DD
{f} 01278 447402
info@bridgwaterartscentre.co.uk
www.bridgwaterartscentre.co.uk
Founded: 1723

Bridport Arts Centre
South Street
Bridport
Dorset DT6 3NR
{t} 01308 424204
info@bridport-arts.com
www.bridport-arts.com
Capacity: 200

Brighton Centre
Kings Road
Brighton BN1 2GR
{t} 0870 9009100
b-centre@pavillion.co.uk
www.brightoncentre.co.uk
Capacity: 4127
Founded: 1977

Brighton Little Theatre
9 Clarence Gardens
Brighton BN1 2EG
{t} 01272 390004
chair@the-little.co.uk
www.the-little.co.uk

Brindley, The
High Street
Runcorn

Cheshire WA7 1BG
{t} 0151 907 8360
www.thebrindley.org.uk
Capacity: 420

Bristol Hippodrome
St Augustines Way
Bristol BS1 1TX
{t} 0870 607 7500
enquiries.bristol@livenation.co.uk
www.livenation.co.uk/venues/venue.aspx?vrid=143&&shortcut=bristol
Capacity: 2000
Founded: 1984

Bristol Old Vic
King Street
Bristol BS1 4ED
{t} 0117 987 7877
admin@bristol-old-vic.co.uk
www.bristol-old-vic.co.uk
Capacity: 645
Founded: 1766

Britannia Pier
Marine Parade
Great Yarmouth NR30 2EH
{t} 01493 842 914
theatre@britannia-pier.co.uk
www.britannia-pier.co.uk
Founded: 1858

Britten Theatre
Prince Consort Road
London SW7 2BS
{t} 020 7591 4335
info@rcm.ac.uk
www.rcm.ac.uk/content.asp?display=Events&wp=-68&pt=
Founded: 1986

Brixham Theatre
New Road
Brixham TQ5 8TA

Broadbent, The
Snarford Road
Wickenby
Lincolnshire LN3 5AW
{t} 01673 885500
box.office@broadbent.org
www.broadbent.org
Capacity: 100
Founded: 1971

Broadgate Arena
Exchange House
12 Exchange Square
London EC2A 2BQ
{t} 020 7505 4068
ljones@broadgateestates.co.uk
www.broadgateevents.co.uk

Broadway Studio
Catford Broadway
Catford
London SE6 4RU
{t} 020 8690 1000
info@broadwaytheatre.org.uk
www.broadwaytheatre.org.uk/whatson.php?location=Studio%20theatre
Capacity: 120
Founded: 1932

Broadway Theatre
Broadway
Barking IG11 7LS
{t} 020 8591 9662
admin@broadwaytheatre.co.uk
www.broadwaytheatre.co.uk
Capacity: 810
Founded: 1932

Broadway Theatre
46 Broadway
Peterborough PE1 1RT
{f} 01733 316123
admin@thebroadwaytheatre.co.uk

Brockley Jack Theatre
410 Brockley Road
London SE4 2DH
{t} 020 8291 6354
admin@brockleyjack.co.uk
www.brockleyjack.co.uk
Capacity: 51
Founded: 2003

Bromley Little Theatre
North Street,
Bromley
Kent BR1 1SD
{t} 020 8460 3047
mail@bromleylittletheatre.co.uk
www.bromleylittletheatre.co.uk
Capacity: 113
Founded: 1938

Brook Theatre
Old Town Hall
Chatham
Kent ME4 4SE
{t} 01634 338338
boxoffice@medway.gov.uk
www.medway.gov.uk/index/leisure/2130-2.html

Brunton Theatre
Ladywell Way
Musselburgh
Edinburgh EH21 6AA
{t} 0131 665 2240
info@bruntontheatre.co.uk
www.bruntontheatre.co.uk
Capacity: 296
Founded: 1971

Burton Taylor Studio
Gloucester Street
Oxford OX1 2BN
{t} 01865 305350
burtontaylor@oxfordplayhouse.com
www.oxfordplayhouse.com

Bush
Shepherds Bush Green
London W12 8QD
{t} 020 7602 3703
info@bushtheatre.co.uk
www.bushtheatre.co.uk
Capacity: 80
Founded: 1972

Buxton Opera House
Water Street
Buxton SK17 6XN
{t} 0845 12 72190
admin@boh.org.uk
www.buxtonoperahouse.org.uk
Capacity: 938
Founded: 1903

Byre
Abbey Street
St Andrews KY16 9LA
{t} 01334 475 000
enquiries@byretheatre.com
www.byretheatre.com
Capacity: 220
Founded: 1933

C

C
Chambers Street
Edinburgh EH1 1HR
{t} 0845 260 1222
boxoffice@cvenues.com
www.cthefestival.com

C central
Carlton Hotel, North Bridge
Edinburgh EH1 1SD
{t} 0845 260 1222
info@CtheFestival.com
www.cthefestival.com

C cubed
Brodie's Close
304 Lawnmarket
Edinburgh EH1 2PQ
{t} 0845 260 1222
boxoffice@cvenues.com
www.cthefestival.com

C too
Johnston Terrace
Edinburgh EH1 2PW
{t} 0845 260 1222
info@cvenues.com
www.cthefestival.com

Cabaret Voltaire
36 Blair Street
Edinburgh EH1 1QR
{t} 0131 220 6176
info@tonthefringe.com
www.thecabaretvoltaire.com/subindex.php

Cafe Royal Fringe Theatre
17 West Register Street
Edinburgh EH2 2AA
www.edinburgh-festivals.com/news.cfm?id=1249742006

Calton Theatre Cafe Bar
Calton Centre
121 Montgomery Street
Edinburgh EH7 5EP
{t} 0131 661 5252
admin@edfringe.com

Camberley Studio Theatre
Knoll Road
Camberley GU15 3SY
{t} 01276 707600
camberley.theatre@surreyheath.gov.uk
www.camberleytheatre.biz
Founded: 1966

Cambridge
Earlham Street
London WC2 9HU
{t} 020 7850 8710
info@rutheatres.com
www.rutheatres.com/venueinfo/cam.htm
Capacity: 1283
Founded: 1930

Cambridge Arts Theatre
6 St Edward's Passage
Cambridge CB2 3PJ
{t} 01223 503333
{f} 01223 579004
info@cambridgeartstheatre.com
www.cambridgeartstheatre.com
Capacity: 673
Founded: 1936

Cambridge Corn Exchange
Wheeler Street
Cambridge CB2 3QB
{t} 01553 764 864
{f} 01223 329074
ellenmcphillips@dial.pipex.com
www.cornex.co.uk
Capacity: 1462
Founded: 1868

Camden People's
58-60 Hampstead Rd
London NW1 2PY
{t} 020 7916 5878
{f} 020 7813 3889
admin@cptheatre.co.uk
www.cptheatre.co.uk
Capacity: 52
Founded: 1994

Campus West Theatre
The Campus
Welwyn Garden City
Hertfordshire AL8 6BX
{f} 01707 357155
campuswest@welhat.gov.uk
www.campuswest.co.uk/theatre

Canal Cafe Theatre
Delamere Terrace, Little Venice
Paddington
London W2 6ND
{t} 020 7289 6054
{f} 020 7266 1717
mail@canalcafetheatre.com
www.canalcafetheatre.com
Capacity: 60
Founded: 2003

Cannonball House
Castlehill, Royal Mile
Edinburgh EH1 1HR

Canolfan Beaumaris Centre
Rating Row
Beaumaris LL58 8AL
{f} 01248 811567
manager@beaumarislc.fsnet.co.uk

Capitol Horsham
North Street
Horsham RH12 1RG
{t} 01403 750 220
michael.gattrell@horsham.gov.uk
www.thecapitolhorsham.com
Capacity: 423
Founded: 1936

Capitol Theatre
Mable TyleCote building
Cavendish St M15 6BG
{t} 0161 247 1305
k.daly@mmu.ac.uk
www.theatre.mmu.ac.uk
Capacity: 200

Carling Academy Birmingham
52-54 Dale End
Birmingham B4 7LS
mail@birmingham-academy.co.uk
www.birmingham-academy.co.uk

Carling Academy Bristol
Frogmore Street
Bristol BS1 5NA
boxoffice@bristol-academy.co.uk
www.bristol-academy.co.uk

Carling Academy Brixton
211 Stockwell Road
London SW9 9SL
mail@brixton-academy.co.uk
www.brixton-academy.co.uk
Capacity: 4921
Founded: 1929

Carling Academy Newcastle
Westgate Road
Newcastle Upon Tyne NE1 1SW
boxoffice@newcastle-academy.co.uk
www.newcastle-academy.co.uk

Carnegie Hall
East Port
Dunfermline KY12 7JA
{t} 01383 314000

carnegiehall@fife.gov.uk
www.carnegiehall.co.uk
Capacity: 500
Founded: 1937

Carnegie Theatre
Finkle Street
Workington CA14 2BD
{t} 01900 602122

Carriageworks, The
3 Millennium Square
Leeds LS2 3AD
{t} 0113 224 3801
carriageworks@leeds.gov.uk
www.carriageworkstheatre.org.uk
Capacity: 300
Founded: 2005

Castle, The
Castle Way
Wellingborough NN8 1XA
{f} 01933 229 888
info@thecastle.org.uk
www.thecastle.org.uk
Capacity: 505
Founded: 1995

Caxton Theatre
128 Cleethorpes Road
Great Grimsby DN31 3HW
{t} 01472 345167
caxton.theatre@ntlworld.com
www.caxtontheatre.com

CBSO Centre
Berkley Street
Birmingham B1 2LF
jn@cbso.co.uk
www.cbso.co.uk/?page=about/cbsoCentre.html
Capacity: 300
Founded: 1998

Cecil Sharp House
Cecil Sharp House
2 Regents Park Road
London NW1 7AY
info@efdss.org
www.efdss.org
Capacity: 420
Founded: 1930

Centotre
103 George Street
Edinburgh EH2 3ES
{t} 0131 225 1550
info@centotre.com
www.centotre.com

Central Hall Westminster
Central Hall Westminster
Storey's Gate
London SW1H 9NH
www.c-h-w.com
Capacity: 2352
Founded: 19091912

Central Studio
Cliddesden Road
Basingstoke RG21 3HF
phil.pennington@qmc.ac.uk
www.centralstudio.co.uk

Central Theatre
170 High Street
Chatham ME4 4AS
{t} 01634 338338
theatres@medway.gov.uk
www.medway.gov.uk/index/leisure/theatres.htm
Capacity: 964
Founded: 1968

Centre Stage
14 Queens Road
Bournemouth BH2 6BE
{t} 01202 540065
Michael@Funnybone.co.uk
www.funnybone.co.uk/generic.php?area=Centre+Stage
Capacity: 150
Founded: 2000

Chads Theatre
Mellor Road
Cheadle Hulme SK8 5AU
info@chads.co.uk
www.chads.co.uk
Founded: 1921

Chapter Arts Centre
Market Road
Canton
Cardiff CF5 1QE
{t} 029 2030 4400
enquiry@chapter.org
www.chapter.org
Capacity: 200
Founded: 1971

Charles Cryer Studio
39 High Street
Carshalton SM5 3BB
{t} 020 8770 4950
e-mail@charlescryer.org.uk
www.suttontheatres.co.uk

Chats Palace
42-44 Brooksby's Walk
Hackney
London E9 6DF
{t} 020 8533 0227
chatspalace@hotmail.com
www.chatspalace.com
Capacity: 96
Founded: 1981

Chelmsford Civic and Cramphorn Theatres
Fairfield Rd
Chelmsford CM1 1JG
{t} 01245 606505
boxoffice@chelmsford.gov.uk
www.chelmsford.gov.uk/index.cfm?articleid=8564
Capacity: 505

Chelsea
World's End Place
King's Road
Chelsea SW10 0DR
{t} 0870 990 8454
admin@chelseatheatre.org.uk
www.chelseatheatre.org.uk
Capacity: 110
Founded: 1990

Chequer Mead Arts Centre
East Grinstead
West Sussex RH19 3BS
{t} 01342 325577
info@chequermead.org.uk
www.chequermead.org.uk
Capacity: 340
Founded: 1996

Chesil Theatre
Chesil Street
Winchester SO23 0HU
info@chesiltheatre.org.uk
www.chesiltheatre.org.uk

Chester Gateway Theatre
Hamilton Place
Chester CH1 2BH
{t} 01244 340392
boxoffice@chestergateway.co.uk
www.chestergateway.co.uk
Capacity: 460
Founded: 1968

Chichester Festival Theatre
Oaklands Park
Chichester PO19 6AP
{t} 01243 781312
box.office@cft.org.uk
www.cft.org.uk
Capacity: 1206
Founded: 1962

Chickenshed
Chase Side
London N14 4PE
{t} 020 8351 6161
info@chickenshed.org.uk
www.chickenshed.org.uk
Capacity: 300
Founded: 1994

Chipping Norton Theatre
2 Spring Street
Chipping Norton
Oxfordshire OX7 5NL
{f} 01608 642324
boxoffice@chippingnortontheatre.com
www.chippingnortontheatre.co.uk

Chisenhale Dance Space
64 - 84 Chisenhale Road
London E3 5QZ
{t} 020 8981 6617
{f} 020 8980 9323
mail@chisenhaledancespace.co.uk
www.chisenhaledancespace.co.uk
Capacity: 150
Founded: 1985

Chorley Amateur Dramatic and Operatic Society
Dole Lane
Chorley
Lancs PR7 2RL
secretary@chorleylittletheatre.com
Capacity: 238

Church Hill Theatre
Morningside Rd
Edinburgh EH10 4DR
{f} 0131 220 1996
admin@edfringe.com
www.edinburgh.gov.uk/CEC/Recreation/Leisure/Church_Hill_Theatre/Church_Hill_Theatre.html
Capacity: 360
Founded: 1892

Churchill Theatre
High Street
Bromley BR1 1HA
{t} 020 8460 6677
jennykeeling@theambassadors.com
www.churchilltheatre.co.uk
Capacity: 785
Founded: 1977

Circomedia – Portland Square
St Paul's Church
Portland Square
Bristol BS2 8SJ
{f} 0117 924 8303
william@circomedia.com
www.circomedia.com/index.cfm/section.Performances
Capacity: 200
Founded: 1797

Circus Space
Coronet Street
London N1 6HD
{t} 020 7613 4141
enquiries@thecircusspace.co.uk
www.thecircusspace.co.uk
Capacity: 350
Founded: 1994

Citizens
119 Gorbals Street
Glasgow G5 9DS
{t} 0141 429 0022
info@citz.co.uk
www.citz.co.uk
Capacity: 450
Founded: 1878

City Art Centre
2 Market Street
Edinburgh EH1 1DE
info@cac.org.uk
www.cac.org.uk

City Hall
Victoria Square, Paragon Street
Hull HU1 3NA
{t} 01482 610610
theatre.secretary@hullcc.gov.uk
www.hullcc.gov.uk/hullcityhall

City Hall Sailsbury
Malthouse Lane
Salisbury SP2 7TU
{t} 01722 434434
thecouncil@salisbury.gov.uk
www.cityhallsalisbury.co.uk
Capacity: 553
Founded: 1937

City Varieties Music Hall
Swan Street
Leeds LS1 6LW
www.cityvarieties.co.uk

Civic Theatre Oswaldtwistle
155-157 Union Rd
Oswaldtwistle BB5 3HZ
tourism@hyndburnbc.gov.uk
www.hyndburnentertainment.com/whatson_oct.html
Capacity: 472

Clerkenwell Theatre
Exmouth Market
Islington
London EC1R 4QE
{t} 020 7274 4888
sharikas80@hotmail.com
Capacity: 60
Founded: 2004

Cliffs Pavilion
Station Road
Southend On Sea SS0 7RA
{t} 01702 390472
chasm@cliffspavilion.demon.co.uk
www.thecliffspavilion.co.uk
Capacity: 1630
Founded: 1964

Clocktower
Katharine Street
Croydon CR9 1ET
{t} 020 8253 1027
boxoffice@croydononline.org.uk
www.croydon.gov.uk/clocktower

Club for Acts and Actors, The
20 Bedford Street
London WC2E 9HP
{t} 020 7836 3172
office@thecaa.org
www.thecaa.org
Capacity: 120
Founded: 1897

Club Theatre
17 Oxford Road
Altrincham
Cheshire WA14 2ED
info@clubtheatre.org.uk
www.clubtheatre.org.uk

Clwyd Theatr Cymru
Civic Centre
Mold CH7 1YA
{t} 01352 756 331
admin@clwyd-theatr-cymru.co.uk
www.clwyd-theatr-cymru.co.uk
Capacity: 580
Founded: 1976

Cochrane Theatre
Southampton Row
London WC1B 4AP
{t} 020 7269 1606
info@cochranetheatre.co.uk
www.cochranetheatre.co.uk
Capacity: 314
Founded: 1963

Cockpit Theatre, The
Gateforth Street
Off Church Street
London NW8 8EH
{t} 020 7258 2925 / 020 7258 2920
{f} 020 7258 2921
mail@cockpittheatre.org.uk
www.cockpittheatre.org.uk
Capacity: 240
Founded: 1970

Colchester Arts Centre
Church Street
Colchester CO1 1NF
{t} 01206 500900
info@colchesterartscentre.com
www.colchesterartscentre.com
Capacity: 400
Founded: 1980

Coliseum
St Martin's Lane
London WC2N 4ES
{t} 020 7632 8300
marketing@eno.org
www.eno.org
Capacity: 2364
Founded: 1904

Colne Little Theatre
River Street
Colne BB8 0DQ
{t} 01282 861424

Colour House Theatre
Merton Abbey Mills
London SW19 2RD
{t} 020 8542 5511
info@colourhousetheatre.co.uk
www.colourhousetheatre.co.uk
Founded: 1995

Colston Hall
Colston Street
Bristol BS1 5AR
boxoffice@colstonhall.org
www.colstonhall.org

Comedy Pub, The
7 Oxendon Street
LONDON SW1Y 4EE
{t} 07092 095401
mail@comedypub.com
Capacity: 150

Comedy Theatre
6 Panton Street
London SW1Y 4DN
www.thecomedytheatre.co.uk
Capacity: 125
Founded: 1884

Company of Players
Balfour Street
Hertford
Herts SG14 3AY
info@cops.org.uk
www.cops.org.uk

Compass Theatre & Arts Centre
Glebe Avenue
Ickenham
Middlesex UB10 8PD
{t} 01895 673200
compasstheatre@hillingdongrid.org
www.compasstheatre.co.uk
Capacity: 200
Founded: 2000

Compton Castle
Marldon
Paignton
Devon TQ3 1TA
admin@facsimiletheatre.co.uk

Concert Hall
Church Street
Brighton BN1 1UE
{t} 01273 709709
info@brighton-dome.org.uk
www.brighton-dome.org.uk
Capacity: 1872

Concert Hall Reading
The Town Hall
Blagrave Street
Reading RG1 1QH
{f} 0118 956 6719
www.readingarts.com
Capacity: 780
Founded: 1882

Congress Theatre
Carlisle Road
Eastbourne BN21 4BS
{t} 01323 412000
theatres@eastbourne.gov.uk
www.eastbournetheatres.co.uk
Capacity: 1689

Connaught Theatre
Union Place
Worthing BN11 1LG
{t} 01903 206206
theatres@worthing.co.uk
www.worthingtheatres.co.uk
Capacity: 512
Founded: 1935

Contact Theatre
Oxford Road
Manchester M15 6JA
{t} 0161 274 0600
bookings@contact-theatre.org
www.contact-theatre.org

Conway Hall
25 Red Lion Square
London WC1R 4RL
{t} 020 7242 8032
{f} 020 7242 8036
conwayhall@ethicalsoc.org.uk
www.conwayhall.org.uk
Capacity: 500
Founded: 1929

Corbett Theatre
Hatfields
Rectory Lane
Debden IG10 3RY
{t} 020 8508 5983
east15@essex.ac.uk
www.east15.ac.uk
Capacity: 120

Corn Exchange
Market Place
Newbury RG14 5BD
{f} 01635 582223
admin@cornexchangenew.co.uk
www.cornexchangenew.com/pages/venueinfo/find_us.htm
Capacity: 150

Cotswold Playhouse
Parliament Street
Gloucestershire GL5 1LW
{t} 0870 432 5405
patrick@cotswoldplayhouse.co.uk
www.cotswoldplayhouse.co.uk

Cottesloe Theatre
National Theatre
South Bank
London SE1 9PX
{t} 020 7452 3400
info@nationaltheatre.org.uk
www.nationaltheatre.org.uk
Capacity: 300
Founded: 1977

Cottier Theatre
93 Hyndland Street
Glasgow G11 5PX
{t} 0141 357 4000
info@thecottier.com
www.thecottier.com
Capacity: 450
Founded: 1865

Courtyard Theatre
Wellington Street
Covent Garden
London WC2E 7PA
{t} 020 7833 0876
info@thecourtyard.org.uk
www.thecourtyard.org.uk
Capacity: 81

Courtyard Theatre
Edgar Street
Hereford HR4 9JR
{t} 0870 1122330
info@courtyard.org.uk
www.courtyard.org.uk
Capacity: 400
Founded: 1998

Courtyard Theatre
10 York Way
London N1 9AA
{t} 020 78330876
{f} 020 78330876
info@thecourtyard.org.uk
www.thecourtyard.org.uk
Capacity: 70

Courtyard Theatre
Hazelwood Lane
Chipstead CR5 3QU
{t} 01737 555680
info.chipstead@btinternet.com
www.chipsteadplayers.com

Cow Barn Reid Concert Hall
Bristo Square
Edinburgh EH8 9AL
{t} 020 7580 0150
david@underbelly.co.uk
www.underbelly.co.uk

CragRats Theatre
Dunford Road
Huddersfield
Holmfirth HD9 2AR
{t} 01484 691323
theatre@cragrats.com
www.cragratstheatre.com
Capacity: 80

Craiglea Clocks
88 Comiston Road
Edinburgh EH10 5QJ
info@craigleaclocks.org.uk
www.craigleaclocks.org.uk

Cranleigh Arts Centre
1 High Street
Cranleigh GU6 8AS
boxoffice@cranleighartscentre.org
www.cranleighartscentre.org

Crescent Theatre
20 Sheepcote Street
Brindleyplace
Birmingham B16 8AE
{t} 0121 643 5859
{f} 0121 643 5860
admin@crescent-theatre.co.uk
www.crescent-theatre.co.uk
Capacity: 450

Cresset
Rightwell
Bretton Centre
Peterborough PE3 8DX
{t} 01733 265705
info@cresset.uk
www.cresset.co.uk
Capacity: 1000

Cricketer's
20 Fairfield South
Kingston upon Thames KT12UL
{t} 020 8977 4766
pendryporter@msn.com
Capacity: 90
Founded: 2004

Criterion Theatre
2 Jermyn Street
London SW1Y 4XA
{t} 0870 060 2313
Admin@criterion-theatre.co.uk
www.criterion-theatre.co.uk
Capacity: 591
Founded: 1874

Criterion Theatre
Berkley Road South
Earlsdon
Coventry CV5 6EF
{t} 024 7667 5175
criteriontheatre@hotmail.co.uk
www.criteriontheatre.co.uk

Cromer Pier Pavilion
The Pier
Cromer NR27 9HE
{t} 01263 512495
boxoffice@thecromerpier.com
www.thecromerpier.com
Capacity: 510
Founded: 1906

Crucible Theatre
55 Norfolk Street
Sheffield S1 1DA
{t} 0114 249 6000
info@sheffieldtheatres.co.uk
www.sheffieldtheatres.co.uk
Capacity: 980
Founded: 1971

Cuba Norte
192-194 Morrison Street
Edinburgh EH3 8EB
{t} 0131 221 0499
info@cubanorte.com
www.cubanorte.com

Cumbernauld Theatre
Kildrum
Cumbernauld G67 2BN
{f} 01236 738408
info@cumbernauldtheatre.co.uk
www.cumbernauldtheatre.co.uk

Customs House
Mill Dam
South Shields NE33 1ES
{t} 0191 454 1234
mail@customshouse.co.uk
www.customshouse.co.uk
Founded: 1994

Cut
New Cut
Halesworth IP19 8BY

{t} 01986 873285
mail@newcut.org
www.newcut.org
Capacity: 220

Dalkeith Arts Centre
White Hart Street, Dalkeith
Edinburgh EH1 1QR

Dance Centre
Chapel Street
Derby DE1 3GU
{t} 01332 370 911
info@derbydance.co.uk
www.derbydance.co.uk
Capacity: 134
Founded: 1991

Dancehouse Theatre
10 Oxford Rd
Manchester M1 5QA
{f} 0161 237 1408
boxoffice@thedancehouse.co.uk
www.thedancehouse.co.uk

Daneside Theatre
Park Road
Congleton
Cheshire CW12 1DP
{t} 01260 278481
info@danesidetheatre.co.uk
www.danesidetheatre.co.uk/diary-2006-1.html#september

Darlington Arts Centre & Civic Theatre
Parkgate
Darlington DL1 1RR
{t} 01325 486555
admin@darlingtonarts.co.uk
www.darlingtonarts.co.uk
Capacity: 439
Founded: 1907

Dartington Arts
The Barn
Dartington Hall
Totnes TQ9 6DE
info@dartingtonarts.org.uk
www.dartington.org

Darwen Library Theatre
Knott Street
Darwen BB3 3BU
{t} 01254 774 684
steve.burch@blackburn.gov.uk
www.darwenlibrarytheatre.com
Capacity: 238
Founded: 1962

David Hall Arts Centre
Roundwell St
South Petherton
Somerset TA13 5AA
{t} 01460 240340
nfo@thedavidhall.org.uk
www.thedavidhall.org.uk

De La Warr Pavilion
Marina
Bexhill On Sea TN40 1DP
{t} 01424 787949
dlwp@rother.gov.uk
www.dlwp.com
Capacity: 1000
Founded: 1935

De Montfort Hall
Granville Road
Leicester LE1 7RU
{f} 0116 233 3182
dmh.office@leicester.gov.uk
www.demontforthall.co.uk

Deco
Abington Square
Northampton NN1 4AE
{f} 01604 624 627
enquiries@thedeco.co.uk
www.thedeco.co.uk
Founded: 1930

Denny Civic Theatre
St Mary's Way
Dumbarton G82 1SG

Derby Playhouse
Eagle Centre
Theatre Walk
Derby DE1 2NF
{t} 01332 363275
info@derbyplayhouse.co.uk
www.derbyplayhouse.co.uk
Founded: 1975

Devonshire Park
Compton Street
Eastbourne BN21 4BP
{t} 01323412000
theatres@eastbourne.gov.uk
www.eastbourne-theatres.co.uk/devonshire.asp
Capacity: 936
Founded: 1884

Dewsbury Little Theatre
Upper Road
Batley Carr WF17 7LT
{t} 01274 865592
{f} 01274 865592
dewsburylittletheatre@btinternet.com
www.kirklees.gov.uk/community/localorgs/orgdetails.asp?OrgID=675

Dilys Guite Players Ltd
Kenwood Park Road
Sheffield S7 1NF
lanterntheatrehire@hotmail.com
Capacity: 92

Diorama Arts Centre
Diorama Arts
3-7 Euston Centre
London NW1 3JG
dmin@diorama-arts.org.uk
www.diorama-arts.org.uk
Capacity: 50

Diverse Attractions
Riddles Court, 322 Lawnmarket
Edinburgh EH1 2PG
{f} 0790 4270218
diverse.attractions@lawnmarket.freeserve.co.uk
www.lawnmarket.freeserve.co.uk

Dolman Theatre
Kingsway
Newport
Gwent NP20 1HY
{t} 01633 251338
www.dolmantheatre.co.uk
Capacity: 400
Founded: 1967

Dominion Theatre
Tottenham Court Road
London W1P 0AG
{t} 0870 607 7400
venuebookings@clearchannel.co.uk
www.dominiontheatre.co.uk
Capacity: 2007
Founded: 1929

Doncaster Civic Theatre
Waterdale
Doncaster DN1 3ET
{f} 01302 367223
www.doncastercivic.co.uk

Doncaster Little Theatre
1 King Street
Doncaster DN1 1JD
{f} 01302 340422
enquiries@thedoncasterlittletheatre.co.uk
www.thedoncasterlittletheatre.co.uk

Donmar Warehouse
41 Earlham Street
London WC2H 9LX
{t} 020 7369 1732
office@donmar.demon.co.uk
www.donmarwarehouse.com
Capacity: 270
Founded: 1870

Dorchester Arts Centre
School Lane
The Grove
Dorset DT1 1XR
{t} 01305 266926
enquiries@dorchesterarts.org.uk
www.dorchesterarts.org.uk

Dorking Halls
Reigate Road
Dorking RH4 1SG
{t} 01306 879200
dorkinghalls@mole-valley.gov
www.dorkinghalls.co.uk

Downstairs at the Kings Head
2 Crouch End Hill
Crouch End
London N8 8AA
{t} 020 8340 1028
admin@downstairsatthekingshead.com
www.downstairsatthekingshead.com

Dragon Hall
17 Stukeley Street
London WC2B 5LT
{t} 020 74047274
info@dragonhall.org.uk
www.dragonhall.org.uk
Capacity: 200
Founded: 2001

Dragon Theatre Barmouth
Jubilee Road
Barmouth
Gwynedd LL42 1EF
{f} 01341 281698
llison@dragob-theatre.fsnet.co.uk
Capacity: 186

Dream Factory
Shelley Avenue
Warwick CV34 6LE
{t} 01926 419555
stewart@playboxtheatre.com
www.playboxtheatre.com

Drill Hall
16 Chenies Street
London WC1E 7EX
{t} 020 7307 5060
admin@drillhall.co.uk
www.drillhall.co.uk

Drum, The
144 Potters Lane
Aston
Birmingham B6 4UU
{f} 0121 333 2440
info@the-drum.org.uk
www.the-drum.org.uk

Drum Theatre
Royal Parade
Plymouth PL1 2TR
{t} 01752 267222
info@theatreroyal.com
www.theatreroyal.com
Founded: 1982

Drummond Theatre
41 Bellevue Place
Edinburgh EH7 4BS
{t} 0131 557 9009
www.edinburgh-festivals.com/cityguide.cfm?type=venue&vid=1399

Duchess Theatre
Catherine Street
London WC2B 5LA
www.duchesstheatre.co.uk
Capacity: 479

Duke of York's
St Martin's Lane
London WC2H 4BG
{t} 020 7836 5122
doymanager@theambassadors.com
www.theambassadors.com/london
Founded: 1892

Dukes Theatre
check website
Lancaster LA1 1QE
{t} 01524 380062
info@dukes-lancaster.org
www.dukes-lancaster.org
Capacity: 500

Dundee Rep
Tay Square
Dundee DD1 1PB
{t} 01382 223530
info@dundeereptheatre.co.uk
www.dundeereptheatre.co.uk
Capacity: 455

Durham City Theatre
City Theatre
Back Silver Street
Durham DH1 3RA
MikeWendy4@aol.com
www.durham-city-theatre.fsnet.co.uk

E

E M Forster Theatre
Tonbridge School, High Street
Kent TN9 1JP
{t} 01732 365555
boxoffice@tonbridge-school.org
www.tonbridgeschoolarts.co.uk
Capacity: 380

E4 UdderBELLY
Bristo Square
Edinburgh EH8 9AL
david@underbelly.co.uk
www.underbelly.co.uk/edinburgh/e4_udderbellys_pasture/index.php

Ealing Studios
Ealing Green
London W5 5EP
{t} 020 8567 6655
info@ealingstudios.com

East Kilbride Village Theatre
51-53 Old Coach Road
East Mains
East Kilbride G74 4DU
{t} 01355 261000
{f} 01355 261280
ekartscentre@southlanarkshire.gov.uk
www.southlanarkshire.gov.uk
Capacity: 96
Founded: 13

East Kilbride Village Theatre
Maxwell Drive
the Village
East Kilbride G74 4HG
{t} 01355 248669
{f} 01355 248677
villagetheatre@southlanarkshire.gov.uk

www.southlanarkshire.gov.uk:80/portal/page/portal/EXTERNAL_WEBSITE_DEVELOPMENT/SLC_ONLINE_HOME/SLC_WHATS_ON/WHATSON_FACILITIES?CONTENT_ID=1485
Capacity: 318

Eastbourne College Theatre
Eastbourne College
Old Wish Road
East Sussex BN21 4JY
{f} 01323 452307
reception@eastbourne-college.co.uk
www.eastbourne-college.co.uk/Home/Content/Beyond%20the%20Classroom/The%20Arts/Drama
Capacity: 120

Eastgate Arts Centre
Eastgate
Peebles EH45 8AD
{t} 01721 722991
mail@eastgatearts.com
www.eastgatearts.com
Founded: 2004

Eastwood Theatre
Mansfield Road
Eastwood NG16 3EA
{t} 0115 941 9419
sue.beresford@nottscc.gov.uk

Eden Court
Bishop's Road
Inverness IV3 5SA
{t} 01463 234234
ecmail@call.co.uk
www.eden-court.co.uk

Edge Arts Centre
William Brookes School
Farley Road, Much Wenlock
Shropshire TF13 6NB
{t} 01952 728509
admin@edgeartscentre.co.uk
www.edgeartscentre.co.uk

Edinburgh Comedy Room
The Tron, Hunter Square, Royal Mile
Edinburgh EH1 1QR
www.edinburghcomedy.com/html/venue_the_tron.html
Capacity: 75

Edinburgh Corn Exchange
11 Newmarket Rd
Slateford
Edinburgh EH14 1RJ
info@tonthefringe.com
www.ece.uk.com
Capacity: 1500

Edinburgh Festival Theatre
13-29 Nicolson Street Edinburgh
Edinburgh EH8 9FT
{t} 0131 529 6000
info@eft.co.uk
www.eft.co.uk

Edinburgh Playhouse
18-22 Greenside Place
Edinburgh EH1 3AA
{t} 0870 606 3424
www.livenation.co.uk/venues/venue.aspx?vrid=338

Electric Theatre
Onslow Street
Guildford
Surrey GU1 4SZ
{t} 01483 444 789
electrictheatre@guildford.gov.uk
www.electrictheatre.co.uk
Capacity: 180

Elgin Town Hall
Trinity Road
Elgin
Morayshire IV30 1UL
{t} 01343 543500

Elgiva Theatre
St Mary's Way
Chesham HP5 1LL
{t} 01494 582900
boxoffice@elgiva.com
www.elgiva.com

Elmwood Hall
89 University Road
Belfast BT7 1NF
{t} 020 9068 9054
p.pinion@u-o.org.uk

Embassy Theatre
64 Eton Avenue
Swiss Cottage
London NW3 3HY
{t} 020 7722 8183
enquiries@cssd.ac.uk
www.cssd.ac.uk/pages/contact2.html
Capacity: 224
Founded: 100

Embassy, The
Grand Parade
Skegness
Lincolnshire PE25 2UG
{t} 0845 674 0505
Enquiries2007@EmbassyTheatre.co.uk
www.embassytheatre.co.uk

Emery Theatre
Annabel Close
Poplar
London E14 6DP
{t} 020 7515 1177
keith@emerytheatre.co.uk
www.emerytheatre.co.uk
Capacity: 100

Empire Theatre
Front Street
Consett DH8 5AB
{t} 01207 218171
{f} 01207 218416
empire@derwentside.gov.uk
www.derwentside.gov.uk/index.cfm?articleid=5157
Capacity: 503
Founded: 1885

Empire Theatre
Butler Road
Halstead
Essex CO9 1LL
{t} 07778 025490
mike@empire-theatre.co.uk
www.empire-theatre.co.uk

Epsom Playhouse
Ashley Avenue
Surrey
Epsom KT18 5AL
{t} 01372 742555
{f} 01372 726228
playhouse@epsom-ewell.gov.uk
www.epsomplayhouse.co.uk
Capacity: 406
Founded: 1984

Erin Arts Centre
Victoria Square
Port Erin
Isle of Man IM9 6LD
{f} +440 1624 836658
information@erinartscentre.com
www.erinartscentre.com

Erith Playhouse
38-4- High Street
Erith
Kent DA8 1QY
{t} 01322 350345
mail@playhouse.org.uk
www.playhouse.org.uk

Etcetera Theatre
265 Camden High Street
London NW1 7BU
{t} 020 7482 4857
{f} 020 7482 0378
etc@etceteratheatre.com
www.etceteratheatre.com
Capacity: 42
Founded: 1986

Everyman Theatre
Regent Street
Cheltenham GL50 1HQ
{t} 01242 512 515
admin@everymantheatre.org.uk
www.everymantheatre.org.uk
Founded: 1891

Exeter Phoenix
Bradninch Place
Gandy Street
Exeter EX4 3LS
boxoffice@exeterphoenix.org.uk
www.exeterphoenix.org.uk

Exhibit Bar & Cinema, The
12 Balham Station Road
London SW12 9SG
{t} 020 8772 6556
alham@exhibitbars.com
www.theexhibit.co.uk
Capacity: 70
Founded: 2005

Exmouth Pavilion
The Esplanade
Exmouth EX8 2AZ
{t} 01395 222477
nfo@ledleisure.co.uk
www.ledleisure.co.uk/Index/exmouth_pavilion.htm

Eye Theatre
Broad Street
Eye
Suffolk IP23 7AF
{t} 01733 313414
boxoffice@eyetheatre.freeserve.co.uk

F

Faircharm Studios
8-10 Creekside
Deptford
London SE8 3DX
{t} 020 8694 6472
info@stonecrabs.co.uk
www.stonecrabs.co.uk

Fairfield Halls
Park Lane
Croydon CR9 1DG
{t} 020 8688 9291
info@fairfield.co.uk
www.fairfield.co.uk
Capacity: 760

Farnham Maltings
Bridge Square
Farnham GU9 7QR
{t} 01252 726234
info@farnhammaltings.com
www.farnhammaltings.com

Farnworth Little Theatre
Cross Street
Farnworth
Bolton BL4 7AJ
{t} 01204 303808
publicity@farnworthlittletheatre.co.uk
www.farnworthlittletheatre.co.uk
Capacity: 108

Farrer Theatre
Common Lane
Eton College
Windsor SL4 6DW
{f} 01753 671059
www.etoncollege.com/default.asp
Capacity: 400

Ferneham Hall
Osborn Road
Fareham PO16 7DB
{t} 01329 824864
{f} 01329 281528
boxoffice@fareham.gov.uk
www.fareham.gov.uk/fernehamhall
Founded: 1982

Finborough Theatre
118 Finborough Road
London SW10 9ED
{t} 020 7244 7439
admin@finboroughtheatre.co.uk
www.finboroughtheatre.co.uk
Founded: 1980

Floral Pavilion
Virginia Road
New Brighton CH45 2LH
{t} 0151 639 4360
floralpavillion@wirral.gov.uk
www.floralpavillion.co.uk
Capacity: 1200

Forest Arts Centre
Old Milton Road
New Milton BH25 6DS
{t} 01425 612393
{f} 01425 616340
judy.kyle@hants.gov.uk
www.forest-arts.co.uk

Forest Upstairs, The
3 Bristo Place
Edinburgh EH1 1EY
info@theforest.org.uk
www.theforest.org.uk

Formby Little Theatre
off Rosemary Lane
Formby
Liverpool L37 3HA
{t} 01704 872161
formbytheatre@lycos.co.uk
www.formbytheatre.co.uk
Capacity: 64

Fortune Theatre
Russell Street
London WC2B 5HH
{t} 01462 421416
info@theambassadors.com
www.theambassadors.com/fortune/info/index.html
Founded: 1989

Forum
Town Centre
Billingham TS23 2LJ
{t} 01642 552663
admin@forumbillngham.freeserve.co.uk
www.forumtheatrebillingham.co.uk

Forum 28
28 Duke St
Barrow-In-Furness LA14 1HH
{t} 01229 820000

nward@barrowbc.gov.uk
www.barrowbc.gov.uk

Four Dwellings High School Drama Studio
Dwellings Lane
Birmingham B32 1RJ
{t} 07833 513230
q2qtheatre@yahoo.co.uk

Friends Meeting House
Ship Street
Brighton BN1 1AF
admin@brightonquakers.net
www.brightonquakers.co.uk
Founded: 1805

Fringe Club
Unit 3, Fishmarket Close
Edinburgh EH1 1QR
{t} 0131 226 0026
admin@edfringe.com
www.edfringe.com

Fringe Shop
180 High Street
Edinburgh EH1 1QS

Frome Memorial Theatre
Christchurch Street West
Frome BA11 1EB
{t} 01373 462795
phoenix46@amserve.com
www.fromememorialtheatre.org.uk

Futurist Theatre
Foreshore Road
Scarborough YO11 1NT
{t} 01723 374500
boxoffice@futuristtheatre.plus.com
www.futuristtheatre.co.uk
Capacity: 2148
Founded: 1903

G

Gaiety Theatre
Harris Promenade
Douglas
Isle of Man IM1 2HH
{t} 01624 625 001
{f} 01624 629028
gaietytheatre@iom.com
www.gov.im/villagaiety
Capacity: 1514
Founded: 1900

Gaiety Theatre
Carrick Street
Ayr KA7 1NU
{t} 01292 612218
gaiety.theatre@south-ayreshire.gov.uk
www.gaietytheatre.co.uk
Capacity: 220
Founded: 1902

Gala Theatre
Millennium Place
Durham DH1 1WA
{t} 0191 3324040
{f} 0191 3324066
enquiries@galadurham.co.uk
www.galadurham.co.uk
Capacity: 500
Founded: 2002

Gallery & Studio Theatre
Leeds Metropolitan University
Civic Quarter
Leeds LS1 3HE
{t} 0113 812 5998
gallerytheatre@leedsmet.ac.uk
www.leedsmet.ac.uk/arts

Garage
The Garage
14 Chapelfield North
Norwich NR2 1NY
{t} 01603 283382
{f} 01603 886089
info@thegarage.org.uk
www.thegarage.org.uk
Founded: 2003

Gardner Arts Centre
University of Sussex
Falmer
Brighton BN1 9RA
{t} 01273 685447
{f} 01273 678551
info@gardnerarts.co.uk
www.gardnerarts.co.uk
Founded: 1969

Garrick
Castle Dyke
Lichfield WS13 6HR
{t} 01543 412121
info@lichfieldgarrick.com
www.lichfieldgarrick.com

Garrick Theatre
Charring Cross Road
London W1D 7DY
www.garrick-theatre.co.uk
Capacity: 678

Garrison Theatre
Toll Clock Centre
26 North Road
Lerwick ZE1 0PE
{f} 1595 694001
richard.wemyss@shetland-arts-trust.co.uk
Capacity: 280

Gate
11 Pembridge Road
London W11 3HQ
{t} 020 7229 5387
gate@gatetheatre.freeserve.co.uk
www.gatetheatre.co.uk
Founded: 1979

Gate Arts Theatre
Dunhill Road
Goole DN14 6ST
helen.gtc@btconnect.com
www.thegategoole.com

Gateway Theatre
41 Elm Row, Leith
Edinburgh EH7 4AH
info@pendfringe.co.uk
www.pendfringe.co.uk

GBS Theatre
Royal Academy of Dramatic Art
Malet Street
London WC1E 6ED
{t} 020 7908 4800
jed@radaenterprises.org
Capacity: 102

Geoffrey Whitworth Theatre
Beech Walk
Dartford DA1 4WB
{t} 01322 526390
colin@nickhill.org.uk
www.thegwt.org.uk
Capacity: 150

George Square Theatre
George Square
Edinburgh EH1 9LH
{t} 0131 662 8740
uoefo@ed.ac.uk
www.festivals.ed.ac.uk/venue_georgetheatre.htm
Capacity: 560

George Wood Theatre
Goldsmiths College
New Cross
London SE14 6NW
{t} 020 7919 7414
{f} 020 7919 7413
drama@gold.ac.uk
www.goldsmiths.ac.uk/departments/drama/facilities.php

Georgian Theatre Royal
Victoria Road
Richmond DL10 4DW
{f}1748
admin@georgiantheatreroyal.co.uk
www.georgiantheatreroyal.co.uk
Capacity: 214
Founded: 1788

Gibson Hall
13 Bishopsgate
London EC2N 3BA
{f} 020 7334 3981
sales@gibsonhall.com
Capacity: 400
Founded: 1865

Gielgud Theatre
The Royal Academy of Dramatic Arts
Chenies Street
London WC1E 6ED
{t} 020 7908 4800
jed@radaenterprises.org
www.yptc.co.uk

Gielgud Theatre
Shaftesbury Avenue
London W1D 6BA
info@gielgudtheatre.com
Capacity: 889
Founded: 1906

Gilded Balloon
13 Bristo Square
Edinburgh EH8 9AL
{t} 0131 622 6555
info@gildedballoon.co.uk
www.gildedballoon.co.uk
Founded: 1986

Gilded Balloon
25 Greenside Place
Edinburgh EH1 3AA
{t} 0131 622 6555
www.gildedballoon.co.uk

Gilmorehill G12
9 University Avenue
Glasgow G12 8QQ
{t} 0141 330 5522
{f} 0141 330 3857
boxoffice@gilmorehillg12.co.uk
www.gilmorehillg12.co.uk
Capacity: 210
Founded: 1997

Gladstone Theatre
Greendale Road
Port Sunlight
Wirral CH62 4XB
{t} 01516438757
enquire@gladstone.uk.com
www.gladstone.uk.com
Capacity: 470
Founded: 1891

Glasgow Royal Concert Hall
2 Sauchiehall Street
Glasgow G2 3NY
{t} 0141 353 8080
{f} 0141 353 8001
arts@grch.com
www.grch.com
Capacity: 2500
Founded: 1990

Glasgow Theatre Royal
282 Hope Street
Glasgow G2 3QA
www.theambassadors.com/theatreroyalglasgow
Founded: 1867

Glee Club
Mermaid Quay
Cardiff Bay CF10 5BZ
duncan@glee.co.uk

Glee Club
Hurst Street
Birmingham B5 4DP
duncan@glee.co.uk

Glyndebourne
Lewes
East Sussex BN8 5UU
{t} 01273 813813
info@glyndebourne.com
www.glyndebourne.com
Founded: 1934

Golden Hinde, The
St Mary Overie Dock
Cathedral Street
London Bridge SE1 9DE
{t} 0870 4466 826
info@goldenhinde.co.uk
www.goldenhinde.org
Capacity: 50

Gordon Craig
Lytton Way
Stevenage SG1 1LZ
{t} 08700 131 030
gordoncraig@stevenage-leisure.co.uk
www.stevenage-leisure.co.uk/CentrenbspLocator/StevenageArtsampLeisureCentre/GordonCraigTheatre/tabid/182/
Capacity: 501
Founded: 1975

Grand Opera House
Great Victoria Street
Belfast BT2 7HR
{t} 02890 241919
info@goh.co.uk
www.goh.co.uk

Grand Opera House
Cumberland Street
York YO1 1SW
{t} 0870 6063595
yorkboxoffice@clearchannel.co.uk
www.getlive.co.uk/york
Founded: 1902

Grand Pavilion
The Esplanade
Porthcawl CF36 3YW
{t} 01656 783 860
grandpavilion@compuserve.com
www.grandpavilion.co.uk
Capacity: 643
Founded: 1932

Grand Theatre
Singleton Street
Swansea SA1 3QJ
{t} 01792 475715
mail@swanseagrand.co.uk
www.swansea.gov.uk/index.cfm?articleid=480
Founded: 1897

Grand Theatre
Lichfield Street
Wolverhampton WV1 1DE
{t} 01902 57 33 00
info@grandtheatre.co.uk
www.grandtheatre.co.uk
Founded: 1982

Grand Theatre
St Leonardgate
Lancaster LA1 1NL
{t} 01524 64695
www.lancastergrand.co.uk
Capacity: 457

Grange Arts Centre
Rochdale Road
Oldham
Lancashire OL9 6EA
{t} 0161 785 4239
boxoffice@coliseum.org.uk
www.grangeartsoldham.co.uk

Grange Court Theatre
1 Grange Road
Ealing
London W5 5QN
{t} 020 8579 3897
{f} 020 8566 2035
admin@dramastudiolondon.co.uk

Grange Playhouse
Broadway North
Walsall WS1 2D
grange@playhouse.gpanet.co.uk

Greenock Arts Guild
Campbell Street
Greenock PA16 8AP
{t} 01475 723 038
admin@greenockartsguild.co.uk
www.greenockartsguild.co.uk
Capacity: 449
Founded: 1955

Greenroom
54-56 Whitworth Street West
Manchester M1 5WW
{f} 0161 615 0516
info@greenroomarts.org
www.greenroomarts.org

Greenside
1b Royal Terrace
Edinburgh EH7 5AB
info@w4greenside.co.uk
www.w4greenside.co.uk

Greenwich Park
The Royal Observatory Gardens
Greenwich Park
London SE10 8QY
lordstrangesmen@hotmail.com
www.royalparks.gov.uk/parks/greenwich_park/events.cfm
Capacity: 300

Greenwich Playhouse
189 Greenwich High Road
London SE10 8JA
{t} 020 8858 9256
boxoffice@galleontheatre.co.uk
Capacity: 87
Founded: 1988

Greenwich Theatre
Crooms Hill
Greenwich
London SE10 8ES
{t} 020 8858 7755
{f} 020 8858 8042
info@greenwichtheatre.org.uk
www.greenwichtheatre.org.uk
Capacity: 421
Founded: 1835

Grimsby Auditorium
Cromwell Road
Grimsby
Lincolnshire DN31 2BH
{t} 0870 380 0017
www.grimsbyontheweb.com/directory/dirhome.asp?id=302&townid=475
Capacity: 2000

Grove Park Theatre
Hill Street
Wrexham LL11 1SN
{t} 01978 351091
boxoffice@groveparktheatre.co.uk
www.groveparktheatre.co.uk
Capacity: 169

Guildford Arms
1 West Register St
Edinburgh EH2 2AA
{t} 0131 556 4312
info@guildfordarms.com
www.guildfordarms.com
Founded: 1898

Guildhall
Civic Centre
Southampton SO14 7LP
{t} 01703 632601
venuebookings@clearchannel.co.uk
www.southampton-guildhall.com
Capacity: 1271
Founded: 1937

Guildhall Arts Centre
St. Peter's Hill
Grantham NG13 6PZ
{t} 01476 406158
boxoffice@theguildhall.biz
www.guildhallartscentre.com
Capacity: 210
Founded: 1991

Gulbenkian Theatre
University of Kent
Canterbury CT2 7NB
{t} 01227 769075
{f} 01227 827444
gulbenkian@kent.ac.uk
www.kent.ac.uk/gulbenkian
Capacity: 340
Founded: 1969

Guthrie Castle
Guthrie
By Forfar
Angus DD8 2TP
{f} 01241 828605
enquiries@guthriecastle.com
www.guthriecastle.com

H

Hackney Empire
291 Mare Street
London E8 1EJ
{t} 020 8510 4500
{f} 020 8510 4530
info@hackneyempire.co.uk
www.hackneyempire.co.uk
Capacity: 1300
Founded: 1986

Hailsham Pavilion
George Street
Hailsham
East Sussex BN27 1AE
{t} 01323 841414
info@hailshampavilion.co.uk
www.hailshampavilion.co.uk

Half Moon
93 Lower Richmond Road, Putney
London SW15 1EU
{t} 020 8780 9383
office@halfmoon.co.uk
www.halfmoon.co.uk

Half Moon Young People's Theatre
43 White Horse Road
London E1 0ND
{t} 020 7265 8138
admin@halfmoon.org.uk
www.halfmoon.org.uk

Halifax Playhouse
Halifax
West Yorkshire HX1 2SH
{t} 01422 365998
martyn@halifaxplayhouse.org.uk
www.users.ministryofsound.net/~steadals/halifaxplayhouse.html

Hall for Cornwall
Back Quay
Truro TR1 2LL
admin@hallforcornwall.org.uk
www.hallforcornwall.co.uk

Hall Green Little Theatre
Pemberley Road
Birmingham B27 7RY
{t} 0121 707 1874
info@hglt.co.uk
www.hglt.org.uk
Capacity: 195

Hambleton Forum
Bullamoor Road
Northallerton DL6 2UZ
{t} 01609 777070
richard.dawson@hambleton.gov.uk
www.hambleton.gov.uk/hambleton/leisure.nsf/webpages/hambletonforum.html
Capacity: 400

Hampden
Hampden Park Ltd
Hampden Park G42 9BA
{f} 0141 620 4001
info@hampdenpark.co.uk
www.hampdenpark.co.uk/about_hampden/
Capacity: 52000

Hampstead Theatre
Eton Avenue
Swiss Cottage
London NW3 3EU
{t} 020 7722 9301
info@hampsteadtheatre.com
www.hampsteadtheatre.com
Capacity: 325
Founded: 1976

Hampton Hill Playhouse
Hampton Hill Playhouse
90 High St
Hampton Hill TW12 1NY
{t} 020 8410 4545
hires@ttc-hhp.org.uk
www.ttc-hhp.org.uk/hhp-general.php3?sess=
Capacity: 200
Founded: 1998

Hanover Community Centre
77 Southover Street
BN2 2UD
{t} 01273 694873
office@hanovercommunitycentre.freeserve.co.uk
share.runtime-collective.com/~joe/cbn/hanover.htm
Capacity: 100

Harbour Arts Centre
114-116 Harbour Street
Ayrshire KA12 8PZ
contactus@north-ayrshire.gov.uk
www.harbourarts.org.uk

Harlequin
Warwick Quadrant, London Road
Redhill RH1 1NN
{t} 01737 765547
harlequin@atlas.co.uk
www.harlequin-theatre.co.uk

Harlequin Theatre
Queen Street
Northwich
Cheshire CW9 5JN
webmaster@harlequinplayers.co.uk
www.harlequinplayers.co.uk

Harlow Playhouse
Playhouse Square
Harlow
Essex CM20 1LS
{t} 01279 446760
playhouse@harlow.gov.uk
www.playhouseharlow.com
Capacity: 412
Founded: 1959

Harpenden Public Halls
Southdown Road
Harpenden
Herts AL5 1PD
{t} 01582 762880
{f} 01582 765464
harpenden.public.halls@
leisureconnection.co.uk
www.harpenden-town.com
Capacity: 384
Founded: 2005

Harrogate Theatre
Oxford Street
Harrogate
North Yorkshire HG1 1QF
{f} 01423 563 205
info@harrogatetheatre.co.uk
www.harrogatetheatre.co.uk

Hartham Park
Corsham
Wiltshire SN13 0RP
{f} 01249 700001
info@harthampark.com
www.harthampark.com

Hartlepool Town Hall Theatre
Raby Road
Hartlepool TS24 8AH
www.thisishartlepool.co.uk/
entertainment/townhalltheatre.asp

Hat Factory
65-67 Bute Street
Luton LU1 2EY
{t} 01582 878100
hatfactory@luton.gov.uk
www.lutonline.gov.uk/hatfactory
Founded: 2004

Hatherop Castle
Hatherop Castle School
Cirencester GL7 3NB
{t} 01285 750206
boxoffice@arcadians.org
www.isbi.com/isbi-viewschool/155-
HATHEROP_CASTLE_SCHOOL.html
Founded: 1946

Havant Arts Centre
East Street
Havant PO9 1BS
{t} 023 92 472 700
info@havantartsactive.co.uk
havantartscentre.co.uk
Founded: 1987

Haverhill Arts Centre
High Street
Haverhill
Suffolk CB9 8AR
{f} 01440 718931
boxoffice@haverhillartscentre.co.uk
www.haverhillartscentre.co.uk
Founded: 1883

Hawth
Hawth Avenue
Crawley RH10 6YZ

{f} 01293 533362
info@hawth.co.uk
www.hawth.co.uk

Haymarket
Wote Street
Basingstoke RG21 7NW
{t} 01256 465566
info@haymarket.org.uk
www.haymarket.org.uk
Capacity: 420
Founded: 1993

Hazlitt Theatre
Earl Street
Maidstone ME14 1PL
{t} 01622 602 178
mandyhare@hazlitt.org.uk
www.hazlitttheatre.co.uk

Hebden Bridge Little Theatre
Holme Street
Hebden Bridge
West Yorkshire HX7 6EE
{t} 01422 843907
phil.vaughan@3-c.coop
Capacity: 120

Helmsley Arts Centre
The Old Meeting House
Helmsley YO62 5DW
{t} 01439 772112
helmsleyarts@yahoo.com
www.helmsleyarts.co.uk/index2.html

Hen & Chickens
109 St Paul's Rd
London N1 2NA
{t} 020 7704 2001
Henandchickens@aol.com
www.henandchickens.com
Capacity: 54
Founded: 1837

Henry's Jazz Cellar
8 Morrison Street
Edinburgh EH3 8BH
{t} 0131 228 9393
info@henrysjazz.co.uk
www.henrysjazz.co.uk

Her Majesty's
Haymarket
London SW1Y 4QR
{t} 020 7494 5400
info@rutheatres.com
www.rutheatres.com/venueinfo/hmt.htm
Capacity: 1148

Herne Bay Little Theatre
Bullers Avenue
Herne Bay
Kent CT6 8UH
{t} 01227 366004
playmakers.membership@fsmail.net
www.hblt.co.uk
Capacity: 72

Heron Theatre
Stanley Street
Beetham
Milnthorpe LA7 7AS
{t} 01539 560328
johndeanuk@aol.com
www.herontheatre.fsnet.co.uk
Capacity: 81

Hexagon
Queens Walk
Reading RG1 7UA
{t} 0118 960 6060
boxoffice@readingarts.com
www.readingarts.com/thehexagon
Capacity: 1200
Founded: 1977

Highbury Theatre Centre
Sheffield Road
Sutton Coldfield
West Midlands B73 5HD
{t} 0121 373 2761
admin@highburytheatre.co.uk
www.highburytheatre.co.uk

Hill Street
19 Hill Street
Edinburgh EH2 3JP
{t} 0131 226 6522
hillstreet@universal-arts.com
www.universal-arts.com
Capacity: 120
Founded: 1970

Hippodrome
Hurst Street
Birmingham B5 4TB
{t} 0121 689 3170
{f} 0870 730 5030
info@birminghamhippodrome.com
www.birminghamhippodrome.com

Hippodrome Circus
St Georges Road
Great Yarmouth NR30 2EU
{t} 01493 844 172
chrisjay@jaysuk.fsnet.co.uk
www.hippodromecircus.co.uk
Capacity: 1000
Founded: 1903

Hippodrome Theatre
Halifax Road
Lancashire OL14 5BB
{t} 01706 814875
Capacity: 485

His Majesty's Aberdeen
Rosemount Viaduct
Aberdeen AB25 1GL
{t} 08452 708200
info@hmtheatre.com
www.hmtaberdeen.com
Capacity: 1475
Founded: 1906

HMT at Hilton
University of Aberdeen
Aberdeen AB24 4FA
{t} 01224 641122
Stanley@abdnboxoffice.com
www.hmtheatre.com

Hobbs Factory
122 Gloucester Avenue
Primrose Hill
London NW1 8HX
{t} 020 7428 5897
thehobbsfactory@yahoo.co.uk
www.thehobbsfactory.com
Founded: 2004

Holland Park Theatre
Stable Yard
London W8 6LU
{t} 0845 230 9769
boxoffice@operahollandpark.com
www.operahollandpark.com

Holyrood Tavern
9a Holyrood Road
Edinburgh EH8 8AE
{t} 0131 556 5044
info@rarebirdsprod.com
www.rarebirdsprod.com/holyrood.htm

Horse Hospital, The
Colonnade
London WC1N 1HX
{t} 020 7833 3644
popculture@thehorsehospital.com
www.thehorsehospital.com
Founded: 1993

Horseshoe Theatre
Ocean Boulevard
Blackpool FY4 1EZ
{t} 0870 444 5566
info@bpdltd.com
www.blackpoolpleasurebeach.com

Howden Park Centre
Howden
Livingston EH54 6AE
{t} 01506 433634
robbie.mcghee@weld.org.uk
www.livingstonalive.co.uk/howdenpc.shtml

Hoxton Hall
130 Hoxton Street
London N1 6SH
{f} 020 7729 3815
info@hoxtonhall.co.uk
www.hoxtonhall.co.uk
Founded: 1863

Hub Courtyard, The
Festival Centre, Castlehill, Royal Mile
Edinburgh EH1 2NE
info@oldtowntours.co.uk
www.oldtowntours.co.uk

Hub, The
12 Hillside Road
Brock Way
Verwood BH31 7PU
{t} 01202 828740
info@verwoodhub.org
www.verwoodhub.org
Capacity: 300
Founded: 2006

Hull New Theatre
Kingston Square
Kingston Upon Hull HU1 3HF
{t} 01482 226655
theatre.secretary@hullcc.gov.uk
www.hullcc.gov.uk/hullnewtheatre
Founded: 1924

Hull Truck Theatre
Spring Street
Hull HU2 8RW
{t} 01482 323638
admin@hulltruck.co.uk
www.hulltruck.co.uk
Founded: 1971

Human Rights Action Centre, The
17-25 New Inn Yard
London EC2A 3EA
vulture_culture_productions@yahoo.co.uk

Humms Theatre
Whiteknights Campus
Reading RG6 6AH
{t} 0123456
humss@auditioncall.com
Capacity: 170
Founded: 1984

I

ICA
The Mall
London SW1Y 5AH
{t} 020 7930 3647
info@ica.org.uk
www.ica.org.uk
Capacity: 168

ICIA
University of Bath
Claverton Down
Bath BA2 7AY
ICIAinfo@bath.ac.uk
www.bath.ac.uk/icia/home

Ifield Barn
Ifield Barn Theatre
Rectory Lane
Ifield RH11 0NN
{t} 01293 525 030
general@ifieldbarn.co.uk
www.ifieldbarn.co.uk
Capacity: 80
Founded: 1968

Ilkley Playhouse
Weston Road
Ilkley
West Yorkshire LS29 8DW
{t} 01943 609539
info@Ilkleyplayhouse.org
www.ilkleyplayhouse.org
Capacity: 148
Founded: 1984

Inn on the Green
3-5 Thorpe Close
underneath the Westway
London W10 5XL
{t} 020 8962 5757
info@iotg.co.uk
www.iotg.co.uk

International Convention Centre
Broad Street
Birmingham B1 2EA
{f} 0121 643 0388
info@theicc.co.uk
www.theicc.co.uk

Ipswich Regent Theatre
3 St Helen's Street
Ipswich IP4 1HE
{t} 01473 433 555
regent@ipswich-ents.co.uk
online.ipswich.gov.uk/eSROIpswich

Islington Tap, The
80 Liverpool Road
Islington
London N1 0QD
{t} 020 8288 9398
hotfudgetheatre@hotmail.co.uk

J

Jacksons Lane
269a Archway Road
London N6 5AA
{t} 020 8340 5226
mail@jacksonslane.org.uk
www.jacksonslane.org.uk
Capacity: 167
Founded: 1990

Jazz Bar, The
1A Chambers Street Edinburgh
Edinburgh EH1 1HU
{t} 0131 220 4298
info@thejazzbar.co.uk
www.thejazzbar.co.uk

Jellicoe Theatre
Lower Constitution Hill
Poole BH14 0QA
whited@bpc.ac.uk
Capacity: 120

Jennie Lee Theatre
Princes Way
Bletchley MK2 2HQ
{t} 01908 613145
bletchley@leisureconnection.co.uk

Jermyn Street Theatre
16b Jermyn Street
London SW1Y 6ST
{t} 020 7434 1443
info@jermynstreettheatre.co.uk

www.jermynstreettheatre.co.uk
Capacity: 70
Founded: 1994

Jerwood Space
171 Union Street
London SE1 0LN
{t} 020 7654 0171
space@jerwoodspace.co.uk
www.jerwoodspace.co.uk
Founded: 2000

JJB Stadium
Loire Drive
Robin Park
Wigan WN5 OUH
{f} 01942 770444
info@jjbstadium.co.uk
www.jjbstadium.co.uk
Capacity: 24826

John Donald & Co
8/10 Bristo Place
Edinburgh EH1 1EY
info@highlandstoneware.com
www.highlandstoneware.com

John Lyon Hall
Keeley Street
London WC2B 4BA
{t} 020 7492 2542
drama@citylit.ac.uk
www.citylit.ac.uk/drama
Capacity: 100
Founded: 2005

John Prescott Theatre
Handbridge Centre
Eaton Road
Chester CH4 7ER
{f} 01244 670676
info@west-cheshire.ac.uk
www.west-cheshire.ac.uk/theatre

John Sowerby Theatre
Ralph Thoresby High School
Community Arts College
Farrar Lane
Holt Park, Leeds LS16 7NQ
{f} 0113 225 9922
headteacher@ralphthoresby.leeds.sch.uk
www.ralphthoresby.leeds.sch.uk/Theatre.html

Jongleurs Comedy Club
Omni Leisure Complex
Greenside Place
Edinburgh EH1 3AA
{t} 0870 787 0707
info@jongleurs.com
www.jongleurs.com

Joogleberry Playhouse
14-16 Manchester Street
Brighton BN2 1TF
{t} 01273687171
info@joogleberry.com
www.joogleberry.com
Capacity: 70
Founded: 2002

Joseph Rowntree Theatre
Haxby Road
York YO31 8TA
{t} 01904 658197
publicity@jrtheatre.co.uk
www.jrtheatre.co.uk

Journal Tyne Theatre, The
Westgate Road
Newcastle upon Tyne NE1 4xe
{t} 0191 274 7066
bookings@newcastlepantomime.com
www.thejournaltynetheatre.co.uk
Capacity: 1500
Founded: 1860

Judi Dench Theatre
104 Crouch Hill
London N22 6XF
{t} 020 8829 0035
Capacity: 60
Founded: 1986

Junction
Clifton Way
Cambridge CB1 7GX
{t} 01223 511 511
spiral@junction.co.uk
www.junction.co.uk
Capacity: 220
Founded: 1990

K

Keay Theatre
Tregonissey Road
St Austell PL25 4DJ
{t} 01726 226713
{f} 01726 226778
info@thekeay.co.uk
www.thekeay.co.uk
Capacity: 224

Keighley Playhouse
Devonshire Street
Keighley BD21 2QW
{t} 08451 267859
shelia.kershaw@keighleyplayhouse.co.uk
www.keighleyplayhouse.co.uk

Kelvin Players Theatre
253b Gloucester Road
Bristol BS7 8NY
{t} 0117 959 3636
kelvinplayers_publicity@hotmail.com
www.kelvinplayers.co.uk/html/productions.htm
Founded: 1929

Kendal Brewery Arts Centre
Highgate
Kendal
Cumbria LA9 4HE
{f} 01539 730257
admin@breweryarts.co.uk
Capacity: 260
Founded: 1993

Kenneth More Theatre
Oakfield Road
Ilford
Essex IG1 1BT
{t} 020 8553 4466
{f} 01708 458262
info@kenneth-more-theatre.co.uk
www.kenneth-more-theatre.co.uk
Capacity: 364
Founded: 1974

Kenton Theatre
New Street
Henley-on-Thames
Oxfordshire RG9 2BP
{t} 01491 575698
info@kentontheatre.co.uk
www.kentontheatre.co.uk

Key
Embankment Road
Peterborough PE1 1EF
{t} 01733 552 439
keytheatre@freenetname.co.uk
www.peterboroughkeytheatre.co.uk
Capacity: 399
Founded: 1973

King George's Hall
Northgate
Blackburn BB2 1AA
{t} 01254 582582
dave.cooper.hughes@blackburn.gov.uk
www.kinggeorgeshall.com

King's
2 Leven Street
Edinburgh EH3 9LQ
{t} 08700 606 650
empire@eft.co.uk
www.eft.co.uk
Capacity: 1336
Founded: 1905

King's
297 Bath Street
Glasgow G2 4JN
{t} 0141 240 1111
duncanmay@theambassadors.com
www.theambassadors.com/kings
Capacity: 1785
Founded: 1904

King's Hall
Beacon Hill
The Downs
Herne Bay CT6 6BA
{t} 01227 374 188
david.clarke@thekingshall.co.uk
www.thekingshall.co.uk
Capacity: 646
Founded: 1912

King's Head
115 Upper Street
Islington
London N1 1QN
{t} 020 7226 1916
{f} 020 7226 8507
info@kingsheadtheatre.demon.co.uk
www.kingsheadtheatre.org
Capacity: 105
Founded: 1970

Kings Lynn Arts Centre
27-29 King Street
King's Lynn PE30 1HA
{t} 01553 764864
entertainment-admin@west-norfolk.gov.uk
www.kingslynnarts.co.uk
Capacity: 738
Founded: 1854

King's Lynn Corn Exchange
Tuesday Market Place
King's Lynn
Norfolk PE3O 1JW
{f} 01553 762141
thecoffeehouse@west-norfolk.gov.uk
www.kingslynncornexchange.co.uk
Capacity: 733

Kings Theatre
338 High Street
Chatham ME4 4NR
{t} 01634 829468
office@spotlites.co.uk
www.spotlites.co.uk
Capacity: 110
Founded: 1999

Kings Theatre
Albert Road
Portsmouth
Hants PO5 2QJ
{t} 023 9282 8282
groups@kings-southsea.com
www.kings-southsea.com

King's Theatre Newmarket
17 Fitzroy Street
Newmarket
Suffolk CB8 0JW
{t} 01638 663337
www.nomadskingstheatre.com

Komedia
44 Gardner Street
Brighton
East Sussex BN1 1UN
{t} 01273 647101
info@komedia.co.uk
www.komedia.co.uk
Capacity: 350
Founded: 1994

L

Laban
Creekside
London SE8 3DZ
{t} 020 8691 8600
{f} 020 8691 8400
info@laban.org
www.laban.org
Capacity: 300
Founded: 2000

Lace Market Theatre
Halifax Place
Nottingham NG1 1QN
{t} 0115 950 7201
info@lacemarkettheatre.co.uk
www.lacemarkettheatre.co.uk

Lakeside Arts Centre
University of Nottingham
Nottingham NG7 2RD
{t} 0115 846 7777
cholden@essex.ac.uk
www.lakesidearts.org.uk
Capacity: 217
Founded: 1971

Lakeside Theatre
University of Essex
Wivenhoe Park
Colchester CO4 3SQ
{t} 01206 873261
cholden@essex.ac.uk
www.essex.ac.uk/Arts

Lambeth Mission
3-5 Lambeth Road
London SE1 7DQ
{t} 020 7735 2166
cindy.office@lambethmission.org.uk
Capacity: 200

LampLight Arts Centre
Front Street
Stanley
Co Durham DH9 0NA
{f} 01207 218897
lamplight@derwentside.gov.uk
www.derwentside.gov.uk/index.cfm?articleid=5156
Capacity: 400

Lamproom Theatre
Westgate
Barnsley
South Yorkshire S70 2DX
{t} 01226 200075
boxoffice@barnsleylamproom.com
www.barnsleylamproom.com

Landmark Arts Centre
Ferry Road
Teddington
London TW11 9NN
{t} 020 8977 7558
lourda@landmarkartscentre.org
www.landmarkartscentre.org
Capacity: 300
Founded: 1889

Landmark Theatre
The Seafront
Wilder Road
Ilfracombe EX34 8BW

{t} 01271 324242
box.qt@northdevontheatres.org.uk
www.northdevontheatres.org.uk
Capacity: 483
Founded: 1998

Landor Theatre
70, Landor Road
London SW9 9PH
{t} 020 7737 7276
info@landortheatre.co.uk
www.landortheatre.co.uk
Founded: 1984

Lanhydrock
Lanhydrock
Bodmin
Cornwall PL30 5AD
{t} 01208 265950
{f} 01208 265959
lanhydrock@nationaltrust.org.uk
www.nationaltrust.org.uk/main/w-vh/w-visits/w-findaplace/w-lanhydrock
Capacity: 500
Founded: 1953

Lantern, The
Kenwood Park Road
Nether Edge
Sheffield S7 1DN
{t} 0114 236 2608
Founded: 1890

Lauderdale House
Highgate Hill
Waterlow Park
London N6 5HG
{t} 020 8348 8716
www.lauderdalehouse.co.uk
Founded: 1582

Lawrence Batley Theatre
Queen's Square
Queen Street
Huddersfield HD1 2SP
{t} 01484 430528
theatre@lbt-uk.org
www.lawrencebatleytheatre.co.uk
Capacity: 477
Founded: 1994

Layard Theatre
Canford School
Canford Magna
Wimborne BH21 3AD
{t} 01202 849134
Capacity: 294
Founded: 1998

Leas Cliff Hall
The Leas
Folkestone CT20 2DZ
{t} 01303 253193
venuebookings@clearchannel.co.uk
www.leascliffhall.co.uk
Capacity: 940
Founded: 1927

Leatherhead Theatre
7, Church Street
Leatherhead KT22 8DN
{t} 01372 365141
{f} 01372 365195
boxoffice@the-theatre.org
www.the-theatre.org
Capacity: 526
Founded: 1890

Leeds Grand Theatre
46 New Briggate Leeds
Leeds LS1 6NZ
{t} 0113 245 3546
boxoffice@leedsgrandtheatre.com
www.leedsgrandtheatre.com

Left Bank
Chambers Street
Edinburgh EH1 3EE
leftbank@hotmail.com

Leicester Haymarket
Belgrave Gate
Leicester LE1 3YQ
{t} 0116 253 0021
enquiry@lhtheatre.co.uk
www.lhtheatre.co.uk
Founded: 2007

Leighton Buzzard Theatre
Lake Street
Leighton Buzzard LU7 1RX
{t} 01582 81880
www.leightonbuzzardtheatre.co.uk
Capacity: 170

Leith Market
12a Dock Place
Commercial Quay
Leith EH6 6LU
info@leithmarket.com
www.leithmarket.com

Lemon Tree
5 West North Street
Aberdeen AB24 5AT
{t} 01224 642230
info@lemontree.org
www.lemontree.org
Capacity: 550
Founded: 1930

Lewes Theatre Club
Lancaster Street
Lewes BN7 2PX
{t} 01273 474882
memsec@lewestheatre.org
www.lewestheatre.org
Capacity: 158

LGBT Centre for Health & Wellbeing
9 Howe Street
Edinburgh EH3 6TE
{t} 0131 523 1100
brian@rememberwhen.org.uk
www.rememberwhen.org.uk

Library Theatre
Central Library
St Peter's Square
Manchester M2 5PD
{t} 0161 236 7110
ltc@library.manchester.gov.uk
www.librarytheatre.com
Capacity: 312
Founded: 1933

Library Theatre
St George's Square
Luton LU1 2NG
{f} 01582 547476
theatre@luton.gov.uk
www.luton.gov.uk/0xc0a80123%200x00022aa5

Lighthouse
Kingland Road
Poole BH15 1UG
{t} 01202 685222
info@pooleartscentre.co.uk
www.lighthousepoole.co.uk
Capacity: 669
Founded: 2002

Lighthouse
The Cubb Buildings
Fryer Street
Wolverhampton WV1 1HT
{t} 01902 716055
info@light-house.co.uk
www.light-house.co.uk

Lighthouse, The
32-34 The Shore, Leith
Edinburgh EH1 1QR
info@lthse.com
www.lthse.com

Lincoln Drill Hall
Free School Lane
Lincoln LN2 1EY
{t} 01522 873894
boxoffice@lincolndrillhall.com
www.lincolndrillhall.com/home

Lion and Unicorn Theatre
42-44 Gaisford Street
London NW5 2ED
{t} 020 7485 9897
act@provocateur.freeserve.co.uk
www.actprovocateur.net
Capacity: 45
Founded: 2002

Little Angel
14 Dagmar Passage
Cross Street
London N1 2DN
{t} 020 7226 1787
angel@puppettheatre.freeserve.co.uk
www.littleangeltheatre.com
Capacity: 100
Founded: 1961

Little Theatre
Dover Street
Leicester LE1 6PW
{t} 0116 255 1302
admin@thelittletheatre.net
www.thelittletheatre.net

Little Theatre
Hoghton Street
Southport PR9 0PA
www.littletheatresouthport.co.uk

Little Theatre Gateshead
Saltwell View
Gateshead
Tyne & Wear NE8 4JS
{t} 0191 478 1499
susanhighbury@tiscali.co.uk
www.littletheatregateshead.com

Live Theatre
27 Broad Chare
Quayside
Newcastle Upon Tyne NE1 3DQ
{t} 0191 232 1232
info@live.org.uk
www.live.org.uk
Capacity: 200
Founded: 1973

Liverpool Empire
Lime Street
Liverpool L1 1JE
www.livenation.co.uk/venues/venue.aspx?vrid=1115

Liverpool Institute for Performing Arts
Mount Street
Liverpool L1 9HF
{t} 0151 330 3000
{f} 0151 330 3131
performances@lipa.ac.uk
www.lipa.ac.uk
Capacity: 500
Founded: 1996

Liverpool Lighthouse
Oakfield Road
Anfield
Liverpool L4 0UF
{t} 0151 476 2342
info@liverpoollighthouse.com
Capacity: 700
Founded: 90

Liverpool Playhouse
5 - 9 Hope Street
Liverpool L1 9BH
{t} 0151 709 4776
{f} 0151 708 3701
info@everymanplayhouse.com
www.everymanplayhouse.com
Founded: 1866

Lochside Theatre
Lochside Road
Castle Douglas DG7 1EU
{t} 01556 504506
info@lochsidetheatre.co.uk
www.lochsidetheatre.co.uk
Capacity: 200

London Oratory Arts Center
Seagrave Road
London SW6 1RX
{t} 020 7385 0102

London Palladium
Argyll Street
London W1A 3AB
{t} 020 7494 5020
info@rutheatres.com
www.rutheatres.com
Capacity: 2298
Founded: 1910

London Venue, The
2a Clifton Rise, New Cross
London SE14 6JP
{t} 020 8692 4077
thelondon.venue@virgin.net
www.thelondonvenue.com

Long Paws Comedy Club
Chamberlain Street
Wells BA5 2PS
info@longpawscomedy.co.uk
www.longpawscomedy.co.uk

Longborough Festival Opera
Longborough
Moreton-in-Marsh GL56 0QF
{f} 01451 830605
enquiries@longboroughopera.com
www.longboroughopera.com
Capacity: 480

Lot, The
4 Grassmarket
Edinburgh EH1 2JU
{t} 0131 225 9922
info@the-lot.co.uk
www.the-lot.co.uk

Loughborough Town Hall
Market Place
Loughborough LE11 3EB
{t} 01509 231914
{f} 01509 240617
townhall@charnwood.gov.uk
www.loughboroughtownhall.co.uk

Lowry
Pier 8
Salford Quays
Manchester M50 3AZ
{t} 0161 876 2020
info@thelowry.com
www.thelowry.com
Capacity: 1730
Founded: 2000

LSO St Lukes
161 Old Street
London EC1V 9NG
{t} 020 7490 3939
lsostlukes@lso.co.uk

Ludlow Assembly Rooms
1 Mill Street
Ludlow
Shropshire SY8 1AZ

{t} 01584 813701
admin@ludlowassemblyrooms.co.uk
www.ludlowassemblyrooms.co.uk
Capacity: 291

Lyceum
Heath Street
Crewe CW1 2DA
{t} 01270 537333
jane.ashcroft@crewe-nantwich.gov.uk
www.lyceumtheatre.net
Capacity: 693
Founded: 1911

Lyceum
21 Wellington Street
London WC2E 7DA
{t} 0870 243 9000
venuebookings@clearchannel.co.uk
www.lyceum-theatre.co.uk
Capacity: 2107
Founded: 1834

Lyceum
Norfolk Street
Sheffield S1 1DA
{t} 0114 249 6000
info@sheffieldtheatres.co.uk

Lyme Park
Disley
Cheshire SK12 2NX
{t} 0870 428 8934
{f} 01663 765035
lymepark@nationaltrust.org.uk
www.nationaltrust.org.uk/main/w-vh/w-visits/w-findaplace/w-lymepark
Capacity: 700
Founded: 1947

Lymington Community Centre
New Street
Lymington SO41 9BQ
{t} 01590 672337
lymcomass@aol.com
www.lymingtoncommunitycentre.org.uk

Lyric
King Street
London W6 0QL
{t} 020 8741 2311
enquiries@lyric.co.uk
www.lyric.co.uk
Capacity: 555
Founded: 1895

Lyric Theatre, The
29 Shaftesbury Avenue
London W1D 7ES
{t} 020 7494 5842
enquiries@nimaxtheatres.com
Capacity: 1306
Founded: 1888

Lyth Arts Centre
by Wick
Caithness KW1 4UD
{t} 01955 641270
william246@btinternet.com
www.lytharts.org.uk

Lyttelton Theatre
National Theatre
South Bank
London SE19PX
{t} 020 7452 3000
info@nationaltheatre.org.uk
www.nationaltheatre.org.uk
Capacity: 898
Founded: 1976

M

Macclesfield Amateur Dramatic Society
Lord Street
Macclesfield
Cheshire SK11 6SY
info@madstheatre.org.uk
www.madstheatre.org.uk
Capacity: 193

MacPhail Centre
Mill Street
Ullapool IV26 2UN
{t} 01854 613336
macphail.centre@ullapoolhigh.highland.sch.uk
www.macphailcentre.co.uk
Capacity: 187
Founded: 2000

Mad George Tavern
373 Commercial Road
London E1 0LE
klubdada@yahoo.co.uk

Maddermarket Theatre
St. John's Alley
Norwich NR2 1DR
{t} 01603 620917
{f} 01603 661357
mmtheatre@btconnect.com
www.maddermarket.co.uk
Capacity: 310
Founded: 1921

Magna Science Adventure Centre
Sheffield Road
Templeborough
Rotherham S60 1DX
{f} 01709 820092
events@magnatrust.co.uk
www.visitmagna.co.uk/corporate/corporate.html

Majestic Theatre
Coronation Street
Retford
Notts DN22 6DX
{t} 01777 706866
majestictheatreuk@yahoo.co.uk
www.majestictheatre.co.uk
Capacity: 648
Founded: 1927

Maltings Arts Theatre
The Maltings
St Albans AL1 3HL
{t} 01727 844222
{f} 01727 836637
maltingsarts@leisureconnection.co.uk
Capacity: 139
Founded: 16

Maltings Concert Hall
Snape Bridge
Snape IP17 1SP
{t} 01728 687110
enquiries@aldeburgh.co.uk
www.aldeburgh.co.uk

Maltings Theatre and Arts Centre, The
Eastern Lane
Berwick-upon-Tweed TD15 1AJ
boxoffice@maltingsberwick.co.uk
www.maltingsberwick.co.uk
Capacity: 258

Malvern Theatres
Grange Road
Malvern
Worcestershire WR14 3HB

{f} 01684 893300
boxoffice@malvern-theatres.co.uk
www.malvern-theatres.co.uk/home1.shtml
Capacity: 800

Manchester Apollo
Ardwick Green, Stockport Road
Manchester M12 6AP
{t} 0870 401 8000
venuebookings@clearchannel.co.uk
www.livenation.co.uk/venues/venue.aspx?vrid=180

Manchester Opera House
Opera House
Quay Street
Manchester M3 3HP
{t} 0870 160 2874
info@livenation.co.uk
www.livenation.co.uk/manchester

Mansfield Traquair Centre
15 Mansfield Place
Edinburgh EH3 6BB
{t} 0131 555 8475
info@mansfieldtraquair.org.uk
mansfieldtraquair.org.uk

Marina Theatre, The
The Marina
Lowestoft
Suffolk NR32 1HH
info@marinatheatre.co.uk
www.marinatheatre.co.uk/index.html

Marine Hall
The Esplanade
Fleetwood
Lancashire FY7 6HF
{t} 01253 771141
{f} 01253 771141
marinehall@wyrebc.gov.uk
www.marinehall.co.uk
Capacity: 700
Founded: 1935

Marine Theatre
Church Street
Lyme Regis DT7 3QA
{t} 01392 277189
info@marinetheatre.com
www.marinetheatre.com
Capacity: 150

Market Harborough Drama Society
Church Square
Market Harborough
Leicester LE16 7NB
john@connect-jf.com
www.harboroughtheatre.com
Capacity: 117

Market Place
Market Street
Armagh City
Co. Armagh BT617AT
{t} 028 3752 1821
admin@themarketplace.com
www.marketplacearmagh.com
Capacity: 400

Market Theatre
6a Sun Street
Hitchin SG5 1AE
{t} 01462 433553
info@markettheatre.co.uk
www.markettheatre.co.uk
Capacity: 65

Market Theatre
Market Street
Ledbury HR8 2AQ
{t} 01531 633760
paul.graham.a7@pins.gsi.gov.uk

Marlborough Theatre
4 Princes Street
Brighton BN2 1RD
{t} 07782 278521
info@marlboroughtheatre.co.uk
www.marlboroughtheatre.co.uk
Capacity: 50

Marlowe Theatre
The Friars
Canterbury
Kent CT1 2AS
{t} 01227 787787
{f} 01227 479662
marlowetheatre@canterbury.gov.uk
www.marlowetheatre.com

Martlets Hall
Civic Way
Burgess Hill
West Sussex RH15 9NN
{t} 01444 242888
martletsboxoffice@midsussex.gov.uk
www.midsussex.gov.uk/page.cfm?pageid=2009

Mary Wallace Theatre
Embankment
Church Road
Twickenham TW1 3DU
{t} 020 8892 2565
mjsmith@a4u.com
www.rss-mwt.org.uk
Capacity: 96
Founded: 1934

Maskers Theatre Company
Unit 1
Emsworth Industrial Estate
Emsworth Road SO15 3LX
maskers.sec@maskers.org.uk
www.maskers.co.uk
Capacity: 476

Mayflower
Commercial Road
Southampton SO15 1GE
{t} 02380 711811
Dennis.Hall@mayflower.org.uk
www.the-mayflower.com
Capacity: 2208
Founded: 1920

McEwan Hall
Bristo Square
Edinburgh EH8 9AJ
{t} 0131 6628740
uoefo@ed.co.uk
www.uoefo.co.uk
Capacity: 2000
Founded: 1914

McManus Galleries
Albert Square
Dundee DD1 1PB
{t} 01382 432084
info@dundeereptheatre.co.uk
www.mcmanus.co.uk
Capacity: 200
Founded: 2006

Medina & Negociants
45 - 47 Lothian Street
Edinburgh EH1 1QR

Medina Theatre
Fairlee Road
Newport
Isle of Wight PO30 2DX
{f} 01983 822821
katie.smith@iow.gov.uk
www.medinatheatre.co.uk
Capacity: 425

Medway Little Theatre
256 High Street
Rochester ME1 1HY

feedback@mlt.org.uk
mlt.org.uk
Capacity: 108
Founded: 1958

Melton Theatre
Asfordby Road
Melton Mowbray
Leicestershire LE13 0HJ

Memorial Hall Theatre
Gladstone Road
Barry
South Wales CF62 8NA
nickbrit@easynet.co.uk

Menier Chocolate Factory
51/53 Southwark Street
London SE1 1TE
{t} 020 7378 1712
office@menierchocolatefactory.com
www.menierchocolatefactory.com
Capacity: 200
Founded: 1870

Mercury Theatre
Balkerne Gate
Colchester CO1 1PT
{t} 01206 577006
{f} 01206 769607
info@mercurytheatre.co.uk
www.mercurytheatre.co.uk
Capacity: 496
Founded: 1972

Merlin Theatre
Bath Road
Frome BA11 2HG
{t} 01373 465949
info@merlintheatre.co.uk
www.merlintheatre.co.uk
Capacity: 241
Founded: 1975

Mermaid, The
Puddle Dock
London EC4V 3DB
{t} 0870 780 9480
Capacity: 160

Merryfield Theatre
28 Vicarage Road
Verwood BH31 6DW
{t} 01202 828740
info@verwoodhub.org
www.verwoodhub.org
Capacity: 300
Founded: 2006

Met Arts Centre
Market Street
Bury BL9 0BW
{t} 0161 761 2216
post@themet.biz
www.themet.biz
Capacity: 240

Middlesbrough Theatre
The Avenue
Linthorpe
Middlesbrough TS5 6SA
{t} 01642 815181
david_lindsey@middlesbrough.gov.uk
www.middlesbrough.gov.uk/ccm/navigation/leisure-and-culture/arts-and-entertainment/theatres
Capacity: 486
Founded: 1957

Middlesbrough Town Hall
Albert Road
Middlesbrough TS1 1EL
unknown@remotegoat.co.uk
Capacity: 1300
Founded: 1889

Middleton Civic Centre
Fountain Street
Middleton M24 1AF
{t} 0161 643 2470
middleton.civic@virgin.net
www.middletoncivic.com

Midlands Arts Centre
Cannon Hill Park
Birmingham B12 9QH
{t} 0121 4403838
enquiries@macarts.co.uk
www.macarts.co.uk
Capacity: 201
Founded: 1964

Mill Arts Centre
Banbury OX16 5QE
{t} 01295 252050
info@millartscentre.org.uk
www.themillartscentre.co.uk/wps/wcm/connect/MillArts/Home
Capacity: 200
Founded: 1990

Millennium Forum
Newmarket Street
Derry BT48 6EB
{t} 028 7126 4455
info@millenniumforum.co.uk
www.millenniumforum.co.uk
Capacity: 367
Founded: 2000

Miller Centre Players, The
30 Godstone Road
Caterham
Surrey CR3 6RA
{t} 01883 349850
Webmail@chads.co.uk
Capacity: 198

Miller, The
96 Snowsfields Road
London Bridge
London SE1 3SS
{t} 020 7407 2690
mail@themiller.co.uk
www.themiller.co.uk
Capacity: 100

Millfield Theatre
Silver Street
Edmonton
London N18 1PJ
{t} 020 8887 7301
info@millfieldtheatre.co.uk
www.millfieldtheatre.co.uk
Capacity: 362
Founded: 1988

Milton at St Vincent
St Stephen Street
Edinburgh EH3 5AB
info@guthrieproductions.com
www.guthrieproductions.com

Milton Hall Studio Theatre
Milton Building, The University of Huddersfield
Queensgate
Huddersfield HD1 3DH
{t} 01484 478449
D.Wainwright@hud.ac.uk
www.hud.ac.uk/mh/drama
Capacity: 120
Founded: 2005

Milton Keynes Theatre
500 Marlborough Gate
Milton Keynes MK9 3NZ
{t} 020 7854 7000
stagedoormk@theambassadors.com
www.theambassadors.com/miltonkeynes/info/index.html

Capacity: 1376
Founded: 1999

Minack Theatre
Porthcurno
Penzance
Cornwall TR19 6JU
{t} 01736 810181
info@minack.com
www.minack.com
Capacity: 750
Founded: 1932

Miskin Theatre
Dartford DA1 2JT
{t} 01322629472
miskintheatre@mac.com
www.miskintheatre.com
Founded: 1915

Mission Theatre
32 Corn Street
Bath BA1 1UF
{t} 01225 428600
nextstagebath@aol.com
www.missiontheatre.co.uk

Mitchell Theatre
North Street
Glasgow G3 7DN
{f} 0141 221 0695
lil@csglasgow.org
Founded: 1877

Montgomery Theatre
Surrey Street
Sheffield S1 2LG
{t} 0114 272 0455
office@scec.org.uk
myweb.tiscali.co.uk/sheffcec/theatre.htm
Capacity: 400
Founded: 1886

Montrose Town Hall
Melville Gardens
Montrose DD10 8HG
{t} 01307 461461
cultural@angus.gov.uk
Capacity: 669

Morecambe Platform
Central Promenade
Morecombe LA4 4DB
www.lancaster.gov.uk/whatson/Content.asp?id=SXCE8B-A77FE628&cat=529

Morlan Centre
Queen's Road
Aberystwyth SY23 2HH
{t} 01970 617996
enquiries@morlan.org.uk
www.morlan.org.uk
Capacity: 200

Motherwell Concert Hall and Theatre
Civic Centre
Motherwell ML1 1TW
motherwellconcerthall@northlan.gov.uk
Founded: 394

Moulton Theatre
10 Cross Street
Moulton
Northampton NN3 7RZ
secretary.h@ukonline.co.uk
www.moulton-theatre.co.uk
Capacity: 71

Mountview
Clarendon Road
Wood Green N22 6XF
{t} 02088290036
www.mountview.ac.uk/general_information_level2.asp?level2_ID=65

Mumford Theatre
Anglia Polytechnic University
East Road
Cambridge CB3 9ED
{t} 01223 352932
info@anglia.ac.uk
web.apu.ac.uk/mumfordtheatre
Capacity: 266

Muni Arts Centre
Gelliwastad Road
Pontypridd CF37 2DP
{t} 01443 485934
enquiries@muniartscentre.co.uk
www.muniartscentre.co.uk

Municipal Hall
61 Albert Road
Colne BB8 0BP
{t} 01282 661 220
phil.storey@pendleleisuretrust.co.uk
www.pendleleisuretrust.co.uk

N

National Museum of Photography Film and Television
Bradford
Bradford BD1 1NQ
{t} 07811 368830
yorkshirefilmlab@hotmail.co.uk
www.yorkshirefilmlab.net
Capacity: 400
Founded: 2006

National Museum of Scotland
Chambers Street
Edinburgh EH1 1JF
info@nms.ac.uk
www.nms.ac.uk

Netherbow Theatre
Scottish Storytelling Centre
43-45 High Street
Edinburgh EH1 1SR
{t} 0131 556 9579
reception@scottishstorytellingcentre.com
Capacity: 99

Netherton Arts Centre
Northfield Road
Netherton
Dudley DY2 9ER
{t} 01384 812846
claire.starmer@dudley.gov.uk
www.dudley.gov.uk/education-and-learning/extra-curricular-activities/dudley-performing-arts/whats-on-offer/tailor-made-options/netherton-arts-centre
Capacity: 340

Nettlefold Hall, The
1-5 Norwood High Street
West Norwood
London SE27 9JX
{t} 020 7926 8070
{f} 020 7926 8071
thenettlefold@lambeth.gov.uk
Capacity: 175

Network Theatre
246a Lower Road
London SE1 8SJ
info@networktheatre.org
www.networktheatre.org

Neuadd Dwyfor
Styrd Penlan
Pwllheli LL53 5DN
{t} 01758 704088
sideau@gwynedd.gov.uk
Capacity: 354
Founded: 1902

New Ambassadors
West Street
London WC2H 9ND
{t} 020 7836 6111
newambassadorsmanager@theambassadors.com
www.newambassadors.com
Capacity: 403
Founded: 1913

New End Theatre
27 New End
London NW3 1JD
{t} 020 7794 0022
administration@newendtheatre.co.uk
www.newendtheatre.co.uk
Capacity: 84
Founded: 1974

New Greenham Arts
113 Lindenmuth Way
Newbury RG19 6HN
{t} 01635 817 480
administrator@ng-arts.org.uk
www.cornexchangenew.com
Capacity: 150
Founded: 1998

New London
Drury Lane
London WC2B 5PW
{t} 020 7405 0072
info@rutheatres.com
www.rutheatres.com
Capacity: 1106
Founded: 1973

New Nomad Theatre
Bishopsmead Parade
East Horsley KT24 6PF
{t} 01483 284717
lauren.fontham@talk21.com
www.nomadtheatre.com

New Players Theatre
Villiers Street
The Arches
London WC2N 6NG
{t} 08700 332626
info@newendtheatre.co.uk
www.newplayerstheatre.com
Capacity: 276
Founded: 1936

New Theatre
Park Place
Cardiff CF10 3LN
{t} 029 2087 8889
ntmailings@cardiff.gov.uk
www.newtheatrecardiff.co.uk

New Theatre Oxford
George Street
Oxford OX1 2AG
jamie.baskeyfield@livenation.co.uk
www.livenation.co.uk/venues/venue.aspx?vrid=648&&shortcut=oxford
Capacity: 1800

New Theatre Royal
Guildhall Walk
Portsmouth PO1 2DD
{t} 0239 264 9000
boxoffice@newtheatreroyal.com
www.newtheatreroyal.co.uk
Capacity: 320

New Theatre, The
Friars Gate
Exeter EX4 3QL
{t} 01392277189
cygnetarts@btinternet.com
Capacity: 70

New Venture Theatre
Bedford Place
Brighton BN1 2PT
{t} 01273 746118
info@newventure.org.uk
www.newventure.org.uk
Capacity: 180
Founded: 1841

New Vic
Etruria Road
Newcastle under Lyme ST5 0JG
{t} 01782 717962
admin@newvictheatre.org.uk
www.newvictheatre.org.uk
Capacity: 597
Founded: 1986

New Victoria Theatre
The Peacocks Centre
Woking
Surrey GU21 1GQ
www.theambassadors.com/newvictoria/index.html

New Wimbledon Theatre
The Broadway
Wimbledon
London SW19 1QG
{t} 0870 060 6646
wimbledonboxoffice@theambassadors.com
www.theambassadors.com/newwimbledon/info/index.html

New Wolsey Theatre
Civic Drive
Ipswich
Suffolk IP1 2AS
{t} 01473 295 900
webmaster@wolseytheatre.co.uk
www.wolseytheatre.co.uk
Capacity: 400

Newark Palace Theatre
Appletongate
Newark NG24 1JY
{t} 01636 655755
palace@nsdc.info
www.palacenewark.com/core.html

Newcastle Theatre Royal
100 Grey Street
Newcastle upon Tyne NE1 6BR
boxoffice@theatreroyal.co.uk
www.theatreroyal.co.uk

Newhampton Arts Centre
Dunkley St
Wolverhampton WV1 4AN
{t} 01902 572090
{f} 01902 572090
admin@newhamptonarts.co.uk
www.newhamptonarts.co.uk
Capacity: 120
Founded: 1999

Nightingale Club, The
Kent Street
Birmingham B5 6RD
{t} 0871 505 5000
simon.baker@nightingaleclub.co.uk
www.nightingaleclub.co.uk

Nightingale Theatre
29-30 Surrey St.
Brighton BN1 3PA
{t} 01273 702563
info@nightingaletheatre.co.uk
www.nightingaletheatre.co.uk
Capacity: 50

Noel Coward Theatre
St Martin's Lane
London WC2N 4AH
{t} 0870 950 0920
alberymanagers@delmack.co.uk

www.delfontmackintosh.co.uk/theatres/albery
Capacity: 886
Founded: 1903

Nomads Tent, The
21 St Leonard's Lane
Edinburgh EH8 9SH
{t} 0131 662 1612
info@nomadstent.co.uk
www.nomadstent.co.uk

Norden Farm Centre for The Arts
Altwood Road
Maidenhead SL6 4PF
{t} 01628 788997
admin@nordenfarm.org.uk
www.nordenfarm.org
Capacity: 225
Founded: 2000

Normansfield Hospital Theatre
2A Langdon Park
Richmond
Teddington TW11 9PS
{t} 020 8977 7558
lourda@landmarkartscentre.org
www.landmarkartscentre.org/hw/visual-arts.html
Founded: 1877

North Edinburgh Arts Centre
15a Pennywell Court Edinburgh
Edinburgh EH4 4TZ
info@northedinburgharts.co.uk
www.northedinburgharts.co.uk

North Wales Theatre
The Promenade
Penrhyn Crescent
Wales LL30 1BB
{t} 01492 872000
info@nwtheatre.co.uk
www.nwtheatre.co.uk
Capacity: 1500

Northbrook Theatre
Littlehampton Road
Goring by Sea
Worthing BN12 6NU
{f} 01903 606141
box.office@nbcol.ac.uk
www.northbrooktheatre.co.uk

Northcott Theatre
Stocker Road
Exeter
Devon EX4 4QB
{f} 01392 255835
admin@northcott-theatre.co.uk
www.northcott-theatre.co.uk/welcome1.shtml

Northern Stage
Barras Bridge
Newcastle NE1 7RH
{t} 0191 230 5151
info@northernstage.co.uk
www.northernstage.co.uk/AboutUs/tabid/53/Default.aspx

Norwich Arts Centre
Reeves Yard
St Benedict's Street
Norwich NR2 4PG
{t} 01603 660 352
boxoffice@norwichartscentre.co.uk
www.norwichartscentre.co.uk
Capacity: 120
Founded: 1980

Norwich Playhouse
42 - 58 St. George's Street
Norwich NR3 1AB
{f} 01603 617728
info@norwichplayhouse.co.uk
www.norwichplayhouse.org.uk/contact_us.php

Norwich Puppet Theatre
St James
Whitefriars, Norwich
Norfolk NR3 1TN
{f} 01603 617578
info@puppettheatre.co.uk
www.puppettheatre.co.uk
Capacity: 197
Founded: 1979

Norwich Theatre Royal
Theatre Royal
Theatre Street
Norwich NR2 1RL
{f} 01603 622777
boxoffice@theatreroyalnorwich.co.uk
www.theatreroyalnorwich.co.uk

Nottingham Arts Theatre
George Street
Nottingham NG1 3BE
boxoffice@artstheatre.org.uk
www.artstheatre.org.uk
Capacity: 321

Nottingham Playhouse
Wellington Circus
Nottingham NG1 5AF
{t} 01159474361
rosiep@nottinghamplayhouse.co.uk
www.nottinghamplayhouse.co.uk
Capacity: 800
Founded: 1962

Novello Theatre
2 High Street
Sunninghill
Berkshire SL5 9NE
{t} 01753 783 726
agengy2@redroofs.co.uk
www.novellotheatre.co.uk
Capacity: 160
Founded: 1987

Novello Theatre
The Aldwych
London WC2B 4LD
{t} 0870 950 0935
info@delfrontmackintosh.com
Capacity: 1060
Founded: 1905

Nuffield Theatre
University Road
Southampton SO17 1TR
{t} 023 8067 1771
info@nuffieldtheatre.co.uk
www.nuffieldtheatre.co.uk
Capacity: 500
Founded: 1964

Number 8
8 High Street
Pershore
Worcestershire WR10 1BG
{t} 01386 555488
enquiries@number8.org
www.number8.org

Oakengates Theatre
Limes Walk
Oakengates
Telford TF2 6EP
{t} 01952 619020

oakthea@wrekin.gov.uk
www.oakengates.ws
Capacity: 164
Founded: 1968

Oasthouse Theatre
Stafford Lane, Off High Street
Rainham
Kent ME8 8AG
www.oasthousetheatre.co.uk
Capacity: 72

Obie Theatre, The
60 The Crescent
Croydon CR0 2HN
{t} 020 8665 5242
admin@brit.croydon.sch.uk
www.brit.croydon.sch.uk
Capacity: 410

Octagon Theatre
Howell Croft South
Bolton BL1 1SB
{t} 01204 556505
{f} 01204 556502
karen.douglas@octagonbolton.co.uk
www.octagonbolton.co.uk
Capacity: 390
Founded: 1967

Octagon Theatre
Hendford
Yeovil BA20 1UX
{t} 01935 422884
octagontheatre@southsomerset.gov.uk
www.octagon-theatre.co.uk
Capacity: 626
Founded: 1974

Old Court Theatre
233 Springfield Road
Chelmsford
Essex CM2 6JT
{t} 01245 606505
info@ctw.org.uk
www.ctw.org.uk

Old Crown, The
33 New Oxford Street
London WC1A 1BH
tom@theoldcrownpublichouse.com
www.theoldcrownpublichouse.com
Capacity: 30

Old Fire Station
40 George Street
Oxford OX1 2AQ
{t} 01865 297170
venuebookings@clearchannel.co.uk
www.newburytheatre.co.uk/theatres/oldfire.htm
Capacity: 169

Old Hall Hotel
The Square
Buxton
Derbyshire SK17 6BD
{t} 01298 22841
{f} 01298 72437
info@oldhallhotelbuxton.co.uk
www.undergroundvenues.co.uk

Old Laundry Theatre
Crag Brow
Bowness-on-Windermere LA23 3BX
{t} 015394 88444 option 5
info@oldlaundrytheatre.com
www.oldlaundrytheatre.com
Capacity: 300
Founded: 1992

Old Market
Upper Market Street
Hove BN3 1AS
{t} 01273 736222
stephen.neiman@theoldmarket.co.uk
www.theoldmarket.co.uk
Founded: 1999

Old Red Lion
418 St John Street
London EC1V 4NJ
{t} 020 7833 3053
helenoldredlion@yahoo.co.uk
www.oldredliontheatre.co.uk
Capacity: 60
Founded: 1979

Old Rep Theatre
Station Street
Birmingham B5 4DY
{t} 0121 605 5116
{f} 0121 605 5121
oldrephelpdesk@birmingham.gov.uk
www.oldreptheatre.org.uk
Capacity: 378
Founded: 1913

Old Sorting Office
Barnes Pond
19-21 Station Road
London SW13 0LF
{t} 020 8876 9885
info@osoarts.org.uk
www.osoarts.org.uk
Capacity: 150
Founded: 2002

Old Town Hall
High Street
Hemel Hempstead HP1 3AE
{t} 01422 228091
othadmin@dacorum.gov.uk
www.dacorum.gov.uk/arts
Capacity: 234
Founded: 1805

Old Vic
The Cut
London SE1 8NB
{t} 0870 0606628
info@oldvictheatre.com
www.oldvictheatre.com
Capacity: 1077
Founded: 1818

Oldham Coliseum
Fairbottom Street
Oldham OL1 3SW
{t} 0161 624 2829
mail@coliseum.org.uk
www.coliseum.org.uk
Capacity: 750
Founded: 1887

Olivier Theatre
London SE1 9PX
{t} 020 7452 3000
boxoffice@nationaltheatre.org.uk
www.nt-online.org
Capacity: 1150
Founded: 1976

Olympus Theatre
Filton College
Bristol BS34 7AT
cpa@uwe.ac.uk
www.filton.ac.uk/swada/olympus/olympusFacilities.php

Open Air Theatre
Open Air Theatre
Inner Circle, Regent's Park
London NW1 4NR
{f} 020 7487 4562
www.openairtheatre.org

Oran Mor
Great Western Road
Glasgow G12 8QX
{t} 0141 357 6200
info@oran-mor.co.uk
www.oran-mor.co.uk
Capacity: 200
Founded: 2004

Orange Tree
1 Clarence Street
Richmond upon Thames TW9 2SA
{t} 020 8940 3633
admin@orange-tree.demon.co.uk
www.orangetreetheatre.co.uk
Capacity: 172
Founded: 1991

Orbital Art Space
150 Easter Road
Edinburgh EH7 5RL
{t} 07766 730054

Orchard Theatre
Home Gardens
Dartford DA1 1ED
{t} 01322 220000
orchard.boxoffice@dartford.gov.uk

Orkney Arts Theatre
Mill Street
Kirkwall KW15 1NL
{t} 01856 873151

Outside Scottish Arts Club
24 Rutland Square
Edinburgh EH1 2BW
info@rebustours.com
www.rebustours.com

Oval House Theatre
Oval House Theatre
52-54 Kennington Oval
London SE11 5SW
{t} 020 7582 0080
{f} 020 7820 0990
info@ovalhouse.com
www.ovalhouse.com
Capacity: 200
Founded: 1960

Oxford House Theatre
Derbyshire Street
London E2 6HG
{t} 020 77399001
info@oxfordhouse.org.uk
www.oxfordhouse.org.uk
Capacity: 200
Founded: 1884

Oxford Playhouse
Beaumont Street
Oxford OX1 2LW
{t} 01865 305305
admin@oxfordplayhouse.com
www.oxfordplayhouse.com
Capacity: 613
Founded: 1920

P

Paddington Studio Theatre
North Wharf Road
London W2 1LF
{t} 020 76418424
studiot@nwcschool.co.uk
Capacity: 100

Paisley Arts Centre
New Street
Paisley PA1 1EZ
{t} 01418871010
info@paisleyartscentre.co.uk
www.paisleyartscentre.co.uk

Palace Theatre
Shaftesbury Avenue
London W1V 8AY
{t} 020 7434 0909
info@rutheatres.com
www.palace-theatre.co.uk
Capacity: 1394
Founded: 1891

Palace Theatre
86A Fordhook Ave
London W5 3LR
{t} 020 8992 3732
kate@fordhook.fsnet.co.uk
www.mansfield.gov.uk/palacetheatre
Capacity: 750
Founded: 1910

Palace Theatre
Leeming Street
Mansfield
Nottinghamshire NG18 1NG
{f} 01623 412922
palacetheatremarketing@mansfield.gov.uk

Palace Theatre
Alcester Street
Redditch
Worcs B98 8AE
{t} 01527 65203
info.centre@redditchbc.gov.uk
www.redditchpalacetheatre.co.uk
Capacity: 399
Founded: 1913

Palace Theatre
Oxford Street
Manchester M1 6FT
{t} 0161 245 6600
manchester.boxoffice@livenation.co.uk
www.manchestertheatres.com/palac etheatre.htm
Capacity: 2600

Palace Theatre.
Palace Avenue
Paignton TQ3 3HF
{t} 01803 665800
info@palace-theatre.org.uk

Park and Dare Theatre
Station Road
Treorchy CF42 6UA
{f} 01443 776922
Capacity: 784

Parr Hall
Palmyra Square South
Warrington WA1 1BL
{t} 01925 443 229
parrhall@warrington.gov.uk
www.pyramid.org.uk
Founded: 1989

Pateley Bridge Playhouse
Church Street
Pateley Bridge HG3 5LB
website.lineone.net/~teddodsworth/hom e.htm
Capacity: 73

Paul Robeson Theatre
Centrespace
24 Treaty Centre
Hounslow TW3 1ES
{t} 020 8583 2345
prtBoxOffice@cip.org.uk
www.hounslow.info/page.aspx?pointerid=5C3CEF93564B4DD8B383B755425C4DA6&thelang=001lngdef
Capacity: 280

Paupers Pit
Paupers Pit
Buxton
Derbyshire SK17 6BD
{t} 07980 29 29 78

thepits@undergroundvenues.co.uk
www.undergroundvenues.co.uk
Capacity: 41

Pavilion
Promenade
Rhyl LL18 3AQ
{t} 01745 330000
garethowen@denbighshire.gov.uk
www.rhylpavilion.co.uk

Pavilion Theatre
Westover Road
Bournemouth BH1 2BU
{t} 01202 456400
boxoffice.bic@bournemouth.gov.uk

Pavilion Theatre
Union Place
Worthing
West Sussex BN11 1LG
theatres@worthing.gov.uk
www.worthingtheatres.co.uk
Capacity: 850171100
Founded: 1926

Pavilion Theatre
121 Renfield Street
Glasgow G2 3AX
{f} 0141 331 2745
manager@paviliontheatre.co.uk
www.paviliontheatre.co.uk

Pegasus Theatre
Magdalen Road
Oxford OX4 1RE
{t} 01865 722 851
patrick.martin@pegasustheatre.org.uk
www.pegasustheatre.org.uk/homepage.phtml
Capacity: 120

Pendley Manor Hotel
Cow Lane
Tring HP23 5QY
{t} 01442 891891
tom@tomattwood.co.uk
www.pendleyshakespearefestival.co.uk
Capacity: 700
Founded: 1945

Penrith Players Theatre
Auction Mart Lane
Penrith
Cumbria CA11 7JG
{t} 01768 865557
feedback@mlt.org.uk

Pentameters Theatre
The Three Horseshoes Pub
28 Heath Street
London NW3 6TE
{t} 020 7435 3648
info@pentameterstheatre.co.uk
www.pentameters.co.uk
Capacity: 60
Founded: 1968

People's Theatre Arts Centre
Stephenson Road
Heaton
Newcastle NE6 5QF
{t} 0191 265 5020
boxoffice@ptag.org.uk
ptag.org.uk/index.htm
Founded: 500

Performance Centre, The
Bretton Hall Campus
West Bretton
Wakefield WF4 4LG
{t} 0113 343 9245
boxoffice@theperformancecentre.co.uk
www.theperformancecentre.com
Founded: 2002

Perth Theatre
185 High Street
Perth PH1 5UW
{t} 01738 621 031
info@perththeatre.co.uk
www.horsecross.co.uk/index.php?option=content&task=view&id=40
Capacity: 480
Founded: 1901

Phoenix
110 Charing Cross Road
London WC2H OJP
{t} 020 7438 9600
pheonixmanager@theambassadors.com
www.theambassadors.com/london
Capacity: 1000
Founded: 1930

Phoenix
Station Road
Bordon
Hampshire GU35 0LR
{f} 01420 478700
info@phoenixarts.co.uk
www.phoenixarts.co.uk

Phoenix Arts
21 Upper Brown Street
Leicester LE1 5TE
{t} 0116 224 7700
Tech@phoenix.org.uk
www.phoenix.org.uk
Capacity: 262
Founded: 1963

Phoenix Theatre
Ivy House
94-96 North End Road
{t} 020 8457 5000
Golders Green NW11 7SX
admin@ljcc.org.uk

Phoenix Theatre
Beaconsfield Street
Blyth
Northumberland NE24 2DS
{t} 01670 367228
PhoenixBlyth@aol.com
phoenixtheatre1.homestead.com/PhoenixTheatre.html

Picadilly Downside
11 Woodcote Lane
Purley
Surrey CR8 3HB
{t} 07930 940710
aletha@lycos.co.uk
Capacity: 500
Founded: 1996

Piccadilly Theatre
Denman Street
London W1D 7DY
{t} 020 7369 1734
piccadillymanager@theambassadors.com
www.theambassadors.com/london
Capacity: 1199
Founded: 1928

Pitlochry Festival Theatre
Port-Na-Craig
Pitlochry PH16 5DR
{f} 01796 484 616
boxoffice@pitlochry.org.uk
www.pitlochry.org.uk

Place
17 Duke's Road
London WC1H 9PY
{t} 020 7121 1000
info@theplace.org.uk
www.theplace.org.uk
Founded: 1969

Playhouse
Northumberland Avenue
London WC2N 5DE
{t} 020 7839 4292
sarah@playhouse-theatre.fsbusiness.co.uk
www.theambassadors.com/london
Capacity: 819
Founded: 1882

Playhouse Theatre
115 Clare street
Northampton
Northamptonshire NN1 3LR
{t} 01604 627791
namdram@btopenworld.com
www.namdram.co.uk

Playhouse Theatre Cheltenham
Bath Road
Cheltenham
Glos GL53 7HG
{t} 01242 522852
info@playhousecheltenham.org
www.playhousecheltenham.org
Capacity: 226
Founded: 1945

Playhouse Theatre, The
The Playhouse
Anfield Road
Cheadle Hulme SK8 5EX
pete.dinsdale@act1theatre.co.uk
www.playersdramatic.co.uk
Founded: 1923

Playhouse, The
104 High Street
Whitstable CT5 1AZ
{f} 01227 275506
actorlee@btinternet.com
www.theplayhousewhitstable.co.uk

Plaza
Winchester Road
Romsey
Hampshire SO51 8JA
{t} 01794 523054
postmaster@plazatheatre.com
www.plazatheatre.com
Capacity: 246
Founded: 1930

Pleasance
Carpenters Mews
Islington
London N7 9EF
{t} 020 7619 6868
info@pleasance.co.uk
www.pleasance.co.uk
Capacity: 280
Founded: 1996

Pleasance
60 Pleasance
Edinburgh EH8 9TJ
{f} 0131 556 4472
festival@pleasance.co.uk
www.pleasance.co.uk
Capacity: 175

Plough Arts Centre
9-11 Fore Street
Great Torrington
Devon EX38 8HQ
{t} 01805 622552
www.plough-arts.org

Plymouth Pavilions
Millbay Road
Plymouth
Devon PL1 3LF
groupsales@plymouthpavilions.com
www.plymouthpavilions.com

Pocklington Arts Centre
Market Place
Pocklington
York YO42 2AR
info@pocklingtonartscentre.co.uk
www.pocklingtonartscentre.co.uk

Point, The
Leigh Road
Eastleigh SO50 9DE
{t} 0238 065 2333
thepointboxoffice@eastleigh.gov.uk
www.thepoint-online.co.uk
Capacity: 318
Founded: 1875

Polar Bear
30 Lisle Street
Soho
London WC2H 7BA
{t} 020 7479 7981
boxoftrickstheatre@yahoo.co.uk

Polka
240 The Broadway
Wimbledon
London SW19 1SB
{t} 020 8543 4888
info@polkatheatre.com
www.polkatheatre.com
Capacity: 300
Founded: 1979

Pomegranate
Corporation Street
Chesterfield S41 7TX
{t} 01246 345 222
pomegranate.theatre@chesterfield.gov.uk
www.pomegranatetheatre.co.uk
Capacity: 546
Founded: 1879

Pontardawe Arts Centre
Herbert Street
Pontardawe
Swansea SA8 4ED
webmaster@npt.gov.uk
Capacity: 450

Prema
South Street
Uley
Gloucestershire GL11 5SS
{t} 01453 860703
info@prema.demon.co.uk

Preston Guild Hall and Charter Theatre
Lancaster Road
Preston
Lancashire PR1 1HT
{t} 01772 203456
www.prestonguildhall.com
Capacity: 780

Priestley, The
Chapel Street
Little Germany
Bradford BD1 5DL
{t} 01274 82 06 66
{f} 01274 82 27 01
info@thepristley.org.uk
www.mypriestley.org.uk
Capacity: 290
Founded: 1929

Prince Charles Cinema
7 Leicester Place
London WC2H 1LB
{t} 0870 8112559
web@princecharlescinema.com
www.princecharlescinema.com
Founded: 1991

Prince Edward
Old Compton Street
London W1V 6HS
{t} 020 7447 5400
info@delfont-mackintosh.com
www.delfontmackintosh.co.uk/theatres/prince-edward
Capacity: 1631
Founded: 1930

Prince of Wales
31 Coventry Street
London W1V 8AS
{t} 020 7839 5972/5987
info@delfont-mackintosh.com
www.delfontmackintosh.co.uk/theatres/prince-of-wales
Capacity: 1160
Founded: 1937

Prince of Wales Centre
Church Street
Cannock WS11 1DE
{f} 01543 574439
princeofwales@cannockchasedc.gov.uk
www.cannockchasedc.gov.uk/princeofwales

Princes Hall
Princes Way
Aldershot GU11 1NX
{t} 01252 329155
dfphillips@rushmoor.gov.uk
www.princeshall.com/thetheatre.htm
Capacity: 593
Founded: 1973

Princes Theatre
Town Hall
Station Road
Clacton on Sea CO15 1SE
{t} 01255 868650
emorgan@tendringdc.gov.uk
www.tendringdc.gov.uk/TendringDC/Leisure/Arts+and+Entertainment/Princes+Theatre

Princess Royal Pavilion
Civic Centre
Port Talbot SA13 1PJ
{t} 01639 763 214
prtadmin@npt.gov.uk
www.npt.gov.uk/theatres
Capacity: 850
Founded: 1987

Princess Theatre
Torbay Road
Torquay TQ2 5EZ
{t} 01803 290290
venuebookings@clearchannel.co.uk
www.torbay.gov.uk/index/leisure/arts-culture/theatres/princesstheatre.htm
Capacity: 1494
Founded: 1961

Priory
Rosemary Hill
Kenilworth
Warwickshire CV8 1BN
{t} 01926 863334
chairman@priorytheatre.co.uk
www.priorytheatre.co.uk

Progress Theatre
The Mount
off Christchurch Road
Reading RG1 5HL
{t} 0870 774 3490
admin@progresstheatre.co.uk
www.progresstheatre.co.uk
Capacity: 98
Founded: 1947

Puppet Barge
78 Middleton Road
London E8 4BP
{t} 020 7249 6876
puppet@movingstage.co.uk

Purple Venues
L'Attache, 3 Rutland Street
Edinburgh EH1 2AE
info@purplevenues.com
www.purplevenues.com

Putney Arts Theatre
Ravenna Road
Putney
London SW15 6AW
{t} 020 8788 6943
mail@putneyartstheatre.org.uk
www.putneyartstheatre.org.uk
Capacity: 50
Founded: 1968

QEH
Jacobs Wells Road
Bristol BS8 1JX
{t} 0117 930 3082
bookings@qehtheatre.com
www.qehtheatre.com
Capacity: 210
Founded: 1847

Quaker Meeting House
7 Victoria Terrace
Edinburgh EH1 2JL
{t} 0131 225 4825
www.quakerscotland.org

Quay Theatre
Quay Lane
Sudbury
Suffolk CO10 2AN
{t} 01787 374745
quayfreeverse@yahoo.co.uk
www.quaytheatre.org.uk

Queen Mother Theatre
Woodside
Hitchin
Hertfordshire SG4 9YA
{t} 01462 434875
www.queenmothertheatre.org.uk

Queen's
University Road
Belfast BT7 1NN
{t} 028 9033 5005
elizabethmoore@qub.ac.uk

Queen's Hall
87-89 Clerk Street
Edinburgh EH8 9JG
{t} 0131 668 2019
admin@queenshalledinburgh.org
www.thequeenshall.net
Capacity: 900
Founded: 1840

Queen's Hall
Cranbrook School
Waterloo Road
Cranbrook TN17 3JD
{t} 01369 702800
yatesn@cranbrook.kent.sch.uk
www.cranbrookschool.co.uk/index.php?option=com_content&task=view&id=144&Itemid=198
Capacity: 350
Founded: 1976

Queen's Hall
Argyll Street
Dunoon
Argyll PA23 7HH

{f} info@queenshalldunoon.co.uk
info@queenshalldunoon.co.uk
www.queenshalldunoon.co.uk

Queens Park Arts Centre
Queens Park
Aylesbury
Buckinghamshire HP21 7RT
{f} 01296 337363
bookings@qpc.org
www.qpc.org
Capacity: 120

Queen's Theatre
Boutport Street
Barnstaple EX31 1SY
{t} 01271 32 42 42
info@northdevontheatres.org.uk
www.northdevontheatres.org.uk
Capacity: 800

Queen's Theatre
Billet Lane
Hornchurch RM11 1QT
{t} 01708 443333
info@queens-theatre.co.uk
www.queens-theatre.co.uk
Capacity: 503
Founded: 1953

Queen's Theatre
Shaftesbury Avenue
London W1D 6BA
{t} 020 7395 5240
info@rutheatres.com
www.delfont-mackintosh.com
Capacity: 990
Founded: 1907

Questors Theatre
12 Mattock Lane
Ealing
London W5 5BQ
{t} 020 8567 0011
{f} 020 8567 2275
editor@questors.org.uk
www.questors.org.uk
Capacity: 350
Founded: 1929

R

RADA Bar
Malet St
London WC1E 6ED
{t} 020 7636 7076
enquiries@rada.ac.uk
www.rada.org
Capacity: 120

Radlett Centre
1 Aldenham Avenue
Radlett
Herts WD7 8HL
{t} 01923 857546
{f} 01923 857592
admin@radlettcentre.com
www.radlettcentre.co.uk
Capacity: 300

Rae Macintosh Music
6 Queensferry Street
Edinburgh EH2 4PA
{t} 0131 225 1171

Raffles Members Club
287 Kings Road
Chelsea
London SW3 5EW
7915243140
ben@theeventsagency.com
Capacity: 250

Rag Factory, The
16-18 Heneage Street
London E1 5LJ
{t} 020 76508749
hello@ragfactory.org.uk
www.ragfactory.org.uk
Founded: 2006

Ramshorn Theatre
98 Ingram Street
Glasgow G1 1ES
{t} 0141 552 3489
{f} 0141 553 2036
ramshorn.theatre@strath.ac.uk
www.strath.ac.uk/culture/ramshorn
Capacity: 80
Founded: 1992

Reardon Smith Theatre
National Museum Cardiff
Cathays Park
Cardiff CF10 3NP
Capacity: 380
Founded: 1932

Red Rose Comedy Club
129 Seven Sisters Road
London N7 7QG
{t} 020 7281 3051
info@redrosecomedy.co.uk
www.redrosecomedy.co.uk
Capacity: 200
Founded: 2000

Redbridge Drama Centre
Church Fields
South Woodford
London E182RB
{t} 02085045451
rdc@redbridgedramacentre.co.uk
www.redbridgedramacentre.co.uk
Capacity: 100

Redgrave Theatre
2 Percival Road
Clifton
Bristol BS8 3LE
{t} 0117 315 7601
redgrave@clifton-college.avon.sch.uk
www.cliftoncollegeuk.com/ NetCommunity/Page.aspx?pid=214
Capacity: 323
Founded: 1966

Regal Theatre
10-16 The Avenue
Minehead TA24 5AY
{t} 01643 706 430
mail@regaltheatre.co.uk
www.regaltheatre.co.uk
Capacity: 410
Founded: 1980

Regent Centre
51 The High Street
Christchurch
Dorset BH23 1AS
{t} 01202 479 819
info@regentcentre.co.uk
www.regentcentre.co.uk
Capacity: 472
Founded: 1986

Regent Theatre
Piccadilly
Stoke-on-Trent ST1 1AP
{t} 0870 060 6649

Regent's Park
Regent's Park
London NW1 4NP
{t} 020 7486 2431
info@openairtheatre.org
www.openairtheatre.org
Capacity: 1187
Founded: 1932

Rhoda McGaw
The Ambassadors
Peacocks Centre
Woking GU21 6GQ
kevinshelfer@theambassadors.com
www.theambassadors.com/rhodamcgaw/info/index.html

Rhodes Arts Complex & Bishop's Stortford Museum
South Road
Bishop's Stortford
Hertfordshire CM23 3JG
info@rhodesbishopsstortford.org.uk
www.rhodesbishopsstortford.org.uk
Capacity: 349

Richmond Theatre
The Green
Richmond
Surrey TW9 1QJ
{f} 020 8948 3601
richmondboxoffice@theambassadors.com
www.theambassadors.com/richmond
Capacity: 850
Founded: 1899

Ripley Arts Centre
24 Sundridge Avenue
Bromley
Kent BR1 2PX
{t} 020 8464 5816
enquiries@bromleyarts.com

Riverfront Theatre
Bristol Packet Wharf
Newport NP20 1HG
{t} 01633 656 757
{f} 01633 257187
the.riverfront@newport.gov.uk
www.newport.gov.uk/riverfront
Capacity: 493
Founded: 2004

Riverhead Theatre
Louth Playgoers Society Limited
Victoria Road, Louth
Lincolnshire LN11 0BX
{t} 01507 600350
admin@louthplaygoers.co.uk
www.louthplaygoers.co.uk/Home.htm

Riverside Studios
Crisp Rd
Hammersmith
London W6 9RL
{t} 020 8237 1000
online@riversidestudios.co.uk
www.riversidestudios.co.uk
Capacity: 200
Founded: 1976

Robert Powell Theatre
Frederick Road Campus, University of Salford
Fredrick Road M5 4WT
{t} 0161 295 6120
I.Currie@salford.ac.uk
Capacity: 220
Founded: 1997

Robin Anderson Theatre, The
261 West Princes Street
Glasgow G4 9EE

Robin Hood Theatre
Church Lane
Averham
Newark NG23 5RD
info@robinhoodtheatre.co.uk
www.robinhoodtheatre.co.uk
Capacity: 150

Rocket
Lady Glenorchy's Church
Roxburgh Place
{t} 0871 750 0077
Edinburgh EH8 9EB
info@rocketvenues.com
www.rocketvenues.com

Roman Eagle Lodge
2 Johnston Terrace
Edinburgh EH1 2PW
info@komedia-rel.com
www.komedia-rel.com

Rondo Theatre
St Saviours Road
Larkhall
Bath BA16RT
{t} 01225 444003
andy@rondotheatre.co.uk
www.rondotheatre.co.uk
Capacity: 105
Founded: 1976

Roscoe Street Gallery
52 Roscoe Street
Liverpool L1 3BT
info@theartorganisation.co.uk

Rose Theatre
Edge Hill
St Helens Road
Ormskirk L39 4QP
{t} 01695 584480
rose@edgehill.ac.uk
www.edgehill.ac.uk/Sites/RoseTheatre/index.htm
Capacity: 204
Founded: 1960

Rose Theatre
Chester Road North
Broadwaters
Kidderminster DY10 2RX
{t} 01562 743745
admin@rosetheatre.co.uk
www.rosetheatre.co.uk
Capacity: 181
Founded: 1981

Rose Theatre
Rose Bruford College
Burnt Oak Lane
Sidcup DA15 9DF
{t} 020 8308 2600
{f} 020 8308 0542
Diane.Stacey@bruford.ac.uk
www.bruford.ac.uk/default.aspx

Rosehill Theatre
Moresby
Whitehaven CA28 6SE
{t} 01946 692422
rosehilltheatre@btopenworld.com
www.rosehilltheatre.co.uk
Capacity: 208
Founded: 1959

Rosemary Branch
2 Shepperton Road
London N1 3DT
{t} 020 7704 6665
{f} 020 7249 4786
cecilia@rosemarybranch.co.uk
www.rosemarybranch.co.uk
Capacity: 55
Founded: 1995

Roses Theatre
Sun Street
Tewkesbury
Gloucestershire GL20 5NX
boxo@rosestheatre.org
www.rosestheatre.org
Founded: 1974

Ross Bandstand
Princes Street Gardens West
Edinburgh EH1 1QR
info@tonthefringe.com
www.tonthefringe.com

Ross Theatre and Bandstand
West Princes Street Gardens
Edinburgh EH1 2EA
administration@edintattoo.co.uk
www.edinburgh.gov.uk/CEC/Recreation/Leisure/Ross_Theatre_and_Bandstand/Ross_Theatre_and_Bandstand.html
Capacity: 2000

Rotherham Arts Centre
Walker Place
Rotherham S65 1JH
{t} 01709 823621
Capacity: 200
Founded: 1976

Rotherham Civic Theatre
Catherine Street
Rotherham S65 1EB
{t} 01709 823640
jayne.globe@rotherham.gov.uk
www.rotherham.gov.uk

Rothes Halls
Rothes Square
Glenrothes
Fife KY7 5NX
{f} 01592 612220
admin@rotheshalls.org.uk
Capacity: 1500

Rothesay Pavilion
Argyle Street
Rothesay PA20 0AX
{t} 01700 504250
eileen.rae@argyll-bute.gov.uk
Capacity: 1250
Founded: 1938

Round Chapel
Round Chapel Old School Rooms
Powerscroft Rd
London E5 0PU
{t} 020 8533 9676
info@theroundchapel.org.uk
www.theroundchapel.org.uk
Capacity: 600

Roundhouse
Chalk Farm Road
London NW1 8EH
{t} 020 7424 9991
info@roundhouse.org.uk
www.roundhouse.org.uk
Capacity: 1800
Founded: 1846

Roundhouse
Ponds Forge
Sports Centre
Sheffield S1 2PZ
{t} 0114 223 3505
www.sheffieldcomedy.com/the_roundhouse.php

Roxy Art House
2 Roxburgh Place
Edinburgh EH8 9SU
{t} 0871 750 0077
info@roxyarthouse.com
www.roxyarthouse.com

Royal Academy of Music
Marylebone Road
London NW1 5HT
{t} 020 7873 7373
box.office@ram.ac.uk
www.ram.ac.uk/events
Founded: 1822

Royal Albert Hall
Kensington Gore
London SW7 2AP
{t} 020 7589 3203
sales@royalalberthall.com
www.royalalberthall.com
Capacity: 8000
Founded: 1871

Royal and Derngate
19-21 Guildhall Road
Northampton NN1 1DP
{t} 01604 624811
postbox@ntt.org.uk
www.royalandderngate.com
Capacity: 1200
Founded: 1983

Royal Concert and Conference Hall
Theatre Square
Nottingham NG1 5ND
{t} 0115 989 5555
enquiries@royalcentre-nottingham.co.uk
www.royalcentre-nottingham.co.uk
Capacity: 2499
Founded: 1865

Royal Court Theatre
1 Roe Street
Liverpool
Merseyside UK L1 1HL
{t} 0151 709 4321
boxoffice@rawhidecomedy.com
www.royalcourtliverpool.co.uk
Capacity: 1250
Founded: 1938

Royal Court Theatre
Royal Court
Sloane Square
London SW1W 8AS
{t} 020 7222 1234
info@royalcourttheatre.com
www.royalcourttheatre.com
Capacity: 411
Founded: 1956

Royal Exchange
St Ann's Square
Manchester M2 7DH
{t} 0161 833 9833
administrator@royalexchange.co.uk
www.royalexchange.co.uk
Capacity: 750
Founded: 1921

Royal Festival Hall
London SE1 8XX
{t} 0870 3800 400
customer@southbankcentre.co.uk
www.southbankcentre.co.uk/visiting-us/finding-your-way-around/royal-festival-hall
Capacity: 917
Founded: 1951

Royal Highland Centre, The
Ingliston
Edinburgh EH28 8AU
{t} 0131 335 6200
info@equestriantheatre.co.uk
www.royalhighlandcentre.co.uk

Royal Hippodrome
108-112 Seaside Road
Eastbourne BN21 3PF
{t} 01323 415500
boxoffice@eastbourne.gov.uk
Capacity: 643

Royal Lyceum
30b Grindlay Street
Edinburgh EH3 9AX
{t} 0131 248 4848
info@lyceum.org.uk

www.lyceum.org.uk
Founded: 1883

Royal Oak, The
Infirmary Street, South Bridge
Edinburgh EH1 1LT
{t} 0131 557 2976
info@royal-oak-folk.com
www.royal-oak-folk.com

Royal Opera House
Bow Street
Covent Garden
London WC2E 9DD
{t} 020 7304 4000
john.seekings@roh.org.uk
www.royaloperahouse.org.uk
Capacity: 2262
Founded: 1999

Royal Shakespeare Theatre
Waterside
Stratford-upon-Avon
Warwickshire CV37 6BB
{t} 01789 403444
info@rsc.org.uk
www.rsc.org.uk
Capacity: 1412

Royal Spa Centre
Newbold Terrace
Leamington Spa CV32 4HN
{t} 01926 334418
boxoffice@royal-spa-centre.co.uk
www.royal-spa-centre.co.uk
Capacity: 800
Founded: 1972

Royal Terrace Hotel
18 Royal Terrace Edinburgh
Edinburgh EH7 5AQ
{t} 0870 850 2608

Royal Welsh College of Music and Drama
Castle Grounds
Cardiff CF10 3ER
{t} 029 2039 1391
boxoffice@rwcmd.ac.uk
www.rwcmd.ac.uk
Capacity: 50
Founded: 1949

Royalty, The
25 The Royalty
Chester Road
Sunderland SR2 7PP
{t} 0111 565 7945
Slundy1045@aol.com
www.royaltytheatre.co.uk

RSC's Dell Theatre, The
Waterside
Stratford-upon-Avon
Warwickshire CV37 6BB
{t} 01789 403403
{f} 01789 403413
info@rsc.org.uk
www.rsc.org.uk
Capacity: 200

Rugby Theatre
Henry Street
Rugby CV21 2QA
{t} 01788 541234
www.rugbytheatre.co.uk
Capacity: 313

Ryde Studio Theatre
Ryde High School
Pell Lane, Ryde
Isle of Wight PO33 3LN
{t} 01883 567331
denman@rydehigh.iow.sch.uk
www.rydehigh.iow.sch.uk/?_id=427

Ryde Theatre
Lind Street
Ryde
Isle of Wight PO33 2NL
{t} 01883 568099
naomi.sondergaard@iow.gov.uk
www.rydetheatre.co.uk/default.aspx
Capacity: 500

S

Sadler's Wells
Rosebery Avenue
London EC1R 4TN
{t} 020 7863 8000
info@sadlerswells.com
www.sadlerswells.com
Capacity: 1560
Founded: 1683

Sage Gateshead
St Mary's Square
Gateshead Quays
Gateshead NE8 2JR
{f} 0191 443 4551
corin.mcewan@thesagegateshead.org
www.thesagegateshead.org

Salford Arts Theatre
Westerham Avenue
off Liverpool street
Salford M5 4TL
{t} 01619 250111
salfordartstheatre@msn.com
Capacity: 130

Salisbury Arts Centre
Bedwin Street
Salisbury
Wiltshire SP1 3UT
{t} 01722 321744
info@salisburyarts.co.uk
www.salisburyartscentre.co.uk
Founded: 1977

Salisbury Playhouse
Malthouse Lane
Wiltshire
Salisbury SP2 7RA
{t} 01722 320333
press@salisburyplayhouse.com
www.salisburyplayhouse.com
Capacity: 517
Founded: 1976

Sallis Benney Theatre
University of Brighton
Grand Parade
Brighton BN2 0JY
g.wilson@bton.ac.uk
www.brighton.ac.uk/gallery
Capacity: 242

Savoy Theatre
Savoy Court
London WC2R OET
{t} 0870 1648787
savoytheatre@hotmail.com
www.thisistheatre.com/londontheatre /savoytheatre.html
Founded: 1881

Savoy Theatre
Church Street
Monmouth NP25 3BU
{t} 01600 750488
info@savoytrust.org.uk
Capacity: 400

Scottish Mask and Puppet Centre
8-10 Balcarres Avenue
Kelvindale
Glasgow G12 0QF
{f} 0141 357 44840141 357 4484

info@scottishmaskandpuppetcentre.co.uk
www.scottishmaskandpuppetcentre.co.uk
Capacity: 250

Scottish Storytelling Centre
43-45 High Street
Edinburgh EH1 1SR
{t} 0131 556 1579
reception@scottishstorytellingcentre.com
www.scottishstorytellingcentre.co.uk

SCR, University of Ulster
Magee
Derry BT48 7JL
{t} 028 713 75658
n.pearce@ulster.ac.uk
Capacity: 30

Secombe Theatre, The
42 Cheam Road
Sutton SM1 2SS
{t} 020 8770 6990
kate.puleston@sutton.gov.uk
www.suttontheatres.co.uk

Sevenoaks Playhouse
London Road
Sevenoaks TN13 1ZZ
{t} 01732 743306
playhouse@kinocinemas.co.uk
www.kinocinemas.co.uk/so
Capacity: 450

Shaftesbury Theatre
210 Shaftesbury Avenue
London WC2H 8DP
{t} 07000 211221
info@toc.dftentertainment.co.uk
Capacity: 1406
Founded: 1911

Shakespeare's Globe
21 New Globe Walk
London SE1 9DT
{t} 020 7401 9919
info@shakespearesglobe.com
www.shakespeares-globe.org
Capacity: 1500
Founded: 1400

Shanbrook Mill Theatre
Mill Road
Sharnbrook
Bedford MK44 1NP
{f} 01234 325358
info@sharnbrookmilltheatre.co.uk
www.sharnbrookmilltheatre.co.uk
Founded: 1979

Shanklin Theatre
Prospect Road
Steephill Road
Shanklin PO37 6AJ
{f} 01883 527267
chris.gardner@shanklintheatre.co.uk

Shaw Theatre
100 - 110 Euston Road
London NW1 2AJ
{t} 020 7388 2555
{f} 020 7388 7555
info@theshawtheatre.com
www.theshawtheatre.com
Capacity: 446
Founded: 1998

Sheldonian Theatre
University of Oxford
Broad Street
Oxford OX1 3AZ
{f} 01865 277295
custodian@sheldon.ox.ac.uk
Capacity: 1000
Founded: 16648

Shepherds Bush Empire
Shepherds Bush Green
London W12 8TT
{f} 020 8743 5384
mail@shepherds-bush-empire.co.uk

Sheringham Little Theatre
2 Station Road
Sheringham
Norfolk NR26 8RE
{t} 01263 822347
enquiries@sheringhamlittletheatre.com
www.sheringhamlittletheatre.co.uk

Sherman Theatre
Senghennydd Road
Cardiff CF24 4YE
{t} 029 2064 6900
boxoffice@shermantheatre.demon.co.uk

Ship Theatre, The
Hollybush Lane
Sevenoaks
Kent TN13 3UL
{t} 01732 454227
bursar@walthamstow-hall.co.uk
www.walthamstow-hall.co.uk/walthamstowhall/DisplayArticle.asp?ID=2829

Shipley Country Park
off Slack Road
Heanor
Derbyshire DE75 7GX
{t} 01773 719961
{f} 01773 715023
call.centre@derbyshire.gov.uk
www.derbyshire.gov.uk/leisure/countryside/parks_sites/country_parks/shipley.asp

Shire Hall
11 Market Place
Howden DN14 7BJ
www.howden-live.com/THE-SHIRE-HALL
Capacity: 200

Shrewsbury Music Hall
The Square
Shrewsbury SY1 1LH
{t} 01743 281281
mail@musichall.co.uk

Shunt Vaults
20 Stainer Street
London SE1 9RL
{t} 020 7378 7776
{f} 020 7378 7776
events@shunt.co.uk
www.shunt.co.uk

Sir John Mills
Gateacre Road
Ipswich IP1 2LQ
{t} 01473 211498
admin@easternangles.co.uk
www.easternangles.co.uk
Capacity: 120
Founded: 1988

Soho Theatre
21 Dean Street
London W1D 3NE
{t} 0870 429 6883
{f} 020 7287 5061
mail@sohotheatre.com
www.sohotheatre.com
Founded: 2000

Solihull Arts Complex
Homer Road
Solihull B91 3RG
{t} 0121 7046962

artscomplex@solihull.gov.uk
www.solihull.gov.uk/arts
Capacity: 339
Founded: 1976

Sound
Swiss Centre
10 Wardour Street
London W1D 6QF
{t} 020 7287 1010
info@soundlondon.com
www.soundlondon.com
Capacity: 130
Founded: 2005

South Hill Park & Wilde Theatre
Ringmead
Bracknell
Berkshire RG12 7PA
{t} 01344 484 858
{f} 01344 411 427
admin@southhillpark.org.uk
www.southhillpark.org.uk
Capacity: 330
Founded: 1973

South Holland Centre
Market Place
Spalding
Lincolnshire PE11 1SS
{t} 01775 764777
shcentre@sholland.gov.uk
www.southhollandcentre.co.uk

South London Gallery
65 Peckham Road
SE5 8UH
{t} 020 7703 6120
mail@southlondongallery.org
www.southlondongallery.org

South London Theatre
2a Norwood High Street
London SE27 9NS
{t} 020 8670 3474
info@southlondontheatre.co.uk
www.southlondontheatre.co.uk
Capacity: 60
Founded: 1881

South Street Arts Centre
21 South Street
Reading RG1 4QU
{t} 01189015234
boxoffice@readingarts.com
www.readingarts.com
Capacity: 120

Southend Palace Theatre
430 London Road
Southend-on-Sea SS0 9LA
{t} 01702 351135
info@palacetheatrewestcliff.co.uk
Capacity: 600
Founded: 1912

Southport Dramatic Club
Little Theatre
Hoghton Street
Southport PR9 0PA
sdcoffice@supanet.com
www.littletheatresouthport.co.uk
Capacity: 396

Southport Arts Centre
Lord Street
Southport
Merseyside PR8 1DB
{t} 01704 540011
christopher.wells@leisure.sefton.gov.uk
www.seftonarts.co.uk
Capacity: 472

Southport Theatre & Floral Hall Complex
Promenade
Southport PR9 0DZ
{t} 01704 540404
southporttheatre@clearchannel.co.uk
www.getlive.co.uk/southport
Capacity: 1200
Founded: 1930

Southside
117 Nicholson Street Edinburgh
Edinburgh EH8 9ER
info@southside-venue.com
www.southside-venue.com

Southwark Playhouse
62 Southwark Bridge Road
London SE1 0AS
{t} 020 7620 3494
admin@southwarkplayhouse.co.uk
www.southwarkplayhouse.co.uk
Capacity: 90
Founded: 1993

Southwick Barn Theatre
24 Southwick Street
Southwick
West Sussex BN42 4TE
{t} 01273 592819
enquiries@southwickcommunitycentre.org.uk
www.southwickcommunitycentre.org.uk
Capacity: 160
Founded: 1950

Spa Pavilion
Undercliff Road West
Felixstowe IP11 8AQ
{t} 0870 145 1151
bridget.rutherford@clearchannel.co.uk
Capacity: 905

Space
269 West Ferry Road
London E14 3RS
{t} 020 7515 7799
adam@space.org.uk
www.space.org.uk
Capacity: 520
Founded: 1994

Space
Lansdown
Stroud
Gloucestershire GL5 1BN
{t} 01453 767576
info@the-space.org
www.the-space.org
Capacity: 150

Spielgeltent
George Square Gardens
Edinburgh EH8 9LH
contact@spiegeltent.net
www.spiegeltent.net

Spilsby Theatre
Church Street
Spilsby PE23 5DY
{t} 01790 752136
www.spilsby.info/theatre

Spinney Hill Theatre
Northampton School
Spinney Hill Road
Northamptonshire NN3 6DG
{t} 01604 624811
postbox@ntt.org.uk
www.royalandderngate.com

Square Chapel
10 Square Road
Halifax HX1 1QG
{t} 01422 349422
info@squarechapel.co.uk

www.squarechapel.co.uk
Capacity: 280
Founded: 1772

St Andrews Crypt
St Andrews Church
Holborn Circus
London EC4A 3AB
{t} 020 7583 3498
AnnelieseC@standrewholborn.org.uk
Capacity: 100
Founded: 2003

St George's Bristol
Great George Street
off Park Street
Bristol BS1 5RR
{t} 0117 923 0359
administration@stgeorgesbristol.co.uk
www.stgeorgesbristol.co.uk
Capacity: 562
Founded: 1976

St George's Concert Hall
Bridge Street
Bradford BD1 1JS
{t} 01274 432000
Administration@bradford-theatres.co.uk
www.bradford-theatres.co.uk/stgeorges.asp
Capacity: 1671
Founded: 1984

St Martin's Theatre
West Street
Cambridge Circus
London WC2H 9NZ
{t} 0870 162 8787
www.vpsmvaudsav.co.uk

St Mary's Cathedral
Palmerston Place
Edinburgh EH12 5AW
info@cathedral.net
www.cathedral.net

St Ninian's Hall
Comely Bank Road Comely Bank
Edinburgh EH4 1AW
stninian@dioceseofedinburgh.org
www.stninians-edinburgh.org.uk

St Oswald's Hall
Montpelier Park Edinburgh
Edinburgh EH10 4LX
{t} 0131 220 3234

St Stephen's
Rosslyn Hill
London NW3 2PP
{t} 08700 600 100
info@richardiii.co.uk
www.richardiii.co.uk

Stables
Stockwell Lane
Wavendon
Milton Keynes MK17 8LT
{t} 01908 583928
stables@stables.org
www.stables.org
Capacity: 396
Founded: 1969

Stables at Prestonfield, The
Prestonfields, Prestonfield Rd
Edinburgh EH16 5UT

Stables Theatre and Art Centre
The Bourne
Hastings TN34 3EY
{t} 01424 423221
info@stables-theatre.co.uk
Capacity: 160

Stafford Gatehouse Theatre
Eastgate Street
Stafford ST16 2LT
{t} 01785 254653
gatehouse@staffordbc.gov.uk
www.staffordgatehousetheatre.co.uk/theatre/boxofficeandbooking.php

Stahl Theatre
West Street
Oundle PE8 4EJ
{t} 01832 273 930
stahl@oundle.co.uk
www.oundleschool.org.uk/arts/theatre/index.php
Founded: 1980

Stamford Arts Centre
27 St Mary's Street
Stamford PE9 2DL
{t} 01780 763203
boxoffice@stamfordartscentre.com
www.stamfordartscentre.com/phase1asp/default.asp

Stand Comedy Club II, The
16 North St Andrew Street
Edinburgh EH2 1HJ
{t} 0131 558 7272
info@thestand.co.uk
www.thestand.co.uk

Stantonbury Campus Theatre
Purbeck
Stantonbury
Milton Keynes MK14 6BN
{t} 01908 224 234
theatre@stantonbury.org.uk
www.stantonbury.org.uk
Capacity: 260
Founded: 1974

Stanwix Arts Theatre
Cumbria Institute of the Arts
Brampton Road
Carlisle CA3 9AY
{t} 01228 400300
ArtsDev@tulliehouse.co.uk
Founded: 1991

Station Theatre
Station Road
Hayling Island
Hampshire PO11 0EH
{t} 023 1246 6363
hayling_drama@which.net
www.hants.gov.uk/hayling_dramatics

Stephen Joseph
Westborough
Scarborough
North Yorkshire YO11 1JW
{t} 01723 370541
response@sjt.uk.com
www.sjt.uk.com
Capacity: 404
Founded: 1936

Sterts Theatre
Upton Cross
Liskeard
Cornwall PL14 5AZ
{t} 01579 362382
sterts@btinternet.com
www.sterts.co.uk

Stockport Garrick Theatre
Exchange Street
Wellington Road South
Cheshire SK3 0EJ
webmaster@stockportgarrick.co.uk
www.stockportgarrick.co.uk
Capacity: 155

Stockport Plaza
Mersey Square
Stockport SK1 1SP
{f} 0161 480 3818
boxoffice@stockportplaza.co.uk
www.stockportplaza.co.uk

Stockton Arc
Dovecot Street
Stockton on Tees TS18 1LL
{t} 01642 522199
box.office@arconline.co.uk

Stoke on Trent Repertory Theatre
Leek Road
Stoke-on-Trent ST4 2TR
www.stokerep.org.uk

Stratford Circus
Theatre Square
Stratford
London E15 1BX
{t} 020 8279 1000
info@stratford-circus.com
www.stratford-circus.com
Capacity: 512
Founded: 2001

Strode Theatre
Strode College
Church Road
Street BA16 0AB
{t} 01458 442 846
info@strodetheatre.co.uk
www.strodetheatre.co.uk
Capacity: 393
Founded: 1963

Studio Salford
11 Bloom St
Salford
Manchester M3 6AN
{t} 0161 839 8726
reservation@studiosalford.com
www.studiosalford.com
Capacity: 60
Founded: 2003

Studio Theatre
20 University Square
Belfast BT7 1PA
{t} 028 9097 1097
m.b.kelly@qub.ac.uk
www.queensfilmtheatre.com
Capacity: 120
Founded: 2004

Sunderland Empire
High Street West
Sunderland SR1 3EX
{t} 0191 520 5555
Paul.Ryan@LiveNation.co.uk
www.visitsunderland.com/culture/empire.html
Capacity: 2000
Founded: 1907

Sundial Theatre
Cirencester College
Stroud Road
Cirencester GL7 1XA
{t} 01285 654228
boxoffice@cirencester.ac.uk
www.cirencestercollege.org.uk/live/index.php?option=com_content&task=category§ionid=7&id=43&Itemid=196
Capacity: 130

Sutton Arts Theatre
South Parade
Sutton Coldfield
West Midlands B72 1QU
{t} 0121 355 5355
info@suttonartstheatre.co.uk

Swan
The Moors
Worcester WR1 3EF
{t} 01905 611427
swan_theatre@lineone.net
www.huntingdonarts.com
Capacity: 350
Founded: 2003

Swan, The
Waterside
Stratford-upon-Avon CV37 6BB
{f} 01789 403413
ticketqueries@rsc.org.uk
Founded: 1879

Swan, The
138 Park Street
Yeovil
Somerset BA20 1QT
{t} 01935 845946
william.scott-robinson@virgin.net
www.swan-theatre.co.uk
Founded: 1969

Sweet ECA
Lauriston Place/Lady Lawson Street
Edinburgh EH3 9DF
{t} 0870 241 0136
info@sweet-uk.net
www.sweet-uk.net
Capacity: 180

Sweet Grassmarket
61 Grassmarket
Edinburgh EH1 3JT
info@sweet-uk.net
www.sweet-uk.net/venues/shows/where.htm

Swindon Arts Centre
Devizes Road
Swindon
Wilts SN1 4BJ
{t} 01793 614837
artscentre@swindon.gov.uk
Capacity: 428
Founded: 1863

T

Tabard Theatre
2 Bath Road
Chiswick
London W4 1LW
{t} 020 8994 5985
tabard.theatre@virgin.net
freespace.virgin.net/tabard.theatre
Capacity: 50
Founded: 1986

Tabernacle
Heol Penrallt
Machynlleth
Powys SY20 8AJ
{f} 01654 702160

Tacchi-Morris Arts Centre
School Road
Monkton
Taunton TA2 8PD
{t} 01823 414144
info@tacchi-morris.com
Capacity: 250

Talbot Rice Gallery
University of Edinburgh
Old College, South Bridge
Edinburgh EH8 9YL
info@trg.ed.ac.uk
www.trg.ed.ac.uk
Founded: 1975

Taliesin Arts Centre
University of Wales Swansea
Singleton Park
Swansea SA2 8PZ
{t} 01792 296883
s.e.crouch@swansea.ac.uk
www.taliesinartscentre.co.uk
Capacity: 330
Founded: 1984

Talisman Theatre and Arts Centre
Barrow Road
Kenilworth CV8 1EG
talisman.theatre@btinternet.com
www.talismantheatre.co.uk

Tameside Hippodrome
Oldham Road
Ashton-Under-Lyne OL6 7SE
{t} 0161 308 3223
karen.whittick@clearchannel.co.uk
www.ticketmaster-direct.co.uk

Tara Arts
356 Garratt Lane
London SW18 4ES
{f} 020 8870 9540
tickets@tara-arts.com

Taurus Bar
1 Canal St
Manchester M1 3HE
{t} 01612364593
info@taurus-bar.co.uk
www.taurus-bar.co.uk
Capacity: 45

Terry O'Toole Theatre, The
Moor Lane
North Hykeham
Lincolnshire LN6 9AX
{t} 01522 883311
{f} 01522 883366
terryotoole@leisureconnection.co.uk
www.terryotooletheatre.org.uk
Capacity: 158268
Founded: 2002

Thame Youth Theatre
Thame A/L
Lord Williams School
Thame OX9 3NW
{f} 01844 213114
thameyouththeatre@fsmail.co.uk
www.thameyouththeatre.co.uk
Capacity: 200

Thameside
Orsett Road
Grays
Essex RM17 5DX
{t} 01375 382 555
mallinson@thurrock.gov.uk
www.thurrock.gov.uk/theatre
Capacity: 323

Theatr Brycheiniog
Canal Wharf
Brecon
Powys LD3 7EW
{t} 01874 611622
enquiries@brycheiniog.co.uk
www.theatrbrycheiniog.co.uk

Theatr Colwyn & Cinema
Abergele Rd
Colwyn Bay
Conwy LL29 7RU
jean.bilsland@conwy.gov.uk
www.theatrcolwyn.co.uk
Founded: 1800

Theatr Fach
Cymdeithas Ddrama Llangefni
Pencraig
Llangefni LL77 7LA
www.theatrfach.co.uk
Capacity: 100

Theatr Felinfach
Dyffryn Aeron
Ceredigion SA48 8AF
{f} 01570 471030
theatrfelinfach@ceredigion.gov.uk

Theatr Gwynedd
Fford Deiniol
Bangor LL57 2TL
{t} 01248 351708
theatr@theatrgwynedd.co.uk
www.theatrgwynedd.co.uk
Capacity: 348
Founded: 1975

Theatr Mwldan
Bath House Road
Cardigan SA43 1JY
{t} 01239 623920
{f} 01239 613600
dilwyn@mwldan.co.uk
www.mwldan.co.uk
Capacity: 1146
Founded: 1992

Theatre 503
Latchmere Pub
503 Battersea Park Road
London SW11 3BW
{t} 020 7978 7040
info@theatre503.com
www.theatre503.com
Founded: 1982

Theatre by the Lake
Lakeside
Keswick CA12 5DJ
{t} 01768 772 282
enquiries@theatrebythelake.com
www.theatrebythelake.com
Capacity: 385
Founded: 1999

Theatre in the Mill
Shearbridge Road
Bradford BD7 1DP
{t} 01274 233188
theatre@bradford.ac.uk
www.bradford.ac.uk/admin/theatre
Capacity: 140
Founded: 2003

Theatre On The Steps
Stoneway Steps
Bridgnorth WV16 4BD
{t} 01746 763257
admin@theatreonthesteps.co.uk
www.theatreonthesteps.co.uk
Founded: 1962

Theatre Royal
The Guildhall
Guildhall Street
Bury St Edmunds IP33 1QF
{t} 01284 769505
booking@theatreroyal.org
www.theatreroyal.org
Founded: 1819

Theatre Royal
Drury Lane
Catherine Street
London WC2B 5JF
{t} 0870 895 5505
info@rutheatres.com
www.wayahead.com/useful/venues/dru.asp

Capacity: 2237
Founded: 1663

Theatre Royal
Aldwych
London WC2B 5LD
{t} 020 7930 8800
info@delfont-mackintosh.com
www.trh.co.uk
Capacity: 890
Founded: 1821

Theatre Royal
Corporation Street
St Helens WA10 1LQ
{t} 01744 756000
info@sthelenstheatreroyal.co.uk
www.sthelenstheatreroyal.co.uk
Capacity: 700

Theatre Royal
Gerry Raffles Square
London E15 1BN
{t} 020 8534 7374
theatreroyal@stratfordeast.com
www.stratfordeast.com
Capacity: 460
Founded: 1884

Theatre Royal
32 Thames Street
Windsor
Berkshire SL4 1PS
{t} 01753 853 888
{f} 01753 831673
info@theatreroyalwindsor.co.uk
www.theatreroyalwindsor.co.uk
Capacity: 633
Founded: 1793

Theatre Royal
St Leonards Place
York YO1 9TL
{t} 01904 623568
{f} 01904 550164
marketing@yorktheatreroyal.co.uk
www.yorktheatreroyal.co.uk
Capacity: 900
Founded: 1744

Theatre Royal
Shakespeare Street
Dumfries DG1 2JH
{t} 01387 254209
info@theatreroyaldumfries.co.uk
Capacity: 220
Founded: 1792

Theatre Royal
Theatre Royal
Sawclose
Bath BA1 1ET
{t} 01225 448844
{f} 01225 444080
boxoffice@theatreroyal.org.uk
www.theatreroyal.org.uk
Founded: 1805

Theatre Royal
New Road
Brighton
Sussex BN1 1SD
{t} 01273 764 400
{f} 01273 764412
brightonstagedoor@theambassadors.com
Capacity: 1000
Founded: 1806

Theatre Royal
Royal Parade
Plymouth PL1 2TR
{t} 01752 267222
info@theatreroyal.com
www.theatreroyal.com
Capacity: 1200
Founded: 1811

Theatre Royal
Jewry Street
Winchester SO23 8SB
{t} 01962 840440
info@theatre-royal-winchester.co.uk
www.theatre-royal-winchester.co.uk
Founded: 1850

Theatre Royal Lincoln
Clasketgate
Lincoln LN2 1JJ
{f} 01522 526576
trl@dial.pipex.com
www.theatreroyallincoln.com

Theatre Royal Margate
Addington Street
Margate
Kent CT9 1PW
Mailinglist@trm-marketing.fsnet.co.uk

Theatre Workshop
34 Hamilton Place
Edinburgh EH3 5AX
{t} 0131 226 5425
mail@twe.org.uk
www.theatre-workshop.com
Founded: 1965

Theatro Technis
26 Crowndale Road
London NW1 1TT
{t} 020 7387 6617
{f} 020 7383 2545
info@theatrotechnis.co.uk
www.theatrotechnis.com
Capacity: 120
Founded: 1906

Third Floor Arts Centre
Central Library
Guildhall Square
Portsmouth PO1 2DX
{t} 023 9268 8070
arts@portsmouthcc.gov.uk
www.portsmouth.gov.uk/living/867.html
Capacity: 120

Thoresby Park
Nr Ollerton
Newark
Nottinghamshire NG22 9EP
gallery@thoresby.com
www.thoresby.com

Thwaites Empire
Aqueduct Road
Ewood
Blackburn BB2 4HT
{t} 01254 680137
thwaitestheatre@yahoo.co.uk
www.thwaitestheatre.co.uk

Titchfield Abbey
Mill Lane
Titchfield PO15 5RA
{t} 01202 456456
info@shakespeareattheabbey.com
www.shakespeareattheabbey.com
Capacity: 200

Tivoli Theatre
West Borough
Wimborne Minster
Dorset BH21 1LT
{t} 01202 885566
boxoffice@tivoliwimborne.co.uk

Tobacco Factory
Raleigh Road
Bedminster BS3 1TF
{t} 0117 902 0344
admin@tobaccofactory.com
www.tobaccofactory.com
Capacity: 50
Founded: 1995

Tolbooth
Jail Wynd
Stirling FK8 1DE
{f} 01786 27 4001
tolbooth@stirling.gov.uk

Tonbridge Oast Theatre
London Road
Tonbridge
Kent TN10 3AN
{t} 01732 363849
chriscarolwickham@hotmail.com
www.oast-theatre-tonbridge.co.uk

Too2Much
11 Walkers Court
London W1F 0SB
{t} 020 7734 0377
info@too2much.co.uk
www.too2much.co.uk

Toot Hill Theatre
Toot Hill School
The Banks
Bingham Notts NG13 8BL
{f} 01949 875551
www.nottinghamshire.gov.uk/home/leisure/arts/stages/stagescompanyinfo/theatrevenues-companyinfo.htm?companyinfoid=21454
Capacity: 145

Torch Theatre
St Peter's Road
Milford Haven
Pembrokeshire SA73 2BU
{t} 01646 695267
info@torchtheatre.co.uk
www.torchtheatre.org.uk
Capacity: 297
Founded: 1977

Torquay Little Theatre, The
St Marks Road
Meadfoot
Torquay TQ1 2EL
{t} 01803 299330
toads2@btinternet.com
www.toadstheatre.co.uk

Torriano Meeting Rooms
99 Torriano Avenue
Kentish Town
London NW5 2RX
{t} 020 7267 2751
roslisa@gmail.com
www.Torriano.org
Capacity: 50

Tower Theatre
54a Canonbury Road
Islington
London N1 2DQ
info@towertheatre.freeserve.co.uk
www.towertheatre.org.uk
Capacity: 136

Toynbee Studios
Artsadmin
28 Commercial Street
London E1 6AB
admin@artsadmin.co.uk
www.artsadmin.co.uk
Capacity: 280
Founded: 1995

Trafalgar Studios
14 Whitehall
London SW1A 2DY
{t} 0870 060 6632
boxoffice@qmuc.ac.uk
www.theambassadors.com/trafalgarstudios
Capacity: 70
Founded: 2005

Tramway
25 Albert Drive
Glasgow G41 2PE
{f} 0141 423 1194
info@tramway.org
www.tramway.org
Founded: 1893

Travellers studio
Harrow Arts Centre
Uxbridge Road
Middlesex HA5 4EA
{t} 020 8428 0124
info@harrowarts.com

Traverse 4
109 Princes Street Edinburgh
Edinburgh EH2 3AA
{t} 0131 228 1404
info@traverse.co.uk
www.traverse.co.uk

Traverse 5
Bristo Square Edinburgh
Edinburgh EH8 9AL
{t} 0131 228 1404
info@traverse.co.uk
www.traverse.co.uk

Traverse 6
Princes St. Edinburgh
Edinburgh EH1 2AB
{t} 0131 228 1404
info@traverse.co.uk
www.traverse.co.uk

Traverse 7
30b Grindlay Street
Edinburgh EH3 9AX
{t} 0131 228 1404
info@traverse.co.uk
www.traverse.co.uk

Traverse Theatre
Cambridge Street
Edinburgh EH1 2ED
{t} 0131 228 1404
michael@traverse.co.uk
www.traverse.co.uk
Capacity: 216
Founded: 1963

Tricycle Theatre
269 Kilburn High Road
London NW6 7JR
{t} 020 7328 1000
admin@tricycle.co.uk
www.tricycle.co.uk
Capacity: 230
Founded: 1980

Trinity Buoy Wharf
Orchard Place
London E14 0JW
{t] 020 7515 7153
sally.ho@urban-space.co.uk
www.trinitybuoywharf.com
Founded: 1997

Trinity Theatre
Church Road
Tunbridge Wells TN1 1JP
{t} 01892 678 678
info@trinitytheatre.net
www.trinitytheatre.net
Capacity: 300
Founded: 1982

Tristan Bates Theatre
1a Tower St
London WC2H 9NP
{t} 020 7240 3940
admin@actorscentre.co.uk
www.tristanbatestheatre.co.uk
Capacity: 70
Founded: 1975

Tron Theatre
63 Trongate
Glasgow G1 5HB
{f} 0141 552 6657
box.office@tron.co.uk
www.tron.co.uk
Founded: 1529

Twentieth Century Fox Theatre
31 Soho Square
London W1D 3AP
{t} 020 7753 7135
projection@fox.com

Twisters
Albert Road
Bournemouth
Dorset BH1 1BZ
{t} 01202 702070
enquiries@comedyclubbournemouth.co.uk
www.twisterscomedyclub.co.uk

U

UCL Bloomsbury Theatre
15 Gordon Street
London WC1H 0AH
{t} 020 7679 2777
info@thebloomsbury.com
www.thebloomsbury.com
Capacity: 535
Founded: 1968

Udderbelly
Old Steine Lawns
Brighton BN2 1EL
penny@underbelly.co.uk
www.underbelly.co.uk/brighton

UEA Studio
Norwich NR4 7TJ
{t} 01603 592272
j.hyde@uea.ac.uk
Capacity: 150

UHArts
Marketing & Communications
University of Hertfordshire
Hatfield AL10 9AB
{t} 01707 281127
uharts@herts.ac.uk
perseus.herts.ac.uk/extrel/uharts_new/uharts_new_home.cfm

Underbelly
56 Cowgate
Edinburgh EH1 1EG
info@smirnoffunderbelly.co.uk
www.smirnoffunderbelly.co.uk

Unex Towerlands
Panfield Road
Braintree CM7 5BJ
{f} 01376 552487
info@unextowerlands.com
www.unextowerlands.com

Unicorn Theatre
147 Tooley St
London SE1 2HZ
{t} 0870 0534534
admin@unicorntheatre.com
www.unicorntheatre.com
Capacity: 300
Founded: 2005

Union Chapel
Compton Terrace
London N1 2UN
{t} 020 7226 1686
spacehire@unionchapel.org.uk
www.unionchapel.org.uk
Capacity: 150
Founded: 1991

Union Theatre
204 Union Street
London SE1 0LX
{t} 020 72619876
sasha@uniontheatre.co.uk

Unity Theatre
1 Hope Place
Liverpool L1 9BG
{t} 0151 709 4988
{f} 0151 709 7182
tickets@unitytheatre.co.uk
www.unitytheatreliverpool.co.uk
Capacity: 182
Founded: 1989

Upstairs at the Gatehouse
The Gatehouse
Highgate Village
London N6 4BD
{t} 020 8340 3488
{f} 020 8340 3466
events@ovationproductions.com
www.upstairsatthegatehouse.com
Capacity: 128
Founded: 1997

V

Valvona & Crolla
19 Elm Row
Edinburgh EH7 4AA
info@valvonacrolla.com
www.valvonacrolla.com

Vaudeville Theatre
404 Strand
London WC2R 0NH
{t] 0870 890 0511
Capacity: 690

Venture Theatre
North Street
Ashby de la Zouch LE65 1HU
{t] 01530 560649
sales@ventureads.plus.com
www.ashbyventuretheatre.org.uk
Capacity: 112

Venue Cymru
The Promenade
Llandudno LL30 1BB
{t] 01492 87200
info@venuecymru.co.uk
www.venuecymru.co.uk
Capacity: 1800
Founded: 1894

Venue, The
5 Leicester Place
London WC2H 7BP
{t} 0870 899 3335
thevenue@aol.co.uk
Capacity: 400

Vera Fletcher Hall
4 Ember Court Road
Thames Ditton KT7 0LQ
{t} 020 8873 7393
errowe@dircon.co.uk
www.esher.ac.uk/verafletcherhall

Victoria Hall
Bagnall Street
Stoke-on-Trent ST1 3AD
{f} 01782 214738
info@theambassadors.com
www.theambassadors.com/victoriahall

Victoria Palace Theatre
Victoria Street
London SW1E 5EA
{t] 0870 845 5577
Founded: 1832

Victoria Theatre
Wards End
Halifax
West Yorkshire HX1 1BU
{t} 01422 351 158
{f} 01422 320 552
admin@victoriatheatre.co.uk
www.victoriatheatre.co.uk
Capacity: 1568
Founded: 1901

Vikingar Barrfields Theatre
24 Greenock Road
Largs KA30 8NE
{t} 01475 689777

Vortex
11 Gillett St
Dalston N16 8JH
{t} 020 7254 4097
info@vortexjazz.co.uk
www.vortexjazz.co.uk
Capacity: 100

Wakefield Theatres
Drury Lane
Wakefield WF1 2TE
{t} 01924 211 311
mail@wakefieldtheatres.co.uk
www.wakefieldtheatres.co.uk

Walkabout
Quay Street
Manchester M3 3HN
{t} 0161 817 4800
natalie_blades@yahoo.co.uk

Walthamstow Assembly Hall
Forest Road
Walthamstow
London E17 4SY
{t} 020 8496 8018
wfdirect@walthamforest.gov.uk
www.lbwf.gov.uk/index/council/about/structure/council-departments/halls-for-hire/walthamstow-assembly-hall.htm

Warehouse Theatre
Dingwall Road
Croydon CR0 2NF
{t} 020 8680 4060
info@warehousetheatre.co.uk
www.warehousetheatre.co.uk
Capacity: 100
Founded: 1977

Warehouse Theatre
Brewery Lane
Ilminster TA19 9AD
vhobbs@tiscali.co.uk
www.thewarehousetheatre.org.uk
Capacity: 155

Warwick Arts Centre
University of Warwick
Coventry CV4 7AL
{t} 024 76 52 3734
arts.centre@warwick.ac.uk
www.warwickartscentre.co.uk
Capacity: 500
Founded: 1974

Waterfront
139-141 Kings Street
Norwich NR1 1QH
{t} 01603 632717
thewaterfront@uea.ac.uk
Capacity: 200
Founded: 1990

Watermans Arts Centre
High Street
Brentford TW8 0DS
{t} 020 8568 1176
info@watermans.org.uk
www.watermans.org.uk
Capacity: 300
Founded: 1984

Watermill Theatre
Bagnor
Near Newbury
Berks RG20 8AE
{t} 01635 46044
jill@watermill.org.uk
www.watermill.org.uk
Capacity: 220
Founded: 1967

Waterside Arts Centre
Sale Waterside
Sale M33 7ZF
{f} 0161 912 1859
watersideartscentre@trafford.gov.uk
www.watersideartscentre.co.uk

Waterside Theatre
8-13 Waterside
Stratford-upon-Avon
Warwickshire CV37 6BA
{t} 01789 290111
{f} 01789 269410
info@watersidetheatre.co.uk
www.watersidetheatre.co.uk
Capacity: 185
Founded: 2004

Waterside Theatre
City College
Whitworth Street
Manchester M1 3HB
{t] 0161 614 8000
a.murry@ccm.ac.uk
www.ccm.ac.uk/ccm_gateway.asp?NavID=1216
Capacity: 100

Watersmeet
High Street
Rickmansworth WD3 1EH
{t} 01923 711063
{f} 01923 727366
www.threerivers.gov.uk
Capacity: 481
Founded: 1975

Watford Palace
Clarendon Road
Watford WD17 1JZ
{t] 01923 225671
www.watfordtheatre.co.uk
Founded: 1908

Wembley Arena
Arena Square
Middlesex HA9 0DH
{t] 020 8782 5500
www.wembley.co.uk/venues/wo.htm

West Cliff
Tower Road
Clacton-On-Sea
Essex CO15 1LE
{t} 01255 474000
administration@west-cliff-theatre-clacton.org.UK
www.west-cliff-theatre-clacton.org.uk
Capacity: 590
Founded: 1928

West End Centre
Queens Road
Aldershot GU11 3JD
{f} 01252 408041
westendcentre@hants.gov.uk
www.westendcentre.co.uk

West Walls Theatre
West Walls
Carlisle
Cumbria CA3 8UB
{t] 01228 523254
boxoffice1@carlislegreenroom.co.uk
www.carlislegreenroom.co.uk

West Yorkshire Playhouse
Playhouse Square
Quarry Hill
Leeds LS2 7UP
{t} 0113 2137800
{f} 0113 213 7210
info@wyp.org.uk
www.wyplayhouse.com
Capacity: 756
Founded: 1990

Westacre River Studios
River Road
Westacre
King's Lynn PE32 1UD
{f} 01760 755800
sarah@westacreriverstudios.co.uk
www.westacreriverstudios.co.uk
Capacity: 145
Founded: 2000

Westbourne Studios
242 Acklam Road
London W10 5JJ
info@westbournestudios.com
www.westbournestudios.com
Capacity: 82

Westminster Kingsway College
The Regents Park Centre
Longford Street NW1 3HB
{t} 0870 060 9801
courseinfo@westking.ac.uk
www.westking.ac.uk
Capacity: 80

Westminster Studio Theatre
425 Harrow Road
London W2 1RR
{t} 020 7641 8424
studiot@nwschool.co.uk
Capacity: 80

Weston Super Mare Playhouse
High Street
Weston Super Mare BS23 1HP
{t} 01934 645544
playhouse@a-somerset.gov.uk
www.theplayhouse.co.uk
Capacity: 658
Founded: 1946

Westovian Theatre Society
Pier Pavilion
South Shields NE33 2JS
beejay4475@hotmail.com
www.westovians.org
Capacity: 286

Westpoint
Westpoint
Clyst St Mary
Exeter EX5 1DJ
{t} 01392 446000
info@westpoint-devonshow.co.uk
www.westpoint-devonshow.co.uk

Wharf Theatre
The Wharf
Devizes SN10 1EB
www.wharftheatre.co.uk

Wharf, The
Canal Road
Tavistock PL19 8AT
{f} 01822 613974
enquiries@tavistockwharf.com
www.tavistockwharf.com
Capacity: 600

Wheatsheaf
25 Rathbone Place
London W1P 1DG
{t} 0871 332 2606
courses@scratchimpro.com

White Bear
138 Kennington Park Road
London SE11 4DJ
{t} 020 7793 9193
mkwbear@hotmail.com
www.whitebeartheatre.co.uk
Capacity: 55
Founded: 1988

White Rock
White Rockswing
Hastings
East Sussex TN34 1JX
{t} 01424 462288
hastingsboxoffice@clearchannel.co.uk
www.hastings.gov.uk/wrt
Capacity: 1066
Founded: 1927

Whitehall Theatre
12 Bellfield Street
Dundee DD1 5JA
{f} 01382 226926
whitehalltheatre@its-showtime.co.uk
www.whitehalldundee.co.uk
Founded: 1928

Whitley Bay Playhouse
Marine Avenue
Whitley Bay NE26 1LZ
{f} 0191 251 4949
office@whitleybayplayhouse.co.uk
www.whitleybayplayhouse.co.uk
Founded: 1913

Wickham Theatre
Cantocks Close
Drama Department Building
Bristol BS8 1UP
{t} 0117 3315084
wickham-theatre@bristol.ac.uk

Wigmore Hall
36 Wigmore Street
London W1U 2BP
{f} 020 7935 3344
boxoffice@wigmore-hall.org.uk

Williamson Park
Williamson Park
Lancaster LA1 1UX
{t} 01524 33318
office@williamsonpark.com
www.williamsonpark.com
Capacity: 500

Willows Arts Centre
George Street
Corby NN17 1QB
{t} 01536 402233
roger@willows-arts.org
www.willows-arts.org

Wilmslow Green Room Theatre
85 Chapel Lane
Wilmslow
Cheshire SK9 5JH
wgrsoc@aol.com
www.members.aol.com/wgrsoc
Capacity: 75

Wilton's Music Hall
Grace's Alley
off Ensign Street
London E1 8JB
{t} 020 7702 1414
info@wiltons.org.uk
www.wiltons.org.uk

Capacity: 300
Founded: 1850

Wiltshire Music Centre
Ashley Rd
Bradford on Avon BA15 1DZ
{f} 01225 860111
info@wiltshiremusic.org.uk
www.wiltshiremusic.org.uk

Wimbledon Studio
103 The Broadway
Wimbledon
London SW19 1QG
{t} 0870 060 6646
info@theambassadors.com
www.theambassadors.com/ wimbledonstudio
Capacity: 40

Winding Wheel
13 Holywell Street
Chesterfield S41 7SA
{t} 01246 345333
winding.wheel@chesterfieldbc.gov.uk
Capacity: 1000
Founded: 1980

Windmill Entertainment Centre
The Green
Windmill Road
Littlehampton BN17 5LM
{f} 01903 725606
windmill@inspireleisure.co.uk
www.inspireleisure.co.uk/index.php ?page_id=83§ion_id=5

Windsor Arts Centre
The Old Court
St Leonards Rd
Windsor SL4 3BL
{f} 01753 621527
www.windsorartscentre.org

Winter Garden
Compton Street
Eastbourne BN21 4BP
{t] 01323 415500
boxoffice@eastbourne.gov.uk
www.eastbourne-theatres.co.uk/glance.asp? search=winter

Winter Gardens
Fort Crescent
5 Hawley Street
Margate, Kent CT9 1HX
{f} 01843 293163
www.margatewintergardens.co.uk

Winter Gardens & Opera House
97 Church Street
Blackpool
Lancashire FY1 1HL
events@leisure-parcs.co.uk
www.wintergardensblackpool.co.uk/ Operahouse.html
Founded: 1878

Woodley Theatre
Headley Road
Woodley
Berkshire RG5 4DN
{t] 0118 9690 8278
woodleytheatre@hotmail.com
Capacity: 100

Woodville Halls
Woodville Place
Gravesend DA12 1DD
{t} 01474 337459/60
woodvillehalls@gravesham.gov.uk
www.gravesham.gov.uk/index.cfm? articleid=256
Capacity: 700
Founded: 1995

Woolstore Country Theatre
High Street
Codford St Peter
Warminster BA12 0NE

Worcester Studio Theatre
Henwick Grove
Worcester
Worcestershire WR2 6AJ
{t} 01905 855 000
d.broster@worc.ac.uk
www.worcester.ac.uk/student/drama/864.html
Capacity: 120
Founded: 2001

Workhouse Theatre
242, Pentonville Road
London N1 9JY
{t} 020 7837 6030
{f} 020 7833 1149
acting@thepoorschool.com
Capacity: 60
Founded: 1986

Worthing Pavilion
Marine Parade
Worthing BN11 3PX
{t} 01903 206 206
theatres@worthing.gov.uk
www.worthingtheatres.co.uk/worthingtheatres/AbouttheTheatres/PavilionTheatre
Capacity: 850
Founded: 1926

Woughton Centre
Rainbow Drive
Leadenhall
Milton Keynes MK6 5EJ
{f} 01908 696146
www.woughtoncentre.co.uk

Wulfrun Hall
Mitre Fold
North Street
Wolverhampton WV1 1RQ
{t} 01902 552121
info@wolvescivic.co.uk
www.wolvescivic.co.uk/index.asp?loc=venues&venueid=2

Wycombe Swan
St Mary Street
High Wycombe
Bucks HP11 2XE
{t} 01494 514444
{f} 01494 538080
enquiries@wycombeswan.co.uk
www.wycombeswan.co.uk
Capacity: 1076
Founded: 1992

Wyeside Arts Centre
Castle Street
Builth Wells LD2 3BN
{t} 01982 552555
box@wyeside.co.uk
www.wyeside.co.uk
Capacity: 249
Founded: 1877

Wyllyotts Centre
Darkes Lane
Potters Bar EN6 2HN
{t} 01707 645005
ginny@isnet.co.uk
www.hertsmereleisure.co.uk/wyllyotts.asp
Capacity: 421
Founded: 1990

Wyndham's Theatre
Charing Cross Road
London WC2H 0DA
{t} 020 7369 1736

wyndhamsmanager@theambassadors.com
www.delfontmackintosh.co.uk
Capacity: 759
Founded: 1899

Wyvern
Theatre Square
Swindon SN1 1QN
{t} 01793 524481
{f} 01793 480 278
venuebookings@clearchannel.co.uk
www.wyverntheatre.org.uk
Capacity: 617
Founded: 1971

XYZ

Y Theatre
East Street
Leicester LE1 6EY
chiefexecutive@leicesterymca.co.uk

Young Actors Theatre
70-72 Barnsbury Road
London N1 0ES
{t} 020 72782101
{f} 020 78339467
info@yati.org.uk
www.yati.org.uk
Capacity: 100
Founded: 1975

Young Vic
1-3 Brixton Road
London SE1 8LZ
{t} 020 7928 6363
info@youngvic.org
www.youngvic.org
Capacity: 500
Founded: 1970

Yvonne Arnaud
Millbrook
Guildford GU1 3UX
{t} 01483 440000
yat@yvonne-arnaud.co.uk
www.yvonne-arnaud.co.uk
Capacity: 80
Founded: 1965

Zoo, The
140 The Pleasance
Edinburgh EH8 9RR
{t] 01432 344885
info@zoovenues.co.uk
www.zoovenues.co.uk
Capacity: 90

Index